THE NANNY DIARIES

ST. MARTIN'S PRESS

NEW YORK

The Nanny Diaries

A NOVEL

EMMA MCLAUGHLIN AND
NICOLA KRAUS

THE NANNY DIARIES. Copyright © 2002 by Emma McLaughlin
and Nicola Kraus. All rights reserved. Printed in the United States
of America. No part of this book may be used or reproduced in
any manner whatsoever without written permission except in the
case of brief quotations embodied in critical articles or reviews.
For information, address St. Martin's Press, 175 Fifth Avenue,
New York, N.Y. 10010.

www.stmartins.com

Book design by Gretchen Achilles

Library of Congress Cataloging-in-Publication Data

McLaughlin, Emma.
    The nanny diaries : a novel / Emma McLaughlin & Nicola Kraus
—1st ed.
        p. cm.
    ISBN 0-312-27858-6
        1. Manhattan (New York, N.Y.)—Fiction.   2. Park Avenue
(New York, N.Y.)—Fiction.   3. Rich people—Fiction.
4. Nannies—Fiction.   I. Kraus, Nicola.   II. Title.

PS3613.C575 N36 2002
813'.6—dc21   2001048652

*To our parents, for always reading at least one bedtime story
(with voices) no matter how tuckered out they were.*

*And to all the fabulous kids who have danced, giggled,
and hiccuped their way into our hearts.*

We root for you still.

A NOTE TO READERS

The authors have worked, at one time or another, for over thirty New York City families, and this story was inspired by what they have learned and experienced. However, *The Nanny Diaries* is a work of fiction, and none of those families is portrayed in this book. Names and characters are the product of the authors' imagination. Any resemblance to actual events or persons, living or dead, is coincidental. Although some real New York City institutions— schools, stores, galleries, and the like—are mentioned, all are used fictitiously.

"You should hear mama on the chapter of governesses: Mary and I have had, I should think, a dozen at least in our day; half of them detestable and the rest ridiculous, and all incubi—were they not, mama?"

"My dearest, don't mention governesses; the word makes me nervous. I have suffered a martyrdom from their incompetency and caprice; I thank Heaven I have now done with them!"

—JANE EYRE

THE NANNY DIARIES

The Interview

Every season of my nanny career kicked off with a round of interviews so surreally similar that I'd often wonder if the mothers were slipped a secret manual at the Parents League to guide them through. This initial encounter became as repetitive as religious ritual, tempting me, in the moment before the front door swung open, either to kneel and genuflect or say, "Hit it!"

No other event epitomized the job as perfectly, and it always began and ended in an elevator nicer than most New Yorkers' apartments.

⟡

The walnut-paneled car slowly pulls me up, like a bucket in a well, toward potential solvency. As I near the appointed floor I take a deep breath; the door slides open onto a small vestibule which is the portal to, at most, two apartments. I press the doorbell. Nanny Fact: she always waits for me to ring the doorbell, even though she was buzzed by maximum security downstairs to warn of my imminent arrival and is probably standing on the other side of the door. May, in fact, have been standing there since we spoke on the telephone three days ago.

The dark vestibule, wallpapered in some gloomy Colefax and Fowler floral, always contains a brass umbrella stand, a horse print, and a mirror, wherein I do one last swift check of my appearance. I seem to have grown stains on my skirt during the train ride from school, but otherwise I'm pulled together—twin set, floral skirt, and some Gucci-knockoff sandals I bought in the Village.

She is always tiny. Her hair is always straight and thin; she always seems to be inhaling and never exhaling. She is always wearing expensive khaki pants, Chanel ballet flats, a French striped T-shirt, and a white cardigan. Possibly some discreet pearls. In seven years and umpteen interviews the I'm-mom-casual-in-my-khakis-but-intimidating-in-my-$400-shoes outfit never changes. And it is simply impossible to imagine her doing anything so undignified as what was required to get her pregnant in the first place.

Her eyes go directly to the splot on my skirt. I blush. I haven't even opened my mouth and already I'm behind.

She ushers me into the front hall, an open space with a gleaming marble floor and mushroom-gray walls. In the middle is a round table with a vase of flowers that look as if they might die, but never dare wilt.

This is my first impression of the Apartment and it strikes me like a hotel suite—immaculate, but impersonal. Even the lone finger painting I will later find taped to the fridge looks as if it were ordered from a catalog. (Sub-Zeros with a custom-colored panel aren't magnetized.)

She offers to take my cardigan, stares disdainfully at the hair my cat seems to have rubbed on it for good luck, and offers me a drink. I'm supposed to say, "Water would be lovely," but am often tempted to ask for a Scotch, just to see what she'd do. I am then invited into the living room, which varies from baronial splendor to Ethan Allen interchangeable, depending on how "old" the money is. She gestures me to the couch, where I promptly sink three feet into the cushions, transformed into a five-year-old dwarfed by mountains of chintz. She looms above me, ramrod straight in a very uncomfortable-looking chair, legs crossed, tight smile.

Now we begin the actual Interview. I awkwardly place my sweating glass of water carefully on a coaster that looks as if it could use a coaster. She is clearly reeling with pleasure at my sheer Caucasianness.

"So," she begins brightly, "how did you come to the Parents League?"

This is the only part of the Interview that resembles a professional exchange. We will dance around certain words, such as "nanny" and "child care," because they would be distasteful and we will never, *ever*, actually acknowledge that we are talking about my working for her. This is the Holy Covenant of the Mother/Nanny relationship: this is a pleasure—*not* a job. We are merely "getting to know each other," much as how I imagine a John and a call girl must make the deal, while trying not to kill the mood.

The closest we get to the possibility that I might actually be doing this for money is the topic of my baby-sitting experience, which I describe as a passionate hobby, much like raising Seeing Eye dogs for the blind. As the conversation progresses I become a child-development expert—convincing both of us of my desire to fulfill my very soul by raising a child and taking part in all stages of his/her development; a simple trip to the park or museum becoming a precious journey of the heart. I cite amusing anecdotes from past gigs, referring to the children by name—"I still marvel at the cognitive growth of Constance with each hour we spent together in the sandbox." I feel my eyes twinkle and imagine twirling my umbrella à la Mary Poppins. We both sit in silence for a moment picturing my studio apartment crowded with framed finger paintings and my doctorates from Stanford.

She stares at me expectantly, ready for me to bring it on home. "*I love children!* I love little hands and little shoes and peanut butter sandwiches and peanut butter in my hair and Elmo—*I love Elmo*— and sand in my purse and the "Hokey Pokey"—can't get enough of it!—and soy milk and blankies and the endless barrage of questions no one knows the answers to, I mean why *is* the sky blue? And Disney! Disney is my second language!"

We can both hear "A Whole New World" slowly swelling in the

background as I earnestly convey that it would be more than a privilege to take care of her child—it would be an adventure.

She is flushed, but still playing it close to the chest. Now she wants to know *why*, if I'm so fabulous, I would *want* to take care of her child. I mean, she gave birth to it and *she* doesn't want to do it, so why would I? Am I trying to pay off an abortion? Fund a leftist group? How did she get this lucky? She wants to know what I study, what I plan to do in the future, what I think of private schools in Manhattan, what my parents do. I answer with as much filigree and insouciance as I can muster, trying to slightly cock my head like Snow White listening to the animals. She, in turn, is aiming for more of a Diane-Sawyer-pose, looking for answers which will confirm that I am not there to steal her husband, jewelry, friends, or child. In that order.

Nanny Fact: in every one of my interviews, references are never checked. I am white. I speak French. My parents are college educated. I have no visible piercings and have been to Lincoln Center in the last two months. I'm hired.

She stands with newfound hope. "Let me show you around . . ." Although we have already met, it's time for the Apartment to play *its* role to full effect. As we pass through each room it seems to fluff itself and shimmy to add shine to the already blinding surfaces. Touring is what this Apartment was born for. Each enormous room leads to the next with a few minihallways just big enough for a framed original so-and-so.

No matter if she has an infant or a teenager—there is never a trace of a child to be found on the Tour. In fact, there's never a trace of anyone—not a single family picture displayed. I'll find out later that these are all discreetly tucked into sterling Tiffany frames and clustered artfully in a corner of the den.

Somehow the absence of a pair of strewn shoes or an opened envelope makes it hard to believe that the scene I am being led through is three-dimensional; it seems like a Potemkin apartment. I consequently feel ungainly and unsure of how to demonstrate the appropriate awe that is expected from me, without saying, "Yes'm, it's awl so awfly luverly, shore is," in a thick cockney accent and curtsying.

Luckily she is in perpetual motion and the opportunity does not present itself. She glides silently ahead of me and I am struck by how tiny her frame seems against the dense furnishings. I stare at her back as she moves from room to room, stopping only briefly in each to wave her hand around in a circle and say the room's name, to which I nod to confirm that this is, in fact, the dining room.

Two pieces of information are meant to be conveyed to me during the Tour: (1) I am out of my league, and (2) I will be policing at maximum security to ensure that her child, who is also out of his or her league, does not scuff, snag, spill, or spoil a single element of this apartment. The coded script for this exchange goes as follows: she turns around to "mention" that there really is no housekeeping involved and that Hutchison really "prefers" to play in his room. If there were any justice in the world this is the point when all nannies should be given roadblocks and a stun gun. These rooms are destined to become the burden of my existence. From this point on, ninety-five percent of this apartment will be nothing more than a blurred background for chasing, enticing, and point-blank pleading with the child to "Put the Delft milkmaid down!!" I am also about to become intimate with more types of cleaning fluid than I knew there were types of dirt. It will be in her pantry—stocked high above the washer-dryer—that I discover people actually import toilet bowl cleanser from Europe.

We arrive in the kitchen. It is enormous. With a few partitions it could easily house a family of four. She stops to rest one manicured hand on the counter, affecting a familiar pose, like a captain at the helm about to address the crew. However, I know if I asked her where she keeps the flour, a half hour of rummaging through unused baking utensils would ensue.

Nanny Fact: she may pour an awful lot of Perrier in this kitchen, but she never actually eats here. In fact, over the course of the job I never see her *eat* anything. While she can't tell me where to find the flour, she can probably locate the laxatives in her medicine cabinet blindfolded.

The refrigerator is always bursting with tons of meticulously chopped fresh fruit separated into Tupperware bowls and at least two packs of fresh cheese tortellini that her child prefers without sauce. (Meaning there is never any in the house for me, either.) There is also the requisite organic milk, a deserted bottle of Lillet, and Sarabeth's jam, and lots of refrigerated ginkgo biloba ("for Daddy's memory"). The freezer is stocked with Mommy's dirty little secret: chicken nuggets and popsicles. As I peer into the fridge I see that food is for the child; condiments are for the grown-ups. One pictures a family meal in which parents meekly stick toothpicks into a jar of Grace's sundried tomatoes while child gorges on a feast of fresh fruit and frozen dinners.

"Brandford's meals are really quite simple," she says, gesturing to the frozen food as she closes the freezer door. Translation: they are able to feed him this crap in good conscience on the weekends because I will be cooking him four-course macrobiotic meals on the weeknights. There will be a day to come when I stare at the colorful packages in the freezer with raw envy as I resteam the wild rice from Costa Rica for the four-year-old's maximum digestive ease.

She swings open the pantry (which is big enough to be a summer home for the family of four who could live in the kitchen) to reveal an Armageddon-ready level of storage, as if the city were in perpetual danger of being looted by a roving band of insanely health-conscious five-year-olds. It is overflowing with every type of juice box, soy milk, rice milk, organic pretzel, organic granola bar, and organic raisin the consulted nutritionist could think up. The only item with additives is a shelf of Goldfish options, including low salt and the not-so-popular onion.

There isn't a single trace of food in the entire kitchen big enough to fill a grown-up hand. Despite the myth of "help yourself," it will take a few starving evenings of raisin dinners before I discover THE TOP SHELF, which appears to be trip wired and covered with dust, but contains the much-coveted gourmet house gifts that have been left for dead by women who see chocolate as a grenade in Pandora's box. Barneys' raisinettes, truffles from Saks, fudge from Martha's Vineyard, all of which I devour like crack-cocaine in the bathroom to avoid the crime being recorded by a possible security camera. I picture the footage being played on *Hard Copy*: "Nanny caught in the act—heady with delusions of entitlement—breaks cellophane wrapper on '92 Easter Godivas."

It is at this point that she begins the Rules. This is a very pleasing portion of the event for any mother because it is a chance to demonstrate how much thought and effort has gone into bringing the child this far. She speaks with a rare mixture of animation, confidence, and awesome conviction—she knows this much is true. I, in turn, adopt my most eager, yet compassionate expression as if to say "Yes, please tell me more—I'm fascinated" and "How awful it must be for you to have a child allergic to air." So begins the List:

Allergic to dairy.
Allergic to peanuts.
Allergic to strawberries.
Allergic to propane-based shellac.
Some kind of grain.
Won't eat blueberries.
Will only eat blueberries—sliced.
Sandwiches must be cut horizontally and have crusts.
Sandwiches must be cut in quarters and have NO crusts.
Sandwiches must be made facing east.
She *loves* rice milk!

He won't eat anything starting with the letter M.

All servings are to be pre-measured—NO additional food is permissible.

All juice is to be watered down and drunk out of a sip glass over the sink or in the bathtub (preferably until the child is eighteen).

All food is to be served on a plastic place mat with paper towel beneath bowl, bib on at all times.

Actually, "if you could get Lucien naked before eating and then hose her down afterward, that would be perfect."

NO food or drink within two hours of bedtime.

NO additives.

NO preservatives.

NO pumpkin seeds.

NO skins of any kind.

NO raw food.

NO cooked food.

NO American food.

and . . . (voice drops to a pitch only whales can hear)

NO FOOD OUTSIDE THE KITCHEN!

I am nodding gravely in agreement. This makes total sense. "Oh, my God, of course," I find myself saying.

This is Phase I of bringing me into the fold, of creating the illusion of collusion. "We're in this together! Little Elspeth is our joint project! And we're going to feed her nothing but mung beans!" I feel as if I am nine months pregnant and just finding out my husband plans to raise the child in a cult. Yet I am somehow flattered that I am being chosen to participate in this project. Completion Phase II: I am succumbing to the allure of perfection.

The tour proceeds to the farthest possible room. The distance of the child's room from the parents' room always runs the gamut from far away to really, really far away. In fact, if there is another floor this room will be on it. One has the image of the poor three-year-old awakening from a nightmare and having to don a pith helmet and flashlight to go in search of her parents' room, armed only with a compass and fierce determination.

The other telltale sign that one is moving into the Child Zone is the change in the decor from muted, faux Asian to either a Mondrian scheme of primary colors or Bonpoint, Kennedy pastels. Either way Martha has been here—personally. But the effect is oddly disquieting; it's so obviously an adult's conception of a child's room, as evidenced by the fact that all the signed first edition Babar prints are hung at least three feet above the child's head.

After having received the Rules I am braced to meet the boy in the bubble. I expect to see a full-out intensive care unit complete with a Louis Vuitton IV hookup. Imagine my shock at the ball of motion that comes hurtling across the room at us. If it's a boy the movement is reminiscent of the Tasmanian Devil, while a girl tends toward a full-tilt Mouseketeers sequence, complete with two pirouettes and a grand jeté. The child is sent into this routine by some Pavlovian response to the mother's perfume as she rounds the corner. The encounter proceeds as follows: (1) Child (groomed within an inch of his/her life) makes a beeline directly for mother's leg. (2) At the precise moment the child's hands wrap around her thigh the mother swiftly grabs the child's wrists. (3) And she simultaneously sidesteps out of the embrace, bringing the child's hands into a clapping position in front of the child's face, and bends down to say hello, turning the child's gaze to me. Voilà. And thus the first of many performances of what I like to call the "Spatula Reflex." It has such timing and grace that I feel as if I should applaud, but instead move directly into my Pavlovian response set off by their expectant faces. I drop to my knees.

"Why don't you two get to know each other a little . . ." This is the cue for the Play-With-Child portion of the audition. Despite the fact that we all know the child's opinion is irrelevant I nevertheless become psychotically animated. I play as if I'm Christmas and then some until the child has been whipped into a foaming frenzy of interaction, with the added stimulant of a rare audience with mother. The child has been trained in the Montessori approach to fun—only one toy is pulled from its walnut cubicle at a time. I over-compensate for the lack of normal childhood chaos by turning into a chorus of voices, dance steps, and an in-depth understanding of Pokémon. Within moments the child is asking me to go to the zoo, sleep over, and move in. This is the mother's cue to break in from where she has been sitting with her mental clipboard and Olympic score cards on the edge of the child's bed to announce that it is "Time to say goodbye to Nanny. Won't it be fun to play with Nanny again?"

The housekeeper, who has been folded into a child-size rocking chair in the corner this entire time, offers up a dejected storybook, making a meek attempt to match my display of fireworks and delay the inevitable crash. Within seconds there is a replay of a slightly more sophisticated version of the Spatula Reflex, this time encompassing a maneuvering of both mother and myself outside the room, punctuated by a slammed door, all in one seamless motion. She runs her hands through her hair as she leads me back into the silence of the apartment with a long, breathy "Well . . ."

She hands me my purse and then I stand with her in the foyer for at least half an hour, waiting to be dismissed.

"So, do you have a boyfriend?" This is the cue for the Play-With-Mother portion of the audition. She is in for the night—there is no mention of a husband's imminent arrival or plans for dinner. I hear about her pregnancy, Lotte Berk, the last Parents' Night meeting, the pain-in-the-ass housekeeper (left for dead in the Child Zone), the wily decorator, the string of nanny disasters before me, and the nursery school *nightmare*. Completion Phase III: I am actually excited that I am not only getting a delightful child to play with, I'm getting a new best friend!

Not to be outdone, I hear myself talking—trying to establish my status as a person of the world; I name-drop, brand-drop, place-drop. Then self-consciously deprecate myself with humor so as not to intimidate her. I become aware that I am talking way, way too much. I am babbling about why I left Brown, why I left my last relationship—not that I'm a leaver no, no, no! I pick something, I stick with it! Yessiree! Did I tell you about my thesis? I am revealing information that will be dragged up repeatedly for months in awkward attempts to make conversation. Soon I am just bobbing my head and saying "Okay-ay!" while blindly groping for the doorknob. *Finally* she thanks me for coming, opens the door, and lets me press for the elevator.

I am caught mid-sentence as the elevator door starts to close, forcing me to shove my bag in front of the electronic eye so I can finish a meaningful thought on my parents' marriage. We smile and nod at one another like animatrons until the door mercifully slides closed. I collapse against it, exhaling for the first time in an hour.

Minutes later the subway barrels down Lexington, propelling me toward school and back to the grind of my own life. I slump against the plastic seat, images from the pristine apartment swimming in my head. These snapshots are soon interrupted by a man or woman—sometimes both—shuffling through the car begging for change while gripping their worldly possessions in a shredded shopping bag. Pulling my backpack up onto my lap, my postperformance adrenaline leveling out, questions begin to percolate.

Just how does an intelligent, adult woman become someone whose whole sterile kingdom has been reduced to alphabetized lingerie drawers and imported French dairy substitutes? Where is the child in this home? Where is the woman in this mother?

And how, exactly, am I to fit in?

✧

Ultimately, there would come a turning point in every job when it seemed that the child and I were the only three-dimensional people running around on the black-and-white marble chessboards of those apartments. Making it inevitable that someone would get knocked down.

Looking back, it was a setup to begin with. They want you. You want the job.

But to do it well is to lose it.

Hit it.

PART ONE

Fall

Then, with a long, loud sniff, that seemed to indicate that she had
made up her mind, she said: "I'll take the position."
   "For all the world," as Mrs. Banks said to her husband later,
"as though she were doing us an honour."

—MARY POPPINS

CHAPTER ONE

Nanny for Sale

"Hi, this is Alexis at the Parents League. I'm just calling to follow up on the uniform guidelines we sent over . . ." The blond woman volunteering behind the reception desk holds up a bejeweled finger, signaling me to wait while she continues on the phone. "Yes, well, this year we'd really like to see all your girls in longer skirts, at least twenty inches. We're still getting complaints from the mothers at the boys' schools in the vicinity . . . Great. Good to hear it. Bye." With a grand gesture she crosses the word "Spence" off her list of three items.

She returns her attention to me. "I'm sorry to keep you waiting. With the school year starting we're just crazed." She draws a big circle around the second item on her list, "paper towels." "Can I help you?"

"I'm here to put up an ad for a nanny, but the bulletin board seems to have moved," I say, slightly confused as I've been advertising here since I was thirteen.

"We had to take it down while the foyer was being painted and never got around to moving it back. Here, let me show you." She leads me to the central room, where mothers perch at Knoll desks fielding inquiries about the Private Schools. Before me sits the full range of Upper East Side diversity—half of the women are dressed in Chanel suits and Manolo Blahniks, half are in six-hundred-dollar barn jackets, looking as if they might be asked to pitch an Aqua Scutum tent at any moment.

Alexis gestures to the bulletin board, which has displaced a Mary Cassatt propped against the wall. "It's all a bit disorganized at the moment," she says as another woman looks up from the floral arrangement she's rearranging nearby. "But don't worry. Tons of lovely girls come here to look for employment, so you shouldn't have any trouble finding someone." She raises her hand to her pearls. "Don't you have a son at Buckley? You look so familiar. I'm Alexis—"

"Hi," I say. "I'm Nan. Actually, I took care of the Gleason girls. I think they lived next door to you."

She arches an eyebrow to give me a once-over. "Oh . . . Oh, Nanny, that's right," she confirms for herself, before retreating back to her desk.

I tune out the officious, creamy chatter of the women behind me to read the postings put up by other nannies also in search of employment.

Babysitter need children
very like kids
vacuums

I look your kids
Many years work
You call me

The bulletin board is already so overcrowded with flyers that, with a twinge of guilt, I end up tacking my ad over someone else's pink paper festooned with crayon flowers, but spend a few minutes ensuring that I'm only covering daisies and none of her pertinent information.

I wish I could tell these women that the secret to nanny advertising isn't the decoration, it's the punctuation—it's all in the exclamation mark. While my ad is a minimalist three-by-five card, without so much as a smiley face on it, I liberally sprinkle my advertisement with exclamations, ending each of my desirable traits with the promise of a beaming smile and unflagging positivity.

Nanny at the Ready!
Chapin School alumna available weekdays part-time!
Excellent references!
Child Development Major at NYU!

The only thing I don't have is an umbrella that makes me fly.

I do one last quick check for spelling, zip up my backpack, bid Alexis adieu, and jog down the marble steps out into the sweltering heat.

As I walk down Park Avenue the August sun is still low enough in the sky that the stroller parade is in full throttle. I pass many hot little people, looking resignedly uncomfortable in their sticky seats. They are too hot even to hold on to any of their usual traveling companions—blankies and bears are tucked into back stroller pockets. I chuckle to myself at the child who waves away the offer of a juice box with a flick of the hand and a toss of the head that says, "I couldn't possibly be bothered with juice right now."

Waiting at a red light, I look up at the large glass windows that are the eyes of Park Avenue. From a population-density point of view, this is the Midwest of Manhattan. Towering above me are rooms—rooms and rooms and rooms. And they are empty. There are powder rooms and dressing rooms and piano rooms and guest rooms and, somewhere above me, but I won't say where, a rabbit named Arthur has sixteen feet square all to himself.

I cut across Seventy-second Street, passing under the shade of the blue awnings of the Polo mansion, and turn into Central Park.

Pausing in front of the playground, where a few tenacious children are trying their best despite the heat, I reach in my backpack for a small bottle of water—just as something crashes into my legs. I look down and steady the offending object, an old-fashioned wooden hoop.

"Hey, that's mine!" A small boy of about four or so careens down the hill from where I see he's been posing for a portrait with his parents. His sailor hat topples off into the patchy grass as he runs.

"That's my hoop," he announces.

"Are you sure?" I ask. He looks perplexed. "It could be a wagon wheel." I hold it sideways. "Or a halo?" I hold it above his blond head. "Or a really large pizza?" I hold it out to him, gesturing that he can take it. He's smiling broadly at me as he grasps it in his hands.

"You, silly!" He drags it back up the hill, passing his mother as she strolls down to retrieve the hat.

"I'm sorry," she says, brushing dust off the striped brim as she approaches me. "I hope he didn't bother you." She holds her hand out to block the sun from her pale blue eyes.

"No, not at all."

"Oh, but your skirt—" She glances down.

"No big deal," I laugh, dusting off the mark the hoop left on the fabric. "I work with kids, so I'm used to being banged up."

"Oh, you do?" She angles her body so her back is to her husband and a blond woman who stands off to the side of the photographer holding a juice box for the boy. His nanny, I presume. "Around here?"

"Actually, the family moved to London over the summer, so—"

"We're ready!" the father calls impatiently.

"Coming!" she calls back brightly. She turns to me, tilting her delicately featured face away from him. She lowers her voice. "Well, we're actually looking for someone who might want to help us out part-time."

"Really? Part-time would be great, because I have a full course load this semester—"

"What's the best way to reach you?"

I rummage through my backpack for a pen and a scrap of note-book on which I can scribble down my information. "Here you go." I pass her the paper and she discreetly slips it in the pocket of her shift, before adjusting the headband in her long, dark hair.

"Wonderful." She smiles graciously. "Well, it was a pleasure to meet you. I'll be in touch." She takes a few steps up the hill and then turns around. "Oh, how silly of me—I'm Mrs. X."

I return the smile before she goes back to take her place in the contrived tableau. The sun filters through the leaves, creating dap-pled sunshine on the three figures. Her husband, in a white seer-sucker suit, stands squarely in the middle, his hand on the boy's head, as she slides in beside them.

The blond woman steps forward with a comb and the little boy waves to me, causing her to turn and follow his gaze. As she shields her eyes to get a better look at me I turn and continue on my way across the park.

◇

My grandmother greets me in her entryway in a linen Mao Tse-tung outfit and pearls. "Darling! Come in. I was just finishing my tai-chi." She gives me a kiss on both cheeks and a solid hug for good measure. "Honey, you're damp. Would you like to shower?" There is nothing better than being offered Grandma's buffet of amenities.

"Maybe just a cold washcloth?"

"I know what you need." She takes my hand, weaving her fin-gers through mine, and leads me to her guest powder room. I've always adored how the small lights of the antique crystal chandelier illume the rich peach chintz. But my favorite part is the framed French paper dolls. When I was little I would set up a salon under the sink, for which Grandma would provide real tea and topics for the discussions I would lead with all of my lovely French guests.

She places my hands under the faucet and runs cool water over my wrists. "Pressure points for distributing fire," she says as she sits down on the toilet seat, crossing her legs. She's right; I begin to cool down immediately.

"Have you eaten?" she asks.

"I had breakfast."

"What about lunch?"

"It's only eleven, Gran."

"Is it? I've been up since four. Thank God for Europe or I'd have no one to talk to till eight."

I smile. "How have you been?"

"I've been seventy-four for two months, that's how I've been." She points her toes like a dancer and slightly lifts the hem of her pants. "It's called Sappho—I had it done at Arden's this morning— what do you think? Too too?" She wiggles her coral toes.

"Gorgeous, very sexy. Okay, as much as I would love to spend the rest of the day in here I've got to drag myself downtown and make my offering to the Tuition Gods." I turn off the sink and shake my hands dramatically over the basin.

She hands me a towel. "You know, I don't remember having a single conversation like the ones you describe when I was at Vassar." She is referring to my endless history of tête-a-têtes with the administrative staff at NYU.

I follow behind her into the kitchen. "Today I'm prepared. I've got my Social Security card, my driver's license, my passport, a Xerox copy of my birth certificate, every piece of mail I've ever received from NYU, and my letter of acceptance. This time I *won't* be told I don't go there, haven't completed the last semester, haven't paid my tuition from last year, haven't paid my library fees, don't have the correct ID number, Social Security number, proof of my address, the right forms, or simply don't exist."

"My, my, my." She opens the fridge. "Bourbon?"

"Orange juice would be great."

"Kids." She rolls her eyes and points me to her old air conditioner sitting on the floor. "Darling, let me get the doorman to help you carry it."

"No, Gran, I got it," I say, trying valiantly to heave the machine into my arms before slamming it back down on the tile. "Yeah, okay, I think I'm going to have to come back later with Josh and get this."

"Joshua?" she asks with a raised eyebrow. "Your little blue-haired friend? He weighs five pounds soaking wet."

"Well, unless we want Dad throwing his back out again, that's about all I have to choose from in the boy department."

"I chant for you every morning, darling," she says, reaching for a glass. "Come on. Let me whip you up some Eggs Benedict."

I glance up at the old Nelson wall clock. "I wish I had time, but I've gotta get downtown before the line at the registrar is around the block."

She gives me a kiss on both cheeks. "Well, then bring that Joshua by at seven and I'll feed you both a proper meal—you're disappearing!"

◇

Josh groans and rolls slowly onto his back from where he has nearly blacked out after dropping the air conditioner outside my front door.

"You lied to me," he wheezes. "You said it was on the third floor."

"Yeah?" I say, shaking out my lower arms while leaning back against the top stair.

He lifts his head an inch off the floor. "Nan, that was six flights. Two flights a floor, which makes this technically, like, the sixth floor."

"You helped me move out of the dorm—"

"Yeah, why was that? Oh, right, because it has an el-e-va-tor."

"Well, the good news is that I'm not planning on moving out of here, *ever*. This is it. You can visit me up here when we're old and gray." I wipe the sweat off my forehead.

"Forget it—I'll be hanging out on your front stoop with the rest of the blue hairs." He drops his head back down.

"Come on." I pull myself up by the banister. "Cold beers await." I unlock all three locks and open the door. The apartment feels like a car that's been sitting in the hot sun and we have to step back to let the scorching air blow past us into the hallway.

"Charlene must have closed the windows before she left this morning," I say.

"And left the oven on," he adds, stepping behind me into the tiny entryway that also does double duty as a kitchen.

"Welcome to my fully equipped closet. Can I toast you a bagel?" I drop my keys next to the two-burner stove.

"What are you paying for this place?" he asks.

"You don't want to know," I say, as we push the air conditioner across the room together in little shoves.

"So, where's the hot roommate?" he asks.

"Josh, not all stewardesses are hot. Some are the matronly type."

"Is she?" He stops.

"Don't stop." We resume pushing. "No—she's hot, but I don't like you assuming she's hot. She flew to France or Spain or some-thing this morning," I huff as we round the corner to my end of the L-shaped studio.

"George!" Josh cries out in greeting to my cat, who's sprawled out on the warm wooden floor in despair. He lifts his gray, furry head half an inch and meows plaintively. Josh straightens up and wipes his forehead with the bottom of his Mr. Bubble T-shirt. "Where do you want this sucker?"

I point to the top of the window.

"*What?* You a crazy lady."

"It's a trick I learned on the Avenue, 'so as not to interfere with the view.' Those without central air go to great lengths to hide it, darling," I explain as I kick off my sandals.

"What view?"

"If you smoosh your face against the window and look left you can see the river."

"Hey, you're right." He pulls back from the glass. "Listen— this whole Josh-heaving-heavy-machinery-up-to-balance-on-sheet-of-glass-thing, not gonna happen, Nan. I'm getting a beer. Come on, George."

He heads back to the "kitchen" and George stretches up to follow him. I use the moment alone to grab a clean tank top out of an open box and pull off my sweaty one. As I crouch behind the boxes to change I catch sight of the red light from my answering machine blinking in a frenzy from the floor. The word "full" glares up at me.

"Running that 900 number again?" Josh reaches over the box to hand me a Corona.

"Practically. I put my ad up for a new position today and the mummies are restless." I take a swig of my beer and slide down between the boxes to hit play.

A woman's voice fills the room: "Hi, this is Mimi Van Owen. I saw your ad at the league. I'm looking for someone to help me look after my son. Just part-time, you understand. Maybe two, three, four days a week, half-days or longer and some nights or weekends, or both! Whenever you have time. But I just want you to know that I'm very involved."

"Well, that's just obvious, Mimi," Josh says, sliding down to join me.

"HithisisAnnSmithI'mlookingforsomeonetowatchmyfiveyearold-sonhe'snotroublereallyandwerunaveryrelaxedhousehold—"

"Ouch." Josh puts his hands up to shield himself and I forward to the next message.

"Hi. I'm Betty Potter. I saw your ad at the Parents League. I have a five-year-old girl, Stanton, a three-year-old boy, Tinford, a ten-month-old, Jace, and I'm looking for someone who can help me, since I'm pregnant again. Now you didn't mention your fee in the ad, but I've been paying six."

"Six American dollars?" I ask the machine, incredulously.

"Hey, Betty, I know a crack-whore down in Washington Square Park who'd do it for a quarter." Josh swigs his beer.

"Hi, it's Mrs. X. We met in the park this morning. Give me a call when you get a chance. I'd like to talk more about the type of job you're looking for. We have a girl—Caitlin—but she's looking to cut her hours and you made quite an impression on our son, Grayer. Look forward to talking to you. Bye."

"She sounds normal. Call her."

"You think?" I ask as the phone rings, making us both jump. I pick up the receiver. "Hello," I say in instant nanny mode, trying to convey utmost respectability with two syllables.

"Hello"—my mother matches my deep, fancy tone—"how'd the air-conditioner mission turn out?"

"Hey." I relax. "Fine—"

"Wait, hold on." I hear a scuffle. "I have to keep moving Sophie—she's determined to sit two inches from the air conditioner." I smile at the image of our fourteen-year-old springer spaniel with her ears blowing out behind her like the Red Baron. "Move it, Soph—and now she's sitting on all the research for the grant."

I take a sip of beer. "How's that coming?"

"Ugh, it's too depressing—tell me something cheerful." Since the Republicans took office my mother's Coalition for Women's Shelters gets even less money than it used to.

"I got some funny messages from mummies-in-need," I offer.

"I thought we discussed this." Her lawyer voice is back. "Nan, you take these jobs and within days you're up at three in the morning worrying if the little princess has tap dancing or a jam session with the Dalai Lama—"

"Mom. Mommm—I haven't even interviewed yet. Besides, I'm

not going to be working as many hours this year, because I have my thesis."

"Exactly! That's exactly it. You have your thesis, just like last year you had your internship and the year before that you had your field study. I don't understand why you won't even consider an academic job. You should ask your thesis professor if you can assist him. Or you could work in the research library!"

"We have been over this a million times." I roll my eyes at Josh. "Those jobs are so competitive—Dr. Clarkson has a graduate student on full fellowship assisting him. Besides, they only pay six dollars an hour—*before* taxes. Mom, nothing I do with my clothes on is going to pay this well until I get my degree." Josh shimmies and pulls off an imaginary bra.

My mother lucked out with a research assistant position that she held on to for all four years of her undergraduate work. However, that was when housing near Columbia cost as much as I am currently paying for utilities. "Do I have to give you the Real Estate Talk again, Mom?"

"Then, for the love of God, be a makeup girl at Bloomingdale's. Just punch in your time card, look pretty, smile, and get your paycheck." She can't imagine that one would ever wake at three A.M. in a cold sweat, wondering if the shipment of oil-free toner had remembered to put on its Nighttime Pull-Ups.

"*Mom*, I enjoy working with kids. Look, it's too hot to argue."

"Just promise me you'll think about it this time before you take a job. I don't want you graduating on Valium because some woman with more money than she knows what to do with left you her kid while she ran off to Cannes."

And I do think about it, while Josh and I listen to all the messages again trying to find the mother who sounds least likely to do just that.

◇ ◇ ◇

The following Monday on my way to meet Mrs. X I make a quick stop at my favorite stationery store to stock up on Post-its. Today my Filofax only has two Post-its: a tiny pink one imploring me to "BUY MORE POST-ITS" and a green one reminding me that I have "Coffee, Mrs. X, 11:15." I pull off the pink one and toss it in the trash as I continue heading south to La Pâtisserie Goût du Mois, our appointed meeting place. As I cut across to Park I begin passing chic women in fall suits, all holding sheets of monogrammed stationery in their bejeweled hands. Each one walks in tandem with a shorter, dark-skinned woman, who nods emphatically back at them.

"Baa-llleeeet? Do-you-un-der-stand!" the woman next to me rudely shouts to her nodding companion as we wait for the light to change. "On Mondays Josephina has Baaaaaa-lleeeeeeet!"

I smile sympathetically at the uniformed woman to show solidarity. No bones about it, training just plain sucks. And it sucks significantly harder, depending on who you're working for.

There are essentially three types of nanny gigs. Type A, I provide "couple time" a few nights a week for people who work all day and parent most nights. Type B, I provide "sanity time" a few afternoons a week to a woman who mothers most days and nights. Type C, I'm brought in as one of a cast of many to collectively provide twenty-four/seven "me time" to a woman who neither works nor mothers. And her days remain a mystery to us all.

"The agency said you can cook. Can you? Cook?" a Pucci-clad mother interrogates on the next corner.

As a working woman herself, the Type A mother will relate to me as a professional and treat me with respect. She knows I've arrived to do my job and, after a thorough tour, will hand me a comprehensive list of emergency numbers and skedaddle. This is the best transition a nanny can hope for. The child sobs for, at most, fifteen minutes, and before you know it we're bonding over Play-Doh.

The Type B mother may not work in an office, but she logs enough hours with her child to recognize it for the job it is and, following an afternoon of hanging around the apartment together, her kids are all mine for the second date.

"Now the dry cleaner's number is on there and the florist and the caterer."

"What about the doctor for the children?" the Mexican woman next to me asks quietly.

"Oh. I'll get you that next week."

Suffice it to say that the quirk factor sharply increases as one moves along the spectrum from A to C. The only thing predictable about training with a Type C mother is that her pervasive insecurity forces everyone to take the longest possible route to getting in sync.

I push open the heavy glass door of the pâtisserie and see Mrs. X already seated, going over her own list. She stands, revealing a lavender knee-length skirt, which perfectly matches the cardigan tied around her shoulders. No longer in her youthful white shift, she looks older than she did in the park. Despite her girlish ponytail I'm guessing she's in her early forties. "Hi, Nanny, thanks so much for meeting me early. Would you like some coffee?"

"That sounds perfect, thank you," I say, taking a seat with my back to the wood-paneled wall and smoothing the damask napkin onto my lap.

"Waiter, another café au lait and could you bring us a bread-basket?"

"Oh, you don't need to do that," I say.

"Oh, no, it's the best. That way you can pick what you want." The waiter brings over a Pierre Deux basket brimming with breads and little jars of jam. I help myself to a brioche.

"They have the best pastry here," she says, taking a croissant. "Which reminds me, I prefer that Grayer stay away from refined flour."

"Of course," I mumble, mouth full.

"Did you have a nice weekend?"

I quickly swallow. "Sarah—my best friend from Chapin—had a

little farewell party last night before everyone goes back to school. Now it's just me and the California people—who have off till October! Tell Grayer to go to Stanford," I laugh.

She smiles.

"So, why'd you transfer from Brown?" she asks, pulling one claw off her croissant.

"They had a stronger child development program at NYU," I reply, trying to tread lightly here, in case I'm talking to a steadfast Brown alum, choosing not to mention the human excrement in the lounge next to my room, or any other of the myriad of charming anecdotes I could share.

"I really wanted to go to Brown," she says.

"Oh?"

"But I won a scholarship to UConn." She drops the croissant to play with the diamond heart dangling from her necklace.

"That's great," I say, trying to imagine a time when she would have needed a scholarship to do anything.

"Well, I'm from Connecticut, so . . ."

"Oh! Connecticut's beautiful," I say.

She glances down at her plate. "Actually, it was New London so . . . Well, after graduation I moved here to run Gagosian—the art gallery." She smiles again.

"Wow—that must have been amazing."

"It was a lot of fun," she says, nodding, "but you can't really do it when you have a child—it's a full-time life, parties, trips, a lot of shmoozing, a lot of late nights—"

A woman in dark Jackie O sunglasses accidentally bumps our table as she passes, causing the china saucers to teeter precariously on the marble.

"Binky?" Mrs. X asks, reaching up to touch the woman's arm as I steady the cups.

"Oh, my God. Hi, I didn't even see you there," the woman says, lowering her dark glasses. Her eyes are swollen and damp from crying. "I'm sorry I couldn't come to Grayer's birthday party. Consuela said it was fabulous."

"I've been meaning to call," Mrs. X says. "Is there anything I can do?"

"Not unless you know a hit man." She pulls a handkerchief out of her Tod's purse and blows her nose. "That lawyer Gina Zuckerman recommended couldn't help at all. It turns out all our assets are actually in Mark's company's name. He's getting the apartment, the yacht, the house in East Hampton. I'm getting four hundred thousand flat—that's it." Mrs. X swallows and Binky continues tearfully. "And I have to supply complete receipts for every penny of child support spent. I mean, really. Am I supposed to get my facials at Baby Gap?"

"That's appalling."

"Then the judge had the nerve to tell me to go back to work! He has no idea what it means to be a mom."

"None of them do," Mrs. X says, tapping her list for emphasis, while I stare intently at my brioche.

"If I had known he was going to go this far, I would have just turned a blind—" Binky's voice breaks and she purses her glossy lips together to clear her throat. "Well, I've gotta run—Consuela has another 'appointment' for her hip replacement." She speaks with venom. "I swear, it's the third one this month. I'm really losing patience with her. Anyway, great to see you." She pushes her sunglasses back into place and, with an air kiss, disappears through the crowd awaiting tables.

"Well . . ." Mrs. X stares after her, her face locked briefly into a grimace before returning her attention to me. "Well, let's just go over the week. I've typed this all up for you, so you can review it later. We'll walk over to school now, so Grayer can see us together and get the sense that I'm trusting you with him. That should relax him. He has a play date at one-thirty, so that'll give you just enough time to have lunch in the park and yet not overwhelm him. Then tomorrow you and Caitlin can both spend the afternoon with him, so you can get a sense of his routine and he can see the authority being shared between you. I'd appreciate it if you didn't discuss the transition with her at this point."

"Of course," I say, trying to absorb it all, the brioches, the briefing, Binky. "Thank you for breakfast."

"Oh, don't mention it." She stands, pulling a blue folder that says "Nanny" out of her Hermès bag and sliding it across the table. "I'm so glad Tuesdays and Thursdays fit into your class schedule. I think it'll be great for Grayer to have someone young and fun to play with—I'm sure he gets tired of boring old Mom!"

"Grayer seems great," I say, recalling his giggles in the park.

"Well, he has his little things, like any kid, I suppose."

I gather my bag, glancing down and noticing her lavender silk heels for the first time. "God, those are beautiful! Are they Prada?" I ask, recognizing the silver buckle.

"Oh, thank you." She turns her ankle. "Yes, they are. You really like them?" I nod. "You don't think they're too . . . loud?"

"Oh, no," I say, following her out of the café.

"My best friend just had a baby and her feet went up a whole size. She let me pick out what I wanted, but I . . . I don't know." She glances down at her shoes in consternation as we wait for the light. "I guess I've just gotten used to wearing flats."

"No, they're great. You should definitely keep them."

She smiles, delighted, as she slides on her sunglasses.

⟡

Mrs. Butters, Grayer's teacher, smiles at me and shakes my hand. "It's a pleasure to meet you." She looks down adoringly. "You are going to love Grayer, he's a very special little boy." She pats her corduroy apron dress, which fits loosely over her puffed-sleeve blouse. With her round, dimpled cheeks and plump, dimpled hands she looks much like a four-year-old herself.

"Hi, Grayer!" I say, smiling down at the top of his blond head. He's wearing a little white oxford button-down Polo shirt, untucked on one side, containing the evidence of a morning hard at work: finger paint, what looks like glue, and one lone macaroni. "How was school today?"

"Grayer, you remember Nanny? You two are going to have lunch at the playground!" his mother prompts him.

He slumps against her leg and glares at me. "Go away."

"Honey, we can have snack together, but Mommy has an appointment. You two are going to have such a good time! Now hop in your stroller and Nanny will give you snack."

As we approach the playground he and I both listen attentively to the long list of Grayer's Likes and Dislikes: "He loves the slide, but the monkey bars bore him. Don't let him pick anything up off the ground—he likes to do that. And please keep him away from the drinking fountain by the clock."

"Um, what should I do if he needs to use the bathroom? Where should he go?" I ask as we pass under the dusty wooden arches of the Sixty-sixth Street playground.

"Oh, anywhere."

I'm just about to ask for a little clarification on the peeing thing when her cell phone rings.

"Okay, Mommy's gotta go," she says, snapping her Startac closed. Her departure is like the suicide drills from gym class—every time she gets just a few feet farther away, Grayer cries and she scurries back, admonishing, "Now, let's be a big boy." Only once Grayer is in complete hysterics does she look at her watch and with a "Now Mommy's going to be late" is gone.

We sit on the only empty bench in the shade, while he sniffles, and eat our sandwiches, which have some sort of vegetable spread in them and, I think, unbologna. As he raises his sleeve to wipe his nose I notice for the first time, dangling from beneath his untucked shirttails, what appears to be a business card pinned to his belt loop.

I reach out. "Grayer, what's with the—"

"Hey!" He swats my hand away. "That's my card." It's dirty and bent and has clearly been around the block a few times, but I think I can make out Mr. X's name in faded type.

"Whose card is that, Grayer?"

"You know." He pounds his forehead, exasperated by my ignorance. "My card. Jeez. Push me on the swings!"

By the time we're done eating and I've given him a few pushes it's time for us to walk over to his play date. I wave as he runs into the apartment. "Okay, bye, Grayer! See you tomorrow!" He screeches to a halt, turns around, sticks his tongue out at me and then runs off. "Okay, have fun!" I smile at the other nanny as if to say "Oh, that? That's just our tongue game!"

Once I'm on the subway to school I pull out the blue folder, which has my pay envelope paper-clipped inside.

MRS. X

721 PARK AVENUE, APT. 9B

NEW YORK, N.Y., 10021

Dear Nanny,

Welcome! The attached is a copy of Grayer's schedule of after-school activities. Caitlin will show you the routine, but I'm sure you've been to most of these places before! Let me know if you have any questions.

Thanks, Mrs. X

P.S. I've also included a list of some possible fun activities.

P.P.S. I really prefer it if Grayer doesn't nap in the afternoons.

I glance at the schedule and she's right—I'm a veteran of every activity on the list.

MONDAY

2–2:45: Music lesson, Diller Quaile, 95th Street between Park and Madison

(*Parents pay an astronomical sum for this prestigious music school where four-year-olds usually sit in stone-cold silence as their caregivers sing nursery rhymes in a circle.*)

5–5:45: Mommy & Me, 92nd Street Y on Lexington

(*As the name implies, mothers are expected to go. Nevertheless, half of the group is nannies.*)

TUESDAY

4–5:00: Swimming lesson at Asphalt Green, 90th Street and East End Avenue

(*One emaciated woman in a Chanel swimsuit and five nannies in muumuus all pleading with toddlers to "Get in the water!"*)

WEDNESDAY

2–3:00: Physical education at CATS, Park Avenue at 64th Street

(*Deep in the bowels of a cold, dank church that smells like feet, thoroughly choreographed games for the pint-sized athlete.*)

5–5:45: Karate, 92nd Street Y on Lexington

(*Kids who quake with fear do fifty push-ups on their knuckles as a warm-up. The one class daddies attend.*)

THURSDAY

2–2:45: Piano lesson at home with Ms. Schrade

(*"Music" to be tortured by.*)

5–6:00: French Class, Alliance Française, 60th Street between Madison and Park

(*Standard afterschool activities conducted in another language.*)

FRIDAY

1–1:40: Ice skating, The Ice Studio, Lexington between 73rd and 74th Street (*Cold as fuck—and damp. Struggle through a thirty-minute "Change of Terror," sharp metal blades flying everywhere, so children can get on ice for forty minutes and come back out to change again.*)

I will let you know when he is scheduled for the:

Optician
Orthodontist
Orthodic fittings
Physical therapist
Ayurvedic practitioner

In the event of a class cancellation the following "nonstructured" outings are permissible:
The Frick
The Met
The Guggenheim Soho
The Morgan Library
The French Culinary Institute
The Swedish Consulate
Orchid Room of the Botanical Garden
New York Stock Exchange Trading Floor
The Angelika (*Preferably the German Expressionist series, but anything with subtitles will do.*)

I shrug and open the envelope, thrilled to discover that despite only working two hours, she's paid me for the whole day. The Envelope is a major perk of being a nanny. Traditionally, we're kept off the books and dealt with strictly in cash, which always keeps me hoping she'll stick in an extra twenty. A girl I knew lived-in with a family whose father slipped a few hundred dollars under her door whenever his wife drank too much and "caused a scene." It's like waiting tables—you just never know when the customer might be overwhelmed with appreciation.

✧ ✧ ✧

"Caitlin? Hi, I'm Nanny," I say. Mrs. X told me that my colleague is blond and Australian, which makes her fairly easy to pick out amid the sea of faces that have had work done and the faces that are doing the work. I recognize her from the Xes' photo session in the park.

She looks up from where she sits on the school steps, sensibly outfitted in an Izod shirt and jeans, a sweatshirt tied round her waist. She's holding Grayer's apple juice in her right hand with the straw already in it. I'm impressed.

Just as she stands to return my greeting, our charge and his class-mates are released by his teacher and the courtyard becomes instantly animated. Grayer comes streaking through the crowd toward Caitlin, but screeches to a halt when he sees me, his enthusi-asm visibly draining out through his Keds.

"Grayer, Nanny'll be coming to the park with us this after-noon—won't that be fun?" I sense from her tone that she isn't quite convinced we're in for a laugh riot. "He's always a bit cranky when school lets out, but he gets over it fine once he's had his snack."

"I'm sure."

It is chaos around us as children are snacked and play dates are made. I'm impressed by the finesse with which she works Grayer from snack to stroller to good-byes. He maintains screaming conver-sation with three of his classmates while getting a sweater put on, a Baggie opened, homework unpinned from his lapel, and a stroller strapped under him. She's like a puppeteer, keeping the play in motion. I debate taking notes. "Right hand on stroller handle, left hand pull down sweater, two steps left and squat."

We head toward the park as they chatter away. She propels him forward with ease, though he can't be a light load with his sand toys, school stuff, and backup supplies of snack.

"Grayer, who's your best friend at school?" I ask.

"Shut up, stupidhead," he says, kicking out at my shins. I walk the remainder of the way well outside his field of stroller vision.

After lunch Caitlin takes me around to meet the other nannies in the playground, most of whom are Irish, Jamaican, or Filipino. They each give me a quick, cold appraisal and I get the sense I won't be making a lot of friends here.

"So what do you do during the week?" she asks suspiciously.

"I'm a senior at NYU," I say.

"I couldn't figure out how she found someone who only wanted to work weekends." What? Weekends what?

She reties her ponytail while she continues. "I'd do it, but I wait tables on the weekends and, really, one needs a bit of a break by Friday. I thought they had a girl who worked weekends in the country, but I guess she didn't work out. Are you planning on driving out with them to Connecticut on Friday nights or taking the train?" She looks pointedly at me as I stare back at her in confusion.

Then it is suddenly clear to both of us why we aren't meant to discuss the "transition." I'm not the pinch hitter, I'm the replacement. A sadness flickers over her features.

I reach to change the subject. "So, what's with the card?"

"Oh, that grotty old thing." She swallows. "He carries it everywhere. He'll be wanting it pinned to his trousers and in his pajamas. It drives the Mrs. crazy, but he refuses to so much as put on his underpants without it." She blinks a few times and then turns away.

We make it full circle back to the sandbox where another family, who I assume from their matching shell suits and overwhelming zest for life are tourists, is playing.

"He's so cute. Is he your only child?" the mother asks in a flat Midwestern accent. I'm twenty-one. He's four.

"No, I'm his—"

"I told you to get out of here, you bad woman!" Grayer hurls his stroller at me, screaming at the top of his lungs.

Blood rushes to my face as I retort with false confidence, "You . . . silly!" The tourist clan focus intently on a group sand-castle project.

I consider taking a playground poll as to whether I should "get out" and, if I choose not to, does this, in fact, make me a "bad woman"?

Caitlin rights the stroller as if his throwing it were part of a fabulous game we're playing. "Well, looks to me like somebody has a bit of energy and wants me to catch him!" She chases him all over the playground, laughing deeply. He slides down the slide and she catches him. He hides behind the monkey bars and she catches him. There is a lot of catching overall. I start to chase her as she chases him, but give up when he looks pleadingly into my eyes, moaning "STOaaaooop." I walk to a bench. As I watch them play I have to hand it to her. She has perfected the magic act that is child care, creating the illusion of an effortless relationship; she could be his mother.

Eventually, Caitlin drags him over to me with a Frisbee in hand. "Well now, Grayer, why don't we teach Nanny the Frisbee game?" We stand in triangular formation as she tosses the Frisbee to me. I catch it and toss it to Grayer, who gracefully receives it by sticking out his tongue and turning his back to both of us. I pick up the Frisbee from where it has landed by his feet and toss it back to her. She throws it to him and he catches it and throws it back to her. It seems to take hours, this halting circuit that comes to a full stop whenever contact is required between him and me. He simply denies that I exist and sticks out his tongue at any effort to prove otherwise. We play on and on because she wants to make it right and thinks maybe she can wear him down to the point where he will at least toss me a Frisbee. I think we have all set our sights just a little too high.

◇ ◇ ◇

Three days later, just as I bend over to pick up the grubby little sneaker Grayer has hurled into the Xes' marble entryway, the front door slams behind me with a loud bang. I jerk upright, still holding his shoe.

"Shit."

"I heard you! You said 'Shit.' You said it!" Muffled sounds of a gleeful Grayer make their way through the heavy door.

I steady my voice and reach for a low, authoritative octave. "Grayer, open the door."

"No! I can stick my fingers out at you and you can't see. I got my thung thitikin out, too." He's sticking his tongue out at me.

Okay, options. Option One, knock on crotchety-matron-across-the-way's door. Right, what am I going to do then? Call Grayer? Invite him over for tea? His little fingers sweep out beneath the door.

"Nanny, try to catch my fingers! Do it! Do it! Come on, catch 'em!" I concentrate every muscle on not stepping on them.

Option Two, go down to the doorman and get extra keys. Right. By the time he finishes describing this to Mrs. X not even Joan Crawford would hire me.

"You're not even playing! I'm going to go take a bath. So don't ever come back here, okay? My mom said you don't ever have to come back." His voice gets quieter as he starts to move from the door. "Going to get in the tub."

"GRAYER!" I scream before I catch my breath. "Don't walk away from this door. Ummm, I have a surprise out here for you." Option Three, wait until Mrs. X gets home and tell her the truth: her son is a sociopath. But just as I settle on Option Three, the elevator door slides open and Mrs. X, her neighbor, and the doorman all step out.

"Nanny? Naaanny, I don't want your surprise. So go away. Really, really, go, get out of here." Well, at least we've all been updated. With a few "ahems" the neighbor lets herself into her apartment and the doorman hands off the package he's been carrying and disappears back into the elevator.

I hold up Grayer's shoe.

As if for a studio audience, Mrs. X whips out her keys and proceeds to remedy the situation. "Well, then. Let's get this door open!" She laughs and unlocks the door. But she swings it open a little too quickly and catches one of Grayer's fingers.

"AHHhhhhhh. Nanny broke my hand! AAAAAHhhhhh—my hand is broke. Get out of HEERRrrreeee! GooOOOOoooo!" He throws himself onto the floor, sobbing, lost in grief.

Mrs. X bends down, as if about to hold him, then straightens up.

"Well, looks like you really tuckered him out at the park! You can go on ahead. I'm sure you have a ton of homework to do. We'll see you Monday, then?" I reach carefully inside the doorway and put his shoe down in exchange for my backpack.

I clear my throat. "He just threw his shoe and I—"

At the sound of my voice Grayer lets out a fresh wail. "LEEAAAVVE! Ahhahhha." She stares down at him as he writhes on the floor, smiles broadly, and pantomimes that I should get the elevator. "Oh, and Nanny, C-a-i-t-l-i-n won't be returning, but I'm sure you have the hang of everything by now."

I close their door and am alone again in the now familiar vestibule. I wait for the elevator and listen to Grayer scream. I feel as though the whole world is sticking its tongue out at me.

✧

"Keep your nose out of it, Nanny Drew." My father slurps the last drops of his wonton soup. "You never know. Maybe this Caitlin had another job lined up."

"I didn't really get that sense . . ."

"You like the kid?"

"Minus the locking-me-out part—yeah, okay."

"So, then, you're not marrying these people. You're just working there—what?—fifteen hours a week?" The waiter places a plate of fortune cookies between us and takes the check.

"Twelve." I reach for a cookie.

"Right. So don't get your knickers in a twist."

"But what do I do about Grayer?"

"They're always a little slow to warm up at first," he says, speaking from eighteen years of experience as an English teacher. He grabs a cookie and takes my hand. "Come on, let's walk and talk. Sophie won't be able to keep her legs crossed much longer." We weave out of the restaurant and head over to West End Avenue.

I put my arm through his as he slips his hands into his blazer pockets.

"Glinda-the-Good-Witch him," he says, chewing his cookie thoughtfully.

"Care to elaborate?"

He shoots me a look. "I was finishing my cookie. Are you paying attention?"

"Yes."

"Because this is good stuff." I stand, waiting, with my arms crossed. "In essence, you are Glinda. You are light and clarity and fun. He is an inanimate object, a toaster who happens to have a tongue hanging out. If he goes too far again—I'm talking the door-locking routine, physical violence, or anything that puts him in danger—BABOOM! Wicked Witch of the West! Two point four seconds—you swoop down in front of his face and hiss that he must never do that again—*ever*. It is *not okay*. And then, before he can bat an eyelash, back to Glinda. You let him know he can have feelings, but that there are boundaries. And that you'll let him know when he has pushed too far. Trust me, he'll be relieved. Now, wait here while I get the Sophster."

He disappears into our lobby and I look up between the buildings to the orange sky above. Within minutes Sophie bursts through the front door, pulling the leash in his hand taut as she waggles over, smiling up at me as she always does. I crouch down, wrapping my arms around her neck, and burrow my head in her brown and white fur.

"I'll walk her, Dad." I give him a hug and take the leash. "It'll be good to be around someone under three feet who doesn't talk back."

"And who only sticks out her tongue for biological necessity!" he calls after me.

✧ ✧ ✧

I stand on the sidewalk outside Grayer's school on the following Monday. I'm ten minutes early, as per Mrs. X's strict instructions, so I flip through my Filofax and chart out the deadlines for my next two papers. A taxi comes to a screeching halt on the corner and I look up at the pandemonium of honking cars around it. Across the median a blond woman stands frozen under the shade of an awning. The cars move again and she's gone.

I crane my head, trying to locate the woman, to be sure if it was Caitlin. But the other side of Park Avenue is now empty, save for a maintenance man polishing a brass hydrant.

"Not you!" Grayer draaaaags himself all the way across the courtyard, as if he were marching toward certain death.

"Hey, Grayer. How was school?"

"Yucky."

"Yucky? What was yucky about it?" I unpin the homework, pass off the juice.

"Nothing."

"Nothing was yucky?" Buckle in stroller, unwrap pears.

"I don't want to talk to you."

I kneel in front of the stroller and look him squarely in the eyes. "Look, Grayer, I know you don't like me very much."

"I HATE YOU!" I am light. I am clarity. I am wearing a big, pink dress.

"And that's okay, you haven't known me very long. But I like you a lot." He starts to kick his leg out at me. "I know you miss Caitlin." He freezes at the sound of her name and I catch his foot firmly in my hand. "It's okay to miss Caitlin. Missing her shows that you love her. But being mean to me hurts my feelings and I know Caitlin would never want you to hurt anyone's feelings. So, as long as we're together, let's have fun." His eyes are like saucers.

As we head out of the courtyard the rain that's been threatening all morning finally breaks and I have to push Grayer back up to 721 Park Avenue as if I'm in the Stroller Olympics.

"Weeeeeeee!" he cries and I make race-car noises and steer sharply around puddles all the way home. By the time we get into the lobby we're both soaked and I pray Mrs. X isn't home to see how I've exposed her child to pneumonia.

"I sure am wet. Are you wet, Grayer?"

"I sure am. I sure am wet." He's smiling, but his teeth are starting to chatter.

"We're gonna get you right upstairs and into a hot bath. Ever had lunch in the bath, Grayer?" I steer him into the elevator.

"Wait! Hold it!" a male voice shouts from around the corner.

I slam the stroller into my ankle trying to angle it away from the door. "Ow, sh—oot!"

"Hey, thanks," he says. I look up from my ankle. The rain has plastered his brown, chin-length hair and frayed blue T-shirt to his six-foot frame. Oh, my.

As the elevator closes he crouches down to speak directly to the stroller. "Hey, Grayer! Whassup?"

"She's wet." Grayer points behind him.

"Hi, wet girl. Are you Grayer's girlfriend?" He smiles at me, tucking his damp hair behind his ear.

"He's not sure if he's ready to make that kind of commitment," I say.

"Well, Grayer, don't let her get away." If you tried to catch me, I promise I would run *very slowly*.

We arrive at the ninth floor way too soon. "Have a great afternoon, guys," he says as we get out.

"You, too!" I cry as the door slides closed. Who are you?

"Grayer, who is he?" Stroller unclasped, wet shirt off.

"He lives upstairs. He goes to big boy's school." Shoes off, pants off, grab lunch bag.

"Oh, yeah? Which one?" Follow naked tush to bathroom, turn on tap.

He thinks for a moment. "Where the boats go. With the light-house." Okaaay. Two syllables, sounds like . . .

"Harbor?" I query.

"Yeah, he goes to Harbard." Hello, I can totally do Boston, especially with the shuttle. We could alternate weekends . . . Jesus! *EARTH TO NANNY, COME IN, NANNY!*

"Okay, Grayer, let's get you in the tub." I heave him over the edge, letting go of my Harvard Hottie for the moment. "Grayer, do you have a nickname?"

"What's a nickname?"

"A name that people call you that isn't Grayer."

"My name is Grayer X. That's my name."

"Well, let's think of one." I pop him in the tub and pass him his organic peanut butter and quince jelly sandwich. He wiggles his toes in the water as he munches the sandwich and I can tell it feels fabulously unorthodox to him. I look around the bathroom and my eyes land on his blue Sesame Street toothbrush.

"What about Grover?" I ask.

He mulls it over, his head cocked to one side, his Serious Thinking Face on, then nods. "We'll try it."

Lord, how my head aches! What a head have I!
My back a t'other side—ah, my back, my back!
Beshrew your heart for sending me about
To catch my death with jauncing up and down!

—THE NURSE, *ROMEO AND JULIET*

CHAPTER TWO

Multitasking

Nanny,
While you're on your play date with Alex today,
please ask Alex's mother who catered her last
dinner—tell her I thought Cajun-infused Asian
was a stroke of genius.
Just to let you know, the parents are
D I V O R C I N G. So sad. Please make sure
Grayer doesn't say anything awkward. I'll swing
by Alex's at 4:30 to take Grayer to his orthodist.
See you then.

"Nanny? Nanny?!" Mrs. X's disembodied voice calls out to me as I jog up the block toward the nursery school courtyard.

"Yes?" I say, spinning around.

"This way." The door of a Lincoln town car pops open and Mrs. X's manicured hand flags me over.

"I'm so glad you're here," I say, leaning down to where she's seated amid her shopping bags in the plush darkness. "Because I need to ask you—"

"Nanny, I just want to reiterate that I'd like you to always get here ten minutes early."

"Of course."

"Well, it's eleven fifty-five."

"I'm really sorry—I was trying to find Grayer's class list. I'm not sure which Alex—"

But she's already busy rooting around in her purse. She pulls a small leather-bound notepad out of her hobo bag. "I want to talk with you briefly about a party I'm throwing at the end of the month for the Chicago branch of Mr. X's company." She uncrosses and recrosses her legs, the lavender Prada shoes making an arc of bright color against the dark interior of the town car. "All the top executives will be there—it's a very important evening and I want it to be perfect for my husband."

"Sounds lovely," I say, unsure why I'm being apprised of this fete.

She lowers her sunglasses to make sure that I have taken in every word.

Should I bring my formal wear to the dry cleaner's?

"So, I may need you to run a few errands for me this month. It's just that I'm so overwhelmed with the preparations and Connie's absolutely no help. So if there's anything I need I'll just leave you a note—it really shouldn't be much."

We both hear the heavy clank of the double doors opening behind me followed by the growing swell of children's laughter.

"I better run, if he sees me he'll just get all upset. Let's go, Ricardo!" she calls to the driver and he pulls out before she's even got her door closed.

"Wait, Mrs. X, I needed to ask you a question—" I call after the retreating taillights.

There are four Alexanders and three Alexandras in Grayer's class.

I know. I checked. And now that Mrs. X has sped off I'm still at a complete loss as to which one is supposed to be our escort for the afternoon.

Grayer, however, seems to know exactly who our date is.

"It's her. I have a play date with her," he says, pointing across the courtyard at a little girl hunkered down over something intriguing at ground level. I grab Grayer and make our way over.

"Hi, Alex. We have a play date with you this afternoon!" I enthusiastically inform her.

"My name's Cristabelle. Alex is wearing a shirt," she says, pointing over at thirty shirt-wearing children. Grayer looks up at me blankly.

"Grayer, Mommy said you have a play date with Alex," I say.

He shrugs. "How about Cristabelle? Cristabelle, want to have a play date?" Apparently, one play date's as good as another.

"Grover, it's not Cristabelle, sweetie. But we can have a play date with Cristabelle another day. Would you like that?" The little girl huffs off. At the age of four she seems already to know that if the date has to be postponed it probably isn't going to happen.

"Okay, Grayer, *think*. Didn't your mom say anything to you this morning?"

"She said I have to use more toothpaste."

"Alex Brandi, does that ring any bells?" I ask, trying to rattle off the names I remember from the class list.

"He picks his nose."

"Alex Kushman?"

"She spits Kool-Aid." He cracks himself up.

I sigh, looking out across the crowded courtyard. Somewhere in this chaos is another pair who shares our plan. I get a flash of us—airport-reception style—me in a chauffeur's cap, Grayer on my shoulders, holding a big sign that says "ALEX."

"Hi, I'm Murnel." An older, uniformed woman appears before us. "This is Alex. Sorry, we had a bit of trouble tearing ourselves away from the blue goop." I notice some of it still clinging to her nylon jacket. "Alex, say hello to Grayer," she says in a thick West Indian accent.

After proper introductions we push our charges over to Fifth Avenue. Like little old men in wheelchairs, they relax back in their seats, look about and occasionally converse. "My Power Ranger has a subatomic machine gun and can cut your Power Ranger's head off."

Murnel and I are comparatively quiet. Despite the fact that we share the same job title, in her eyes I probably have more in common with Grayer, as there are at least fifteen years and a long subway ride from the Bronx between us.

"How long you been taking care of him?" She nods down in the direction of Grayer's stroller.

"A month. How about you?"

"Oh, nearly three years now. My daughter looks after Alex's cousin, Benson, up on Seventy-second. You know Benson?" she inquires.

"I don't think so. Is he is in their class?"

"Benson's a girl." We both laugh. "And she goes to school across the park. How old are you?"

"Just turned twenty-one in August." I smile.

"Ooh, you're my son's age. I should introduce you. He's real smart, just opened his own diner out by LaGuardia. You got a boyfriend?"

"Nope, haven't met one lately who isn't more trouble than he's worth," I say. She nods in agreement. "That must not be an easy thing to do—open a restaurant, I mean."

"Well, he's a real hard worker. Gets it from his mother," she says proudly, bending over to pick up the drained juice box Alex has tossed into the street. "My grandson's hard working, too, and he's only seven. He's doing real well in his classes."

"That's great."

"My neighbor always says he's so good about doing his home-work—she stays with him in the afternoons till my daughter can get home from Benson, round nine, usually."

"Nanny! I want more juice!"

"Please," I say, reaching into the stroller bag.

"Please," Grayer mumbles as I pass him a second juice box.

"Thank you," I correct him and Murnel and I exchange smiles.

I'm the last of our crew to walk through Alex's front door. There is very little in this neighborhood that I haven't seen, but I'm com-pletely unprepared for the large strip of duct tape running down the middle of the front hall.

According to New York State law, if one spouse moves out the other can claim abandonment and will most likely get the apart-ment. Some of these places go for fifteen to twenty million, forcing years of bitter cohabitation while each spouse tries to wear down the other by, for example, bringing in their half-naked exercise instruc-tor/lover to live.

"Okay, now you boys can play anywhere on that side," she says, gesturing to the left side of the apartment.

"Nanny, why is there a stripe—" I fix Grayer with a quick Look of Death as I unbuckle his stroller and then wait until Alex is behind me to raise my finger to my lips and point to the tape.

"Alex's mommy and daddy are playing a game," I whisper. "We'll talk about it at home."

"My dad's not sharing," Alex announces.

"Now who wants grilled cheese? Alex, go show Grayer your new photon gun," Murnel says as the boys run off. She turns toward the kitchen. "Make yourself at home," she says, rolling her eyes at the tape.

I wander into the living room, which is faux Louis XIV meets Jackie Collins, with a nice, wide stripe of electrical tape down the middle to give it that certain je ne sais quoi. I sit down on what I hope is the Switzerland area of the couch and instantly recognize the work of Antonio. He's the assistant to one of the most popular decorators and will, for a minor consideration, pop by frequently to "plump" your pillows. He is, in essence, a professional pillow plumper.

I try to heave the twenty-pound copy of *Tuscan Homes*, the current coffee table book of choice, into my lap without bruising myself. After a few minutes of flipping through pictures of villas, I become aware of a little nose resting on the arm of the couch. "Hey," I quietly acknowledge the nose.

"Hey," he replies, coming around the couch to slump face-first onto the cushion next to me, his arms outstretched.

"What's the story?" I ask, looking down at his back, so small against the wide black velvet stripes.

"I was supposed to bring my toys."

"Huh."

He climbs up into my lap, snuggling under *Tuscan Homes*, and helps me turn pages. I feel the softness of his hair under my chin and give his ankle a gentle squeeze. I'm not feeling incredibly motivated to get this play date back on track.

"Lunch!" we hear called from behind us. "What are you all doing in there? Alex!" Murnel calls off toward his room. We stand up.

"I forgot to bring my toys," Grayer offers. Murnel puts her hands on her hips.

"That boy. Come on, Grayer, we'll get this straightened out." Grayer and I follow her past the kitchen where something is buzzing loudly. "Hold on, hold on," she says with a sigh. She goes directly to the intercom, a small box above a tray laden with grilled-cheese sandwiches and sliced fruit.

She presses the button. "Yes, ma'am?"

"Has the motherfucker called?" a woman's voice crackles out of the wall.

"No, ma'am."

"Goddammit! Ever since he froze my fucking cards I'm supposed to get a fucking check. How hard is that? I mean, how am I supposed to feed Alex? Fucker. Did you pick up my La Mer?"

"Yes, ma'am."

Murnel picks up the tray and we follow her silently down to Alex's room. I am the last one in. Half the room is completely bare, a line of model cars down the middle serving as impromptu duct tape, and Alex, shirtless and shoeless, paces in front of a stockpile of all his earthly possessions. He halts and looks up at us.

"I told the fucker he has to bring his own toys."

✧ ✧ ✧

Nanny,

Please call the caterers and double-check what kind of utensils and linens they'll be bringing for Mr. X's party. Please see that they drop off all the linens in advance so Connie can rewash them.

Grayer has his St. David's interview today, after which I'll be running to a meeting with the florist. So Mr. X will drive by and drop Grayer off to you at precisely 1:45 on the <u>northwest</u> corner of Ninety-fifth and Park.

Please be sure to be standing as close to the curb as possible so that the driver can see you. Please get there by 1:30 just in case they're early. I'm sure this goes without saying, but Mr. X should not have to get out of the car.

In the meantime, I'll need you to start assembling the following items for the gift bags.

Except for the champagne, you should be able to find most of these at Gracious Home.

Annick Goutal soap
Piper Heidsieck, small bottle
Morocco leather travel picture frame, red or green
Mont Blanc pen—small
LAVENDER WATER
See you at 6!

I reread the note, wondering if I'm supposed to pull out my magic decoder ring to figure out how many of each item she wants me to buy.

She doesn't answer her cell, so I decide to call Mr. X's office after getting his number off the phone list posted inside the pantry door.

"What?" he answers after one ring.

"Um, Mr. X, it's Nanny—"

"Who? How did you get this number?"

"Nanny. I look after Grayer—"

"Who?"

Unsure how to clarify without seeming impertinent, I barrel on. "Your wife wants me to pick up the stuff for the gift baskets for the party—"

"What party? What the hell are you talking about? Who is this?"

"On the twenty-eighth? For the Chicago people?"

"My wife told you to call me?" He sounds angry.

"No. I just needed to know how many people are coming and I couldn't—"

"Oh, for crissake."

My ear fills with dial tone.

Right.

✧

I walk over to Third, trying to figure out how many of each thing I'm supposed to buy, as if it were a logic puzzle. It's a sit-down dinner, so it can't be a ton of people, but it must be more than, say, eight, or so, if she's having caterers and renting tables. I think she's renting three tables and they probably seat six or eight each, so that'll be eighteen or twenty-four . . . So, either I show up empty-handed tonight or I pick a number.

Twelve.

I stop in front of the liquor store. Twelve. That feels right.

I lug the twelve bottles of Piper Heidsieck to Gracious Home, a housewares store, whose two initial branches are bizarrely right across Third Avenue from each other. They carry everything from luxury items at luxury prices to everyday household items at luxury prices. All so a woman can walk in, buy a ten-dollar bottle of cleanser, and walk out with a cute shopping bag, feeling as if she's had some fun.

I start pulling out picture frames and clearing out all their soap, but I have no idea what or where lavender water is. I look down at the list.

LAVENDER WATER. Like the other women I've worked for, I'm sure she used all caps without thinking, threw the underline in as an afterthought, but, to me, she's screaming. It's as if, suddenly, her life depends on LAVENDER WATER or MILK or EDAMAME. I'm tempted to put my hands up to my ears as their heads rise out of the notepaper, like something from *Terminator 2*, screaming, "CLOROX!!!!!!!"

I commence combing the shelves in pursuit of lavender water and find that Caswell-Massey only makes freesia water, but she definitely wanted lavender. Crabtree and Evelyn have lavender drawer liners, but that's clearly not it. Roger and Gallet make a lavender soap and Rigaud, I'm informed, "doesn't do lavender." Then finally, on the very bottom shelf of another wall, with Grayer scheduled to drop and roll out of the town car in exactly five minutes, I see The Thymes Limited Lavender Home Fragrance Mist, Parfum d'Ambiance. This has got to be it; it's the only watery-type lavendery thing here. I'll take it. Make that twelve.

Nanny,

I'm not sure where I gave you the impression that it was appropriate for you to bother my husband.

I spoke with him and we're setting you up with a cell phone, so the next time you're in doubt we'd appreciate it if you just call me.

Justine at Mr. X's office will give you the correct head count. But it will definitely be closer to thirty than twelve.

Also, please find a moment today to exchange whatever you bought yesterday for Lavender Linen Water by L'Occitane. (We only need one bottle as it's a cleaning tool, not a party favor.)

"Hi, Mom?"

"Yeah?"

"I'm talking to you on a cell phone. Know why?"

" 'Cause you're one of them now?"

"No. Because I'm so not one of them I can't be trusted to perform even the simplest task, say, pick out lavender water."

"Lavender what?"

"You pour it in your iron and it makes your rented tablecloths smell like the south of France."

"Useful."

"And I am being made to feel incompetent over this wh—"

"Bud?"

"Yeah?"

"No complaining from the cute-girl-with-her-own-cell-phone."

"Fiiine."

"Love ya. Bye."

The girl with her own cell phone calls her best friend, Sarah, at Wesleyan. "Hi, you've reached Sarah, impress me. Beep—"

"Hey, it's me. At this very moment I am walking down the street and talking to you. Just like I could on a train, a boat, or even from the makeup floor at Barneys, because . . . I got a cell phone. She gave me a cell phone! See, that's not a perk you get as a professor's assistant. Bye!"

Then I ring Grandma. "Sorry I'm not here to chat, but tell me something fabulous anyway. Beep—"

"Hi, Gran, c'est moi. I'm out on the street talking to you on my brand-new cell phone. Now all I need is a Donna Karan bikini and we can hit the Hamptons. Woohoo! Talk to you later! Bye!"

And then home to check my messages.

"Hello?" my roommate's voice answers.

"Charlene?" I ask.

"Yes?"

"Oh, I was just calling to check my messages."

"You don't have any."

"Oh, okay, thanks. Guess what? I'm on my new cell phone! She gave me a cell phone!"

"Did she tell you what kind of calling plan she got you?" Charlene asks flatly.

"No, why?" I scramble to check Mrs. X's notes.

"Because nonplan calls cost seventy-five cents a minute and cell phone bills are itemized, incoming and outgoing, so she'll know exactly who you've been talking to and what it cost her—"

"Gottagobye—" And thus my brief love affair with my cell is brought to a screeching halt.

Mrs. X starts ringing constantly with new requests for the dinner party. In rapid succession I buy the wrong-colored gift bags for the presents, the wrong ribbon to tie the bags closed, and the wrong shade of lilac tissue paper to stuff them with. Then, in a stunning crescendo, I buy the wrong-sized place cards.

Usually when she calls she refuses to talk to Grayer, despite his desperate pleadings from the stroller, because "it would just confuse him." And then he cries. Sometimes she calls just to talk to Grayer. Then I push the stroller as he listens earnestly to the cell phone, as if he were getting a stock report.

Wednesday afternoon:

Ring. ". . . the impact on the cerebellum . . ." Ring. ". . . can be charted here in . . ." Ring.

"Hello?" I whisper, crouching down with my head beneath the desk.

"Nanny?"

"Yes?"

"It's Mrs. X."

"Um, yeah, I'm in class."

"Oh! Oh. Well, the thing is, Nanny, the paper hand towels you picked out for the guest bathroom aren't the right shade of toile . . ."

Nanny,

I'll be coming by at three with the car to pick up Grayer for his portrait. Please bathe him, brush his teeth, and dress him in the outfit I've left on the bed, but be careful not to let him wrinkle it. Give yourself enough time to get him ready, but not so much that he has a chance to get messy. Maybe you should start at 1:30.

Also, here are some handouts from last night's Parents League meeting: "Mommy, Are You Listening?—Communication and Your

Preschooler." I've highlighted applicable
passages—let's discuss!
After the portrait we'll be going to Tiffany's
to pick out a gift for Grayer's father.

One would think that the customer service mezzanine at Tiffany's would have enough chairs to accommodate all of us, their adoring public. However, soft lighting and fresh flowers do little to offset the fact that it's more crowded in here than JFK on Christmas Eve.

"G, you're making marks on the wall with your sneakers. Stop it," I say. We've been waiting for Mrs. X's name to be called so she can get the gold watch engraved that she'll be presenting to Mr. X at the party. It's been over half an hour and Grayer is really starting to get antsy.

She grabbed a seat when we came in, but suggested that I "keep an eye on Grayer," who, she insisted, should remain "where he'll be more comfortable"—in the lounge chair that is his stroller. I tried standing against the wall for a while, but as soon as the blonde with the Fendi handbag plopped herself on the floor to study her *Town and Country* I slid down.

Mrs. X has been perma-attached to her cell phone, so I'm keeping the aforementioned eye, and hand, on Grayer. The very same Grayer who has taken to using his saddle shoes to push off from the cream paisley wallpaper in order to see how far back he can roll before hitting someone.

"Nanny, let gooo."

"Grover, I've asked you three times to stop. Hey, let's play I Spy. I spy something green—" I spy cheek implants.

He struggles to reach down to where my hand is now serving as a brake on the right stroller wheel. His face is getting red and I can see he is nearly ready to explode. She took him to pose for portraits after school let out and we've been stuck running errands for the party ever since. After being in school all morning, frozen in smiles all afternoon, and then literally strapped in, he can't be blamed for hitting his limit.

"Come on, this one is hard. I spy something green. Betcha can't find it." I tighten my grip on the stroller wheel as he hurls himself over the front bar, then gets snapped back by the straps, his resolve to free himself hardening. People standing near us shuffle away as much as the crowd will allow. I keep a smile on my face as my fingers get pinched into the carpet. Starting to feel a little like James Bond holding the ticking bomb, I assess potential escape routes to a less public venue for his impending tantrum. Five . . . four . . . three . . . two—

"I. WANT. TO. GET. OUT!" He thrusts himself forward to emphasize each word.

"X? Mrs. X, we'll see you now at desk eight." A girl my age (with whom, at this moment, I would trade positions in an absolute heartbeat) motions for Mrs. X to follow her to the long row of mahogany desks around the corner.

"LET GO. I want to get out! I don't want to play! I don't want the stroller!"

Mrs. X pauses as she rounds the corner to place her right hand over the speaker of her cell. She turns to me, beaming, and whispers as she points to Grayer. "*Emoting.* He's emoting to communicate his *boundaries!*"

"Right," I mouth back as I reach to loosen the stroller straps before he hurts himself. She disappears down the dark blue hall as I wheel our Emoting Grayer to the stairwell where he will be able to communicate those boundaries while his father's new watch gets the attention it deserves.

Nanny,

The caterers will be setting up the tables this afternoon, so please keep Grayer out of their way. The head of the Chicago office will be coming by to do the seating arrangement.

I was wondering if you could throw something together for Grayer's dinner, since I won't be home till eight. He loves Coquilles St. Jacques. And I think we have some beets in the fridge. That should be simple. See you at 8. Also, don't forget to do his flashcards. Thanks a bunch!

Coquilles say what?! Whatever happened to mac and cheese with a side of broccoli?

In desperate search of a cookbook I pull open the teak cupboard doors, trying not to mark the trompe d'oeil walls, but there isn't a single cookbook to be found, not even the token *Joy of Cooking* or *Silver Palate*.

She owns what I estimate, based on a Christmas stint at Williams-Sonoma, to be over $40,000 in appliances, yet everything continually looks as though it's just been unpacked. From the La Cornue Le Château custom color stove with electric and gas ovens that start at $15,000, to the full set of Bourgeat copper cookware for $1,912, everything is of the best quality. But the only appliance that looks broken in is the Capresso C3000 espresso machine that retails for $2,400. And, no, for that price, it does not find you a man. I asked.

I open all the cabinets and the drawers, trying to familiarize myself with the equipment, as if holding each Wüsthof knife might tell me the secret to the St. Something I'm supposed to be preparing.

My search for a recipe leads me out to her office where I find nothing but a marked-up Neiman Marcus catalog and Connie, the Xes' housekeeper, on her knees scrubbing the doorknob with a toothbrush.

"Hi, do you know where Mrs. X keeps her cookbooks?" I ask.

"Mrs. X don't eat and she don't cook." She redips the toothbrush in a jar of polish. "She got you cookin' for the party?"

"No—just dinner for Grayer—"

"Can't see what's so special about this party. She hates having

people here. We had, maybe, three dinners since she been here."
She nods her head as she deftly scrubs around the keyhole. "There's
a bunch of books in the second guest room—try there."

"Thanks."

I continue roaming from room to cavernous room until I get to
the guest suite. I skim the titles in the floor-to-ceiling bookcase:

Why Should You Have the Baby? Stress and the Fertility Myth
They're Your Breasts Too: The New Wet Nurse Guide
*Sooner or Later We All Sleep Alone: Getting Your Infant Through the
    Night*
Taking the Bite Out of Teething
The Zen of Walking—Every Journey Begins with a First Step
The Idiot's Guide to Potty Training
*The Benefits of the Suzuki Method on Your Child's Left Brain
    Development*
The Body Ecology Diet for Your Toddler
Making the Most of Your Four-Year-Old
How to Package Your Child; The Preschool Interview
Make it or Break it: Navigating Preschool Admissions

. . . And everything else you could possibly imagine in this
genre to fill up four bookshelves right up through:

City Kids Need Trees; The Benefits of a Boarding School Education
The SATs—Setting the Scene for the Rest of Your Child's Life

I stand in silence with my mouth open, forgetting, for a full
moment, the coquilles and beets. Huh.

✧

"I'm really concerned that you're going to fail out of school and be
making other people dinner for the rest of your life! This is a red flag

here, Nan. Now, if memory serves, you signed on to provide child care for this woman. That's all, right? Is she paying you any more for this extra service?"

"No. Mom, this is not a good time to be having—"

"I mean, you should spend a day down here at the shelter kitchen. Get some perspective."

"Okay, this is not a good time to be having—"

"At least you'd be helping people who really need it. Maybe you should just pause for a second, look inside yourself, check in—"MOM!" I tighten my chin to keep the phone from slipping out from under one ear as I grip a boiling pot of beets in my hands. "I can't really look inside myself right now, because I am *just* calling to find how to prepare coquilles say what, for the love of Christ!"

"I'm helping," Grayer says, a small hand coming up over the edge of the counter, groping for the paring knife I've just put down.

"Gotta go."

I lunge for the knife, sending twenty coquilles flying onto the floor.

"Cool! It's just like the beach, Nanny! Don't pick 'em up, leave 'em. I'm gonna go get my bucket." He scampers out of the kitchen as I drop the knife in the sink and crouch to collect the mollusks. I pick up one, then another, but as I grab for the third the first slides out of my hand, across the floor, and directly into a gray snakeskin high heel. I jerk up to see a redheaded woman in a gray suit standing squarely in the doorway.

Grayer comes skipping around the corner holding his sand bucket, but freezes behind her when he sees my face.

"I'm sorry, can I help you?" I stand, motioning for Grayer to come to me.

"Yes," she says, "I'm here to do the seating arrangement." She saunters past me into the kitchen, pulling off her Hermès scarf and tying it around the handle of her slate-gray Gucci briefcase.

She kneels to retrieve a coquille and turns to hand it to Grayer. "Did you lose this?" she asks.

He looks up at me. "It's okay, Grove," I say, reaching out and taking it from her. "Hi, I'm Nanny."

"Lisa Chenowith, general manager of the Chicago office. And you must be Grayer," she says, setting her briefcase down.

"I'm helping," he says, using his bucket to scoop up the remaining seafood.

"I could use a helper." She smiles down at him. "Are you looking for a new job?"

"Sure," he mumbles into his bucket.

I dump the shells in the colander and turn off the stove. "If you just give me a minute, I'll show you to the dining room."

"Are you cooking for the party?" she asks, gesturing to the sink overflowing with pans.

"No—it's his dinner," I say, scraping burned beets out of the pot.

"What ever happened to peanut butter and jelly?" she laughs, putting her briefcase down on the table.

"Nanny, I want peanut butter and jelly."

"Sorry, didn't mean to start a revolution," she says. "Grayer, I'm sure whatever Nanny is making you will be delicious."

"Actually, pb & j sounds perfect," I say, pulling out the peanut butter from the fridge. Once I've seated Grayer in his booster seat at the banquette I lead her to the dining room, where the long walnut table has been replaced by three round ones.

"Well, well," she murmurs as she steps in behind me. "She had them set up a whole day early—that must have cost thousands." We both look down at the lavender-scented tables, festooned with shining silverware, sparkling crystal, and gilt-edged charger plates. "I'm sorry I won't be here."

"You won't?"

"Mr. X wants me back in Chicago." She smiles at me, then turns her attention to the rest of the room, admiring the Picasso over the mantel and the Rothko above the sideboard.

I follow her to the living room and then the library. She takes in each jewel-toned room as if appraising it for auction. "Beautiful," she says, fingering the raw silk drapes, "but a little overdone, don't you think?"

Unaccustomed as I am to being asked my opinion in this household, I reach for the right words. "Um . . . Mrs. X has very definite tastes. Actually, since you're here, would you mind telling me if this looks okay?" I ask, bending behind Mr. X's desk to retrieve a gift bag.

"What is it?" she asks, pulling her hair over her shoulder to peer inside.

"It's a gift bag for the guests. I wrapped them this morning, but I'm not sure if I did it right, because I couldn't find the right tissue paper and the ribbon Mrs. X wanted was out of stock—"

"Nanny?" She cuts me off. "Is anyone on fire?"

"Sorry?" I say, taken aback.

"They're *just* gift bags. For a bunch of old geezers," she laughs, "I'm sure they're perfect—relax."

"Thanks, it just seemed like it was pretty important."

She glances over my shoulder at the shelf of family pictures behind me. "I'm just going to check in with the office and then I'll do the place cards. Is Mrs. X coming back soon?"

"Not till eight."

She picks up the phone and bends over the mahogany desk to peer at a framed picture of Mr. X with Grayer atop his shoulders at the foot of a ski slope.

"NAN-NY, I'M FIIII-NISHED!"

"Okay, well, let me know if you need anything else," I say from the doorway as she slips off her black pearl earring and dials.

"Thank you!" she mouths, giving me a thumbs-up.

Nanny,
As a rule I don't like Grayer to have too many
carbohydrates before bed. Tonight I've left all

his food already measured out on the counter. If you could just put the beets, the kale, and the kohlrabi in the steamer for twelve minutes that should be perfect, but please try to stay out of the caterers' way.

You should probably give Grayer his dinner in his room. Actually, I might need to bring my dinner guests through when I give the tour. So it's probably best for you both to take your plates into his bathroom while you eat—in case of spills.

P.S. I'm counting on you to stay until Grayer is asleep and make sure that he doesn't intrude on the meal.

P.P.S. I'll need you to pick up Grayer's Halloween costume tomorrow.

"Martini, straight up—no olive." Having steamed Grayer's dinner into an unrecognizable mush, burned my hand in the process, and nearly scalded Grayer several times, then having to dine atop his toilet seat, I am truly ready to "take the edge off." I shift on the bar stool, wondering if, perhaps, I could work for that redhead from Chicago—move to Illinois, try on investment banking, and spend my days preparing her pb & j.

I reach into my bag for my pay envelope and fish out a twenty for the bartender. It's thicker this week and I count over three hundred in cash. I realize that while I'm exhausted and probably on my way to some sort of substance-abuse problem, the upside of working three times as many hours as I'd agreed to is that I'm making three times as much money. It's only the second week of the month and the rent is already covered. And there is that pair of black leather pants I've had my eye on . . .

I just need half an hour of quiet before I can go home to Charlene and her hairy pilot boyfriend. I don't want to talk, I don't want to listen, and I most definitely do not want to cook. I mean, good God, having your hairy boyfriend sleep over when you share a studio apartment. Not okay. Not okay at all. I am counting the days until she's slotted for the Asia route.

"Yo, yo, check this out!" The blond homeboy in the Brooks Brothers ensemble motions for his "posse" to check out his Palm Pilot at the corner table. Classic.

Normally, I avoid Dorrian's and its preppy clientele like the clap. But it was directly on my path home and the bartender makes a terrific martini. And I did have to "take my edge off." Besides, off-season is usually pretty safe, once they all return to school.

I count five white baseball hats huddled over their friend's new toy. Despite only being in college, they all have portable cellular devices of some kind or another hanging off their yuppy utility belts. The years change, the corduroy jackets of the seventies giving way to the flipped-up collars of the eighties, the plaid shirts of the nineties, and the Gore-Tex of the new millennium, but their mentality is as ageless as the red-checked tablecloths.

I am so riveted that I automatically follow their gaze when they turn to the door. In keeping with the tenor of my day, who should walk in but my very own Harvard Hottie, sans *chapeau blanc*. And he knows them. Ugh. I take a long swig as the vision I'd been savoring of him healing children in Tibet morphs into one of him in a suit on the floor of the New York Stock Exchange.

"Is that good? You like that?" Oh God, there's one standing right next to me. Roll 'em up, kids, roll 'em up.

"What?" I ask, noting his South Carolina baseball hat, which proudly proclaims COCKS across the front in three-inch crimson letters.

"Maaar-tiii-niiis. Pretty hard stuff, don't you think?" he says a little too close to my face and then screams over my head, "Yo! Get off your asses and give me a hand with these drinks, you lazy bitches!" H. H. comes over to assist with the beer transport.

"Hey, Grayer's girlfriend, right?" He smiles broadly.

He remembered! No, bad Nanny. Stock exchange, stock exchange. Yet I can't help noting a comparative lack of gadgets adorning his Levi's.

"I'm happy to report that he's out for the count after one reading of *Goodnight Moon*." I smile back in spite of myself.

"I hope Jones here isn't giving you a hard time." Jones cracks up at the unintended double entendre. "He can be a bit much," he says, glaring over my shoulder at Jones. "Hey, you should join us."

"Yeah, I'm kind of tired."

"Please, just for a quick drink." I eye the group skeptically, but I'm swayed as his hair falls in his eyes when he picks up the pitchers.

I follow him over and they make room for me to sit down. A round of boisterous introductions ensue in which I am compelled to shake every clammy hand at the table.

"How do you know our boy, here?" one hat asks.

" 'Cause we all go *way* back—"

"Back in the day." They bob their heads like chickens, repeating "back in the day" about a thousand times.

"They think there was a day," H. H. says quietly, turning his head to me. "So how's work going?"

"Work!" The ears of a hat prick up. "Where do you work?"

"Are you in an analyst program?"

"No—"

"Are you a model?"

"No, I'm a nanny." There's an audible stir.

"Dude!" one guy says, punching H. H. on the shoulder.

"Dude, you never told us you knew a nanneehhh."

I realize from their glazed smiles that they've just cast me in every nanny-themed porn film ever screened in their frat house basements.

"So," the drunkest begins, "is the dad hot?"

"Has he hit on you?"

"Um, no. I haven't met him yet."

"Is the Mom hot?" another one asks.

"Well, I don't think so—"

"What about the kid? Is the kid hot? Has he ever made a pass at you?" They all speak at once.

"Well, he's four, so—" There is a hardness to their tone that dispels any illusion of good-natured fun. I turn to the gentleman who brought me over here, but he seems frozen, blushing deeply with his brown eyes downcast.

"Are any of the dads hot?"

"Right. If you'll excuse me—" I stand up.

"Come on"—Jones stares me down—"you're trying to tell us you never fucked any of the dads?" My last nerve snaps.

"How original of you. You want to know who the dads are? They're you in about two more years. And they're not fucking the nanny. They're not fucking their wives. They're not fucking anyone. Because they get fat, they go bald, they lose their appetites and drink, a lot, because they have to, not because they want to. So enjoy yourselves, boyz. 'Cause back in the day is gonna be lookin' real good. Now please don't get up." My heart pounds as I pull on my sweater, grab my bag, and walk out the door.

"Hey, hold on!" H. H. catches up to me as I storm across the street. I turn, waiting for him to tell me that they all have terminal cancer and a reign of terror was their last request. "Look, they didn't mean anything by that." Which he doesn't.

"Oh." I nod at him. "So they talk to every girl like that? Or just the ones who work in their buildings?"

He crosses his bare arms and hunches up against the cold. "Look, they're just friends from high school. I mean, I barely hang out with them any—"

The Bad Witch comes flying out. "Shame on you."

He stammers, "They're just really drunk—"

"No. They're just really assholes."

We stare at each other and I wait for him to say something, but he seems paralyzed.

"Well," I finally say, "it's been a long day." I'm suddenly utterly exhausted and keenly aware of pulsing pain from the burn on my hand.

I force myself not to look back as I walk away.

Nanny,

The party was a great success. Thank you so much for your help.

These shoes really are too much for me and Mr. X doesn't care for the color. If they're your size you're welcome to them, otherwise, please take them to Encore resale shop on Madison and 84th. I have an account.

By the way, have you seen the Lalique frame that was sitting on Mr. X's desk? The one with the picture of Grayer with his father from Aspen? It seems to be missing. Can you call the caterers and see if they took it home by accident?

I'll be recuperating at Bliss, so my phone will be off for the rest of the afternoon.

PRADA! P-R-A-D-A. As in Madonna. As in *Vogue*. As in, watch me walk off in style, you khaki-wearing, pager-carrying, golf-playing, *Wall Street Journal*–toting, Gangsta-Hip-Hop–listening, Howard Stern–worshiping, white-hat-backward-sporting, arrogant jerk-offs!

Nana also troubled Mr. Darling in another way. He had some-
times a feeling that she did not admire him.

—*PETER PAN*

CHAPTER THREE

Night of the Banking Dead

After picking up some small pumpkins to decorate on the way home from school, Grayer and I return to the apartment just in time for me to sign an invoice for over four thousand dollars. Grayer and I follow in awe as a deliveryman wheels a pair of six-foot wooden crates through the kitchen and deposits them in the front hall. After lunch, we play Guess What's in the Crate. Grayer guesses a dog, a gorilla, a monster truck, and a baby brother. I guess antiques, new bathroom fixtures, and a small cage for Grayer (although I keep that one to myself).

I leave Grayer in the capable hands of his piano teacher at four-fifteen and return, as instructed, at five o'clock. I'm dressed like a grown-up for the Halloween party at Mr. X's office in my new leather pants and secondhand Prada shoes. I let myself in, only to come face-to-crate with a frenzied Mrs. X, who's trying to pry one open with a butcher knife and a toilet plunger.

"Do you want me to call the super?" I ask, carefully angling myself past her. "He might have a crowbar."

"Oh, my God, could you?" she pants up from where she's crouched on the floor.

I go into the kitchen and buzz the super on the intercom, who promises to send up the handyman.

"He's on his way. So, um, what's in there?"

She huffs and puffs as she works at the crate, "I had—ugh— replicas of Mufasa and Sarabi costumes—ow, dammit!—from the Broadway production of *The Lion King* . . . unh—custom made." She's going red in the face. "For this stupid party, argh."

"Wow, that's great. Where's Grayer?" I ask tentatively.

"He's waiting so you both can get dressed! We've got to hurry— we all need to be changed and ready to leave by six." All?

As the service doorbell rings I turn and walk slowly down the long hall to Grayer's room, where he's had the good sense to hide from his plunger-wielding mother. I apprehensively push back the door to reveal not one, but *two* Teletubby costumes half lifting off Grayer's bed, like partially deflated balloons from the Macy's Thanksgiving Day parade.

Dear God. She must be kidding.

"Nanny, we're gonna match!" If I wanted to get dressed up in bizarre costumes I could be making *way* more money than this.

With a long sigh I begin to wrestle Grayer into his yellow costume, trying to convince him it's just like putting on feet pajamas, only rounder. I can hear Mrs. X running through the apartment. "Do we have any pliers? Nanny, have you seen the pliers? The costumes are wired into the crate!"

"Sorry!" I shout toward the direction of her voice, which changes constantly, like a passing siren.

Thud.

Moments later she bursts into the room looking like a mud hut, headdress askance. "Do I wear makeup with this? Do I wear makeup with this?!"

"Um, probably just some neutral tones? Maybe that nice lipstick you wore to lunch the other day?"

"No, I mean something, you know . . . *tribal?*" Grayer looks up at his mother in complete bewilderment, his eyes wide.

"Mommy, is that your costume?"

"Mommy's not finished yet, honey. Let Nanny do your makeup, so she can help me." She runs out. Mrs. X has bought us Cray-Pas face paint so I can transform us into Inky Blinky and Tiggy Wiggy or whatever the hell they're called. But as soon as I start in on Grayer's face he gets a massive attack of the face itchies.

"Laa-Laa, Nanny. I'm Laa-Laa." He raises both mitted hands to his nose. "You're Tinky Winky—"

"Grov, please don't touch your face. I'm trying to make you look like a Teletubby."

The mud hut rushes back in. "My God, he looks awful! What are you doing?"

"He keeps mushing it," I try to explain.

She looks down at him, straw stalks trembling. "GRAYER ADDISON X, DO NOT TOUCH YOUR FACE!" And she's off again.

His chin starts to quiver—he may never touch his face again, ever.

"You look really cool, Grove," I say softly. "Let's just get this done, okay?"

He nods and tilts his cheek to me so I can finish.

"Is it naguma matoto?" she shouts from the hall.

"Hakuna matata!" we shout back.

"Right! Thank you!" she replies. "Hakuna matata, hakuna matata."

The phone rings and I can hear her on the hall extension, straining to sound calm. "Hello? Hello, darling. We're nearly ready . . . But I— . . . Right, but I got the costumes you wanted . . . No, I . . . Yes, I understand, it's just that I . . . Right, no, we'll be right down."

Slow footsteps on the marble floor toward Grayer's wing, then the headdress reappears around the door frame. "Daddy's running a little late, so he's just going to swing by in ten minutes and pick us up downstairs, okay? I'll need everybody in the front hall in nine minutes." Nine minutes (of slithering myself into this stinky, cumbersome purple albatross and smearing my skin in white lard) later and we reassemble awkwardly around the crates in the front hall—small yellow Laa-Laa, large purple asshole, and Mrs. X in a dignified Jil Sander pantsuit.

"Is it too warm for my mink?" she asks, adjusting my hood so the purple triangle, the size of a shoe box, stands "straight."

It requires both of the Xes' doormen's hands on my haunches to shove me in the limo at the Xes' feet. I scramble up onto the seat as the driver starts the car.

"Where's my card?" Grayer asks, just as we pull away from the curb.

I can't tell if it's because of the layer of neoprene over my ears or if I'm just in shock, but Grayer's voice seems to be coming from very far away.

"My card. Where is it? Wheeeerrrre!" He begins to rock back and forth like a weeblewobble on the limousine seat we share across from his parents.

"Nanny!" Mrs. X's tone snaps me back. "Grayer, tell Nanny what you're feeling."

I angle my body on the leather seat in Grayer's direction, as the purple bubble around my head obscures all peripheral vision. Uh, yes? His face is red beneath his makeup and he's out of breath. He scrunches his eyes and roars, "NANNY! I DON'T HAVE MY CARD." Christ.

"Nanny, he always has to have that card pinned to his clothes—"

"I'm so sorry." I angle my girth to him. "Grayer, I'm sorry."

"My ccaaaAAARRrrdd!" Grayer bellows.

"Hey," a deep, disembodied voice commands. "That's enough of that." Miiiiiiissssttter Eeeexxxxxxx, at last we meet.

The whole limo holds its breath. This man of mystery, who has, for the most part, eluded me and, I daresay, the rest of my riding companions for the past two months, deserves a full freeze-frame. He sits facing me in a dark suit and very expensive shoes. Actually, he's facing the *Wall Street Journal,* which fully obscures the rest of him— up to the shiny receding hairline, spotlit by the reading light inches from his head. There's a cell phone wedged beneath his ear, to which he seems only to be listening. "Hey" is his first utterance since we all got in. Or, in some cases, were shoved in.

Sitting there behind his paper he is, without question, the CEO of this family. "What card?" he asks his paper. Mrs. X looks pointedly at me and it is evident that Grayer's meltdown falls into my domain, which alternates between middle management and cleaning staff.

Thus we make a right onto Madison and head back uptown to 721, where the doormen are only too happy to have a shot at pulling my arms and legs to extract me from the limo.

"Wait right here, guys," I say, once upright, "I'll be back in a minute."

I get upstairs, spend ten sweaty minutes rummaging through Grayer's room, forcing me to reapply my Cray-Pas, locate The Card in the laundry hamper, and am ready to rock and roll. (Roll, mostly.)

The elevator door opens and, of course, there stands H. H., my Harvard Hottie.

His jaw drops.

Just kill me.

"What? You never saw a Halloween costume before?" I bristle, lumbering in with my head held high.

"No! Um, well, it's, it's October twenty-third, but—"

"So??!!"

"I ummmm, yeah, yes I have, I—" he stammers.

"He-llo! Are you ever not speechless?" I attempt to shimmy so that I can face the wall. Of course, in this five-by-seven box I make it all of two degrees away from him.

He is quiet for a moment. "Look, I'm really sorry for the other night. Sometimes those guys can be real assholes when they drink. I know that's no excuse, but, I mean, they're just old friends from high school—"

"And?" I say to the wall.

"And . . ." He seems stumped. "And you shouldn't judge me based on one drunken night at Dorrian's."

I shimmy back to face him. "Um, yeah—that's one drunken night when your buddies from 'back in the day' called me a ho. Listen, sometimes I hang out with friends whose politics I don't agree with, but only up to a point. If, oh, say, *gang rape* were on the agenda for the evening, I would speak up!"

"Well!"

"Well?"

"Well, for someone who didn't like it when snap judgments were made about you, it's pretty hypocritical of you to judge me so quickly based on their behavior."

"Fair enough." I take a deep breath and try to straighten to my full height. "Let me clarify, I'm judging you on the fact that you didn't step in to shut them up."

He looks back at me. "Okay, I should've said something. I'm sorry things got so out of hand." He tucks his hair behind his ear. "Listen, come out with me tonight and let me make it up to you. I'm hanging out with some college friends—it's a whole different crowd, I promise." The door slides open and both a woman in a cashmere wrap and her standard poodle glare with annoyance because there is no room for them around my costume. The door slides closed. I realize I have only two more floors to acquiesce.

"Obviously, I have a really decadent affair ahead of me." I gesture with one three-fingered hand to my purple torso. "But I can try to stop by around ten."

"Great! I'm not sure exactly where we're going. We were thinking of Chaos, or The Next Thing, but we'll definitely be at Nightingale's till eleven."

"Well, I'll try to make it." Despite the fact that I am not com-pletely clear where, in his list of destinations, I should aim to make it to. The doors open to the lobby and I attempt a sexy waddle to the car, trying to remember to lead with my hips.

I wait until H. H. is safely around the corner and then, after one last ass-push from the doormen, we are on our way. I take a little bit of pleasure from the fact that Mrs. X is forced to lean across and pin the card on Grayer herself as she has the use of all ten of her fingers.

"Honey, I finally found out who the Brightmans used to book their safari—" she begins, but Mr. X gestures to the phone and shakes his head. Not to be outdone she pulls her Startac out of her Judith Leiber pumpkin clutch and dials. The puffy, primary-colored side of the car sits in prolonged silence.

". . . I don't think her decorator did a very good job . . ."

". . . take another hard look at those numbers—"

". . . and mauve?"

". . . at that APR? Is he nuts?"

". . . bamboo for a kitchen!"

". . . buy back ten billion over the next three years . . ."

I look down at Grayer and poke his yellow tummy with a purple finger. He looks up and pokes me back. I squeeze his felt chub, he squeezes mine.

"So." Mr. X flips his phone closed with a loud click and looks at me. "Do they have Halloween in Australia?"

"Um, I, uh, think they have something called All Souls' Day, but, um, I don't think people dress up or, uh, trick-or-treat, tradi-tionally," I answer.

"Honey," Mrs. X intercedes. "This is *Nanny*. She took over from C-a-i-t-l-i-n."

"Oh, right, right, of course. You're prelaw?"

"I want to sit next to Mommy!" Grayer suddenly bursts out.

"Grove, stay next to me and keep me company," I say, looking down.

"No! I want to sit next to Mommy now."

Mrs. X looks over at Mr. X, who has retreated back behind his paper. "We don't want to get your fun makeup on Mommy's coat—stay with Nanny, sweetie."

After a few more rounds, he finally tuckers out and the four of us sit in silence as the car glides down to the very bottom of the city, where the dense, narrow streets of Lower Manhattan give way to the imposing towers of the Financial District. The neighborhood appears deserted, except for the funereal line of town cars forming outside Mr. X's company.

Mr. and Mrs. X slide out and march ahead of us into the building, leaving Grayer and me unassisted to maneuver our spherical bodies out of the car and onto the sidewalk.

"Nanny, say three and I'll push! Say three, Nanny! SAY IT!"

With his little feet in my backside and my face nearly on the sidewalk it's no wonder he can't hear me when I scream, "Three!"

I smush my face to the left to see Grayer sticking his lips out the crack in the window. "Didja say it, Nanny? Didja?"

I can sense a flurry of activity behind my enormous haunches, accompanied by snippets of the mastermind at work. "Okay, now I'm Rabbit . . . and you . . . you're Pooh . . . and . . . *are you counting?* . . . and . . . after all the honey . . . stuck in the tree—THAT'S THREE, NANNY, on THREE!" He could be constructing a catapult out of cocktail napkins back there for all I know—

WHOMP!

"I did it! Nanny, I did it!"

I right myself, reach down with my three-fingered hand for his, and we waddle with pride toward the entrance. Mr. and Mrs. X have kindly held the elevator for us and we ride up to the forty-fifth floor with another couple whose children couldn't attend. "Homework."

We all step out into a cavernous reception area, which has been transformed into a Tim Burton film—the marble walls are covered in cut-out bats and fake cobwebs, every inch of the ceiling drips in streamers, spiders, and skeletons. There are numerous bar tables strategically placed at regular intervals around the room, each aglow with a hand-carved pumpkin centerpiece.

It seems as though every unemployed actor in the tristate area has been called in to entertain the troops. At the reception desk Frankenstein pretends to answer phones, Betty Boop walks by with a tray of drinks, and Marilyn is singing "Happy Birthday, Mr. President" to a cluster of Mr. X's colleagues in the corner. Grayer looks around with a bit of trepidation until Garfield comes by with a tray of peanut butter and jelly sandwiches.

"You can take one. Go ahead, Grayer," I encourage him. He has some trouble with the gloves on, but manages to secure one and munches, slowly mushing his body tighter against my leg.

The far wall is a breathtaking, floor-to-ceiling view of the Statue of Liberty. I seem to be the only one appreciating it, but then I'm also one of the few nannies with a visible face. Apparently Mrs. X was not alone in her concept for the evening; all the nannies are in huge rented costumes at least three feet in circumference; the child is a small Snow White, nanny is a large Dwarf, the child is a small farmer, nanny is a very large cow, the child is a small Pied Piper, nanny is a large rat. However, the winners, hands down, are the Teletubbies. I exchange wan smiles across the room with two Tinky Winkys from Jamaica.

A couple with a small Woodstock and large Snoopy in tow comes over to us.

"Darling, you look fabulous!" says the wife to Mrs. X, or maybe Grayer.

"Happy Halloween, Jacqueline," Mrs. X replies, giving her an air kiss.

Jacqueline, wearing a tiny pink pillbox hat with her black Armani, barrels on to Mr. X. "Darling, you're not in costume, you bad boy!" Her own betrothed is wearing a captain's hat with his pinstriped suit.

"I'm dressed as a lawyer," Mr. X says. "But really, I'm an investment banker!"

"Stop!" Jacqueline says, giggling. "You're such a stitch!" She looks down at Laa-Laa and Woodstock. "You little darlings should go check out the games area—it's fabulous!" I look over at Snoopy, who's listing under the weight of the giant head. "We got a much better company this year to organize the whole thing. They did Blackstone's 4th of July Bungee Jump and Cocktails."

"I heard that was lovely. Mitzi Newmann's gotten addicted. She had a free-fall bridge installed in Connecticut. Go ahead, Grayer," Mrs. X encourages. He stares up at all the macabre mayhem and doesn't look entirely convinced that he wants to be separated from his parents right now.

"Go on, sport, and if you're good, I'll take you to see the executive dining room," Mr. X says, prompting Grayer to look up at me.

"Where Daddy has lunch," I explain. I take his hand and follow our Peanuts team to the children's area, which is cordoned off with a little picket fence. As Barbie opens the gate I look at her. "Good idea," I say, "let's keep out the grown-ups."

The whole twenty-foot area is filled with activity tables and games that seem mostly to involve throwing things. (A miscalculation on someone's part, I think, as a small Big Bird goes down.) I notice very quickly that the grown-up drink trays aren't circulating in here and lean out over the fence to swipe a little relief. Occasionally parents swing by, like maître d's, to ask if the child is enjoying him/herself and remark, "A marshmallow ghost! Ooooh, scary!", then turn back to each other to add, "You just have no idea what our renovation is costing—it's really staggering. But Bill wanted a screening room." And they shrug, roll their eyes, and shake their heads.

Mrs. X has come in with Sally Kirkpatrick, a woman I recognize from Grayer's swimming class, to watch her three-foot Batman try to obliterate his ring-toss opponents. I come up behind them to check in about bedtime.

"Your new girl's really good at getting Grayer in the pool," Mrs. Kirkpatrick says.

"Thanks, I wish I could take him, but Tuesday's my day at the Parents League and with ice skating on Fridays and French on Thursdays and CATS on Wednesday I need one day to do something for myself."

"I know, I'm so busy. I'm on four different committees this season. Oh, can I put you down for a table for the Breast Ball?"

"Of course."

"So what happened to Caitlin? Your new girl didn't seem to know."

"Sally, it was a nightmare. I'm lucky I found Nanny when I did! Caitlin, whose work I never found to be exemplary, by the way, but I put up with it, because, well, one does. Anyway, she had the nerve to ask for the last week of August off after I already gave her the first two weeks of January when we went to Aspen."

"You're kidding."

"Well, I just felt she was trying to take complete advantage of me—"

"Ryan, play fair—that was Iolanthe's ring," Sally shouts at her Batman.

"But I positively did not know what to do," Mrs. X continues, sipping Perrier.

"So you fired her?" Sally asks, eagerly.

"First I talked to a professional problem consultant—"

"Oh, who'd you use?"

"Brian Swift."

"I hear he's great."

"He was fantastic—helped me put the whole thing into perspective. He made it clear that my authority as house manager had been called into question and I had to bring in a replacement to drive the point home."

"Brilliant. Don't let me forget to get his number from you. I'm having such problems with Rosarita. The other day I asked her to run up to Midtown to pick up a few things while Ryan was in hockey class and she said she didn't want to because she didn't think she'd have enough time to get back. I mean, does she think I don't know how long it takes to get around?"

"I know, it's appalling. After all, when the kids are in class they're just sitting there, on our dime. I mean, really."

"So, are you done with all your interviews?" Sally asks.

"Well, we have Collegiate on Tuesday, but I'm not sure if I want him on the West Side," Mrs. X says, shaking her head.

"But it's such a good school. We'd be thrilled if Ryan got in there. We're hoping the violin gives him an edge."

"Oh, Grayer plays the piano—I had no idea that was important," Mrs. X says.

"Well, it depends on his level. Ryan's already competing regionally . . ."

"Oh, I see. That's fantastic."

Apprehensive of what I might say to Mrs. X at this moment on two vodka tonics, I tiptoe backward and spot Grayer, still slinging beanbags like a pro, which leaves me free to grab another drink and observe the grown-up side of the room. Everyone is dressed in black, the men are tall, the women slim, they all stand with the left arm folded across their abdomen, the left hand supporting the right elbow so the right hand can wave a drink around as they talk. As the pumpkin centerpieces slowly burn down they begin to cast long shadows of bankers and banker wives and everyone is starting to look to me like a Charles Addams cartoon.

I realize I'm getting woozy from the heat and the alcohol, but my purple posterior doesn't fit into any of the pint-size plastic chairs. So I sit on the floor a few feet away from the cupcake table where Grayer has stationed himself while his pitching arm recovers. There is so much commotion around us from the Busby Berkeley staff of hired activity folk that I must consciously fix my stare on Grayer while he decorates his fourth cupcake. I lean my head against the wall and watch with pride as he assertively grabs sprinkles and silver balls, while other children wait for their nannies, crouched beside them, to hand over tubes of frosting as if their charges were about to perform surgery.

Eventually, Grayer's frosting frenzy slows and he is left staring with glossy eyes at the black and orange cardboard centerpiece, his gooey hands motionless atop the table. Little beads of sweat are forming on his face—he must be boiling in that costume. I crawl over and whisper in his ear, "Hey, Buddy, why don't you take a break from all that cake making and come hang out with me for a bit?" He drops his forehead on the table, narrowly missing his candy corn masterpiece.

"Come on, Grove," I say, slipping him into my arms and shuffling back to the wall on my knees. I unzip his hood and use a napkin to wipe the dripping makeup from his forehead and frosting from his hands.

"I gotta bob for an apple," he mumbles as I lay him down with his head resting on the white rectangle of my costumed lap.

"Sure, just close your eyes for a few minutes first."

I take a swig from my newest drink, letting the room soften a bit more as I fan us both with a prospectus left beneath a nearby cabinet. Grayer's body becomes heavy as he drifts off. Closing my eyes, I try to picture myself in this room at some important business-type thing, but can't seem to conjure anything other than leading a board meeting as Tinky Winky.

I must keep nodding off, because I start to dream about Mrs. X, in a mink Laa-Laa costume, trying to convince me that I really should let her speak to H. H.'s posse about the whole "ho-thing" as "setting boundaries" is "her middle name." Then Mr. X dances in to the tune of "Monster Mash," pulling off his head to reveal that he is actually my Harvard Hottie, demanding to be taken to the bathroom. I jolt awake.

"Nanny, I gotta pee." "Monster Mash" blares down on us. I

locate a clock under the cobwebs. Nine goddamn thirty. Okay, so it's—what? Twenty minutes up the FDR, ten to get out of this thing, and another twenty to get downtown to Nightingale's? He'll still be there, right?

"Okay! Let's get this show on the road. Let's find a bathroom and get moving!"

"Nanny, slow down." I pick up my dragging Grayer and sling him onto my purple hump as I dart between the downed and wounded, who are either mid- or post-sugar crash.

"Coming through, coming through. Have you seen the bathroom?" I inquire of a five-foot Indian woman in a Barney costume trying to placate a screaming three-foot Barney who can't seem to bite a doughnut off a string and has taken the matter directly to heart. She points over her shoulder at a line winding endlessly around the corner. I look around for out-of-the-way potted foliage, preparing a speech about how this is "just like the playground."

Grayer points behind me. "The bathroom is that way, in my daddy's office."

I plop him down, instructing him to lead the way, "like someone is chasing us." He takes off down the deserted corridor with his hands between his legs. It's darker and quieter than the room we have just escaped, and I speed-walk to keep Grayer in sight. Halfway down the hall he pushes a door open and I run to catch up, practically rolling over him when he freezes in the darkened doorway.

"Well, hello there, Grayer." A woman's voice startles us. Mr. X flips on the lamp as she comes around the desk in black fishnets, leotard, and a bowler hat. I recognize her instantly. "Hello, Nanny," she says, tucking her loose red hair under the hat.

Grayer and I are speechless.

Mr. X steps out from behind the desk, readjusting himself and surreptitiously wiping lipstick from his mouth. "Grayer, say hello."

"I love your costume," she says brightly before Grayer can even speak. "See, I'm 'Chicago' because that's our biggest market!"

"She's not wearing any pants," he says quietly, pointing at her netted legs and looking up at me.

Mr. X swiftly picks up Grayer without looking at any of us, including Grayer, and with a "Time to call it a night, sport. Let's find your mother" heads back toward the party.

"Um, we had to find a bathroom. Grayer has to go," I call after them, but he doesn't look back. I turn to Ms. Chicago, but she's already past me, clicking down the hall in the opposite direction.

Fuck.

I sit down on the leather couch and slump my face in my hands.

I don't want to know this I don't want to know this I don't want to know this.

I grab a shooter from the deserted tray of chilled vodka shots on the coffee table and down it.

Thankfully, within minutes the Xes and I are flying up the FDR and Grayer has completely passed out with his head in my lap. I suspect there may be a stain on the seat when we get out, but, hey, we were all adequately warned.

Mr. X leans his head back against the leather upholstery and closes his eyes. I crack the window an inch to let some fresh air blow over me from the East River. I am a little drunk. Yeah, I'm a little more than a little drunk.

In the distant background, I hear the tentative chatter of Mrs. X. "I was talking to Ryan's mother and she says Collegiate is one of the top schools in the country. I'm going to call tomorrow and set up an interview for Grayer. Oh, and she told me that she and Ben are taking a house in Nantucket this summer. It turns out that Wallington and Susan have summered there for the last four years and Sally says it's a delightful break from the Hamptons. She said it's so pleasant just to get away from the Maidstone every once in a while, so the children can experience some diversity. And Caroline Horner has a house up there. Sally said Ben's brother is going to Paris this summer, so you could take his membership at their tennis club. And Nanny could come, too! Wouldn't you like to join us for a few weeks on the ocean this summer, Nanny? It will be so relaxing."

My ears perk up at the sound of my name and I find myself responding with unmitigated enthusiasm.

"*Totally*. Relaxing and fun. F-U-N. Bring it on!" I say, trying to give a purple thumbs-up, as I imagine me, the ocean, my Harvard Hottie. "Naaantucket—swim, sand, and surf. I mean, what's not to love? *Sign . . . me . . . up*." Beneath my half-closed eyes I see her look at me quizzically before turning to the snoring Mr. X.

"Well, then." She pulls her mink up close around her and speaks to the city racing by outside the window. "That settles it. I'll call the realtor tomorrow."

A half hour later my cab whizzes back down the FDR in the opposite direction toward Houston Street as I check for traces of greasepaint in my compact. I lean forward to catch a glance at the cabbie's clock and the glowing green letters read back 10:24. Go, Go, Go.

My heart starts to race and the adrenaline sharpens my senses considerably; I feel the bump of each pothole and can smell the last passenger's cigarette. The combination of the surreal tenor of the evening, the numerous drinks I have consumed, the leather pants I'm poured into, and the promise of a potential hookup with Harvard Hottie all add up to a lot of pressure. I am, in no uncertain terms, on a mission. Whatever reservations I had, political, moral, or otherwise, have melted past my lace underwear and into my Prada shoes.

The cab pulls up at Thirteenth Street, on a particularly seedy stretch of Second Avenue, and I toss the driver twelve bucks and jog inside. Nightingale's is one of those places I vowed never to set foot in again after I graduated from high school. The beer's served in plastic cups, drunk men armed with darts make getting safely to the bathroom a challenge, and, if you do make it, the door doesn't close. It is the proverbial Shit Hole.

It takes all of two seconds for me to swing my head around and see that there is no Harvard Hottie to be found. Think. Think. They were going to start at Chaos. "Taxi!"

I leap out on the corner of West Broadway and take my place on line behind a clump of people who have actually come here voluntarily. I'm waved behind the ropes with a clique of scantily clad girls, while a frustrated throng of guys try to take on one of the bouncers.

"Let's see some ID."

I pull open my purse and hand the six-eight bouncer a juice box, Hot Wheels, and Handi Wipes, before uncovering my wallet.

"That'll be twenty bucks." Fine. Fine! I throw him two hours in a Teletubbies outfit and make my way up a darkened staircase lined with inappropriate black-and-white photographs of naked women with trumpet lilies. The bass beat from the house music is like aural rape and as I'm propelled along by the bump-ba-bump it reminds me of the old cartoons where Tom's music would bounce Jerry right out of his matchbox bed.

I start wending my way into the crush of people, looking for— what? Brown hair, a Harvard T-shirt? The crowd is a mishmash of tourists and NYU students from Utah and gay guys—the balding, married ones from the Island—and they all went shopping on Eighth Street. It's not an attractive crowd. The strobe makes it feel as if they're flashing in front of me, like my own private slide show— ugly person, ugly person, ugly person.

I try to make my way onto the dance floor, for which I pay a price. Not only is the crowd unattractive, it is supremely uncoordinated. But enthusiastic. Uncoordinated and enthusiastic, a lethal combination.

I maneuver carefully through the flailing limbs toward the bar at the far end of the room, making an effort to stay in motion—you're only vulnerable to "unwelcome advances" if you stand still or, heaven forbid, dance, in which case you are guaranteed to have an unfamiliar pelvis pressed firmly against your ass within seconds.

"Martini, straight up, no olive." I need a little pick-me-up to put the edge back on.

"Martinis? Pretty hard stuff, don't you think?" Oh, my God—it's Mr. COCKS. I thought H. H. was hanging out with his *college* friends tonight. "Is that good? You like that?"

"WHAT? I CAN'T HEAR YOU!" I mouth as I start scanning over his white hat for H. H. in the crowd.

"MARTINIS! HARD STUFF!!" Right.

"SORRY! NOT A WORD!" I don't see him anywhere, which means I'm going to have to remind Hard Martini over here about Dorrian's.

"HARD!!!" Sure, big guy. Whatever you say.

"LISTEN, WE MET AT DORRIAN'S—I'M LOOKING FOR YOUR FRIEND!"

"RIGHT, THE NAAAANNNEEEEHHH." Yep, that's me.

"IS HE HERE?" I shout.

"THE NANNNEEEHHH."

"YEAH, I'M LOOKING FOR YOUR FRIEND! IS . . . HE . . . HERE?"

"RIGHT, YEAH, HE WAS HERE WITH SOME OF HIS COL-LEGE BUDDIES, BUNCH OF ART HOUSE PUSSIES, THEY WENT TO SOME FUCKING ART GALLERY POETRY THING—"

"THE NEXT THING?" I shout into his ear, hoping to perma-nently deafen him.

"YEAH, THAT'S IT. BUNCH OF BIDDIES IN BLACK TURTLENECKS DRINKING FUCKING IMPORTED COFFEE—"

"THANKS!" And I'm off.

I get outside into the cold air and look with relief at the

bouncer as he undoes the ropes. I take out my wallet and do an inventory. Okay, I can walk it in ten and save the money, but these shoes are—

"Hello?" I look over to see . . . me, in flannel pajamas, on Charlene's futon, watching educational television with George. "Hello? Can we talk for a second here? You got up at five-thirty this morning. Did you even eat a full meal today? When was the last time you had a glass of water and your feet are *killing* you."

"So?" I ask myself as I puff along Spring Street.

"Sooo, you are tired, you are drunk, and, if you don't mind my saying, you're not looking all that great. Go home. Even if you find him—"

"Look, you flannel-wearing, couch-warming, lo mein–eating loser, you are sitting at home *alone*. I know from sitting home, okay? My feet are bleeding, I'm down with that, I cannot fully inhale due to the leather pants, and there is a permanent lace indentation up the crack of my ass—but I deserve this date! This date will happen because I still have greasepaint behind my ears. I've *earned* this! What if I can't find him . . . *ever again*? What if he never finds me? Sure, I want to be home, I want to be on the couch, but I need to hook up first! I have the rest of my life to watch TV!"

"Yeah, you don't really seem all that—"

"Well, of course not! Who would be at this hour? It's not about that! I have to win. He has to see me in my leather pants—he cannot, cannot, *cannot* go to bed tonight with the last image he has of me being in a huge purple Teletubby costume! Out of the question. Good night."

I harden my resolve and turn onto Mercer, heading up to the bouncer—an art gallery with a bouncer, don't even get me started.

"Sorry, lady, we're closed for a private function tonight."

"But—But—But I—" I'm dumbfounded.

"Sorry, lady." And that is that.

"Taxi." I bum a cigarette off the driver and exhale as the city goes by in reverse. I honestly think, years from now, taxi rides like this will be the defining memory of my early twenties.

I mean, really, if you wanted to see me, commit to a place!

I flick the ash out the window. It's the whole Buffet Syndrome—for New York City boys Manhattan is an all-you-can-eat. Why commit to one place when there *might* be a cooler one around the corner? Why commit to one model, when a better/taller/thinner one *could* walk in the door at any moment?

So, in order to avoid having to make a choice, a *decision*, these boys make a religion of chaos. Their lives become governed by this bizarre need for serendipity. It's a whole lot of "We'll just see what happens." And in Manhattan that *could* be hanging out with Kate Moss at four A.M.

So, if I "happen" to run into him three weekends in a row then I *might* end up a girlfriend. The problem, then, is that their reverence for anarchy forces those of us lucky enough to "happen into" relationships with them to become the planners—or *nothing* would happen. We become their mothers, their cruise directors—their nannies. And it runs the gamut from H. H. not being able to commit to one club for one evening to Mr. X always being late, being early, or not being there at all.

I take a drag of my borrowed Parliament and think of *Lion King* costumes, fishnets, and leather pants, the hours of planning poured into this night. The cab pulls into Ninety-third Street and I fish for the last of my crumpled twenties. As the cab drives away the city suddenly seems very quiet. I stand there for a moment on the sidewalk—the air is bracingly cold, but it feels good. I sit down on the steps of my building and look over at the dim lights of Queens, winking at me across the East River. I wish I had another cigarette.

I get upstairs and unbutton my pants, kick off my shoes, reach for water, for pajamas, for George. And on the ninth floor of the electric porcupine that is New York City, Mrs. X is still sitting wide awake in the upholstered chair across from the beige bed, watching as the covers rise and fall with each snore, while somewhere Ms. Chicago unpeels her fishnets and gets into bed alone.

PART TWO

Winter

"Ooooooooo I just love Nanny I absolutely do . . . She is my mostly companion."

—ELOISE

CHAPTER FOUR

Holiday Cheer at $10 an Hour

I turn the key and lean into the Xes' heavy front door, as has become my habit, but it only swings open a foot before getting stuck.

"Huh," I say.

"Huh," Grayer echoes behind me.

"Something's blocking the door," I explain as I reach my arm around and begin to grope blindly to identify the obstructing object.

"MOOOOMMMMMM! THE DOOR WON'T OPENNNN!!!" Grayer, wasting no time, uses his own approach.

I hear the slide of Mrs. X's stocking feet. "Yes, Grayer, Mommy's coming. I simply couldn't carry all my elfing past the door in one trip." She pulls the door open and is revealed, knee deep in piles of shopping bags on the foyer floor—Gucci, Ferragamo, Chanel, Hermès, and endless silver boxes with purple ribbon, the signature Bergdorf's holiday wrap. She holds what must have been the offending item, a large Tiffany blue package, under her arm and greets us. "Can you believe people actually get engaged this time of year? As if there isn't enough to do, I *also* had to run *all* the way to Tiffany's to pick up a sterling serving tray. They should at least have had the decency to wait till January—it's just one more month, really. I'm so sorry, Grayer, that I couldn't come to your party. I'm sure you had a wonderful time with Nanny!"

I put my backpack down in the coat closet and slip off my boots before crouching to help Grayer with his jacket. He gingerly protects the ornament we have just spent the past three hours constructing with his classmates (and their nannies) at his school's Family Christmas Party. He drops to the floor so I can pull off his wet boots.

"Grayer constructed quite the masterpiece," I say. "He's really a wizard with Styrofoam and glitter!" I look up at her as I place his boots on the mat.

"It's a snowman. His name is Al. He has a cold so he has to take lots of vitamin C." Grayer describes Styrofoam Al as if announcing him as the next guest on Letterman.

"Ah." She nods, shifting the Tiffany's package to her hip.

"Why don't you go look for a spot for Al to hang out?" I help him up and he shuffles off toward the living room with his artwork held in front of him like a Fabergé egg.

I stand up, brush myself off, and face Mrs. X, ready to give the report.

"I wish you could have seen him this morning. He was totally in his element! He loved the glitter. And he really took his time with making it. You know Giselle Rutherford?"

"Jacqueline Rutherford's daughter? Of course—oh, her mother is too much. When it was her turn to do snack she brought in a chef and set up an omelette bar in the music corner. I mean, really. The rule is you are supposed to come with the snack *prepared*. Tell me, tell me."

"Well, Ms. Giselle insisted that Grayer do his snowman according to her color scheme—orange, because she's spending this Christmas in South Beach."

"Oh, how tacky." Her eyes are wide.

"She pulled Al right out of Grayer's hands and he landed smack in the middle of her orange glitter. I thought Grayer would lose it, but he just looked up at me and announced that Al's orange specks were simply crumbs from all the vitamin C he had to take for his cold!"

"I think he just has a knack for color." She begins to organize her bags. "So, how are finals going?"

"I'm in the home stretch and can't wait to be done."

She stands up and arches her back a little, making a fearful cracking sound. "I know, I'm just exhausted! It seems like the list just keeps on growing every year. Mr. X has a huge family and so many colleagues. And it's already the sixth. I cannot wait for Lyford Cay. Cannot wait. I'm exhausted." She gathers up her bags. "When are you off until?"

"January twenty-sixth," I say. Just two more weeks to go and then I have a whole month off from school and you.

"You should go to Europe this January. Do it while you're still a student, before you have Real Life to worry about."

Oh, so maybe my pending Christmas bonus will cover a plane ticket to Europe? Six hours in a Teletubby costume says I'm worth it.

She continues. "You should see Paris when it's snowing, there's nothing as charming."

"Except Grayer, of course!" We laugh together, as I try to sell her on her own child. The phone rings, interrupting us.

Mrs. X grabs a few more bags in each hand, tightens her arm around the Tiffany's package, and heads back toward her office. "Oh, Nanny, the tree's been set up. Why don't you and Grayer go down to the basement and bring up the ornaments?"

"Sure!" I call after her as I walk to the living room. The tree is a magnificent Douglas fir that looks as if it were growing right out of the floor. I close my eyes and inhale for a second before addressing Grayer, who's having an animated exchange with Al, the lone tree decoration teetering on the very tip of a low branch.

"Hey, looks like your man Al is getting ready to jump." I reach for the bent paper clip serving as Al's lifeline.

"DON'T! He doesn't want you to touch him. Only me," he instructs. We spend the next fifteen tedious minutes relocating Al while ensuring that *only* Grayer's hands do all the work. I stare up at the many feet of bare greens towering above us and wonder if anyone would notice if the rest of the Xes' ornaments didn't make it on this year. At the rate we're going, it might conceivably take Grayer well into his twenties.

I look down at him as he whispers to Al. "Okay, buddy," I say, "let's go to the basement and bring up the rest of your ornaments so they can keep Al company. They'll be there to talk him down if he gets too close to the edge again."

"To the basement?"

"Yup. Let's go."

"I got to get my stuff. Got to get my helmet and belt. You go to the door Nanny, I'll meet ya . . . got to get the flashlight . . ." He runs to his room as I ring for the elevator.

Grayer glides back out into the vestibule just as the elevator door opens. "Oh, my God, Grove! All this for the basement?" He puts one sock-covered foot down to stop his skateboard in front of the elevator door. His bicycle helmet sits slightly askew and he has shoved a huge flashlight into his waistband, along with a yo-yo and what looks to be a monogrammed washcloth from his bathroom.

"Okay, let's go," he says with complete authority.

"I'm thinking we should at least be wearing shoes for this adventure."

"Nah, don't need 'em." He rolls inside and the door closes behind both of us before I can catch it. "It's so cool down there, Nanny. Oh, man, oh, man." He nods his helmeted head in anticipation. Grayer has taken to peppering his commentary with "oh, mans" as of late, thanks to Christianson, a four-year-old of remarkable charisma who has a good foot in height over the rest of his classmates. In fact, when Al first made impact with the fateful orange glitter both Giselle's and Grayer's first utterance was a simultaneous "Oh, man."

The elevator stops at the lobby and Grayer rolls ahead of me, propelling himself with one foot, while keeping both hands on his waistband so that his packed pants don't succumb to gravity. By the time I catch up, he's already gotten Ramon to lead the way to the caged service elevator. "Ahh, Mr. Grayer. You must have important business down there, huh?"

Grayer is busy adjusting his tools and offers only a distracted "Yup."

Ramon smiles in his direction and then winks conspiratorially at me. "He's very serious, our Mr. Grayer. You got a girlfriend yet, Mr. Grayer?" The elevator jerks as we reach the basement. He slides the gate open and we step out into the bright, cold corridor, rich with the aroma of dryer sheets. "Cage 132—down to the right. Be careful now, don't get lost, or I'll have to come find you . . ." He winks again and, with a suggestive wiggle of his eyebrows, pulls the door closed, leaving me beneath a dangling lightbulb.

"Grayer?" I yell down the corridor.

"Nanny! I'm waiting. Come onnnn!" I follow his voice around the maze of floor-to-ceiling cages lining the walls. Some are more packed than others, but each has the requisite luggage, ski equipment, and random pieces of bubble-wrapped furniture. I round the bend and see Grove lying on his stomach atop his skateboard under a sign that says 132, pulling himself along the wired wall by his hands. "Oh, man, it's gonna be so fun when Daddy comes home and does the tree. Caitlin gets us started and Daddy does the high-ups and we have hot chocolate *in the living room*."

"Sounds pretty cool. Here, I have the key," I say, holding it out toward him. He jumps up and down as I unlock the cage and then proceeds to deftly make his way in around the boxes. I let him lead as he's clearly made this trek before and I wouldn't know a storage locker from an Easy-Bake oven.

I sit down on the cold cement and lean back on the cage door facing that of the Xes. My parents used to daydream about storage space, sitting with both feet up on the trunk packed to bursting with our summer clothes that served as our coffee table. On occasion, we'd allow ourselves to talk about what we could do with one extra closet—much as a family in Wyoming might fantasize about winning the lottery.

"Do you know what you're looking for, Grove?" I call into the piles, as I haven't heard anything in a few minutes. Loud clanging noises break the silence. "Grayer! What's going on in there?" I start to stand up as his flashlight comes rolling out of the darkness and stops at my feet.

"Just getting my stuff out, Nanny! Turn the light on me, I'm going to get the blue box!" I click the high beam on and point it into the cage as directed, illuminating two dirtied socks and a little khaki rear end tunneling into the middle of the pile.

"Are you sure that's safe, Grayer? I think maybe I should . . ." What, crawl in behind him?

"I got it. Oh, man, there's lotsa stuff back here. My skis! These are my skis, Nanny, for when we go to Aspirin."

"Aspen?"

"Aspen. Found it! Going to pass 'em out. Get ready. You get ready, Nanny, here they come." He is far into the boxes. I hear fumbling and then a glass ball comes flying out of the darkness at me. I drop the flashlight and catch it. It is handblown and has a Steuben mark on it, along with a red hook. Before I can look up another one comes flying out.

"GRAYER! FREEZE!" With the flashlight rolling around on the floor, casting a weird light on Grayer's boxes, I realize I've been letting Mickey Mouse run the show. "Back it up, mister, back it right on up. It's your turn to hold the flashlight."

"Noooooo."

"Gray-er!" It's the Wicked Witch voice.

"FINE!" He tunnels back out.

I hand him the flashlight. "Now let's try this again, only this time you'll be me and I'll be you."

When we get back up to the apartment Grayer marches ahead to establish a plan of attack while I gingerly set the box of ornaments down in the front hall.

"Nanny?" I hear a small voice call for me.

"Yes, G?" I follow him into the living room where a flamboyant Johnny Cash is on a ladder, decorating Grayer's tree.

"Pass me that box of doves," he says, not even turning to look at us. Grayer and I, standing safely by the door, survey the living room floor, which is littered with doves, gold leaves, Victorian angels, and strings of pearls.

"Get down. My dad does the high-ups."

"Hold on a sec, Grayer," I say as I pass off the birds to the man in black. "I'll be right back."

"You better get down or my daddy's gonna be mad at you," I hear Grayer challenge as I knock on Mrs. X's office door.

"Come in."

"Hi, Mrs. X? Sorry to bother you—" The room, ordinarily pristine, has been taken over by her "elfing" and stacks and stacks of Christmas cards.

"No, no, come in—what is it?" I open my mouth. "Have you met Julio? Isn't he a genius? I'm so lucky I got him—he is the *the* tree expert. You should see what he did at the Egglestons—it was just breathtaking."

"I—"

"While I've got you, can I ask? Is a plaid taffeta skirt just too cliché for a Scottish Christmas party? I can't decide—"

"I—"

"Oh! You should see—I bought *the* cutest twinsets today for Mr.

X's nieces. I hope they're the right color. Would you wear winter-weight cashmere pastels?" She pulls out a TSE shopping bag. "I might exchange them—"

"I was just wondering," I cut in, "Grayer was really looking forward to decorating the tree. He said it was something he did with Caitlin last year and I was wondering if maybe I could just get him a small tree for his room that he could hang a couple of ornaments on, just for fun—"

"I really don't think it would be a good idea to be traipsing needles all over that part of the house." She searches for a solution. "If he wants a tree activity, why don't you take him to Rockefeller Center?"

"Well . . . Yeah, no, yeah, that's a great idea," I say as I open the door.

"Thanks—I'm just so overwhelmed!"

When I get back in the living room Grayer is holding a silver baby spoon on a string and tapping on Julio's ladder. "Hey! How about this? Where does this go?" he asks.

Julio looks down in disgust at the spoon. "That doesn't really gel with my vision—" Grayer's eyes start to well up. "Well, if you must. In the back. On the bottom."

"G, I've got a plan. Grab Al, I'll get your coat."

✧

"Grandma, Grayer. Grayer, this is Grandma."

My grandmother crouches down in her black satin pajama pants, her pearls clicking together as she extends her hand. "Pleased to meet you, Grayer. And darling, you must be Al." Grayer blushes deeply. "Well, are we doing Christmas or what? Everybody in who wants rugelach."

"Thanks so much, Gran. We were in desperate need of a surface to decorate." The doorbell rings behind us as I reach to take off Grayer's coat.

"A surface! Don't be ridiculous." She reaches over Grayer's head to open the door and there stands a huge tree with two arms wrapped around it. "Right this way!" she says. "Now, Grayer," she whispers, "you cover Al's eyes. It's all about the surprise." We kick off our boots and follow closely behind them into the apartment. I've got to hand it to her—she has the deliveryman place it squarely in the middle of the living room. She sees him out and returns to join us.

"Grandma, you really didn't have to get a—"

"If you're going to do something, darling, then do it all the way. Now, Grayer, let me hit the special effects and we'll get this soiree started." Grayer holds his hands carefully over Al's eyes as my grand-mother turns on Frank Sinatra—"Can't find Bing," she mouths— and hits the lights. She's lit candles all about the room, setting a beautiful glow around our family pictures, and as Frank croons "The Lady Is a Tramp," it's breathtaking.

She leans down to Grayer. "Well, sir, whenever you're ready, I believe Al should meet his tree." We both make drum-roll noises as Grayer takes his hands off Al's eyes and asks him exactly where he would like to hang out first.

An hour later the two of us are lounging on cushions beneath the green boughs, sipping hot chocolate, while Grayer relocates Al at whim.

"So, how's the drama with your H. H.?"

"I can't get a read on him. I want him to be different from those boys, but there's really no good reason why he would be. Of course, if I never see him again it's pretty irrelevant."

"Keep riding the elevator, dear. He'll show up. So, how are finals going?" she asks.

"Only one more and I'm done. It's been insane—the Xes have been out at Christmas parties every night. I only study after Grayer goes to sleep, which, ultimately, is probably better than trying to con-centrate over the sounds of Charlene and her hairy boyfriend—" She looks at me. "Don't even get me started."

"Well, just don't wear yourself out. It's not worth it."

"I know. But the bonus is bound to be good this year—she's mentioned Paris."

"Oh là là, très bien."

"Nanny, Al wants to know why Daddy isn't doing the high-ups," Grayer asks quietly from behind the tree. I look over at her, unsure how to answer him.

"Grayer"—she smiles at me reassuringly—"has Nan told you about wassailing?"

He emerges. "What did you say?" He comes up close to her and puts his hand on her knee.

"Wassailing, darling. When you wassail—*you* make Christmas! You, little Grayer, are the very best gift you can give. All you do is knock on someone's door, someone you want to share the joy of Christmas with, and when they open it you sing your heart out. Wassailing—you've got to try it!" He lies down next to me and we look up through the branches with our heads together on a pillow.

"Grandma, you show me. Sing something," he says. I turn my head and smile at her. From where we lie she seems to be glowing as she leans against the chaise surrounded by candles. She begins to sing along with her Frank to "The Way You Look Tonight." Grayer closes his eyes and I fall just a little bit more in love with her.

✧ ✧ ✧

A week later, in excited pursuit of Mr. X, Mrs. X and Grayer march eagerly ahead of me along the same corridor I chased Grayer down at the Halloween party. Boughs of greens and twinkling colored lights now hang where fake cobwebs had been.

Mrs. X pushes Mr. X's heavy office door open.

"Darling, come in." He stands, backlit by the setting sun, which pours in through the floor-to-ceiling windows behind his desk. I am immediately struck by his capability to exude relaxed power in this room with the lights on as well as off. He looks through me in Grayer's general direction. "Hey, sport."

Grayer tries to hand off the bag of Christmas presents we've brought for the charity his father's company supports, but Mr. X has already picked up the blinking phone.

I take the presents and lean down to unbuckle Grayer's toggle coat.

"Justine said something about cookies in the conference room. Why don't you take Grayer down there? I have to take this call and then I'll join you," Mr. X instructs, his hand over the mouthpiece. Mrs. X drops her mink on the couch and we file back out toward the sound of Christmas carols coming from behind the double doors at the end of the hall.

Mrs. X is a sugarplum vision in her Moschino green suit with red holly-berry trim and mistletoe buttons. To top it off, the heels of her shoes are miniature snow globes with a reindeer in one and Santa in the other. I am just grateful not to be dressed up as Frosty the Snowman, and wear my Christmas-tree pin with pride.

With a grand smile she pushes the doors open into the conference room, at the far end of which sits a small gaggle of women, whom I assume to be secretaries, opening a tin of cookies and playing Alvin and the Chipmunks on a tape player.

"Ooh, I'm sorry. I'm looking for the Christmas party," Mrs. X says, stopping short at the head of the table.

"Would you like a cookie? I made them myself," a jolly-looking robust woman with Christmas-tree-light earrings calls back.

"Oh." Mrs. X seems confused.

The doors swing open again, narrowly missing Grayer and me. I inhale sharply as Ms. Chicago steps in to join our cluster. She maneuvers around us to get to Mrs. X, her tight flannel suit leaving little more to the imagination than her Halloween costume did.

"I heard there were cookies," she says as a sturdy-looking

brunette comes flying in behind her, pushing us all forward against the table.

"Mrs. X," the brunette says, slightly out of breath.

"Justine, Merry Christmas," Mrs. X greets her.

"Hi, Merry Christmas, why don't you come with me to the kitchen and we'll get some coffee?"

"Don't be silly, Justine." Ms. Chicago smiles. "There's coffee right here." She walks over to the chrome pot and pulls out a Styrofoam cup. "Won't you go see what's taking them so long with those numbers?"

"Are you sure you don't want to come with me, Mrs. X?"

"Justine." Ms. Chicago raises an eyebrow and Justine walks slowly back out the double doors.

"Are we early?" Mrs. X inquires.

"Early for what?" Ms. Chicago asks, pouring two cups of coffee.

"For the family Christmas party."

"That's next week—I'm surprised your husband didn't tell you. Shame on him!" She laughs, handing the coffee to her. Grayer squeezes past Ms. Chicago's exposed knees, swaggering down to the other end of the table to wow the secretaries out of a cookie.

Mrs. X stammers, "Well, um, my husband must have gotten the dates confused."

"Men," Ms. Chicago snorts.

Mrs. X shifts the Styrofoam cup to her left hand. "I'm sorry, have we met?"

"Lisa. Lisa Chenowith," Ms. Chicago smiles, "I'm Managing Director of the Chicago branch."

"Oh," Mrs. X says, "nice to meet you."

"I'm so sorry I couldn't get to your dinner party—I heard it was lovely. Unfortunately, that slave-driver husband of yours insisted I hightail it back to Illinois." She tilts her head to the side and smiles brilliantly like a canary-filled cat. "The gift bags were adorable—everyone just loves the pens."

"Oh, good." Mrs. X raises her hand protectively to her collarbone. "You work with my husband?" And with that I decide to make helping Grayer pick out the perfect reindeer cookie my personal mission.

"I'm heading up the team working on the Midwest Mutual merger. Isn't it awful? Well, I'm sure you know."

"Truly," Mrs. X says, but her voice rises, betraying her uncertainty.

"Getting them down to eight percent was such a coup. You must have had some sleepless nights over that one," she says, shaking her Titian hair in sympathy. "But I told him if we push the sell date up and save them the liquidation costs, they might bend—and they did. They bent right over."

Mrs. X stands very straight, her hand clenched tightly around the Styrofoam. "Yes, he's been working very hard."

Ms. Chicago struts to our end of the table, her lizard-skin pumps silent on the plush carpet. "And you're Grayer. Do you remember me?" she bends down to inquire.

Grayer places her. "You don't wear pants." Oh, sweet Jesus.

Just then the door opens and Mr. X strides in, his broad frame towering in the doorway. "Ed Strauss is on the phone—he wants to go over the contract," he calls down the table to Ms. Chicago.

"Fine," she says, smiling, as she walks slowly back up the room past Mrs. X. "Merry Christmas, everybody." As she reaches Mr. X she adds, "It was so lovely to finally meet your family."

His jaw clenched, Mr. X closes the door swiftly behind them.

"Daddy, wait!" Grayer attempts to follow him out of the room, but the Dixie cup of grape juice slips from his grasp, staining both his shirt and the beige carpet a deep purple. Mercifully, we all turn our attention to the spill, gathering paper napkins and seltzer. Grayer stands whimpering while multiple manicured hands dab at his front.

"Nanny, I'd really appreciate it if you kept a closer eye on him. Just get him cleaned up—I'll be waiting in the car," Mrs. X instructs, placing her untouched cup of coffee on the table, like Snow White putting down the apple. When she looks back up she has pasted on a beaming smile for the secretaries. "See you all next week!"

✧ ✧ ✧

The next afternoon, having finished his lunch, Grayer announces our plans as he climbs down from his booster seat.

"Wassailing."

"What?"

"I want to wassail. I'm going to make my own Christmas. I knock on the door, you open it, and I sing my heart out." I'm amazed that he's retained this from our visit over a week ago, but my grandmother does have a way of nestling herself into people's memories.

"Okay, what door would you like me to stand behind?" I ask.

"My bathroom," he says over his shoulder as he heads off with purpose toward his wing. I follow him and position myself in the bathroom as directed. A few moments later I hear his little knock.

"Yes," I say, "who's there?"

"NANNY, you are just supposed to open the door! Don't talk, just open it!"

"Right. Ready when you are." I sit back on the toilet seat and start checking my hair for split ends, sensing that this game may be slow to get off the ground.

Again, a small knock. I lean forward and nudge the door open, almost knocking him over.

"NANNY, that's mean! You're trying to push me! I don't like that. Start over."

Eleven knocks later, I finally get it right and am rewarded with a screaming rendition of "Happy Birthday" that shakes the window-pane.

"Grover, why don't you try a little dancing while you wassail?" I ask when he finishes. "Really wow 'em?" I hope he might quiet down if he has to divert some energy to staying in motion.

"Wassailing is not dancing, it is singing your heart out." He puts his hands on his hips. "Close the door and I'll knock," he says, as if suggesting this routine for the first time. We play wassailing for about half an hour until I remember that Connie, the housekeeper, is here and sic Grayer on her. I hear him from across the apartment, screaming "Happy Birthday" over her roaring vacuum and after five rounds go back to collect what is rightfully mine.

"Want to play cars?"

"No. I want to wassail. Let's go back to my bathroom."

"Only if you dance, too."

"Oh, man, oh, man, there is NO dancing when I wassail!"

"Come on, mister, we're calling Grandma."

One short phone call later and Grayer is not only dancing and singing the actual "Here we come a wassailing among the leaves so green," which is infinitely less painful, but I have been inspired with a delicious plan.

As I give Grayer's wassailing outfit (green and red striped turtleneck, felt reindeer antlers, candy-cane suspenders) a final once-over for "ultra wassailyness," Mrs. X comes bustling in, Ramon in tow, laden with boxes.

Her cheeks are rosy, her eyes are glistening. "Oh, it is a zoo out there, a zoo! I nearly got into a fight with a woman at Hammacher Schlemmer—put them down over there, Ramon—over the last ScrewPull, but I just let her have it, I thought there is no point descending to her level. I think she was from out of town. Oh, I found the most darling wallets at Gucci. Does Cleveland understand Gucci? I wonder—thank you, Ramon. Oh, I hope they like them— Grayer what have you been up to?"

"Nothing," he says, while practicing his soft-shoe by the umbrella stand.

"Before lunch we made unsweetened cookies and decorated them and then we've been practicing carols and I read him *The Night Before Christmas* in French," I say, trying to jog his memory.

"Oh, wonderful. I wish someone would read to me." She takes off her mink and nearly hands it to Ramon. "Oh, that's all, Ramon, thank you." She claps her hands together. "So, what are you up to now?"

"I was going to let Grayer practice his caroling—"

"WASSAILING!"

"—on some of the elderly in the building, who might appreciate a little holiday cheer!"

Mrs. X is beaming. "Oh, excellent! What a good boy you are and that'll keep him o-c-c-u-p-i-e-d. I have *so much to do*! Have fun!"

I let Grayer press for the elevator. "Which floor, Nanny?"

"Let's start with your friend on eleven."

We have to buzz three times before we hear "Coming!" from inside the apartment. As soon as the door opens it's apparent the hour and a half of "practicing" was well worth it. H. H. leans against the door frame in faded Christmas-tree boxers and a well-worn Andover T-shirt, rubbing sleep out of his eyes.

"HERE WE COME A-WASSAILING! AMONG THE LEAVES SO GREEN!!!" Grayer is red faced, swaying back and forth, with his jazz hands splayed and antlers waving. For a split second it crosses my mind that he might literally sing his heart out.

"LOVE AND JOY COME TO YOU!!!" His voice ricochets around the vestibule, bouncing off every surface so that it sounds as if he's a chorus of emphatic wassailers. A wassailing riot. When it appears he has reached his conclusion, H. H. bends down and opens his mouth.

"AND GOD BLESS YOU!!!" This move mistakenly places him at ground zero to be blasted with the spit and sweat of Grayer's effort, which is then followed by an even louder finale.

"Well, good morning to you, too, Grayer!"

Grayer collapses onto the vestibule floor, panting to catch his breath. I smile beguilingly. Make no bones about it; I am a girl with a mission. I am here to get a Date. A Real Date with a plan and a location and everything.

"We're caroling—" I begin.

"Wassailing," a small exasperated voice pipes in from the floor. "Wassailing around the building."

"Can I have a cookie now?" Grayer sits up, ready to be rewarded for his efforts.

H. H. turns into his apartment. "Sure. Come on in. Don't mind my pajamas." Oh, if you insist. We follow his boxer-clad body into what is essentially the Xes' apartment, only two floors higher, and one would never guess that we were even in the same building. The walls in the front hall are painted a deep brick red and are decorated with *National Geographic*-type black-and-white photographs between kilim tapestries. There are sneakers lining the floor and dog hair on the carpet. We make our way into the kitchen where we practically trip over a huge, graying yellow Lab lying on the floor.

"Grayer, you know Max, right?" Grayer hunkers down and with uncharacteristic gentleness rubs Max's ears. Max's tail animatedly pounds the tiles in response. I look around; instead of the large island that Mrs. X has in the middle of the room, there's an old refectory table piled high at one end with the *Times*.

"Cookies? Anyone want cookies?" H. H. asks, brandishing a Christmas tin of David's cookies that he has pulled from a teetering pile of holiday baked goods on the sideboard. Grayer runs over to help himself and I force myself to focus.

"Just one, Grover."

"Oh, man."

"Do you want milk with that?" He heads to the fridge and returns with a full glass.

"Thank you so much," I say. "Hey, Grayer, anything you want to say to our host?"

"Thanks!" he mumbles, his mouth full of cookie.

"No, man, thank you! It's the least I can do after such a powerful performance." He smiles over at me. "I can't remember the last time someone sang to me when it wasn't my birthday."

"I can do that! I can do 'Happy Birthday'—" He puts his glass down on the floor and places his hands into the jazz position in preparation.

"Whoa! We have done our fair share of wassailing already—" I put my hand out to shield us from another round.

"Grayer, it's not my birthday today. But I promise I'll let you know when it is." Teamwork, I love it.

"Okay. Let's go, Nanny. Got to wassail. Let's go now." Grayer hands H. H. his empty glass, wipes his gloved hand across his lips, and heads for the door.

I stand up from the table, not really wanting to leave. "I'm sorry I never caught up with you that night; their party ran really late."

"That's all right, you didn't miss anything. The Next Thing was having a private party, so we just ended up getting pizza at Ruby's." As in the Ruby's that is exactly twenty feet from my front stoop. The irony.

"How long are you home for?" I ask without batting an eyelash.

"NA-NNY. The elevator's here!"

"Just a week and then we go to Africa."

The elevator door waiting, my heart pounding. "Well, I'm around if you want to hang out this weekend," I say as I step in beside Grayer.

"Yeah, great," he says from the doorway.

"Great." I nod my head as the door slides closed.

"GREAT!" Grayer sings as a warm-up to our next performance.

✧ ✧ ✧

Short of writing my number on a piece of paper and shoving it under his door, I leave 721 Park on Friday night knowing there is no way I am going to see H. H. before he leaves for Africa. Ugh.

That night I make Sarah, who's home for Christmas vacation, accompany me to a holiday party being given downtown by some guys in my class. The whole apartment is festively decorated in glowing jalapeño-pepper lights and someone has glued a cutout of a large penis onto the picture of Santa in the living room. It takes less than five minutes to decide that we don't want a Bud Light from the bathtub, a fistful of corn chips from a filmy bowl, or to take any of the frat boys up on their gracious offers of quick oral sex.

We head Josh off on the stairs.

"No fun?" he asks.

"Well," Sarah says, "I love to play strip quarters as much as the next girl, but—"

"Sarah!" Josh cries, giving her a hug. "Lead on!"

Several hours later find me doing a martini-sodden rendition of the wassailing story for Sarah in a corner booth at the Next Thing while Josh hits on some fashionista at the bar. "And *then* . . . he gave him a cookie! That must mean *something*, right?" We do an interpretive dance of every subtle nuance of the entire five-minute exchange until we have completely wrung the encounter of any meaning it might possibly have had. "*So then* he said 'Great' and then I said 'Great.' "

⟡ ⟡ ⟡

Saturday morning I wake with my shoes still on, a killer hangover, and only one day to buy presents for my entire family, the Xes, and the many little people I've taken care of over the years. The Gleason girls have already sent over two glitter pens and a rock with my name painted on it—I've got to get my act together.

I wolf down tomato sauce on toast, drink a liter of water, grab a double shot of espresso on the corner, and ba-da-bing, I am alive with the Holiday Spirit.

An hour later I emerge from Barnes and Noble Junior a good $150 lighter, prompting me to do a little math as I walk down Park. Forget Paris, I'm going to need that stupid bonus just to pay off Christmas.

I walk down Madison to Bergdorf's to get a Rigaud candle for Mrs. X. It may be tiny, but at least she'll know it wasn't cheap. As I stand on line for the all-important silver gift wrap I try to figure out what to get the four-year-old who has everything. What would make him really happy, short of his father actually making an appearance to do the high-ups? Well . . . a night-light, because he's scared of the dark. And maybe a bus-pass holder that could keep that card protected before it completely disintegrates.

As I'm on Fifty-eighth and Fifth, the logical thing would be to cross the street to FAO Schwarz's enormous Sesame Street section to find him a Grover night-light, but I can't, can't, *can't.*

I debate which would be faster, taking the train to a Toys "Я" Us in Queens or navigating a few thousand square feet of bedlam just a block away. Against my better judgment, I drag myself across Fifth to wait in line with the entire population of Nebraska in the cold for over half an hour before being ushered into the revolving doors by a tall toy soldier.

"Welcome to our world. Welcome to our world. Welcome to our world of toys," blasts relentlessly from mysteriously placed speakers, making it sound as if the eerie, childlike singing is coming from within my own head. Yet it cannot drown out the tortured cries of "But I waaaant it!! I neeeeed it!!" that also fill the air. And this is only the stuffed-animal floor.

Upstairs is total chaos; children are firing ray guns, throwing slime, sports equipment, and siblings. I look around at parents who share my "let's just get through this" expression and employees trying to make it to lunch without sustaining serious bodily injury. I slither to Sesame Street Corner where a little girl of about three has prostrated herself on the floor and is sobbing for injustice everywhere.

"Maybe Santa will bring you one, Sally."

"NoooOOOoooOOOOoooOOOoooooooooOOOoooooOOOO!" she howls.

"Can I help you?" asks a salesgirl wearing a red shirt and glazed smile.

"I'm looking for a Grover night-light."

"Oh, I think we sold out of Grover." The last half hour of standing in line says you didn't. "Let's take a look." Yes, let's.

We go to the night-light section where we are faced with an entire wall of Grover. "Yeah, sorry, those went fast," she says, shaking her head as she begins to wander off.

"Yeah, this is one," I say, holding it up.

"Oh, is he the blue guy?" Yes, he's the blue guy. (Don't even get me started! No one at Barnes and Noble Junior had even heard of *Lyle, Lyle, Crocodile*. Come on, you work in a children's bookstore, it's not like I'm asking for *Hustler*.)

I take my place in line for gift wrap and use the opportunity to practice my transcendental meditation amid more children wracked with sobs.

✧ ✧ ✧

On Monday morning Mrs. X pops her head into the kitchen while I'm cutting fruit. "Nanny, I need you to run an errand for me. I went to Saks to pick up the gifts for our help and, like a ninny, I forgot the bonus checks. So I've put handbags on hold and I'd like you to make sure that each check is put inside the right bag. Now, I've written it all down and the name of each person is on the outside of each envelope. Justine gets the Gucci shoulder bag, Mrs. Butters gets the Coach tote, housekeeper gets the LeSportsac and the Hervé Chapeliers are for the piano and the French teachers. Make sure they gift-wrap everything and then just come home in a cab."

"No problem," I say, excitedly estimating where I fit in between Gucci and LeSportsac.

◇ ◇ ◇

Tuesday afternoon Grayer has Allison over, an adorable Chinese girl from his class who will proudly tell anyone who asks, "I have two daddies!"

"Hello, Nanny," she always says, curtsying. "How's school? Love your shoes." She just kills me.

The phone rings as I'm rinsing out their hot carob mugs. "Hello?" I say, hanging the towel neatly on the oven door.

"Nanny?" I hear a tentative whisper.

"Yes," I whisper back, because one does.

"It's Justine, from Mr. X's office. I'm so glad I got you. Can you do me a favor?"

"Sure," I whisper.

"Mr. X asked me to go pick out some things for Mrs. X and I don't know her size or what designer she likes, or the colors." She sounds genuinely panicked.

"I don't know," I say, surprised to find I don't have her measurements committed to memory. "Wait, hold on." I go pick up the extension in the master bedroom.

"Justine?"

"Yes?" she whispers. Is she under her desk? In the ladies' room?

"Okay, I'm going in the closet." Her "closet" is actually a large chocolate-brown dressing room, complete with a long velvet bench. Mrs. X's paranoia is such that I'm sure she's convinced I not only snoop around in here on a daily basis, but am, in fact, wearing her underwear right now. On the contrary, I'm in a cold sweat and debate putting Justine on hold again so I can call Mrs. X on her cell phone to confirm that she's really, really far away.

Regardless, I start gently riffling the merchandise and answering

Justine's questions. "Size two . . . Herrera, Yves Saint Laurent . . . Shoe size seven and a half, Ferragamo, Chanel . . . Her purses are Hermès—no outside pockets and she hates zippers . . . I don't know, pearls, maybe? She likes pearls." And so on and so forth.

"You've been a lifesaver," she gushes. "Oh, one more thing. Is Grayer doing chemistry?"

"Chemistry?"

"Yeah, Mr. X told me to go buy him a chemistry set and some Gucci slippers."

"Right." We both laugh. *The Lion King*," I say. "He loves anything to do with *The Lion King, Aladdin, Winnie-the-Pooh*. He's four."

"Thanks again, Nanny. Merry Christmas!" After clicking off I take one last look around at the tower of cashmere sweaters, each one wrapped with tissue and individually stored in its own clear drawer, the wall of shoes, each stuffed with a satin triangle, the racks of fall, winter, and spring suits, going from lightest to darkest, from left to right. I tentatively pull open a drawer. Each pair of panties, every bra, every pair of stockings, is individually packed in a Ziplock baggy and labeled: "Bra, Hanro, white," "Stockings, Fogal, black."

The doorbell rings and I jump about sixteen feet, panting with relief when I hear Grayer let Henry, Allison's father, in. I slide the drawer shut and walk calmly out to the hall, where a bemused Henry is watching Grayer and Allison trying to tag each other with their scarves.

"Okay, Ally, I have to get dinner started. Let's get it together." He finally catches her, steadying her between his knees to tie her scarf.

I hand over her small loden coat as Henry secures her hat and ushers her into the vestibule.

"Say good-bye to Allison, Grayer." I nudge him and he waves frenetically with both hands.

"Good-bye, Gray-er. Thank you for a lovely afternoon! *Au revoir*, Nanny!" she cries as the elevator opens.

"Thanks, Nan," Henry says, turning and accidentally swinging one of Allison's boots right into another member of the X family.

"Oh!" Mrs. X flinches.

"I'm so sorry," Henry says, as Allison buries her head in his neck.

"No, please, I'm fine. Did you all have a good time?"

"Yes!" Grayer and Allison shout.

"Well," Henry says, "I better get back and start dinner. Richard'll be home soon and I need to get the ornaments down."

"Your nanny's day off?" she asks with a knowing smile.

"Oh, we don't have a nanny—"

"You have *two* daddies to do the high-ups?" Grayer interrupts him.

"My goodness," Mrs. X says quickly, "however do you manage?"

"Well, you know, they're only this age once."

"Yes." She looks a little pinched. "Grayer, say good-bye!"

"I already did, Mommy. You're late."

The door slides shut.

✧ ✧ ✧

Much later that night I ride down in the elevator half-asleep, entertaining the fantasy of walking along the Seine humming "La Vie en Rose." It's twenty past twelve on the twenty-second. Only twenty-four more hours to go until a month off and money in my pocket.

" 'Night, James," I say to the doorman, just as he opens the door for H. H., rosy cheeked and carrying a Food Emporium bag.

"Hey, there. Just get off work?" he asks, smiling.

"Yup." Please don't let me have steamed chard between my teeth.

"That was some fine wassailing. You train him?"

"Impressed?" I ask carefully with my upper lip curled down.

Enough patter, *when's the date?*

"Listen," he says, loosening his scarf, "are you doing anything right now, 'cause I just have to run upstairs. My mom's in a Christmas baking frenzy and we ran out of vanilla."

Oh. Now?

Okay, now works for me.

"Yeah, great." As the numbers go from one to eleven and back again I quickly run to the beveled mirror and groom like a madwoman. I hope I'm not boring. I hope he's not boring. I try to remember if I shaved this morning. Ugh, I'll be so bummed if he's boring. And let's try not sleeping with him. Tonight. I'm applying a furtive swipe of lip gloss as the elevator approaches "L."

"Hey, have you eaten yet?" he asks as James opens the door for us.

" 'Night, James," I call over my shoulder. "It depends on what you mean by eating. If you consider a fistful of Goldfish and a few dry tortellini a meal then I'm stuffed."

"What are you up for?"

"Well." I think for a moment. "The only places with open kitchens right now are coffee shops and pizza. Take your pick."

"Pizza sounds good. Is that okay?"

"Anything not in this building sounds fabulous."

⟡

"Here, sit on my jacket," he says as he closes the empty pizza box. The Metropolitan Museum steps are cold and it's starting to seep up through my jeans.

"Thanks." I tuck his blue fleece under me and look down Fifth Avenue at the twinkling holiday lights of the Stanhope Hotel. H. H. pulls the container of Ben and Jerry's Phish Food out of a brown paper bag.

"So what's it like working on the ninth floor?"

"Exhausting and weird." I look back at him. "That apartment has all the holiday warmth of a meat locker and Grayer has a lone Styrofoam snowman hanging in his closet, because she won't let him put it anywhere else."

"Yeah, she's always struck me as a little high-strung."

THE NANNY DIARIES

"You have no idea, and with the holidays it's like working for a drill sergeant with ADD—"

"Come on, it can't be that bad." He nudges me with his knees.

"Excuse me?"

"I used to baby-sit in the building. You eat some food, play some games—"

"Oh, my God. That is not my job *at all.* I spend more time with this kid than *anybody.*" I slide an inch away from him on the step.

"What about on the weekends?"

"They have somebody in Connecticut. They're only alone with him for the drive out and back—and they do that at night so he's asleep! There's no coming together. I thought maybe they were just waiting for a holiday, but apparently not. Mrs. X is having Christmas by herself at Barneys, so she's been sending us all over town, with the rest of America, mind you, just to get him out of the house."

"But there's so much cool stuff to do with a kid this time of year."

"He's *four.* He slept through the *Nutcracker,* the Rockettes scared the shit out of him, and he developed some kind of weird heat rash while waiting for three hours to see Santa at Macy's. But mostly we just stand in line for the bathroom. *Everywhere.* Not a cab to be found, not a—"

"Sounds like you have definitely earned some ice cream." He hands me a spoon.

I have to laugh. "I'm sorry, you're the first grown-up without shopping bags that I've talked to in a good forty-eight hours. I'm just a little Christmased out at the moment."

"Oh, don't say that. This is such an awesome time of year to be living in the city, all the lights and the people." He gestures to the sparkling Christmas decorations on Fifth Avenue. "It makes you appreciate that we're lucky enough to live here year round."

I dig into the carton, tracing a swirl of caramel. "You're right. Up until two weeks ago I would have said it was my favorite time of year." We pass the Phish Food back and forth and look over at the

wreaths in the Stanhope's windows and the little white bulbs burn-
ing on the awning.

"You seem like a holiday kind of girl."

I blush. "Well, Arbor Day is really when I go all out."

He laughs. Oh, sweet God, you are hot.

He leans in. "So, do you still think I'm an asshole?"

"I never said you were an asshole." I smile back.

"Just an asshole by association."

"Well . . ." AAAAAAHHH!!!! HE'S KISSING ME!!!!!

"Hi," he says softly, his face still almost touching mine.

"Hi."

"Can we please start over and put Dorrian's really, really far
behind us?"

I smile. "Hi, I'm Nan . . ."

✧ ✧ ✧

"Nanny? Nanny!"

"Right. What?"

"Your turn. It's your turn." Poor G, this is the third time he's had
to snap me back from the steps of the Met where my brain has taken
up permanent residence.

I move my gingerbread man from an orange square to a yellow
square. "Okay, Grove, but this is the last game and then we've got to
try on those clothes."

"Oh, man."

"Come on, it'll be fun. You can do a little fashion show for me."
The bed is piled with Grayer's wardrobe from last summer and we
need to figure out what, if anything, still fits so that he can be properly outfitted for his vacation. I know putting together a resort
wardrobe is hardly how he wants to spend his last afternoon with
me, but orders are orders.

After we put away the game I kneel on the floor and help him in and out and in and out of shorts, shirts, swimming trunks, and the world's tiniest navy blue blazer.

"Owww! Too small! It hurts!" His arm chub has been compressed like a hot-dog bun with a rubber band around the middle by the little white Lacoste tee.

"Okay, okay, I'm getting you out, be patient." I peel him out of the shirt and hold up a stiff Brooks Brothers oxford.

"I don't like that one so much," he says, shaking his head, then, slowly, "I think . . . it's . . . too . . . *small*," he says intently.

I look down at the buttons on the sleeve and the starched collar. "Yeah. I think you're right—way too small. You probably shouldn't wear it anymore," I say conspiratorially, folding the offending item and putting it on the reject pile.

"Nanny, I'm bored." He puts his hands on either side of my face. "No more shirts. Let's play Candy Land!"

"Come on, just one more, G." I help him into the blazer. "Now walk down to the end of the room and back—let me see how gorgeous you are." He looks at me like I'm crazy, but starts to walk away, looking back over his shoulder every few steps to make sure I'm not up to something.

"Work it, baby!" I shout when he reaches the wall. He turns and eyes me warily until I whip out an imaginary camera and pretend to take pictures. "Come on, baby! You're fabulous. Show it off!" He takes his jazz-hands pose at the end of the carpet. "Woohoo!" I catcall as if Marcus Shenkenberg had just lost his towel. He giggles, throwing himself into the show as we make pouty lips at each other.

"You're gorgeous, dahling," I say, leaning down to take off the blazer and kissing the air by both his cheeks.

"You'll be back really soon, right, Nanny?" He shakes his arm free. "Tomorrow?"

"Here, let's look at the calendar again so you can see how fast it's going to go and you'll be in the Bahamas—"

"Litferrr Cay," he corrects.

"Right." We lean in to look at the Nanny Calendar I made. "And then Aspen, where there'll be real snow and you can sled and make snow angels and a snowman. You're going to have an awesome time."

"Hello?" I hear Mrs. X call out. Grayer runs to the front hall and I take a moment to fold the last little shirt and then follow him.

"How was your afternoon?" she asks brightly.

"Grayer was a very good boy—we tried on everything," I say, leaning against the doorway. "The pile on the bed is the stuff that fits."

"Oh, excellent! Thank you so much."

Grayer is bouncing up and down in front of Mrs. X and pulling on her mink. "Come see my show! Come in my room!"

"Grayer, what have we discussed? Have you washed your hands?" she asks, evading his grasp.

"No," he answers.

"Well, then, should you be touching Mommy's coat? Now, if you sit on the bench I have a surprise for you from Daddy." She rummages through her shopping bags as Grayer slumps onto the paisley cushion. She pulls out a bright blue sweatsuit.

"Remember how you're going to big boy's school next year? Well, Daddy just loves Collegiate." She flips the sweatshirt around to reveal the orange lettering. I step forward to help Grayer pull it over his head. She stands back while I roll the sleeves up into little doughnuts at his wrists.

"Oh, you are going to make your daddy so happy." Grayer, delighted, whips out his jazz hands and starts to pose as he had done in the bedroom. "Honey, don't fling your arms about." She looks down at him in consternation. "It's weird."

Grayer looks to me for an explanation.

Mrs. X follows his gaze. "Grayer, it's time to say good-bye to Nanny."

"I don't want to." He stands in front of the door and crosses his arms.

I kneel down. "It's only for a few weeks, G."

"Noooooo! Don't go. You said we could play Candy Land. Nanny, you promised." The tears start to roll down his cheeks.

"Hey, you want your present now?" I ask. I go in the closet, take a deep breath, put on a big smile, and pull out the shopping bag I brought with me.

"This is for you, Merry Christmas!" I say, handing Mrs. X the Bergdorf's box.

"You shouldn't have," she says, setting it down on the table. "Oh, yes, we have something for you, too."

I look surprised. "Oh, no."

"Grayer, go get Nanny's present." He runs off. I pull the other box out of the bag. "And this is for Grayer."

"Nanny, here's your present, Nanny. Merry Christmas, Nanny!" He comes running in holding a Saks box and thrusts it at me.

"Oh, thank you!"

"Where's mine?! Where's mine?!" He jumps up and down.

"Your mom has it and you can open it after I leave." I quickly pull on my coat as Mrs. X is already holding the elevator.

"Merry Christmas," she says as I get in.

"Bye, Nanny!" he says, waving wildly, like a marionette.

"Bye, Grayer, Merry Christmas!"

I can't even wait till I get outside. I'm imagining Paris and handbags and many trips to Cambridge. First I open the gift tag. *"Dear Nanny, I don't know what we would do without you! Love, the Xes."* I rip the wrapping paper, pull the box apart, and start grabbing fistfuls of tissue.

There's no envelope. Oh, my God, *there's no envelope!* I shake the box upside down. Tons of tissue comes cluttering out and then something black and furry falls to the elevator floor with a thud. I drop to my knees, like a dog over a bone. I reach down, pushing the mess I've made aside to uncover my treasure and . . . and . . . and . . . it's earmuffs. Only earmuffs.

Just earmuffs.

Earmuffs!

EARMUFFS!!!!!!

Mammy felt that she owned the O'Haras, body and soul, that
their secrets were her secrets; and even a hint of mystery was
enough to set her upon the trail so recklessly as a bloodhound.
                                          —*GONE WITH THE WIND*

CHAPTER FIVE

Downtime

"Grandma's been looking all over for you so we can cut the cake," I
say, stepping into my grandmother's dressing room, where my father
has found respite from the joint New Year's Eve/Fiftieth Birthday
Party she insisted on throwing for the "one son God blessed her
with."

"Quick, close the door! I'm not ready yet—too many of those
people out there." Despite the many mingling artists and writers, the
majority of attendees this evening are donning tuxedos, which is the
one thing, as my father will emphatically inform you, he does not
wear. For anyone. Ever. "Who are we, the goddamn Kennedys?" has
been his thoughtful retort whenever my grandmother attempted to
involve him in the planning of this black-tie affair. I, on the other
hand, never have to be asked twice to step into a gown and am all
too eager for the rare occasions on which I can hang up my sweatpants and head out like a lady.

"Not to be too much of an enabler, but I come bearing gifts," I
say, handing him a glass of champagne. He smiles and takes a long
gulp, placing the glass down on top of her mirrored dressing table
beside his propped-up feet. He drops the *Times* crossword he's been
working on, motioning for me to sit. I plop onto the plush cream car-

pet in a pile of black chiffon and take a sip out of my own flute, while muffled laughter and big band music wafts in.

"Dad, you really should come out—it's not so bad. That writer guy is here, the one from China. And he's not even wearing a tie—you could hang out with him."

He takes off his glasses. "I'd rather spend time with my daughter. How's it going, pixie? Feeling better?"

A fresh wave of rage washes over me, breaking the celebratory mood I've enjoyed for most of the evening. "Ugh, that woman!" I slump forward. "I worked, like, eighty hours a week for the past month and for what? I'll tell you for what. *Earmuffs!*" I sigh exasperatedly, looking out through my hair to where the row of black kitten heels along the wall transitions into a colorful array of Chinese slippers.

"Ah, yes. It's been a whole fifteen minutes since we had this conversation."

"What conversation?" my mother asks as she slips in the door with a plate of hors d'oeuvres in one hand and an open bottle of champagne in the other.

"I'll give you a clue," he says, wryly, while holding up his glass for a refill. "You wear them instead of a hat."

"God! Are we back on this again? Come on, Nan, it's New Year's Eve! Why don't you take a night off?" She falls back on the chaise, tucking her stocking feet up under her, and hands him the plate.

I sit up and reach for the bottle. "Mom, I *can't*! I can't let it go! She might as well have just spit in my face and put a bow on my nose. Everyone knows you get a hefty Christmas bonus; it's just how it's done. Why else would I have put in so much extra time? The bonus is for the extra, it's the recognition! Every stupid person that works for them got money *and* a handbag! And I got—"

"Earmuffs," they chime in as I pour myself another glass.

"You know what my problem is? I go out of my way to make it seem natural that I'm raising her son while she's at the manicurist.

All the little stories I tell and the 'Sure, I'd be happy tos' make her feel like I live there. And then she forgets that I'm doing a job—she's totally convinced herself she's letting me come over for a play date!" I grab a bit of caviar from Dad's plate. "What do you think, Mom?"

"I think you've got to confront this woman and lay down the law or *let it go* already. Honestly, you should hear yourself, you've been talking about this for days. You're wasting a perfectly good party on her, and somebody in this family, other than your grandmother, should take advantage of the band out there and dance." She looks pointedly at my dad as he pops the last crab puff in his mouth.

"I want to! I want to lay down the law, but I don't even know where to begin."

"What's to begin? Just tell her that this is not working for you and if she wants you to continue as Grayer's nanny then a few things are going to change."

"Right," I say with a snort. "When she asks me how my vacation was I just launch into a diatribe? She would slap me."

"Well, then you're really in business," Dad pipes in. "Because you can sue for assault and none of us will ever have to work again."

My mother, now fully involved, plows on. "Then you just smile warmly, put your arm around her and say, 'Gee, you make it hard to work for you.' Let her know in a friendly way that this is not okay behavior."

"Mooommmm! You have no idea who I'm working for. There is no putting your arm around this woman. She's the Ice Queen."

"All right. That's it. Throw her the mink," Mom commands. "It's Rehearsal Time!" These rehearsals are the cornerstone of my upbringing and have helped me to practice everything from college interviews to breaking up with my sixth-grade boyfriend. Dad tosses me the stole that's been hanging next to him and reaches over to pour us another round.

"Okay, you're Mrs. X, I'm you. Hit it."

I clear my throat. "Welcome back, Nanny. Would you mind taking my dirty underwear with you to Grayer's swimming class and scrubbing it while you're in the pool? Thanks so much, the chlorine just works wonders!" I pull the mink up around my shoulders and affect a fake smile.

My mother's voice is calm and rational. "I want to help you. I want to help Grayer. But I need some help from you, so that I can keep doing my job to the best of my abilities. And this means that we need to try together to make sure that I am working the hours upon which we both agreed."

"Oh, you *work* here? I thought we had adopted you!" I raise my pinky to my mouth in mock alarm.

"Well, while it would be an honor to be related to you, I am here to do a job, and if I'm going to be able to keep doing it then I know you'll be more conscious of respecting my boundaries from now on." Dad claps loudly. I fall back on the floor.

"That'll never work," I groan.

"Nan, this woman's not God! She's just a person. You need a mantra. You need to go in there like Lao-tzu . . . Say no to say yes. Say it with me!"

"I say no to say yes. I say no to say yes," I murmur with her as I stare up at the floral wallpaper on the ceiling.

Just as we hit a fever pitch, the door flies open and music floods the room. I roll my head to see my grandmother, cheeks flushed to match her layers of red satin, leaning against the door frame.

"Darlings! Another masterpiece of a party and my son's hiding in the closet at his fiftieth, just like he did at his fifth. Come, dance with me." In a cloud of perfume, she sashays over to my father and kisses him on the cheek. "Come on, birthday boy, you can leave your tie and cummerbund here, but at least dance a mambo with your mother before the clock strikes twelve!"

He rolls his eyes at the rest of us, but the champagne has worn him down. He pulls off his tie and stands up.

"And you, lady." She looks down on me sprawled at her feet. "Bring the mink and let's boogie."

"Sorry to disappear, Gran. It's just this whole earmuffs thing."

"Good lord! Between your father and his tuxedo and you and your earmuffs, I don't want to discuss apparel with this family again until next Christmas! Up and at 'em, gorgeous, the dance floor awaits."

Mom helps me to my feet, whispering in my ear as we follow them back to the party. "See, no to say yes. Your dad's chanting it right now."

✧

Many dances and bottles of champagne later I float back to my apartment in a bubbly haze. George slides up to my heels as soon as I unlock the door and I carry him back to my corner of the room. "Happy New Year, George," I mumble as he purrs under my chin.

Charlene left this morning for Asia and I am giddy with the three weeks of little freedoms this affords me. As I kick off my heels I see the light on my answering machine flashing in a soft blur. Mrs. X.

"What do you think, George, shall we risk it?" I bend over to let him down before pressing the "new message" button.

"Hi, Nan? Um, this is a message for Nan. I think this is the right number . . ." H. H.'s slurred voice fills the apartment.

"Oh, my God!" I scream, turning to check my appearance in the mirror.

"Right. So um, yeah . . . I'm just calling to say 'Happy New Year.' Um, I'm in Africa. And—wait—what time is it there? Seven hours, that's ten . . . eleven . . . twelve. Right. So I'm with my family and we're about to head into the bush. And we've been having some beers with the guides. And it's the last outpost with a phone . . . But I just wanted to say that I bet you had a hard week. See! I know how you've been working hard and I just wanted you to know, um . . .

that I know . . . that you do . . . work hard, that is. Um, and that you have a happy New Year. Okay, so then—I hope this is your machine. Right. So that's all, just wanted you to know. Um . . . bye."

I stumble to my bed in utter euphoria. "Oh, my God," I mumble again in the darkness, before passing out with a grin plastered to my face.

⟡

Ring. Ring. Ring. Ring.

"Hi, you've reached Charlene and Nan. Please leave a message." Beep.

"Hi, Nanny, I hope you're in. I'm sure you're probably in. Well, Happy New Year." I crack one eye open. "It's Mrs. X. I hope you've had a good vacation. I'm calling because . . ." Jesus, it's *eight o'clock* in the morning! "Well, there's been a change of plans. Mr. X apparently needs to go back to Illinois for work. And I, well, Grayer's— we're *all* very disappointed. So, anyway, we won't be going to Aspen and I wanted to see what you're up to for the rest of the month." On New Year's Day! I stick my hand outside the covers and start flailing for the phone. I unplug the receiver and throw it on the floor.

There.

I pass out again.

Ring. Ring. Ring. Ring.

"Hi, you've reached Charlene and Nan. Please leave a message." Beep.

"Hi, Nanny, it's Mrs. X. I left you a message earlier." I crack one eye open. "I don't know if I mentioned, but if you could let me know today . . ." Jesus, it's *nine-thirty* in the morning! On New Year's Day! I stick my hand outside the covers and start flailing for the phone and this time actually manage to pull the right plug out.

Ahh, peace.

"Hi, you've reached Charlene and Nan. Please leave a message."
Beep.

"Hi, Nanny, it's Mrs. X," Jesus! It's ten o'clock in the morning!
What is wrong with you people? This time I can hear Grayer crying
in the background. Not my problem, not my problem, earmuffs. I
stick my hand outside the covers and start flailing for the answering
machine. I find the volume. "Because you didn't say if you had any plans
and I just thought—" Ahh, silence.

Ring. Ring. Ring. Ring.
WHAT THE FUCK?
Oh, my God, it's my cell phone. It's my goddamn cell phone.
Ring. Ring. Ring. Ring.
Aaaahhhhh! I get out of bed, but I can't find the source of the
goddamn ringing. Such a headache.
Ring. Ring. Ring. Ring.
It's under the bed. It's under the bed! I start trying to crawl
under the bed, still in my evening dress, to where George made a
soccer goal with the cell. I extend my arm, grab it, still ringing, and
throw it in the laundry hamper, dumping everything on the floor in
on top of it.
Ahah!! Sleep.
Ring. Ring. Ring. Ring.
I get out of bed, march over to the hamper, retrieve the phone,
go in the kitchen, open the freezer door, throw in the phone, and go
back to sleep.

I awake five hours later to a very patient George waiting at the end of
my bed for breakfast. He tilts his head and meows. "Been on a ben-
der?" he seems to ask. I pad to the kitchen in my very rumpled black
chiffon to feed George and make some coffee. I open the freezer and
see the green glow of the phone from behind the ice trays.

"Number of calls received: 12," the face reads. Oh, Lord. I make some coffee and go sit on my bed to listen to the messages on my machine.

"Hi, again. Hope I'm not repeating myself. So, Mr. X has decided he won't be able to make it to Aspen and I really don't want to be out there by myself. The groom and the groundsman live all the way down the road and, well, I'd feel very isolated. So I'll be in the city. Anyway, I'd appreciate it if you could come in a few days a week. How's Monday for you? Let me know. The number here again is—"

I don't even think or chant. I just reassemble the phone and dial the number for the Lyford Cay Inn.

"Hello?"

"Mrs. X? Hi, it's Nanny. How are you?"

"Oh God, the weather here is just awful. Mr. X has barely been able to play a round of golf and now he'll be missing his skiing, as well. Grayer's been trapped inside the whole time, and they promised us someone full-time, like last year, but there's a shortage or something. I don't know what I'm going to do." I can hear *Pocahontas* in the background. "So, did you get my message?"

"Yes." I brace my pounding temples between my thumb and pinky finger.

"You know, I think there's something wrong with your phone. You really should have it looked at. I was trying to call you all morning. Anyway, Mr. X is leaving today, but I'm staying the weekend and won't be back until Monday. Our plane gets in at eleven, so could you meet us at the apartment at noon?"

"Well, actually"—earmuffs—"I already made plans since I wasn't supposed to start back until the last Monday of the month."

"Oh. Couldn't you at least give me a week or two?"

"Well, the thing is—"

"Can you hold on a moment?" It sounds like she's put her hand over the phone. "We don't have another video." Mr. X says something I can't quite make out. "Well, play it for him again," she hisses.

"Um, Mrs. X?"

"Yes?"

I know we'll be having this conversation for the next thirty-six hours unless I reach for a small white one. "I took your suggestion about Paris. So I can't start back until, let's see, two weeks from Monday. Until the eighteenth." No to say yes. "Also, we didn't really have time before you left to discuss how much more an hour I'd be getting this year."

"Uh-huh?"

"Well, typically I go up two dollars every January. I hope that's not a problem."

"Well . . . No, no, of course. I'll talk to Mr. X. Also, I'd appreciate it if you could go by the apartment tomorrow—you know, while you're out and about—and refill the humidifiers."

"Um, I'm actually going to be on the West Side, so—"

"Great! See you in two weeks. But please do let me know if you can start any sooner."

◇ ◇ ◇

James holds the door open as I pass. "Happy New Year, Nanny. What're you doin' back so soon?" He seems surprised to see me.

"Mrs. X needs her humidifiers filled," I say.

"Oh, does she now?" He gives a wicked grin.

The first thing I notice when I open the Xes' front door is that the heat is actually on. I step slowly into the silence, feeling a bit like a thief. I am just slipping my arms out of my coat when Ella Fitzgerald's "Miss Otis Regrets" comes blaring out of the stereo system.

I freeze. "Hello?" I call. I clutch my backpack and follow the wall into the kitchen, hoping to grab a knife. I've heard about doormen in buildings like this using the apartments when the tenants are away. I swing open the kitchen door.

There's an open bottle of Dom Pérignon on the counter, pots are bubbling on the stove. What kind of sick person steals into an apartment to cook?

"It's not ready yet. Ce n'est pas fini," a man says in a thick French accent as he emerges from the maid's bathroom drying his hands on his checked trousers and adjusting his white chef's coat.

"Who are you?" I ask over the music, taking a step backward toward the door. He looks up.

"*Qui* est *vous?*" he asks, putting his hands on his hips.

"Um, I work here. *Who* are *you?*"

"Je m'appelle Pierre. Your mistress hired me to faire le dîner." He returns to chopping fennel. The kitchen is a phantasm of productivity and delicious aromas. It's never looked so happy.

"Why you stand there like a fish? Go." He waves his knife at me.

I leave the kitchen to go find Mrs. X.

I cannot believe she's back. Of course, why bother to call Nanny? Ooh no, it's not like I have anything better to do than keep her oil paintings moist. Oh, oh, I am *definitely* not working tonight if that's her game. It's probably just one, big ruse to get me to work. She's probably got Grayer tied up in a net over the humidifier and is planning to drop him on my head the minute I pour the water in.

"*SHE RAN TO THE MAN WHO HAD LED HER SO FAR ASTRAY,*" the stereo blares, following me from room to room.

Well, fine. I'll just let her know I came by like I said I would and then I'm out of here.

"Hello?" I practically leap right out of my skin. There she is, strutting out of the bedroom, a silk kimono tied carelessly at her waist, her emerald earrings sparkling in the hall light. My heart jumps to my throat.

It's Ms. Chicago.

"Hi," she says, as friendly as she was in the conference room three weeks ago. She glides past me, out toward the dining room.

"Hi," I say, scampering behind her, untying my scarf. I round the corner just as she throws open the French doors onto the dining room, revealing a table set for a romantic dinner for two. A huge bouquet of peonies, the purply black of squid ink, sits among a ring of glowing votives. She leans across the gleaming mahogany to straighten the silverware.

"I'm just here for the humidifiers!" I call out over the stereo.

"Wait," she says, going over to the hidden control panel in the bookcase and expertly adjusting the volume, tone, and bass. "There." She turns to me, smiling placidly. "What were you saying?"

"The humidifiers? Are, um, dry? They run out of . . . water? And the pictures, well, they can really, uh, suffer? If they're dry? I was just supposed to water them. Only once. Just now, today, 'cause that should last them till . . . Okay! So, I'll just do that, then."

"Well, thank you, Nanny. I'm sure Mr. X appreciates that, and I do, too." She retrieves her errant glass of champagne from the sideboard. I kneel and unplug the humidifier from the floor.

"Okay, then," I grunt, heaving the machine into my arms and letting myself out into the kitchen.

I refill all ten water tanks, schlepping them back and forth to the laundry room, while Ella keeps right on trucking from "It Was Just One of Those Things," through "Why Can't You Behave?" and "I'm Always True to You, Darlin', in My Fashion." My mind is reeling. This is not her house. This is not her family. And that most definitely was not her bedroom that she came out of.

"Are you done yet?" she asks as I plug in the last one. "Because I was wondering if you could run to the shop for me." She follows me to the door as I grab my coat. "Pierre forgot to get heavy cream. Thanks." She hands me a twenty as I open the door.

I look down at the money and then at Grayer's little frog umbrella in the stand, the one that has two big frog eyes that pop up when he opens it. I hold the money out to her. "I can't—I have, um, an appointment, a doctor thing." I catch a glimpse of myself in the gilt mirror. "Actually . . . I just can't."

Her smile strains. "Keep it, then," she says evenly. The elevator door opens, while she attempts to look casual leaning against the door frame.

I put the bill down on the hall table.

Her eyes flash. "Look, Nanny, is it? You run home and tell your boss that you found me here and all you'll be doing is saving me the trouble of leaving behind a pair of panties." She steps back into the apartment, letting the door slam shut behind her.

✧ ✧ ✧

"Like, literally panties?" Sarah asks me the next day as she tries on yet another shade of pink lipstick at the Stila counter.

"I don't know! Do I have to look for them? I feel like I have to look for them."

"How much are these people paying you? I mean, do you have a line? Is there a line they could cross?" Sarah is furiously puckering. "Too pink?"

"Baboon butt," I say.

"Try one of the plummy shades," the makeup artist behind the counter suggests. Sarah reaches for a tissue and starts over.

"Mrs. X is coming back tomorrow. I feel like there's *something* I'm supposed to be doing," I say, leaning against the counter in exasperation.

"Um, quitting?"

"No, out here in the real world, where I pay rent."

"TOOOOOTS!!!!!" Sarah and I freeze and look across the atrium to where two piles of shopping bags are calling Sarah's high-school nickname, which rhymes with "boots." The bags make their way around the balcony toward us, parting to reveal Alexandra and Langly, two of our classmates from Chapin.

Sarah and I exchange glances. In high school they lived in

Birkenstocks and followed the Dead. Now they stand before us, Alexandra at nearly six feet and Langly at barely five, in shearling coats, cashmere turtlenecks, and a shitload of Cartier.

"TOOTS!" they cry again as Alexandra envelops Sarah in a big hug, nearly clonking her on the head with one of her shopping bags.

"Toots, what's up?" Alexandra asks. "So, do you have a man?"

Sarah's eyelids lift. "No. Well, I mean there was someone, but . . ." She's starting to sweat, foundation beading on her brow.

"I have a faaabulous man—he's Greek. He's soo gorgeous. We're going to the Riviera next week," Alexandra coos. "So, what are you up to?" she asks me.

"Oh, same old, same old. Still working with kids."

"Huh," Langly says quietly. "What're you gonna do next year?"

"Well, I'm hoping to work with an after-school program." Their eyes narrow, as if I had just switched languages unexpectedly. "Focusing on using creative arts? As a tool for self-expression? And, um, building community?" I am getting completely blank looks. "Kathie Lee's really involved?" I offer as a last-ditch effort to . . . what?

"Right. What about you?" Langly almost whispers to Sarah.

"I'm going to work at *Allure*."

"Oh, my God!!" they squeal.

"Well," Sarah continues, "I'm only going to be answering the phones, but—"

"No, that's awesome. I. Love. *Allure*," Alexandra says.

"What are you guys doing next year?" I ask.

"Following my man," Alexandra says.

"Ganja," Langly says softly.

"Well, we better run—we're meeting my mom at Côte Basque at one. Oh, Toots!" Sarah is once again molested by Alexandra and they head off to poke at their seafood salads.

"You're too funny," I say to Sarah. "*Allure?*"

"Fuck 'em. Come on, let's go eat somewhere fabulous."

We decide to treat ourselves to a chic lunch of red wine and robiola cheese pizzas at Fred's.

"I mean, would you actually leave your *underwear* in someone's *house?*"

"Nan," Sarah says, shutting me up. "I just don't understand why you care. Mrs. X works you like a mule *and* gave you dead-animal headgear for a bonus! What is your loyalty?"

"Sarah, regardless of what kind of a whackjob employer she might be, she's still Grayer's mom and this woman is having sex with her husband in her bed. And in Grayer's home. It makes me heart-sick. Nobody deserves that. And that freak! She wants to get caught! What's up with that?"

"Well, if my married boyfriend was dawdling about leaving his wife I guess I might want him to get caught, too."

"So, if I tell, Ms. Chicago wins and Mrs. X will be devastated. If I don't tell it's humiliating for Mrs. X—"

"Nan, this is not even within a million miles of your responsibility. You don't have to be the one to tell her. Trust me—it's not in your job description."

"But if I don't and the panties are floating around and she finds out that way . . . Ugh! How awful! Oh, my God, what if Grayer finds them? She's so evil I bet she'd put them somewhere he'd find them."

"Nan, get a grip. How would he even know they were hers?"

"Because they're probably black and lacy and thonged and he might not get it now, but one day he'll be in therapy and it'll just *kiiilll* him. Get your coat."

◇

Sarah greets Josh in the front hall with a glass of wine. "Welcome to Hunt the Panties!, where we play for fabulous prizes, including ear-muffs and a trip to the broom closet. Who's our first contestant?"

"Ooh, me, me!" Josh says as he takes off his jacket. I am on my hands and knees in the front hall closet, looking through every coat pocket and boot. Nothing. "Jesus, Nan, this place is amazing—it's like the fucking Metropolitan Museum."

"Yup, and about as cozy," Sarah says, as I run frantically into the living room.

"We don't have time to shoot the breeze!" I call over my shoulder. "Pick a room!"

"So, do we get points for any undergarments, or must they have a scarlet A on them?" Josh asks.

"Extra points for crotchless and edible." Sarah explains the rules for the game I am not finding amusing.

"All right!" I say. "Listen up! We are going to be methodical. We are going to start in the rooms that get the most use, where the panties would be uncovered the soonest. Joshua, you take the master bedroom, Mrs. X's dressing room, and her office. Sarah Anne!"

"Reporting for duty, sir!"

"Kitchen, library, maid's rooms. I'll take the living room, the dining room, the study, and the laundry room. Okay?"

"What about Grayer's room?" Josh asks me.

"Right. I'll start there."

I turn on each light as I pass, even the rarely used overheads, illuminating the darkest corners of the Xes' home.

⟡

"Nan, you can't say we didn't try," Josh says, passing me a cigarette as we sit by the recycling bins in the back stairwell. "She was probably bluffing, hoping you'd tell Mrs. X so she can start redecorating."

Sarah lights another cigarette. "Besides, whoever finds them in this apartment deserves to find them—they're so well hidden. Are you sure this woman works with Mr. X and not the CIA?" She passes me back the lighter.

Josh is still holding the porcelain Pekingese dog he picked up on his search. "Tell me again."

"I don't know, two, maybe three thousand dollars," Sarah says.

"Unbelievable! Why? Why? What am I missing?" He looks down at the dog in complete disbelief. "Wait, I'm gonna go get something else."

"You better put that back *exactly* where you found it," I say, too tired to chase after him to be sure he does. "I'm sorry I made you waste your night looking for panties," I say, stubbing out the cigarette on the metal railing.

"Hey," she says, putting her arm around my shoulder. "You'll be fine. The Xes have jewelry that has jewelry—they'll be fine."

"What about Grayer?"

"Well, he has you. And you've got H. H."

"Okay, I don't got nuthin'. I have an answering-machine tape in my jewelry box and a plastic spoon I carry around in my purse as a souvenir and that might be as far as it goes."

"Yeah, yeah, sure. Can I mention the plastic spoon at the wedding?"

"Honey, if we make it that far you can *carry* the plastic spoon at the wedding. Come on, let's get Josh and wipe our fingerprints on our way out of here."

When I get home the answering machine is blinking.

"Hi, Nanny, it's Mrs. X. I don't know if you've left for Paris yet. I couldn't reach you on your cell phone again. We may have to get you a new one with better coverage. I'm calling because Mr. X gave me a week at the Golden Door for Christmas. Isn't that wonderful? Lyford Cay is so awful and I still haven't recovered from the holidays—I'm just exhausted, so I've decided to go next week. Mr. X will be around, but I was wondering if you'll be back, just so I can tell him you'll be available if he needs you. Just so we know it's covered. I'll be in my room this evening. Call me."

My first instinct is to call her and tell her never to leave her house again.

"Mrs. X? Hi, it's Nanny."

"Yes?"

I take a deep breath.

"So, will that work?" she asks.

"Of course," I say, relieved that she isn't asking about my housecall.

"Great. So, I'll see you Monday morning—a week from tomorrow. My flight's at nine, so if you could arrive by seven that would be great. Actually, we better say six forty-five, just to be on the safe side."

◇ ◇ ◇

I roll over for the eighth time in the last fifteen minutes. I'm so tired that my body feels weighted, but every time I'm about to drift off, Grayer's hacking cough echoes through the apartment. I reach over to pull the clock back toward me and the red numbers read 2:36 A.M. Jesus.

I hit the mattress with my hand and roll onto my back. Staring up at the Xes' guest-room ceiling, I try to add up the few hours of sleep I've managed to get in the past three nights and the total makes me even heavier. I'm bone tired from spending twenty-four/seven keeping Grayer entertained as his mood has blackened and fever risen.

When I arrived she greeted me at the elevator with a list in her hand, her bags already waiting in the limo downstairs. She just wanted to "mention" that Grayer had a "tiny bit of an earache" and that his medicine was by the sink, along with his pediatrician's number—"just in case." And the kicker: "We really prefer that Grayer not sit in front of the television. You two have fun!"

I knew "fun" was hardly going to be the word for it as soon as I found him lying on the floor next to his train set, listlessly rolling a caboose on his arm.

"Any idea when Mr. X will be home tonight?" I had asked Connie, dusting nearby.

"Hope you brought your pajamas," she replied, wagging her head in disgust. I've come to look forward to Connie's arrival over the past few days; it's a relief to have another person in the apartment, even if she is only a whir of dusting and vacuuming. As the temperature has held steady at seven degrees Fahrenheit, we've been under house arrest since my arrival. This would have been bearable, ideal even, if H. H. hadn't had to go right back up to school for reading period. He said I could take Grayer upstairs to pet Max, but I don't think either one of them is up to it. Grayer's "tiny" earache may have improved, but his cough has only worsened.

And, needless to say, his father has been completely MIA—he simply failed to return home my first night. Numerous phone calls to Justine have unearthed only the voice mail of a suite at the Four Seasons in Chicago. Meanwhile the reception desk at the spa is screening Mrs. X's calls as if she were Sharon Stone. I took Grayer back to the doctor this afternoon, but his only advice was for Grayer to finish the pink amoxicillin and wait it out.

Another round of raspy coughs—he's even more congested now than he sounded at dinnertime. It's so dark and so late and this place is just so big that I'm starting to feel as if no one will ever come back to get us.

I get up, draping the cashmere throw around my shoulders like a cape, and shuffle over to the window. Pulling the heavy chintz drapes to the side, I let the streetlight from Park Avenue spill into the room and rest my forehead against the cold windowpane. A cab pulls up to the building across the street and a boy and girl stumble out. She's in tall boots and a skimpy jacket, leaning against him as they swerve past the doorman and into the building. She must be freezing. My forehead chills quickly from the glass and I pull back, touching it with my hand. The curtain falls closed, taking the light with it.

"Naaanny?" Grayer's small, scratchy voice calls out.

"Yes, Grover, I'm coming." My voice echoes in the big room. I shuffle through the darkness of the apartment, lit up in weird shadows from passing cars outside. The warm glow of his Grover night-light greets me along with the whir of his Supersonic 2000 air filter. The minute I step through his doorway my stomach drops—he is not okay. His breathing is labored and his eyes are watering. I sit on the corner of the bed. "Hey, sweetheart, I'm here." I put my hand on his forehead. It's boiling. The moment my fingers touch him he starts to whimper.

"It's okay, Grover, you're just real sick and I know it's yucky." But I don't know any more. His wheezing alarms me. "I'm going to pick you up now, Grover." I reach my arms under him, the cashmere wrap dropping to the floor. He starts to cry fully, the movement agitating him as I pull him up to me. I go into automatic pilot, running through options. The pediatrician. The emergency room. Mom.

I carry him to the hall extension and lean against the wall for support as I dial. My mother answers on the second ring.

"Where are you? What's wrong?"

"Mom, I can't get into it, but I'm with Grayer and he's been sick with an ear infection and this cough and they've had him on antibiotics, but the cough keeps getting worse and I can't get a message through to Mrs. X because the receptionist says she's been in some sort of sensory-deprivation tank all day and he can't seem to breathe and I don't know if I should take him to the hospital because his fever won't go down and I haven't slept in two nights and—"

"Let me hear him cough."

"What?"

"Put the phone to his mouth so he can cough." Her voice is calm and steady. I hold the phone near Grayer's mouth and within a second he has erupted into a deep cough. I feel the vibrations of this effort where his chest is pressed to mine.

"Oh, God, Mom, I don't know what to—"

"Nanny, that's the croup. He has the croup. And you need to take a deep breath. You may not fall apart right now. Breathe with me, in—"

I focus on her voice, taking a deep breath in for Grayer and myself. "And out. Listen, he's okay. You are okay. He just has a lot of fluid in his chest. Where are you right now?"

"Seven twenty-one Park Avenue."

"No, where in the apartment?"

"In the hall."

"Is this a cordless phone?"

"No, she doesn't like the way they look." I can feel the panic start to well up again as he whimpers.

"Okay, I want you to go into his bathroom, turn on the shower so it's comfortably warm—not too hot, just warm, and then sit on the side of the bathtub with him in your lap. Keep the door closed so it gets nice and steamy. Stay in there until he stops wheezing. You'll see, the steam will help. His fever is trying to break and it will be down by morning. Everything is going to be just fine. Call back in an hour, okay? I'll be waiting."

I feel somewhat soothed knowing that there is something I can do for him. "Okay, Mom. I love you." I hang up and carry him back though the darkness to his bathroom.

"I'm going to flick the light on, Grayer. Close your eyes." He turns his sweaty face into my neck. The light is blinding after being up for so long in the dark and I have to blink a few times before I can focus in on the gleaming silver of the faucet. I grip his body as I lean over to turn on the shower and then sit down, balancing on the edge of the tub with him on my lap. When the water hits our legs he really begins to cry.

"I know, sweetie, I know. We are going to sit here until this wonderful steam makes your chest feel good. Do you want me to sing?" He just leans against me and cries and coughs as the steam fills the bright tile around us.

"I . . . want . . . my mommmmmm." He shudders with the effort, seemingly unaware that I am here. My pajama pants soak in the warm water. I drop my head against his, rocking slowly. Tears of exhaustion and worry drip down my face and into his hair.

"Oh, Grove, I know. I want my mom, too."

◇ ◇ ◇

The sun shines in through the shutters as we munch on cinnamon toast among Grover's stuffed animals.

"Say it again, Nanny. Say it—ciwomen toast."

I laugh and poke him gently in the tummy. His eyes are bright and clear and my relief at his 98.6 has made us both giddy. "No, G, cinnamon, come on—say it with me."

"Call it 'women toast.' You say it with *me*—" His hand pats my hair absentmindedly as the crumbs dribble around us.

"Women toast? You crazy kid, what's next? Men eggs?"

He giggles deeply at my joke. "Yeah! Men eggs! I'm so hungry, Nanny, I'm dying. Can I have some eggs—men eggs?"

I crawl over him, grabbing his plate as I stand.

"Hello! Hello, Mommy's home!" I freeze. Grayer looks up at me and, like an excited puppy, scrambles to get down from the bed. He runs past me and meets her as she comes to his door.

"Hello! What are those crumbs doing all over your face?" She spatulas him and turns to me. I see the room through her eyes. Pillows, blankets, and wet towels all lying on the floor where I finally crashed when Grayer fell asleep at six this morning.

"Grayer's been pretty sick. We were up late last night and—"

"Well, he looks just fine now, except for those crumbs. Grayer, go in the bathroom and wash your face so I can show you your present." He turns to me with wide eyes and skips to the bathroom. I'm amazed he can even set foot in there.

"Didn't he take his medicine?"

"Yes, well, he has two more days to go. But his cough got really bad. I tried to call you."

She bristles. "Well, Nanny, I think we've discussed where we prefer for Grayer to eat. You can go now, I've got it covered."

I focus on smiling. "Okay, I'll just go and get changed." I walk past her with the plate in my hand, hardly recognizing the apartment filled with sunlight. I stuff everything into my bag, pull on jeans and a sweater and leave the bed unmade as my one act of rebellion.

"Bye!" I call out, opening the door. I hear Grayer's naked feet hitting the marble as he runs out in his pajamas beneath a cowboy hat that is much too big.

"Bye, Nanny!" He throws his arms open for a hug and I hold him tight, amazed at the difference a few hours have made in his breathing.

"Mrs. X? He still has two more days of antibiotics so—"

She emerges at the other end of the hall. "Well, we have a big day planned—we've got to get a haircut and go to Barneys to pick up a present for Daddy. Come on, Grayer, let's get dressed. Good-bye, Nanny."

My shift is over—point taken. He follows her to his room and I stand alone in the hall for a moment, pick up my bag, and override the temptation to put the antibiotics by her cell phone.

"Bye, partner." I pull the door closed quietly behind me.

The old nurse went upstairs exulting with knees toiling, and pat-
ter of slapping feet, to tell the mistress of her lord's return.

—ODYSSEY

CHAPTER SIX

Love, Park Avenue Style

I press down the backspace button and watch as my fifth attempt at
a topic sentence deletes itself letter by letter. Jean Piaget . . . what to
say, what to say?

I slouch back, rolling my neck on the top of the chair, and stare
out at the gray clouds drifting slowly above the roofs of the brownstones across the street. George bats at my dangling hand. "Piaget," I
say out loud, waiting for inspiration to hit as I dart my hand at him
playfully. The phone rings and I let the machine pick it up. Either
it'll be Mrs. X calling to check if I have any lifeblood she hasn't
sucked yet or my mother calling to weigh in on the situation.

"Hi, this is Charlene and Nan. Leave a message."

"Hey, working girl. I just want—" My favorite voice fills the
room and I reach across my desk to grab the phone.

"Hi, yourself."

"Hey! What are you doing home at one forty-three on a Tuesday?"

"What are you doing, calling me all the way from Haa-vaad, at
one forty-three on a Tuesday?" I push back my chair and trace a wide
circle on the hardwood floor with my socks.

"I asked you first."

"Well, turns out Jean Georges lost the Xes' reservations for

Valentine's Day so she immediately sent me home with a typed-up list of four-star restaurants to harass." I look over at my backpack, where the document remains folded away.

"Why didn't she just call them herself?"

"I have long since ceased to ask why."

"So, where did you make them?"

"Nowhere! Valentine's Day is tomorrow. I suppose she's in denial that these places only take reservations thirty days in advance and that she already made me spend January fourteenth—a Sunday, thank you very much—calling them. And even then all I could get her was a ten P.M. and I had to swear to the reservationist on my firstborn that I'd have them out by eleven. Yup, no go. They'll be lucky to get a booth at Burger King." I picture Mr. X absentmindedly dunking his fries in ketchup as he reads the business section.

"So have you found the panties?"

"No. You're going to be really sad when we no longer need to talk about panties, aren't you?" He laughs.

"Actually," I continue, "yesterday we had a false alarm in which yours truly dove headfirst onto Snoopy's magician cape in a blind panic."

"They may not be black, you know. You should really try to think outside the box—they could be pastel or tiger print or see-through—"

"See! You enjoy this conversation way too much," I admonish.

"So then what are you doing if you're not making reservations or hunting panties?"

"Trying to write a paper on Jean Piaget."

"Ah, yes, Jean."

"What, you haven't heard of him? And they call that pile of bricks an Ivy League."

"Not *an* Ivy League, dahling, *the* Ivy League—" he says, affecting a Thurston Howell III lockjaw.

"Right. Well, he's the grandfather of child psychology, so to speak. I'm writing on his theory of egocentrism—how children see the physical world exclusively from their own, limited perspective."

"Sounds like your boss."

"Yes, and interestingly, she can't wash her hair by herself, either. There's probably some sort of study here. Ugh! I'm just in total procrastination mode. Being given the luxury of a whole free afternoon makes me feel like I have time to dawdle. Anyway, enough about me, to what do I owe the pleasure of this phone call?"

The phone beeps loudly, interrupting him.

"—about this internship. This guy came to speak today and it was pretty amazing. He—"

BEEP.

"—war crimes in Croatia. So there's a tribunal at The Hague to prosecute war criminals—"

BEEP. No machine to protect me now.

"I'm sorry! Hold on one sec?" I press the flash button and hold my breath.

"Nanny! I'm so glad I caught you." Mrs. X's voice brings me back from my midday rendezvous. "I'm thinking Petrossian because it's really mostly caviar and I think most people expect a full meal for this occasion. But that's fine for us! Have you already called them? You should call them next. Can you? Call them right now?"

"Sure. I'm holding with Le Cirque on the other line so—"

"Oh! Fabulous! Okay. Well, see if they even have something by the kitchen, we'll take that."

"Great. I'll let you know."

"Wait! Nanny! Well, don't say the kitchen thing right away, see if they have something better and then, you know, if there isn't anything better, then ask about the kitchen."

"Oh, okay, sure, I'll keep at it. I'll let you know as soon as I find something."

"All right. You know you can reach me on my cell, too." I sense she is getting ready, once again, to give me her number.

"Okay, great. I've got your numbers right here. Bye." I click back over. "Sorry, where were we? Something about criminals?" I move to my bed and lift George onto my stomach.

"Yeah, so I think I'm going to apply for this internship at The Hague for the summer. After this class on the conflict in Croatia it would be amazing to get closer to it, you know? To be able to do something. I mean, it's totally competitive, but I think I might give it a shot." Swoon.

"I'm swooning."

"Good." There is a warm silence between us. "Anyway, as soon as I got out of class, I had to call and tell you about it."

"Now that's the part I like."

"It sucks that you have to work Valentine's. I really want to hang out with you."

"Yeah, well, I'm not the one going to Cancún for spring break."

"Come on, how was I supposed to know I was going to meet you?"

"Don't even try to use not being psychic as a defense."

Despite the many phone calls, talking is about as far as we've gotten since the museum. First he had exams, then I had Grayer's flu—not exactly sexy. Two weekends ago he came down for the night, but Charlene's flight was canceled and I ended up making a romantic dinner for four. I thought of going up there, but he has three roommates and I *refuse* to have my first night with him be (*a*) punctuated by the sounds of Marilyn Manson blaring through the wall at three A.M. and (*b*) followed by a morning of watching them make coffee, using their underwear as a filter. Killing me.

BEEP.

"Shit. Sorry! Hold on one more time." I click over. "Hello??" I say, bracing myself.

"So? Is it by the kitchen?" She is slightly breathless.

"What? No, um, I'm still on hold with them."

"Petrossian?"

"No, Le Cirque. I'll call you just as soon as I get through."

"All right. But remember, don't start with the kitchen question. And I was thinking that you should try '21', it's unromantic. Maybe they'll still have something. So '21' next, okay? Well, Petrossian would be next and then '21'. Yes, '21' is my third choice."

"Great! I should get back to Le Cirque."

"Yes, yes. Call me the minute you know."

"Bye!" Deep breath. Click over. "Yes, hanging out. That would work for me."

"Good to know. Hey, I've got to run to my next class. Listen, I'll definitely be home in April for a few days, we'll figure something out. Good luck with Jean."

"Hey!" I catch him before he hangs up. "I think The Hague is really great."

"Well, I think you're really great. I'll call you later. Bye."

"Bye!" I hang up and George stretches from where he has been curled up by my head and jumps off the bed onto the floor.

The phone rings again. I stare at the machine.

". . . Charlene and Nan. Please leave a message."

"This is your mother. You may not recognize me as it is not two in the morning and you do not have a suffocating child on your lap, but I assure you that I am one and the same. Listen, bud, today, tomorrow, next week, we *will* have this conversation. In the meantime I leave you with two little words of wisdom regarding this job of yours. 'Not okay.' I love you. Over and out." Right, this job of mine. What to do about this reservation thing?

"Grandma?"

"Darling!"

"I need to get a table for two for Valentine's dinner anywhere that they don't have paper place mats. What can you do for me?"

"Going right for the jackpot today, are we? Can't we start with something smaller, like an afternoon wearing the crown jewels?"

"I know, it's for Grayer's mom. It's a long story, but she's going to hunt me until I get her a seat somewhere."

"That earmuffs woman? She doesn't deserve the crumbs off your plate."

"I know, but can you please just wave your magic wand for me?"

"Hmm, call Maurice at Lutèce and tell him I'll send him the recipe for the cheesecake next week."

"You rock, Grandma."

"No, darling, I swing. Love you."

"Love you, too." One more call and it's back to les petites ego-centrics.

✧ ✧ ✧

The city is on Valentine's overdrive as I walk over to Elizabeth Arden to meet my grandmother. Since the last Christmas decoration came down in January every store has had a Valentine's theme in the window; even the hardware store has a red toilet-seat cover on display. In Februaries past I would wait with exasperation on line behind men and women buying oysters/champagne/condoms, when I only wanted to pay for my grapefruit/beer/Kleenex and get on with my life. This year, I've got nothing but patience.

This is the very first Valentine's Day on which I have not been single. However, in observance of the traditional survival agenda for the one-day-when-being-single-is-just-not-okay, Sarah and I mailed each other Tiger Beat pinups and I am accompanying Grandma to our annual pampering.

"Darling, Saint Valentine's Rule Number One," she imparts as we sip our lemon water and admire our lacquered toes. "It's more important to show *yourself* a little love than to have a man who gives you something in the wrong size and color."

"Thanks for the pedicure, Gram."

"Anytime, darling. I'm going to go back upstairs for my seaweed wrap. Let's just hope they don't forget me like last time. Really, they should put a little buzzer in your hand. Imagine being found, covered in seaweed and wrapped in a tarp by some poor janitor. Rule Number Two: Never take the last appointment of the day."

I thank her profusely, bundle up, bid her farewell, and go to pick up my hot date from nursery school. He comes running out at noon, holding a large, crooked paper heart that leaves a trail of glitter behind him.

"Whatcha got there, buddy?"

"It's a Valentine. I made it. You can hold it." I take the heart and pass him the juice box I've been keeping warm in my pocket as he settles in the stroller.

I look down at the heart, assuming it's for Mrs. X.

"Mrs. Butters spelled for me. I told her what to say and she spelled for me. Read it, Nanny, read it."

I almost can't speak. "I LOVE NANNY FROM GRAYER ADDISON X."

"Yup. That's what I said."

"It's beautiful, Grover. Thank you," I say, starting to get teary behind the stroller.

"You can hold it," he offers as he grips the juice box.

"You know what? I'm going to put it safely in the stroller pocket so it doesn't get hurt. We've got a special afternoon ahead of us."

Despite the fact that it's one of the coldest days of the year, I'm under strict instruction not to bring him home until after French class. So I've made an executive decision to ignore all the usual guidelines and take him to California Pizza Kitchen for lunch and then down Third Avenue to the new Muppet movie. I was worried he might be scared of the dark, but he sings and claps all the way through.

"That was so funny, Nanny. So funny," he says, as I buckle him back into his stroller and we sing the theme song all the way to French class.

After I drop him off with Mme. Maxime to faire les Valentines I run across Madison to Barneys to pick up a little something for H. H.

"Can I help you?" the notoriously bitchy blonde behind the

Kiehl's counter half asks, half spits. She has never been forgiven for once accusing Sarah of shoplifting the toner she was trying to return.

"No, thanks, just browsing." I set my sights on another salesperson, a tall Eurasian man in an expensive-looking black shirt. "Hi, I'm looking for a Valentine's present for my boyfriend." I love saying it. Boyfriend, boyfriend, boyfriend. Yeah, I have the cutest boyfriend. My boyfriend doesn't like wool socks. Oh, my boyfriend works at The Hague, too!

"Okay, well, what kind of products does he prefer?" Right, I'm back.

"Oh, I don't know. Um, he smells nice. He shaves. Maybe some shave stuff?"

He shows me every conceivable product an aspiring model pulling in extra cash at Barneys might ever want to use.

"Um, really? Lip liner?" I ask. "Because he plays lacrosse . . ."

He shakes his head at my shortsightedness and pulls out more esoteric pastes and lotions.

"I don't want to imply that there's anything wrong with him, you know, give him something that fixes anything. He doesn't need fixing." I finally settle on a stainless steel razor and watch him wrap it in red tissue paper and tie a red bow around the black box. *Parfait.*

I greet Grayer outside his classroom with his coat held out. "Bonsoir, Monsieur X. Comment ça va?"

"Ça va très bien, Nanny. Merci beaucoup. Et vous?" he asks, waving his magic fingers at me.

"Oui, oui, très bien."

Maxime leans her head out of the classroom to the row of cubbies where I'm bundling Grayer. "Grayer is really coming along with his verbs." She smiles down at him from atop her Charles Jourdan pumps. "But if you could take some time with him to practice the noun list each week, that would be *fantastique.* If either you or your husband—"

"Oh, I'm not his mother."

"Ah, mon Dieu! Je m'excuse."

"Non, non, pas de problem," I say.

"Alors, see you next week, Grayer."

I try to push him home quickly because a frigid wind is whipping down Park.

"As soon as we get upstairs," I say, crouching in the elevator to loosen his scarf, "I'm going to put some Vaseline on your cheeks, okay? You're getting a little chapped."

"Okay. What are we going to do tonight, Nanny? Let's fly! Yeah, I think we should fly as soon as we get upstairs." Lately I've been balancing him on my feet and "flying" him in his room.

"After bath, G, that's flying time." I push the stroller over the threshold. "What do you want for dinner?"

I'm hanging up our coats when Mrs. X walks into the front hall in a floor-length red evening gown and Velcro curlers, already in the heat of preparation for her Valentine dinner date with Mr. X.

"Hi, guys. Did you have a good day?"

"Happy Valentine's Day, Mommy!" Grayer shouts in greeting.

"Happy Valentine's Day. Oops, be careful of Mommy's dress." Spatula.

"Wow, you look beautiful," I say, pulling off my boots.

"You think so?" She looks down in consternation at her midriff. "I still have a little time—Mr. X's flight from Chicago doesn't land for another half hour. Could you come help me for a minute?"

"Sure. I was just going to get dinner started. I think Grayer's pretty hungry."

"Oh. Well, why don't you just order something in? There's money in the drawer." Well, I never.

"Great! Grayer, why don't you come help me order?" I keep a hidden stash of menus in the laundry room for emergencies.

"Pizza! I want pizza, Nanny! Pleeeaaase?"

I raise an eyebrow at him because he knows I can't say "But you had pizza for lunch" in front of his mother.

"Great. Nanny, why don't you call for a pizza, pop in a v-i-d-e-o and then come help me," she says as she leaves the room.

"Hahaha, pizza, Nanny, we're having pizza," he laughs and claps wildly at his unbelievable good fortune.

"Mrs. X?" I push the door open.

"In here!" she calls out from the dressing room. She's standing in another floor-length red gown and there's a third hanging up behind her.

"Oh, my God! Wow, it's beautiful." This one has thicker straps and red velvet leaf appliqués trailing around the skirt. The color is a stunning combination with her thick black hair.

She looks in the mirror and shakes her head. "No, it's just not right." I look carefully at her in the dress. I realize I've never seen her arms or sternum before. She looks like a ballet dancer, tiny and all sinew. But she isn't filling out the dress in the bust and it's hanging all wrong.

"I think maybe it's the bustline," I say tentatively.

She nods her head. "Breast-feeding," she says derisively. "Let me try on the third. Would you like some wine?" I notice the open bottle of Sancerre on the dresser.

"No, thank you. I shouldn't."

"Oh, come on. Go take a glass off the bar."

I walk through to the piano room where I can hear the strains of "I'm Madeline! I'm Madeline!" coming from the library.

When I get back she's come out in a beautiful Napoleonic raw-silk gown, looking like Josephine.

"Oh, much better," I say. "The empire waist really suits you."

"Yeah, but it isn't very sexy, is it?"

"Well . . . no, it's beautiful, but it depends on the look you're going for."

"Breathtaking, Nanny. I want to be breathtaking." We both smile as she slips behind the Chinese screen. "I've got one more."

"Are you going to keep all of these?" I eye the zeros on the dangling price tags.

"No, of course not. I'll return the ones I don't wear. Oh, that reminds me." She sticks her head around the screen. "Can you take the rest back to Bergdorf's for me tomorrow?"

"No problem. I can do it while Grayer's at his play date."

"Great. Can you zip me?" she calls out. I put down my wine and go around to zip her into a stunningly sexy 1930s red sheath.

"Yes," we both say as soon as she looks in the mirror.

"It's beautiful," I say. And mean it. It's the first one that uses her proportions to its advantage, making her look sylphlike, rather than emaciated. Looking at her reflection, I realize that I am rooting for her, rooting for them.

"So what do you think? Earrings or no earrings? I need to wear this necklace because my husband gave it to me." She holds up a strand of diamonds. "Isn't it beautiful? But I don't want to overaccessorize."

"Do you have any little studs?"

She starts going through her jewelry box and I take my wine over to the velvet bench.

"These?" She holds up a pair of diamond studs—"Or these?"—and rubies.

"No, definitely the diamonds. You don't want to overdo the red."

"I went to Chanel today and got the perfect lipstick and look!" She sticks out her foot. Her toes are painted in Chanel Redcoat.

"Perfect," I say, taking a sip. She puts in the studs and gives herself a quick swipe with the lipstick.

"What do you think?" She turns for me. "Oh, wait!" She goes over to the Manolo Blahnik bag on the floor and pulls out a box containing a pair of exquisite black silk sandals. "Too much?"

"No, no. They're gorgeous," I say, as she slips them on and turns for me again.

"So, what do you think? Anything missing?"

"Well, I'd take the curlers out." She laughs. "No, really, it's perfect." I give her another once-over. "Um, it's just that . . ."

"What?"

"Do you have a thong?"

She quickly looks backward in the mirror. "Oh, my God. You're right." She starts rifling through the plastic bags in her lingerie drawer. "I think Mr. X gave me a pair on our honeymoon." Oh, brilliant, Nan! Brill-i-ant! Send her combing through the panty drawer.

"You can always go commando," I suggest urgently from the velvet bench where I'm downing the rest of my wine.

"Got 'em!" she says and holds up an exquisite, delicate black La Perla thong with cream silk embroidery, which I am *pray*-ing is hers.

The doorbell rings. "NANNYYY! The pizza's here!"

"Thanks, Grayer!" I call back.

"These will do. I'm all set. Thank you so much."

After Grayer and I polish off half a medium pie I remove a small cardboard box from my backpack. "And now a special Valentine's dessert," I say, producing two chocolate cupcakes with red hearts on them. Grayer's eyes widen at the departure from chopped fruit and soy cookies. I pour us each a glass of milk and we dig in.

"Oh, what have we here?" We both freeze, cupcakes midway to our mouths.

"Nanny bwought thpecial walentine's cucakes," Grayer explains defensively with a mouth full of chocolate.

Mrs. X has pulled her long hair up into a loose chignon and finished her makeup. She looks lovely. "Oh, that's so nice. Did you thank Nanny?"

"Thank you," he sprays.

"The car should be here any minute." She perches on the edge of the banquette, every muscle tensed for the intercom buzzer. She reminds me of myself in high school, all dressed up, just waiting to get the call to find out whose parents were out of town, where we were meeting, where *he* was going to be.

We awkwardly finish our cupcakes while she sits anxiously beside us.

"Well . . ." She stands as I'm cleaning Grov off before releasing him from his booster seat. "I'm just going to go wait in my office. Will you let me know when they buzz up?" She exits, taking a quick glance backward at the intercom.

"Of course," I say, wondering just how late Mr. X will dare to push it.

"Okay, let's fly now, Nanny. Let's fly—can we?" He puts his arms out and does circles around me as I clear the plates.

"G, you might be a little full. Why don't you go get your coloring books and we'll hang out in here so we can hear the buzzer, okay?"

For an hour Grayer and I sit in silence, passing crayons back and forth, looking up intermittently at the silent intercom.

At eight o'clock Mrs. X calls me into her office. She's sitting on the edge of her office chair, an old *Vogue* open on the desk. Her mink lies waiting on the armchair.

"Nanny, would you call Justine to find out if she knows anything? The number's on the emergency list in the pantry."

"Sure, no problem."

I don't get an answer at work so I try her cell phone.

"Hello?" I can hear silverware clanking in the background and hate that I'm interrupting her Valentine's dinner.

"Hello, Justine? It's Nanny. I'm so sorry to bother you, but Mr. X is running late and I was wondering if you might know what flight he's on."

"That's all back at the office—"

"Mrs. X is just getting a little anxious," I say, trying to impart the urgency of the situation.

"Nanny! I can't find the red crayon!" Grayer calls from the banquette.

"Look, um, I'm sure he'll be in touch." There's a pause wherein I hear the restaurant in full swing behind her. "I'm sorry, Nanny, I really can't help you." And then I just know, I know it in the pit of my stomach.

"Naa-nny, I'm stuck. *I need the red!*"

"Okay, thanks."

"Well?" Mrs. X asks from over my shoulder.

"Justine wasn't in the office so she doesn't have his itinerary." I walk around her to search through the bucket of crayons on the table, while Grayer slumps over his coloring book. Maybe this is it. Maybe I should just say something. But what? What do I actually know for a fact, here, really? What I know is that Ms. Chicago was here over a month ago—things could've changed since then. How do I know he's not just running late? "Hey, why don't you check the Weather Channel?" I suggest, bending down to retrieve the red crayon, which has rolled under the bench. "Maybe there are delays out of O'Hare?" I reach my arm up over the table and place the crayon next to Grayer's fist. I stand back up. "I'll call the airline. Who does he fly?"

"Justine would know. Oh, and can you call Lutèce and make sure they don't give away our reservation?" She walks hurriedly out toward the library. Grayer slides down and runs across the floor to follow her.

Justine's voice mail comes on three times, but, as she's basically left me to fend for myself, I keep calling.

"Hello?" She sounds annoyed.

"Justine, I'm so sorry. What airline does he fly?"

"American. But Nanny, I really wouldn't . . ." Her voice trails off.

"What?"

"I'm sure he'll call. I wouldn't bother to . . ."

"Okay. Well, thanks, bye."

I get the number from information, because I don't know what else to do.

"Hello, thank you for calling American Airlines. This is Wendy speaking. How may I help you?"

"Hello. Yes, I'm calling to find out if there any delays on the flights from Chicago to New York tonight, or if a passenger X changed his flight?"

"I'm sorry, but I can't give out information on particular passengers."

"Well, can you tell me if there are any delays?"

"Hold on, I'll check." The other line beeps.

"Hello, this is the Xes' residence. May I ask who's calling please?" I say.

"Who's this?" a male voice asks.

"Hi, it's Nanny—"

"Who?"

"Nanny—"

"Whatever. Listen, tell Mrs. X my plane is snowed in here in Chicago. I'll call her tomorrow."

"I'm sure she'd like to talk to—"

"Can't now." The line goes dead.

I click back.

"Hello, miss? Thanks for holding. There are no delays. All flights are running on schedule."

"Thank you," I say, hanging up. Shit. Shit. Shit.

I walk slowly through the living room and go stand outside the library, where Mrs. X and Grayer are seated on the navy leather couch, studying the weather in the Midwest.

"So stay tuned, because after the break we'll be talking to Cindy in Little Springs about what it's doing on her back porch," a perky voice says from the television. I feel queasy.

"Nanny?" She rounds the door frame, nearly knocking into me. "It just occurred to me—call Justine and get the number of his hotel. The weather's fine—maybe his meeting ran late."

"Um, actually Mr. X just called on the other line, while I was on hold with the airline, and that's what he said. His meeting ran late. So he said he'll call tomorrow night and, uh—"

She raises her palm up to silence me. "Why didn't you come get me?"

"He, um, he said he had to go—"

"I see." She presses her lips together. "And what else did he say?"

I can feel small beads of perspiration rolling down my sides. "He said, um, he was just going to spend the night there." I cast my eyes down to avoid her gaze.

She takes a step closer. "Nanny, I want you. To tell me. *Exactly.* What he said."

Please don't make me do this.

"Well?" She waits for an answer.

"He said he was snowed in and he'll call you tomorrow," I say quietly.

She shudders.

I glance up. She looks as if I've just slapped her and I return my eyes to the floor. She walks back into the library, picks up the remote and turns off the television, silencing and darkening the room. She remains immobile, silhouetted against the lights of Park Avenue, her red silk gown shimmering in the somber blue room, her hand still gripping the remote.

Grayer's wide eyes stare up at me in the darkness from where he sits, hands carefully crossed in his lap. "Come on, Grayer. Let's get ready for bed." I extend my hand and he wriggles off the couch and follows me without protest.

He is uncharacteristically quiet while we brush teeth and put on pajamas. I read him *Maisy Goes to Bed* about a little mouse with a simple mission.

" 'Maisy brushed her teeth.' Did Grayer brush his teeth?"

"Yes."

" 'Maisy washed her face and hands.' Did Grayer wash his face and hands?"

"Yes." And so on until he's yawning and his eyes are opening and closing.

I stand to kiss him on the forehead and realize his hand is clenching my sweater. I gently uncurl his fingers. "Good night, Grover."

I walk tentatively out into the cold, gray light of the marble foyer. "Mrs. X?" I call out. "I'm leaving. Okay?" No answer.

I walk down the long, dark hall to her bedroom, through the numerous hot pools of light illuminating the paintings.

The door is open. "Mrs. X?" I enter her bedroom and can hear the sound of muffled crying coming from behind the closed dressing-room door. "Um, Mrs. X? Grayer's asleep. Do you need anything?" Quiet. "I'm just gonna go, okay?" I stand right up against the door and can hear her weeping quietly on the other side. The image of her curled up on the floor in her beautiful gown makes me put my hands to my chest.

"Nanny?" a voice, straining to sound cheerful, calls out. "Is that you?"

"Yes." I pick up our empty wine glasses from the bedside table, careful to keep them from clinking.

"Okay, you go on ahead. See you tomorrow."

"Um, there's still some pizza left. Do you want me to warm it up for you?"

"No, that's okay. Good night."

"Are you sure? 'Cause it's no trouble."

"No, that's really fine. See you tomorrow."

"Okay, good night." I walk back down the long beige hall to the kitchen, place the glasses in the sink, and put out a fruit plate, just in case. I decide to wait till I get downstairs to cancel their expired reservation.

I go back into the hall, grab my coat and boots, and pull my paper heart out from Grayer's stroller pocket. It sprinkles the black-and-white tile with a light dusting of red glitter. I kneel and press my hand over the sparkles, quickly lifting them up and brushing them into my backpack.

Her low sobs give way to a deep, animal-like keening as I gently close the door behind me.

They all felt that there was no sense in their living together, and that any group of people who had met together by chance at an inn would have had more in common than they, the members of the Oblonsky family and their servants. The wife did not leave her own rooms and the husband stayed away from home all day. The children strayed all over the house, not knowing what to do with themselves.

—ANNA KARENINA

CHAPTER SEVEN

We Regret to Inform You

On Monday at noon I wait in the school courtyard, having watched Mrs. Butters pat each of her heavily bundled students on the head and send them off to waiting nannies, and still no Grayer.

"Mrs. Butters?" I ask.

"Yes?"

"Was Grayer in school today?"

"No." She grins at me.

"Okay, thanks," I say.

"Sure."

"Great."

"Well, then . . ." She nods her head, indicating this productive exchange is over and toddles back into the building, her velvet patchwork scarf blowing out behind her. I stand for a moment, unsure of what to do. I am just reaching for my cell phone when suddenly I am dealt a stunning blow to the back of my leg.

"Hi-yaa!"

I turn to see a small woman reproving a very large boy crouched in a menacing karate stance. "No, Darwin," she says, "no chopping the people."

"Where's Grayer? I want to play with his toys."

"I'm sorry, can I help you?" I say, rubbing my leg.

She gently pushes the boy's fingers off her face while patiently replying, "I am Sima. This is Darwin. We were supposed to play with Grayer today."

"I want to see his toys. NOW!" her charge screams up at me with both hands in a karate stance.

"It's nice to meet you, Sima. I'm Nanny. I guess Grayer must have stayed home today, but I didn't know he had a play date. Let me just call his mother." I dial the number, but Mrs. X's voice mail picks up and I click off. "Okay, well, let's go home, then!" I say, trying to be cheerful, but unsure of what we'll find once we get there. I help Sima with Darwin's bag and we trek through the slush to 721. I take an instant dislike to Darwin, as I have spent all of three minutes with him and am already in a perpetual state of flinching. Sima, on the other hand, is completely soft, almost graceful, in her efforts to deflect Darwin's chops.

I stick my key in the door and open it slowly, calling, "Hello? I'm here with Darwin and Sima!"

"Oh, my," Sima murmurs beside me as we make eye contact. The stench of roses is overwhelming. While Mr. X failed to return from what is becoming the longest business trip on record, he has, in his absence, been sending two dozen long-stemmed roses to 721 Park every morning since Valentine's Day. Mrs. X refuses to have them in her or Grayer's wing, but also can't seem to bring herself to throw them out. More than thirty vases fill the living room, dining room, and kitchen. Consequently, the air-conditioning is on, but that only seems to blow the cloying stench from one side of the apartment to the other.

Based on what I've pieced together from the florist cards, Mr. X promised to take his wife and child out to Connecticut this past weekend for "family time," making the last two heavenly days the first weekend I've had completely off in the month since Valentine's.

"GRAYER! GRAAYYRR!" Darwin bellows at the top of his lungs before ripping away from his coat and running in the direction of Grayer's room.

"Please take your coat off and have a seat, I'll just go check with Grayer's mom and let her know that we're home." I put his bag down next to the bench in the front hall and slip my boots off.

"That's okay. I'll just keep my coat on, thank you." Her smile tells me that I don't need to explain the frigid temperature or the mortuary flowers. I attempt to weave my way around the vases toward Mrs. X's office, only to find it empty.

I follow the sound of the boys' hyena giggles to Grayer's room, where his bed is serving as a barricade in the war between a pajama-clad Grayer and Darwin.

"Hi, Grover."

He's busy bombing Darwin with stuffed animals and looks up only briefly to acknowledge me. "Nanny, I'm hungry. I want breakfast now!"

"You mean lunch? Where's your mom?" He dives to avert a flying stuffed frog.

"I dunno. And I *mean* breakfast!" Huh.

I find Connie in Mr. X's office, turning Grayer's fort back into a couch. The room is the messiest I've seen any part of the apartment since I've been here. Small plates with leftover pizza crusts line the floor and every Disney video is strewn about, separate from its case.

"Hey, Connie. How was your weekend?" I ask.

"You're lookin' at it." She gestures to the mess. "I was here all weekend. Mr. X didn't show, and she don't want to be alone with Grayer. She made me come all the way back from the Bronx at eleven Friday night. I had to take my kids over to my sister's.

Wouldn't even pay for a taxi. She didn't say boo to that boy all weekend." She picks up a plate. "Last night I finally just told her I had to go home, but she didn't like it."

"Oh, my God, Connie, I'm so sorry. That sucks. She should've called me—I could at least have done the nights."

"What? And let the likes of you know she can't get her own husband home?"

"Where is she?"

She points me toward the master bedroom. "Her Highness came in an hour ago and went straight to her room."

I knock on the door. "Mrs. X?" I ask tentatively. I push it open and it takes a moment for my eyes to adjust to the darkness. She is sitting on the ecru carpet, surrounded by shopping bags, her flannel nightgown peeking out from under her fur coat. The heavy grosgrain shades are drawn.

"Could you close the door?" She leans back against the bureau, breathing deeply into a wad of lavender tissue paper pulled from one of the bags. She wipes her nose and looks up at the ceiling. Afraid that anything that I ask will be the wrong question, I wait for her to lead.

She stares off into the darkness and then asks in a flat voice, "How was your weekend, Nanny?"

"Okay—"

"We had a great weekend. It was . . . fun. Connecticut was beautiful. We went sledding. You should've seen Grayer and his father. It was adorable. Really, a great weekend."

O-kaaay.

"Nanny, is there any way you could come tomorrow morning and just . . ." She seems exhausted. "Maybe help Grayer get off to school. He's just so . . . He wanted his pink pants and I didn't have the strength—"

"I SHOT YOU! YOU SHOULD BE DEAD!"

"NO! YOU ARE DEAD! DIE! DIE!"

The boys' voices get louder, as does the sound of stuffed animals being pelted down the hall.

"Nanny, take them out. Just . . . take them to the museum or something. I can't . . . I need to—"

"DIE NOW! I SAID DIE!"

"Absolutely. We can totally take them out. Can I get you any—"

"No. Please, just go." Her voice catches and she grabs more tissue from her bags.

As I gingerly close the door behind me, Grayer jumps out at the far end of the long hall. His eyes go to the door and then to me. He hurls his Winnie-the-Pooh at my head with a little too much force.

I take a quick breath. "All right, tough guy, let's get you dressed." I take his hand, leading him and Winnie back to his room.

"You have pajamas on, stupidhead," Darwin offers supportively as I hustle Grayer toward the closet.

In addition to putting on his current uniform of choice, the Collegiate sweatsuit he's been wearing almost daily since Christmas, he pulls one of his father's ties off a hook and loops it around his neck.

"No, Grove, you can't wear that," I say. Darwin tries to grab it out of his hands. "No, Darwin, that's Grayer's tie."

"See? See?" Grayer says victoriously. "You said it. It's mine. My tie. Mom said. She gave it to me." Not wanting to go back in her room to get the real story, I fix a quick knot, letting the tie dangle low beside his business card.

"All right, fellas, shake a leg. We got places to be, things to do! I have a very exciting afternoon planned, but the first one with his coat on will be the first to find out about it!" The boys scramble past me to tackle the floral obstacle course. I grab an armful of the stuffed toys off the floor and toss them back onto the bed on my way out.

In the front hall Sima is attempting to keep Darwin from smothering Grayer, who is flattened against the door. "He must breathe, Darwin."

"So, I was thinking, maybe Play Space?" I announce, realizing I still have my coat on as Darwin releases Grayer.

"YEAH!" The boys jump up and down on top of each other.

"Okay." Sima nods. "Play Space sounds very good." I hand her Darwin's jacket and pull on my boots.

While there are two Play Spaces, one on East Eighty-fifth and one on Broadway in the Nineties, we head up to the one on the East Side, as it has marginally cleaner sand. These indoor playgrounds are Manhattan's version of a fully equipped basement rec room. And, like everything else in the big city, it's for rent. So, similar to motels with hourly rates, a twenty gets you and your charge a good two hours to exhaust each other on their equipment.

Sima stands on the sidewalk with the boys while I get the strollers out of the trunk of the cab.

"IS NOT!"

"IS TOO!"

"Can I help you?" she asks, evading Darwin's kick.

"No," I grunt. "That's okay." I'm just grateful to be out of his reach.

I maneuver the strollers to the sidewalk and we each grab a small hand. Probably to deter perverts from window-shopping, the Space is up on the second level and can only be reached by climbing an *enormous*, blue-carpeted staircase of child-size stairs that seems to stretch all the way up to wherever nannies go when they die. Grayer, undaunted, grabs the child-height railing and starts hauling himself up.

"Darwin, go up. Go up," Sima instructs. "Not down. Up." Darwin, completely disregarding her, plays some sort of leapfrog game that threatens to throw the methodical Grayer backward into a neck-breaking fall. I follow closely behind, dragging the collapsed strollers, my heels hanging off the edge of each stair.

When we eventually get to the top I park the strollers in the Stroller Corral and prepare to check in. Because of the inclement weather the place is packed and we get on a long line of overbundled children, exasperated nannies, and the occasional mother putting in her hour of quality time.

"Elizabeth, we can make wee-wee after we check in. Please just hold it!"

"Hello and welcome to Play Space! Who's checking in?" an overenthusiastic man in his mid-thirties asks from behind the bright red counter.

"He is!" I say, pointing down at Grayer. The man looks confused. "We are," I say, passing him Mrs. X's membership card. He looks her up in the files and once I hand over twenty dollars we each get name tags for ourselves and one to put on the stroller in case it wants to make friends.

"Hello, my name is **Grayer**. I'm with **Nanny**," his reads.

"Hello, my name is **Nanny**. I'm with **Grayer**," mine reads. We are instructed to wear them prominently and I plaster mine directly over my left ventricle, while Grayer prefers to stick his on the edge of his shirt, just above the dangling card and next to his father's tie. After Sima and Darwin are similarly linked, the four of us go and put our coats in our designated cubbies, along with our boots. In the food area I fork over another twenty for our lunch—two small peanut butter and jelly sandwiches and two juice boxes.

"DIE! DIE!"

"KILL HIM IN HIS BLOODY HEAD!"

"All right, enough already!" The Wicked Witch has a headache. "If you two can't eat lunch like nice, peace-loving young gentlemen, Darwin and Sima will have to sit at another table." They manage to argue in dulcet tones for the remainder of the meal while Sima and I exchange wan smiles across the table. She picks at her bologna sandwich and I make a few attempts to begin a conversation, but Darwin chooses these opportune moments to fling Goldfish in her face.

Before we can release them into the pen we go wash hands. The Technicolor bathrooms all have little sinks, low toilets, and high latches. Grayer pees like a champ and then lets me push up his sleeves so he can wash his hands.

"NO! I DON'T WANT TO! YOU DO IT! YOU PEE!" We can hear Darwin in the next bathroom.

I lean over and kiss Grayer on the top of his head. "Okay, G, let's hit the slopes," I say, as I pass him a paper towel so he can dry his hands and whatever else got sprayed by the sink.

"Daddy says that in Aspirin."

"Does he. Come on." I throw out the towel and extend my hand, but he doesn't move.

"When's my daddy taking me to Aspirin?" he asks.

"Oh, Grove . . ." I crouch down. "I don't know, I'm not sure if you are going skiing this year." He continues to look at me questioningly. "Have you asked your mom?"

He angles his body away from me, crossing his arms over the tie. "My mom says not to talk about him, so don't. Don't talk about him."

"Grayer, come on!" Darwin yells, kicking the door at its base.

"Hey! People have to pee out here!" A woman starts pounding above him.

"Grover, if you have questions, it's always okay to—" I say, standing and unlatching the door.

"Don't talk to me," he says, running past me to join Darwin by the gate.

"You have some nerve!" The woman who's been waiting hustles her child past me to the toilet. "I think it's unconscionable to keep a little girl waiting that long!" She narrows her heavily made-up eyes at me. "Who do you work for?" I take in her shellacked hair, her inch-long fingernails, her Versace blouse. "I mean it, who do you work for?"

"God," I mutter, pushing past her to let Grayer into the pen.

Sima and I lift the boys onto the bright blue slide. I look over at her to gauge if she's one of those caregivers who feel compelled to stay within two feet of their charges at all times, tagging along on every move.

"I think they should . . ." she says, pausing, clearly trying to read me, as well.

I nod, waiting for the sign.

". . . be okay if they are together? What do you think?"

"I agree," I say with relief, given Grayer's mood and Darwin's aggression. "Can I treat you to dessert?"

Once we've settled at a table in full view of the slide, I pass Sima a cupcake and a napkin. "I'm glad you don't mind letting the boys play. I usually try to set Grayer free and then come up here where I can keep an eye on him and do my homework. But there's always some nosy caregiver who's, like, 'Um, Grayer's in the . . . *sandbox.*' And I'm supposed to fly across the room with a cry of 'Not . . . THE SAND-BOX!' " I laugh, covering my mouth to keep crumbs from falling out.

Sima giggles. "Yesterday, at a play date, the mother wanted me to color with Darwin, but if I put my crayon on his drawing, he screams. But she made me sit there all afternoon, holding the crayon near the paper." She unwraps her cupcake. "Have you been with Grayer for very long?"

"Seven months—since September. How about you?" I ask in return.

"Two years now I have been with Mr. and Mrs. Zuckerman." She nods her head and her dark hair falls in front of her face. I'm guessing that she's in her early forties. "We used to play with the other girl, she was very nice. What was her name?" She smiles and takes a sip from her miniature carton of milk.

"Caitlin. Yeah, I think she went back to Australia."

"She had a sister there who was very sick. In the hospital. She was saving up to visit her last time we had a play date."

"That's terrible, I had no idea. She was wonderful, Grayer still really misses her—" Out of the corner of my eye I see Darwin, poised on the yellow plastic step above Grayer, pulling Mr. X's tie taut around G's neck. For a brief moment Grayer's choking—his face turning red as he reaches up his hands to clutch at his throat.

Then the knot of the tie gives way in one swift tug. Darwin rips it from around Grayer's red neck and runs, laughing, to the other side of the room, disappearing into the climbing apparatus. Sima and I leap up, dispatching ourselves to the opposing fronts.

"Grove, it's okay," I call out as I approach.

He gives forth a blast of rage toward Darwin that silences the entire room. "GIVE THAT *BACK*!! THAT'S MY *DADDY'S*!! GIVE IT *BACK*!!!!!!!" He starts to sob and shake. "MY DADDY'S SO MAD AT YOU!! HE'S SO MAD!!!!"

He collapses, shaking with the force of his tears. "My daddy's so mad, he's so mad."

I pull him onto my lap and start murmuring in his ear as I rock him. "You are such a good boy. Nobody is mad at you. Your daddy's not mad at you. Your mommy's not mad at you. We all love you so much, Grove."

I carry him up to the food area, where Sima is waiting with the tie.

"I . . . want," he gasps, his breath coming in gulps, "my . . . mommy." I knot the tie gently around his neck and help him up onto one of the green benches next to me, making a pillow for him with my sweater.

"Sih-muh? Are you Sih-muh?" the woman from the bathroom asks.

"Yes?"

"Your Darwin is on the slide by himself," she announces.

"Thank you." Sima smiles graciously.

"By him-self," the mother says again, as if Sima is deaf.

"Okay, thank you." Sima rolls her eyes at me, but goes over to make sure Darwin doesn't somehow hurt himself on the three-foot slide, while I rub Grayer's back as he falls asleep.

I watch as she reaches out a hand to help Darwin place his legs over the top in preparation for his descent. He rejects her offer by smacking her squarely on the head, then laughs and flies down the slide. She stands for a moment with both hands on her head and then walks slowly back to our table and sits down.

"Darwin seems a little intense," I say. Actually, he seems like a potential homicidal maniac, but she must have stayed for a reason and ten dollars an hour isn't enough to subject oneself to gross bodily harm.

"Oh, no. He's just having a lot of anger because he has a new baby brother at home." She reaches up to rub her head.

"Have you ever talked to them about how he hits you?" I ask tentatively.

"No. Well, they are so busy with the new baby. And he can be a very good boy." She takes little breaths as she speaks. This is hardly the first time I've seen this; every playground has at least one nanny getting the shit kicked out of her by an angry child. Clearly she doesn't want to talk about it, so I change the topic.

"You have such a beautiful accent." I fold up the wrapper from my cupcake into a little square.

"I moved here from San Salvador two years ago." She wipes her hands with a napkin.

"Do you still have family there?" I ask.

"Well, my husband and sons are there." She blinks a couple of times and looks down.

"Oh," I say.

"Yes, we all came together, to find work. I was an engineer in San Salvador. But there were no more jobs and we hoped to make money here. Then my husband was rejected for the green card and had to go back with our sons, because I could not work and take care of them."

"How often do you see them?" I ask as Grayer shifts fitfully in his sleep.

"I try to go home for two weeks at Christmastime, but this year

Mr. and Mrs. Zuckerman needed me to go to France." She folds and unfolds Darwin's sweater.

"Do you have pictures of your children? I bet they're beautiful." I am not sure what the positive spin is on this situation or where to take this conversation. I know if my mom were here she would have already rolled Sima up in the Story Time rug and smuggled her to the first safe house she could find.

"No, I don't keep a picture on me. It's too . . . hard . . ." She smiles. "Someday when Grayer comes to play at Darwin's house, I will show you then. What about you? Do you have children?"

"No. Me? No, thank God." We both laugh.

"A boyfriend, then?"

"I'm working on that," and I begin to tell her about H. H. We share slices of our own stories, the parts of our lives the Zuckermans and the Xes neither partake in nor know about, amid all the bright lights and colors, surrounded by a cacophony of screaming. It starts to snow outside the big windows and I tuck my stocking feet beneath me while she rests her chin on her outstretched arm. Thus I while away the afternoon with a woman who has a higher degree than I will ever receive, in a subject I can't get a passing grade in, and who has been home less than one month in the last twenty-four.

⬧ ⬧ ⬧

For the past week I've been arriving at seven to dress Grayer for school, before dropping him off with Mrs. Butters and running madly down to class. Mrs. X never emerges from her room in the mornings and is out every afternoon, so I was surprised when Connie told me she was waiting for me in her office.

"Mrs. X?" I knock on the door.

"Come in." I push the door open with slight trepidation, but find her seated at the desk, fully dressed in a cashmere cardigan and slacks. Despite her best efforts with cream blush, she still looks drawn.

"What are you doing home so early?" she asks.

"Grayer had a run-in with some green paint so I brought him home to change before ice skating—" The phone rings and she motions for me to stay.

"Hello? . . . Oh, hi, Joyce . . . No, the letters haven't come yet . . . I don't know, slow zip code, I guess . . ." Her voice still sounds hollow. "All the schools she applied to? Really? That's fabulous . . . Well, which one are you going to choose? . . . Well, I don't know as much about the girls' schools . . . I'm sure you'll make the right decision . . . Excellent. Bye."

She turns back to me. "Her daughter got into every school she applied to. I don't get it, she isn't even cute . . . What were you saying?"

"The paint—don't worry, he wasn't wearing the Collegiate sweatshirt when it happened. He made a really beautiful tree picture—"

"Doesn't he have a change of clothes at school?"

"Yeah, I'm sorry—he used them last week when Giselle dumped glue on him and I forgot to replace it."

"What if he hadn't had time to change?"

"I'm sorry. I'll bring it tomorrow." I start to leave.

"Oh, Nanny?" I stick my head back in. "While I've got you, I need to have a talk with you about Grayer's applications. Where is he?"

"He's watching Connie dust." Your chair-rail moldings. With a toothbrush.

"Good, have a seat." She gestures to one of the upholstered wing chairs across from her desk. "Nanny, I have something terrible to tell you." She casts her eyes down to her hands twisting in her lap.

I can't breathe. I brace myself for panties.

"We got some very bad news this morning," she says slowly, struggling to get the words out. "Grayer got rejected from Collegiate."

"No." I quickly wipe the look of relief off my face. "I don't believe it."

"I know—it's just awful. *And*, to make matters even worse, he's been wait-listed at St. David's and St. Bernard's. Wait-listed." She shakes her head. "So now our fingers are crossed for Trinity, but if, for some reason, that too doesn't work out, then we're just going to be left with his safeties and I'm not enthusiastic about the college placements at those schools."

"But he's adorable. He's smart and articulate. He's funny. He shares well. I just don't get it." I mean, lose the tie, what's not to love about this kid?

"I've been going over everything all morning, just trying to make sense of it." She looks out the window. "Our application coach told us he was a shoo-in for Collegiate."

"My father did say this was the most competitive year they've ever had. They were inundated with qualified applicants and probably had to make some really tough choices." Keeping in mind that the applicants are *four* and you can't exactly ask them if they have any thoughts on the federal deficit or where they see themselves in five years.

"I thought your father liked Grayer when he met him," she asks pointedly, referring to the rainy afternoon I took him over to my house to pet Sophie.

"He did. They sang 'Rainbow Connection' together."

"Hmmm. Interesting."

"What?"

"No, nothing. Just interesting, that's all."

"My dad's not really involved at all with the admissions process."

"Right. Well, I wanted to talk to you because I'm concerned that dressing him in that Collegiate sweatshirt may have set Grayer's expectations in a certain direction and I want to ensure that—" She's interrupted by the phone. "Hold on." She answers it. "Hello? Oh, hi, Sally . . . No, our letters haven't come yet . . . Oh, Collegiate. Congratulations, that's excellent . . . Well, Ryan's a very special little boy . . . Yes, that *would* be great. I know Grayer would love to go to school with Ryan . . . Yes, dinner would be lovely . . . Oh, the four of us? I'll have to check my husband's schedule. Let's talk after the weekend . . . Great. Bye!" She takes a deep breath and clenches her jaw. "Where was I?"

"Grayer's expectations?"

"Oh, yes. I'm concerned that your encouragement of his fixation on Collegiate may have set him up for a potentially deleterious self-esteem adjustment."

"I—"

"No, please don't feel bad. It's really my fault for allowing you to do it. I should have been more on top of you." She sighs and shakes her head. "But I spoke to my pediatrician this morning and he suggested a Long-term Development Consultant who specializes in coaching parents and caregivers through this transition. She'll be coming by tomorrow while Grayer's in piano and she's asked to speak with you separately to assess your role in his development."

"Great. That sounds like a good idea." I go through the doorway. "Um." I stick my head back in. "Should I not let him wear it today?"

"What?" She reaches for her coffee.

"The sweatshirt."

"Oh. Well, he can wear it today and then we'll let the consultant tell us how to handle this situation tomorrow."

"Okay, great." I go back out to where Grayer, seated in the banquette, is watching Connie polish the stove, while absentmindedly playing with the tie around his neck, and wonder if perhaps we're not focusing on the wrong piece of apparel.

✧ ✧ ✧

I sit in the chair next to Mrs. X's desk, waiting for the consultant, and surreptitiously try to read, upside down, the notes scrawled on Mrs. X's notepad. Even though it's probably nothing more than a glorified grocery list, the fact that I have been left alone in here makes me feel as if I should be covert. If I had a camera hidden in a button on my sweater I would frantically try to photograph every-thing on the desk. I'm starting to make myself laugh at the idea of it when the woman enters, briefcase first.

"Nanny." She reaches out to firmly shake my hand. "I'm Jane. Jane Gould. How are you today?" She speaks just a little too loudly, eyeing me over her glasses as she puts her briefcase down on Mrs. X's desk.

"Fine, thanks. How are you?" I am suddenly very cheerful and also a little too loud.

"Just fine. Thank you for asking." She crosses her arms over her cranberry-colored blazer and nods rhythmically at me. She has very big lips made up in the exact same cranberry, bleeding into the lines around her mouth.

I nod back at her.

She looks down at her watch. "So, Nanny. I'm just going to get my pad out here and we'll get started." She proceeds to mention each action as she does it until she's seated in Mrs. X's chair, pen poised.

"Nanny, our objective over the course of the next forty-five minutes is to assess Grayer's perceptions and expectations. I would like you to share with me the understanding you currently hold of your role and responsibilities surrounding Grayer's critical path with regard to the next stratum of his schooling."

"Okay," I say, replaying her statement in my head to locate the question.

"Nanny, in your first quarter at the X residence, how would you characterize your performance in relation to Grayer's academic activity?"

"Good. I mean, I was picking him up from school. But, honestly, there wasn't a lot of academic activity to—"

"I see, so you do not consider yourself an active, dynamic participant in his process. How would you describe your agenda during his scheduled playtime?"

"Right . . . Grayer really likes to play trains. Oh, and dress up. So I try to do activities that he enjoys. I wasn't aware that he had an agenda for playtime."

"Do you engage him in puzzles?"

"He doesn't like puzzles so much."

"Math problems?"

"He's a little young—"

"When was the last time you practiced circles?"

"I'm sure sometime in the last week we had the crayons out—"

"Do you play the Suzuki tapes?"

"Only when he takes a bath."

"Have you been reading to him from the *Wall Street Journal?*"

"Well, actually—"

"*The Economist?*"

"Not really—"

"*The Financial Times?*"

"Should I be?"

She sighs heavily and scribbles furiously on her pad. She begins again. "How many bilingual meals are you serving him a week?"

"We speak French on Tuesday night, but I usually serve veggieburgers."

"And you are attending the Guggenheim on what basis?"

"We go to the Museum of Natural History—he loves the rocks."

"What methodology are you following to dress him?"

"He picks out his clothes or Mrs. X does. As long as he'll be comfortable—"

"You don't utilize an Apparel Chart, then?"

"Not really—"

"And I suppose you are not documenting his choices with him on a Closet Diagram."

"Yeah, no."

"Nor are you having him translate his color and sizes into the Latin."

"Maybe later this year." She looks back at me and nods for a while. I shift in my seat and smile. She leans across the desk and takes off her glasses.

"Nanny, I'm going to have to raise a flag here."

"Okay." I lean in to meet her.

"I have to question whether you're leveraging your assets to escalate Grayer's performance." Having let the cat out of the bag, she leans back and rests her hands in her lap. I sense that I should feel insulted. 'Leverage my assets?' Umm, anyone?

"I'm sorry to hear that," I say earnestly, as the one thing abundantly clear is that I should be feeling sorry.

"Nanny, I understand you are getting your degree in arts-in-education so, frankly, I'm surprised by the lack of depth surrounding your knowledge base here." Okay, now I know I'm insulted.

"Well, Jane." She straightens at the sound of her name. "I am trained to work with children who have far fewer resources at their disposal than Grayer."

"I see, so you don't perceive this opportunity to be in an arena in which you are a value-add." What?

"I want to add value to Grayer, but he's really stressed out right now—"

She looks skeptically at me. "Stressed?"

"Yes, he's stressed. And I feel—and I am only an undergrad here, Jane, so I'm sure you'll take this with a grain of salt—the best thing I can give him is some downtime so that his imagination can grow without being forced in one direction or another." Blood rushes to my face and I know I've gone too far, but being made to feel like an idiot by yet another middle-aged woman in this office is just a bit more than I can handle.

She scribbles a few more notes and smiles evenly at me. "Well, Nanny, I advise you to integrate time for reflection as you continue to work with Grayer. Here are a series of Best Practices from other caregivers that I suggest you review and internalize. This is explicit knowledge, Nanny, explicit knowledge from your peers that must become tacit for you if Grayer is to reach his optimal state." She hands me a bunch of papers with a big clip at the top and stands, sliding her glasses back on.

I stand up, too, feeling I need, somehow, to clean this up. "I didn't mean to seem defensive. I care very deeply for Grayer and follow all of Mrs. X's instructions. The past few months he's insisted on the Collegiate sweatsuit almost every day. And Mrs. X even got him a few more so he would have one to wear when the others were in the wash. So I just want to be sure that you know I—"

She puts out her hand for me to shake. "Right. Thank you for your time this afternoon, Nanny."

I shake her hand. "Yes, thank you. I'll read these through tonight. I'm sure they'll be very helpful."

✧

"Come on, Grove, finish up so we can go play a game." Grayer has been pushing around his last tortellini for about five minutes. Thanks to Jane, it's already been a long afternoon for both of us. I look down at him, resting his blond head on his arm and staring horizontally at the last of his dinner. "Whatsa matter? Not hungry?"

"No." I reach for his plate. "No!" He grabs the edge, causing his fork to drop to the table.

"Okay, Grayer, just say 'Nanny, I'm not finished.' I can wait." I sit back down.

"Nanny!" Mrs. X comes bustling in. "Nanny." She's about to speak when she sees Grayer and the lone tortellini. "Did you have a good dinner, Grayer?"

"Yes," he says into his arm.

But she's already focused her attention back to me. "Could you come out here for a minute?" I follow her into the dining room where she turns and stops so abruptly I accidentally step on her foot.

"I'm sorry, are you okay?"

She grimaces. "I'm fine. I just finished with Jane and it's paramount that we have a family meeting, to break the news to Grayer together about the r-e-j-e-c-t-i-o-n. So I'll need you to call Mr. X's office and find out when he could be scheduled to attend. The number's in the pantry—"

"Mrs. X?" Jane calls as she comes into the hall.

"Sure. No problem. Right away." I quickly slip back into the kitchen. Grayer is still making slow circles with his fork, the tortellini in orbit. I hover over him for a moment while listening to Jane and Mrs. X in the hallway.

"Yes, I've just spoken with Nanny. I'm going to see how soon my husband can come home for this meeting," Mrs. X says, waxing professional.

"His presence is really unnecessary as long as Grayer perceives his primary caregiver to be present. You should just go ahead and speak with him yourself." Jane's voice moves toward the front door and I head for the phone.

"Mr. X's office, Justine speaking. How may I help you?"

"Justine? Hi, it's Nanny."

"Hi. How are you?" she asks over the din of a printer.

"Hanging in there. How about you?"

"Busy," she sighs. "The merger is making things crazy around here. I haven't been home before midnight in two weeks."

"That sucks."

"Well, hopefully Mr. X'll get a huge retention bonus and spread a little of it around." Don't count on it. "So, is Mrs. X liking the flowers?"

"What?"

"The roses—I thought it was overkill, but Mr. X just told me to put in a standing order."

"Yeah, it kind of feels like a standing order," I confirm.

"I'll make sure tomorrow's bouquet has more variety. What's her favorite flower?"

"She likes peonies," I whisper as Mrs. X breezes past Grayer to stand in front of me, expectantly.

"Where am I going to find peonies in March?" Justine sighs again as the printer makes a clacking sound. "Ugh, I can't believe this thing is broken again. Sorry, never mind, I'll do it. Anything else?"

"Oh, right. Mrs. X wants to schedule a family meeting about . . ."—I glance over her shoulder at the pasta pusher—"the little one. When could he be here?"

"Let's see . . . I could push a meeting up . . ." I can hear her flipping pages. "Tuh, tah, tah . . . Yeah, I can get him back to New York by Wednesday at four. I'll have him there."

"Great. Thanks, Justine."

"Anytime."

I hang up the phone and turn to her. "Justine said that he can be here Wednesday at four."

"Well, if that's really the soonest he can make it . . . I guess that will have to do." She glances down to adjust her sparkling engagement ring. "Jane said it was *crucial* that he be here, so . . ."

Right.

✧ ✧ ✧

"I mean, the *Wall Street Journal*! He's four!"

"Jesus," my dad exclaims just as Sophie pushes her nose between our legs. "Your mom still wants you out of there."

"I can handle it." I jog forward a few steps and Sophie circles, ready for her next run. "And there's no way I could leave Grayer right now."

Dad runs to the bottom of the hill. "Sophie! Come on!" Sophie looks confused. "Over here!" he calls. Sophie turns 180 degrees from my heels and takes off in his direction against a cold gust of wind that blows her ears even farther back. As soon as she reaches him, running just below his gloved hands, I call to her and she gallops back up toward me, and then the two of us run down the slope until we are beside him on the main promenade that runs along the uptown stretch of Riverside Park.

"Ready for your interview tomorrow?" Sophie rolls into his shins in an effort to catch up.

"I'm kind of nervous, but Professor Clarkson's been practicing with us in class. I'd really like to have my job for next year lined up soon." I hunch my shoulders against another gust of cold wind.

"You'll knock 'em dead. Go long!" I run back up the hill toward the edge of the trees and look back down just as the streetlight turns on, making it appear darker around us.

I look up into the yellow glow, composing a wish along the lines of "star light, star bright." "Oh, electric gods of the tristate area, I'm just wishing for a real, honest-to-goodness job with set hours and an office where the boss's underwear isn't drying in the bathroom. Someday I'd like to be able to help more than one child at a time— children who don't come accessorized with their own consultants. Thank you. Amen."

◇ ◇ ◇

The subway car is suddenly flooded with sunlight as we surface high over the streets of the South Bronx. I feel that twinge of excitement I always do when a train car moves aboveground, flying over the city on its skinny rails like an amusement-park ride.

I pull my lesson plan out of my backpack and stare at it for the millionth time. The opportunity to join a conflict-resolution team for city schools is exactly the kind of job I've been training for. Plus, it would be good to work with teenagers and take a break from the tiny folk.

The train pulls to a stop and I step out into the cold sunshine. I make my way down the steps of the platform to the street and discover that I am not four blocks away from my interview, but fourteen. I must have misunderstood the woman on the phone. I check my watch, picking up the pace. I was too nervous this morning to have breakfast, but the ninety-minute trek has revived my appetite. I walk/run down the long streets, knowing I should eat or risk passing out mid-lesson.

Fully out of breath, I run into a tiny newspaper stand, grab a bag of peanuts, and stuff them in my backpack. One door down I ring the buzzer next to a taped piece of hand-colored paper that reads "Communities Against Conflict."

A voice blares unintelligibly out through the static and the door clicks, letting me into a stairwell, once painted green, and lined with posters of children in playgrounds looking gravely into the camera. I examine each print as I climb the stairs and, judging by the haircuts and bell-bottoms, guess these are promo posters circa the early seventies, around the time that this organization was founded. I buzz again at the top step and am greeted by loud barking, before a large hand pulls the door slightly ajar.

"Snowflake, stay! STAY!"

"I'm here for the interview?" I say, looking around for another door, assuming I've mistakenly interrupted a resident in the building. A pale woman's face appears in the crack.

"Yeah, Communities Against Conflict. You're in the right place, come on in, just be careful of Snowflake; he's always trying to free himself."

I shimmy through the small opening she's made in the door and practically come face-to-face with a humongous black shepherd and the rest of an equally large woman in overalls and waist-length, graying blond hair. I smile, bending down to pet Snowflake, who is trying to get past her widely planted legs.

"NO!" she screams.

I jolt up.

"He's not really a people person. Are you, Snowflake?" She pats the dog gruffly on his head with her free hand, as the other holds a stack of manila folders. Having adequately warned me, she lets Snowflake check me out while I stay perfectly still.

"I'm Reena, the executive director of Communities. You are?" She fixes me with an intense stare. I try to get a read on her, attempting to figure out who she would like me to be.

"Nan. I think I was supposed to meet with Richard." I aim for solid and warm, without a hint of cheerful.

"Nan? I thought your name was Naminia. Shit. RICHARD!" Reena bellows at me and I almost duck. She turns back to her files. "He'll be here in a minute. RICHARD!" she screams again, this time into the filing cabinet.

"Okay! I'll just have a seat." I try to demonstrate that I am someone who can take care of herself, as I sense independence is of value here. I turn around to discover that the two chairs designated to the few feet serving as a waiting area are both piled with overflowing boxes of yellowing brochures. I opt for standing by the wall and getting out of Reena's way, as this seems to be a Communities value, as well.

A door flies open at the far side of the room and a man with a pasty complexion, who looks related to Reena and whom I presume to be Richard, emerges. He squints at me in his glasses, breathing heavily with the effort of getting around her and the dog to greet me. He is sweating profusely and has a wilted cigarette stuck behind his ear.

"Naminia!"

"Nan," Reena grunts over a file.

"Oh, Nan . . . I'm Richard, the artistic director. Well, I see you've met Reena and Snowflake. Why don't we get right to it! Let's go into the Feelings Room and get you set up." He shakes my hand and exchanges glances with Reena.

I follow him to the Feelings Room, which is about the same size as the office, but without all the desks.

"So have a seat there, Nan." I do, ready to tell my whole, wonderful story. Ready to knock 'em dead.

"Now let me tell you about myself . . ." Richard begins. He leans back in the plastic folding chair and proceeds to explain about his decades spent in social work, how he met up with Reena at a rally against the superintendent, their years traveling the globe to gather methodologies for conflict resolution, and the host of "virtually thousands of kids" that he has personally trained to "make the world a better place." He also goes on extensively about his misguided childhood, the "illegitimate" son who doesn't call him anymore, and his recent attempts to quit smoking. I zone in and out, keeping a beaming smile on my face and developing a fixation on the peanuts in my bag.

About an hour later he finally says, "So I see here that you are minoring in gender studies, what does that mean?"

He scans the résumé I faxed in, squinting to read the blurred print. I follow his gaze to the top of the page to discover that I am "Naminia of 4ish East 90 something Street." Ahh, Naminia.

"Well, I'm in the home stretch of a major in child development and I was very interested in supplementing this work—"

"So you're not a feminist bitch, then?" He has a good, hearty laugh, taking a Kleenex out of his pocket and wiping down his forehead.

I attempt a weak laugh. "As I was saying, I've been completing my thesis with Professor Clarkson and have been interning this semester at an after-school program in Brooklyn—"

"Right. So let's get you up and running! Let me grab Reena and we'll get started with your session." He stands. "REEENA!" Loud barking ensues in the other room.

I pull my lesson plan out of my backpack while Snowflake bursts in, followed by Reena. I walk to the other side of the room and write my notes on the rolling blackboard.

I take a deep breath. "I have prepared a session on peer pressure for fourteen-year-olds in grade nine. As you'll see on the board here

I have written these key terms. I would begin by asking the group to work together to construct—"

"Teacher! Teacher!" Richard is waving wildly from the back of the room.

"I'm sorry, are you not ready for me to start?" I ask, unsure of what is happening.

He balls up a piece of paper and throws it at Reena, who starts to mock cry.

"Teacher! Reena said a bad word!" Reena continues to boo-hoo, causing Snowflake to circle her, barking.

"I'm sorry, Richard, it was my understanding that we were just doing an overview." But they are in their own world, throwing paper at each other and fake crying.

I clear my throat. "Okay, the session you asked me to prepare was for teenagers, um, but I can modify it for preschoolers." I glance at my notes and frantically try to downscale the plan for a different age group. I turn back to face two huge adults and one huge dog, hiding behind chairs and launching paper.

"Um, excuse me? Excuse me? OKAY, CLASS!" I say loudly, giving sway to my frustration. They turn back to me.

Reena stands up, breaking character. "How are you feeling right now, Nan?"

"Sorry?" I ask.

Richard gets out his notebook. "How do you feel about us in this moment? What does your gut say?" They look at me expectantly.

"Well, I think perhaps I misunderstood the directives—"

"Shit, Nan. Do you have rage in there? Do you hate us? We are just not feeling the love. I want to hear it from you. How is your relationship with your mother?"

"Reena, frankly I'm unclear how this relates to my abilities to—"

Reena puts her hands on her large hips and Snowflake circles her heels. "We're a family here. There are no boundaries in the Feelings Room. You've got to come in here with trust and love and just go for it. Here's the thing, Nan. We're really not looking to hire white women right now."

She is so comfortable with this statement that I'm tempted to ask how many openings they have for white, feminist bitches. Even more bizarre, why a person of color might have a better time discussing their maternal issues with complete strangers. White strangers, nonetheless.

Richard stands, soaked with sweat and coughing a smoker's cough. "We have just gotten way too many résumés from white girls. You don't speak Korean, do you?" I shake my head, speechless.

"Nan, we're trying to model diversity here, to represent an ideal community. SNOWFLAKE, HEEL!" Snowflake wanders back from where he has been sniffing around my bag. He passes me with his head down, swallowing the last of my peanuts.

I look at both of their very white faces against the backdrop of bright rainbows painted on the peeling wall behind them. "Well, thank you for the opportunity, you have a very interesting organization here." I quickly gather my things.

They walk me to the door. "Yeah, maybe next semester, we'll be doing some fund-raising work on the East Side. Would you be interested in that?" I picture introducing Reena to Mrs. X at the Met so she can ask her about her rage.

"I'm really looking for fieldwork right now. Thanks, though." I get out the door and go directly to Burger King for an extra large fries and a Coke. Folded into an immobile red seat I sigh deeply, comparing Reena and Richard with Jane and Mrs. X. Somewhere out there must be people who believe in a middle ground between *demanding* children to "feel their rage" and overprogramming children so everyone can pretend they don't have any. I take a long sip of my soda. Apparently, I'm not going to be finding it anytime soon.

◇ ◇ ◇

"See, if I have two jellybeans and you have one jellybean, together we have three jellybeans!" I hold out the jellybeans to make my point.

"I like the white ones and the ones that taste like banana. How do they do that, Nanny? How do they make it taste like banana?" Grayer lines up the colored candy like railroad tracks on his bedroom carpet.

"I dunno, G. Maybe they mush up a banana and they mush up the jelly and then they mush it all together and cook it in a bean shape?"

"Yeah! A bean shape!" So much for math. "Nanny, try this one!" Yesterday's peony arrangement came with a Grayer-size tin of jellybeans.

"How about the green ones? How do they make those—" We both hear the door slam. Only three hours late, not bad.

"DADDY!!" He runs out of the room and I follow into the hall.

"Hey, sport. Where's your mother?" He pats Grayer on the head while loosening his tie.

"Here I am," she says and we all turn. She is wearing a powder-blue pencil skirt, kitten heels, a cashmere V-neck sweater, eye shadow, mascara, and blush. Va-voom. If this were the first time my husband had been home in three weeks, I'd get dolled up, too. She smiles shakily beneath her rose lipstick.

"Well, let's get this started," he says, barely glancing at her before heading to the living room where Jane left her charts and diagrams. Grayer and his mother scamper in behind Mr. X and I am left behind in the front hall. I take a seat on the bench, resuming my role as lady-in-waiting.

"Darling," Mrs. X begins with a bit too much enthusiasm. "Shall I have Connie get you a drink? Or perhaps some coffee? CONNIE!" I jump about three feet and Connie comes flying out of the kitchen, her hands still wet.

"Jesus, do you have to be so shrill? No. I just ate," Mr. X says.

Connie stops just short of entering the room. We exchange glances and I make room for her on the bench.

"Oh. Oh, all right. So, Grayer, Mommy and Daddy want to talk to you about where you're going to school next year." Mrs. X attempts a second opening.

"I'm going to Collegiate," Grayer offers, trying to be helpful.

"No, sweetie. Mommy and Daddy have decided that you are going to St. Bernard's."

"Burnurd?" he asks. There is a moment of silence. "Can we play trains now? Daddy, I got a new train, it's red."

"So, sweetie. You can't wear the blue sweatshirt anymore, okay?" she says. Connie rolls her eyes at me.

"Why?"

"Because it says Collegiate on it and you're going to St. Bernard's—" Mr. X says with exasperation.

"But I like it."

"Yes, sweetie. We'll get you a St. Bernard's sweatshirt."

"I like the blue one!"

I lean in and whisper to Connie. "Oh, for the love of God, let him wear it inside out. Who cares?" She throws her hands up.

Mrs. X clears her throat. "Okay, sweetie. We'll talk about this later." Connie disappears back into the kitchen.

"Daddy, come see my trains! I'll show you the new one. It's red and really, really fast!" Grayer flies past me toward his room.

"That was a complete waste of time. He clearly could care less," Mr. X says.

"Well, Jane felt it was important—" she retorts defensively.

"Who the hell is Jane?" he asks. "Look, do you have the slightest idea of what it means to be in the middle of a merger? I don't have time for this—"

"I'm sorry, but—"

"Do I have to be on top of everything?" he growls. "The one thing I delegated to you was his schooling and now it's all fucked up."

"It was a very competitive year!" she cries. "Grayer doesn't play the violin!"

"What the fuck does the violin have to do with anything?"

"Maybe if you'd spend an hour of your precious time with us he might have done better in his interviews," she spits back.

"My precious time? My *precious time?* I am bashing my brains out eighty hours a week so you can stand there in your pearls, with your eight-thousand-dollar curtains and your 'charity work,' and question how I spend my time?! Who's going to pay his tuition bills, huh? You?"

"Honey." She softens. "I know you're under a lot of pressure. Look, since you're already home, why don't we talk about it over a nice relaxing dinner? I made a reservation at that place you love, down by the river." Her kitten heels make little clicks as she walks over to him. Her voice drops. "We could get a room at the Pierre, maybe the one with the double Jacuzzi bath . . . I've really missed you."

It's quiet for a minute and then I distinctly hear the sound of them kissing. Their low laughter drifts into the hallway.

I'm just about to sneak off to Grayer's room when Mrs. X coos, "Should I send a donation to St. Bernard's with the tuition check, so we get off on the right foot with them?"

"The right foot?" He's again indignant. "Correct me if I'm wrong, but haven't they already accepted him—"

"But if we have another boy—"

"Look, I've got to get back to the office. The car's waiting downstairs. I'll call you later." Mr. X swiftly passes me, still wearing the overcoat he presumably never took off. The door slams loudly behind him.

"Daddy? WAIT!!!!" Grayer comes running out with his red train. "DADDY!!!" He throws himself, screaming, against the front door.

Mrs. X walks slowly into the hall and stands for a moment, glaring through Grayer at the front door until her eyes glaze over, then walks right past both of us to her bedroom.

"DADDY!!!" He convulses with sobs, bending over, while holding tightly onto the doorknob. "I WANT *DADDY!!!*" I sit down on the floor and reach out to hold him. He drops his head between his dangling arms and away from me. "NOOOoooo. I want my DADDY!!!" We hear the elevator door slide closed. *"DON'T LEAVE!!!!"*

"Ssshhh, I know." I circle my arms to pull him onto my lap. "I know, Grove." We sit on the floor as his tears make a dark, wet spot on the knee of my jeans. I rub his back and murmur, "It's okay, Grove. Shhh, it's okay to be sad. We'll just sit here and be sad for a little while."

"Okay," he says into my pant leg.

"Okay."

PART THREE

Spring

Mammy had her own method of letting her owners know exactly where she stood on all matters. She knew it was beneath the dignity of quality white folks to pay the slightest attention to what a darky said, even when she was just grumbling to herself. She knew that to uphold this dignity, they must ignore what she said, even if she stood in the next room and almost shouted.

—GONE WITH THE WIND

CHAPTER EIGHT

Frosting on the Cake

Connie,
Rather than ironing Grayer's sheets today, I'd like you to pack the following items for Mr. X:
his suits
shirts
ties
underwear
socks
And anything else he uses. These items should be packed and down with the doorman by three o'clock. Please see that you only use his luggage (see monogram).

"Nanny, have you seen Grayer's bow tie? I put it out last night." Mrs. X and Grayer are due at the April Tea for New St. Bernard's Families in twenty minutes. Mrs. X is rummaging through Grayer's drawers while I try to wrestle him into an ultrastarched oxford, complete with stays in the collar, and Connie, I assume, is somewhere in Mr. X's closet filling his monogrammed luggage.

"I need an elephant," Grayer says, pointing to the sketch pad on his diminutive table.

"One second, Grayer," I say, "Let me buckle your belt—"

"No, not that one." She sticks her head out from Grayer's walk-in closet.

"That's the one you put out." I add, "On the bed. Sorry."

"It doesn't go."

Kneeling down in front of him, I look him over—blue pin-striped shirt, khaki pants, white socks, brown belt. I don't see the problem, but I unbuckle him.

"Here," she says, handing me a green and red striped canvas belt. I point down at the belt buckle. "See, G for Grayer."

"G?" he asks, looking down. "I need my card." I reach for the bus-pass holder on the dresser, which contains the vestiges of Mr. X's business card.

"No," she says, emerging from the closet. "Not today. It's like the interviews. Remember the interviews? No card."

"I want my card!"

"You can keep it in your pocket like a secret agent," I say, tucking it out of sight.

"I still can't find his f-ing bow tie."

"Nanny, I *need* an elephant." I pick up a gray crayon and draw an amorphous blob with big ears and a trunk, the extent of my artistic expertise. She starts throwing ties out of the closet.

"I want to wear my tie," he says, referring to the one that hangs to the floor.

"No. *Not today.*" She goes storming out into the entrance hall where I can hear her voice echo off the marble. "CONNIE! CONNIE!"

"Yes, ma'am?" Grayer is quiet, I keep my crayon in motion.

"I have just spent half an hour looking for Grayer's bow tie. Do you happen to know where it is?"

"No, ma'am."

"Is it too much to ask that you keep track of Grayer's clothes? Do I have to be on top of everything? The one thing I delegate to you—" She sighs heavily and then there's a moment of silence. "Why are you standing there? Go look for it!"

"I'm sorry, I just don't know where it could be, ma'am. I put it in his room with the other ones."

"Well, it's not there. And this is the second time that a piece of Grayer's clothing has gone missing this month. Now, if you're feeling that this is all too much responsibility for you, I'm sure we can rethink your role here."

"No, ma'am. I'll look for it. It's just that the clothes need to be packed by three and it's two-thirty now. If Mr. X needs them—"

"Are you questioning who you work for? *You* work for *me*. And *I* am telling you to look for the tie. And if this confuses you, please let me know. Because, as far as I can recall, I am the one who pays you!"

I stand up shakily and start going through Grayer's closet myself. He comes and stands beside me, leaning his head against my hip. Connie joins us in Grayer's room, pulling the closet door further open.

"Connie, I'll look here," I say softly. "You take the laundry room."

As she crosses back through the front hall Mrs. X continues. "We could call Mr. X and see which he gives more of a shit about, whether his clothes get packed or whether his son has the right fucking tie to wear to his new school! Maybe he'll talk to you. Maybe he'll take your call, Connie."

"I'm sorry, ma'am." Five minutes of thorough, breathless searching uncovers nothing.

"Anything?" Mrs. X's face appears where she has lifted the dust ruffle.

"No, sorry," I say from under Grayer's bed.

"Goddammit! Grayer, come on, we have to go. Just put him in the one with the green polka dots." I slide out on my stomach.

"I want my daddy's tie!" He tries to reach for the peg where his father's tie hangs.

"No, G. You can wear it later." I gently pull his hand away, trying to motivate him toward the door.

"I want it now!" He starts to sob, red blotches appearing on his face.

"Shh, please, Grove?" I kiss his damp cheek and he stands still, tears making their way down into the starched collar. I straighten the knot and go to take him in my arms, but he pushes me away.

"No!" And he runs out of the room.

"Nanny?" Mrs. X calls, shrilly.

"Yes?" I walk to the hall.

"We'll be back at four in time for ice skating. Connie?" She shakes her head as Connie emerges from the laundry room, as if she is simply too disgusted and disappointed to speak. "I just don't know what to say. It seems to me we are having these sorts of problems on a regular basis now and I need you to do some serious thinking about your commitment level to this job—"

Mrs. X's cell phone emits a sharp ring.

"Hello?" she answers while motioning for me to help her on with her mink. "Oh, hi, Justine . . . Yes, they'll be down by three . . . Yes, you can tell him she's packed everything . . ." She walks away from us into the vestibule. "Oh, Justine? Could you see that I get his room number at the Yale Club? . . . In case Grayer has an emergency and I need to get a hold of him . . . Well, why would I call *you*?" She takes a deep breath. "Well, I'm glad you see that doesn't make any sense . . . Frankly, I don't want your apology. What I want is my husband's phone number . . . I refuse to discuss this with you!" She slams her cell phone closed with such force that it drops to the marble floor.

Both women kneel to grab the phone just as the elevator door opens, but Mrs. X gets there first. With a shaking hand she picks it up and drops it into her clutch. She puts her other hand to the floor to steady herself, her icy blue eyes even with Connie's brown ones. "We seem to be unable to communicate, Connie," she hisses through clenched teeth. "So let me be crystal clear. *I* want *you* to gather *your* things and get out of *my* house. I want *you* out of *my* house. That's what *I* want."

She stands with a shake of her mink and pushes a stunned Grayer into the elevator as the door closes.

Connie pulls herself up by the foyer table and walks past me back into the apartment.

I take a moment to collect myself before slowly shutting the front door.

I walk through the kitchen and find Connie standing with her back to me in the maid's room, her broad shoulders quivering in the small space. "God, Connie. Are you okay?" I ask quietly in the doorway.

She turns to me—her pain and outrage so rawly palpable on her face that I'm struck silent. She slumps down on the old tweed fold-out couch and undoes the top button of her white uniform.

"I've been here twelve years," she says, shaking her head. "I was here before her and I thought I'd be here after."

"Do you want something to drink?" I ask, stepping into the narrow gap between the couch and the ironing board. "Some juice maybe? I could try to get into the liquor cabinet."

"*She* wants *me* to leave? *She* wants *me* to leave?" I sit down on Mrs. X's steamer trunk. "I've wanted to leave since the first day she got here," she snorts, reaching for a half-ironed T-shirt and wiping her eyes. "Let me tell you something—when they went to Lyford whatever—I didn't get paid. I *never* get paid when they go away. Not my fault they're on vacation. I'm not on vacation. I still have three kids and plenty of bills to pay. And this year—this year—she asked him to declare me! They never declare me! Where am I supposed to come up with that kind of money now? I had to borrow money from my mother to pay all these taxes." She sits back and pulls off her apron. "When Mrs. X and Grayer flew to the Bahamas last year and I was going there too to see my family, she made me fly with them. Grayer spilled juice all over hisself at takeoff and she didn't have a change for him and he's sitting there cold and wet and crying and she just pull on that sleep thing over her eyes and ignore him the whole flight. And I didn't get paid for that! Oh, was I mad—that's why I'm not a nanny. You ever hear about Jackie?" I shake my head. "Jackie was his baby nurse, but she stayed till Grayer was two."

"What happened to her?"

"Well, she got a boyfriend. That's what happened to her." I look at her quizzically. "For two years she just worked, she'd only been here maybe a few years and didn't have too many friends. So she practically lived here and she and Mrs. X got on okay. I think they got together about Mr. X traveling and Jackie dating no one special— you know, man troubles. But then Jackie met someone—he looked like Bob Marley—and now she can't work Friday nights and she don't like to work the weekend if the Xes don't be in Connecticut. So Mrs. X starts in with how inconvenienced she is. But really, she jealous. Jackie had that glow, you know. She had that look about her and Mrs. X couldn't stand it. So she fired her. Nearly broke Grayer's heart. After that—he was like a little devil child."

"Wow." I take a deep breath.

"Oh, you ain't heard the bad part. Jackie called me six months later. She couldn't get a new job because Mrs. X wouldn't give her a reference. You know, no reference, they think Jackie stole or something. So she got two years missing on her résumé. And the agency didn't want to send her out no more." She stands up and wipes her hands slowly down her skirt. "That woman is pure evil. They have six nannies in four months before Caitlin—no one stayed. And one got fired for giving him a corn muffin in the park. Don't you never feed him if you want to keep your job, you hear? And Mr. X—keeps porn in his shoe closet, the naaasty kind."

I'm trying to take this all in. "Connie, I'm so sorry."

"Don't you be sorry for me." She tosses the crumpled t-shirt onto the couch and marches with purpose into the kitchen. "You just watch out for yourself." I follow her.

She opens one of the empty Delft cookie jars on the counter and pulls out a handful of black lace, slamming it down on the table in front of me.

PANTIES!

"And I found these under the bed—"

"Right under the bed?" I can't help asking.

She tilts her head down at me. "Mm-hm. Now he's got the other one running all around here, acting like she owns the place. It took me two days to get the stink of her perfume out of here before Mrs. X got back."

"Should somebody tell her? Do you think somebody should tell Mrs. X about this woman?" I ask, dizzy with relief at finally being able to consult a colleague.

"Now, you listen here. Ain't you been here for the last hour? It's not my problem. And don't you make it your problem, either. It's none of our business. Now you better pack up Mr. X's things—I gotta get out of here." She reaches around and unties her apron, dropping it onto the counter.

"So, what are you gonna do?"

"Oh, my sister, she works up the block, she always knows people who are lookin' for housekeepers and whatnot. I'll find something. It'll be less money, if that's possible. But I'll find something. I always do."

She walks into the maid's room to collect her things, leaving me staring down at the black silk thong, screaming like profane graffiti against the peach marble table.

✧ ✧ ✧

Nanny,

Today you have a play date with Carter after tennis. Please be there by three. The Miltons live at 10 East 67th Street and I think you'll be staying for supper. I'm having dinner at Bolo.

I still can't find Grayer's bow tie. Did you take it home? Please check.

Thanks

Grayer is still crying when we *finally* get a cab. While I'm not allowed to walk him down doormanless side streets, his after-school activities routinely maroon us in desolate, cabless neighborhoods where any minute I'll be forced to choose between Grayer or my life. I haul him into the taxi, throw the tennis racket in after him, and pull the rest of the equipment in with me.

"Sixty-seventh and Madison, please." I look at Grove. "How's your head? Any better?"

"It's okay." He slows down to a whimper, but it sounds like a whimper with staying power. He was looking the wrong way when the pro turned on the ball feeder.

"How about golf, G? I think we should try golf. Smaller balls, less damage." He looks up at me with wet eyes. "Come here." He leans across the seat and puts his head in my lap. I run my fingers through his hair and play with his ears just like my mom used to do. The motion of the car soothes him and before we even reach Midtown he's asleep. He must be wiped. What a different life we'd all be living if he was only allowed to nap.

I pull back my raincoat sleeve to look at my watch. What will an extra fifteen minutes matter?

"Driver? Can you make a loop up to 110 and then back down the West Side and across the Sixty-eighth Street transverse?"

"Sure, lady. Whatever you say." I look out the window at the gray sky and pull my coat closer around me as round raindrops hit the windshield, still waiting for April showers to feel like they could lead to May flowers.

"Grover, wake up. We're here." He's a little groggy and wiping his eyes when I press the town house's doorbell, the racket slung over my shoulder.

"Hello?" an English voice says from the intercom.

"Hi! It's Nanny and Grayer." There's no reply. I reach over and press the talk button again. "We have a play date with Carter."

"Really?" There's a pause. "Well, come on up, then." The buzzer sounds and I push the heavy glass door open, while Grayer stumbles ahead of me into the marble entrance foyer. Past the grand staircase, at the back of house, is a solarium, whose long windows reveal a garden. Raindrops steadily fill the stone fountain.

"Hello?" a young voice asks. I look up from where I'm wrestling Grayer's coat zipper. A little boy Grayer's age with blond, curly hair is standing on the landing, his hand looped through the banister, leaning away on a diagonal. "Hi. I'm Carter." I've never seen this boy before and realize Grayer hasn't, either.

"I'm Grayer."

"Hello?" The same English voice calls down the stairs. "Just leave your gear anywhere and come on up." I throw our wet coats on the floor and drop our gear beside it.

"Go ahead, G." He runs up after Carter. I begin my ascent; on the first floor I pass a Venetian living room at the front of the house and a Deco dining room at the back. As I reach the second floor, featuring the Empire master bedroom and a man's study done in the African vein, lots of antelope heads and a zebra-skin rug, I'm audibly panting. I chug up to the third level, which has a large mural of Winnie-the-Pooh painted on the landing, and I'm guessing it is Carter's floor.

"Keep going!" I hear encouragement being shouted from above.

"You're almost there, Nanny! Lazy!"

"Thanks, G!" I call up. I finally drag myself, sweating, to the fourth floor, which has been opened up into a large family room cum kitchen.

"Hi, I'm Lizzie. Stairs a bit much, eh? Want some water?"

"That would be lovely. I'm Nanny." I extend the hand that isn't clutching my abdomen. She's maybe a few years older than me, wearing a gray flannel skirt, sky-blue oxford shirt, and a navy cardigan tied around her shoulders. I recognize her as part of the community of high-class British imports who regard this as a noble profession, requiring training and certification, and they dress accordingly. The boys have already run off to the corner, where a village of plastic Playskool houses are set up, to play what sounds like Sack the Serfs.

"Here." Lizzie hands me the water. "I thought we'd just let them blow off steam for an hour and then plunk them in front of *The J-u-n-g-l-e B-o-o-k*."

"Sounds great."

"I don't know what I'm going to do when Carter learns how to spell. Learn sign language, I guess."

I stare at the rococo kitchen cabinets, the distressed French tiles, the egg and dart moldings. "This is an amazing house. Do you live in?"

"I have a little flat on the top floor." I look over at the stairs and realize that, yes, there is another floor.

"You must be in amazing shape."

"Try doing it with a knackered four-year-old in your arms."

I laugh. "I've never met Carter before. Where does he go to school?"

"Country Day," she says, taking my empty glass.

"Oh, I used to look after the Gleason girls—they went there. It's a nice place."

"Yeah—Carter, get off him!" I look over just as Grayer is released from a death grip.

"Wow, Carter, how'd you do that? Show me, show me!" Grayer's eyes are alight at the discovery.

"Oh, great," I say. "Now he'll be leaping out to put me in a choke hold."

"A swift kick to the groin and they're down in no time," she says, winking at me. Where has she been this whole year? I could have had a playground buddy. "Hey, you want to see the terrace?"

"Sure." I follow her out to a stone balcony overlooking the garden and the back of the brownstones on the other side of the block. We stand under the awning as the rain splatters the tips of our shoes.

"It's beautiful," I say, my breath coming in little puffs of vapor. "It's a real nineteenth-century enclave."

She nods. "Cigarette?" she asks.

"You can smoke?"

"Sure."

"Carter's mom doesn't mind?"

"Please." I take one.

"So, how long have you been working here?" I ask as she strikes the match.

"About a year. It's a little nuts, but compared to the other jobs I've had. . . . I mean, when you live in, you know." She shakes her head, blowing smoke into the drizzle. "They run your life while you live in a closet off the kitchen. At least here I've got a great space. Those round windows?" She points with her cigarette. "That's my bedroom and that, there, is my sitting room. And my bath has a Jacuzzi. It was meant to be a guest suite, but, well, guests are a little out of the question."

"Wow. Not a bad deal."

"Well, it's full-time duty."

"Are they nice?"

She starts laughing. "I guess he's not bad—he's never really around, which makes her a bit off her rocker. That's why they needed a live-in—"

"Yoo-hoo! Lizzie! Are you out there?" I freeze, trying not to exhale, a tiny trail of smoke escaping from my nostrils.

"Yeah, Mrs. Milton. We're outside." She casually stubs out her cigarette on the balustrade and throws it into the garden. I shrug and follow suit.

"There you are!" she says as we come back into the kitchen. Mrs. Milton, a Matel blonde, sits on the floor in a peach-silk robe, sniffing and delicately wiping her nose, while the boys run around her. "Now, who's this?" Her voice has a slight Southern lilt.

"That's Grayer," Lizzie says.

"And I'm Nanny." I extend my hand.

"Oh, Grayer! Grayer, I saw your momma at Swifty's. Well, every time we're at Lotte Berk we keep saying we have to get our boys together. And then there she was having lunch and we said, well, we just have to make a plan, and here you are! Grayer!" She picks him up and holds him upside down, in fluffy mules, no less. Grayer seems to be trying to make eye contact with me, clearly uncertain how to respond to this outpouring of affection. She puts him down. "Lizzie! Lizzie, darlin', don't you have a date tonight?"

"Yeah, but—"

"Shouldn't you be getting ready?"

"It's only four."

"Nonsense. Go relax. I want to spend some time with my Carter. Besides, Nanny can help me." She hunkers down. "Hey, boys, you wanna make a cake? We have cake mix, right, Lizzie?"

"Always."

"Great!" Her silk robe billows out behind her as she crosses to the kitchen, revealing long, tanned, and very naked legs. I realize as she turns that she is completely au naturel beneath her robe. "Now, let's see . . . eggs . . . milk." She pulls everything out and sets it on the counter. "Lizzie, where are the pans?"

"In the drawer under the oven." She grabs my wrist and whispers, "Don't let her burn herself." Before I have chance to ask if and why this is likely she's run upstairs to her room.

"I like chocolate cake," Grayer says, casting his vote.

"We only have vanilla, sugar." Mrs. Milton holds up the red box.

"I like vanilla," says Carter.

"At my birthday," Grayer continues, "I had a cake. It looked like a football and it was reallyreally big!"

"Woohoo! Let's have some music." She pushes a button on the Bang & Olufsen stereo above the counter and Donna Summer comes blaring out. "Come on, sugar pie. Come and dance with Momma." Carter shakes his arms and bobs his knees. Grayer starts off slowly with a head wiggle, but by "On the Radio" he lets the jazz hands fly.

"Lookin' good, boys!" She takes a hand of each and the three of them bounce through all of Donna Summer's Greatest Hits right up through "She Works Hard for the Money," while I quietly start cracking eggs and greasing the pan. I put the cake in the oven and turn around in search of an oven timer, to see Mrs. Milton twirling near the Playskool village. I have a Miss Clavel feeling.

"I'm just going to go use the powder room," I say to no one in particular. I open every door off the pantry, attempting to locate a bathroom.

Turning on the light in a small room, I discover four man-nequins in a **V** configuration wearing sequined gowns, each with a banner across her middle. Miss Tucson. Miss Arizona. Miss Southwest. Miss Southern States. There are tiaras and scepters, framed news clippings and a baton, all carefully displayed in glass cases.

I slowly inspect every dress, each sash, and then go over to the far wall, which is covered in glossy, framed photographs of Mrs. Milton—the Vegas showgirl. Which, I guess, is where you go after being Miss Southern States. There is row after row of photographs of her in various sequined costumes and headdresses, wearing thick makeup and false lashes. In each she's sitting on some celebrity's lap, everyone from Tony Bennett to Rod Stewart. And then I see it, halfway down the wall, almost hidden, a snapshot of Mrs. Milton in a short, skintight white dress, Mr. Milton, his eyes rolled back in his head, and the preacher. The caption on the frame reads, "The All-Night Chapel of Love, August 12, 199-."

I turn out the light and find the bathroom.

When I come back out Mrs. Milton is peering forlornly in the oven.

"You did it."

"Yes, ma'am." I just said "ma'am."

"You did it." She seems to be having trouble absorbing the information.

"It's almost done," I offer reassuringly.

"Oh, goodie! Who wants frosting?" She pulls six tubs of different-flavored frosting out of the fridge. "Carter, get the food dye." Grayer and Carter mambo over. She grabs sprinkles, silver balls, and candy confetti from the cupboards and starts squirting the food dye Carter hands her directly into the tubs. "Ooohwee!" She's laughing uncontrollably now.

"Mrs. Milton," I say, standing back with apprehension, "I think it's time for Grayer and me to go."

"Tina!"

"I beg your pardon?"

"Call me Tina! You can't leave," she calls over her shoulder as she scoops a fingerful of frosting into her mouth.

"I DON'T WANT TO GO HOME!" Grayer panics, his fists tightly clenching a bouquet of plastic spoons.

"See, nobody has to leave. Now, who . . . wants . . . frosting?" She reaches into two of the containers, pulling out two handfuls of frosting and catapulting them, one at Carter, one at Grayer. "Frosting fight!" She hands a tub to each boy and the frosting starts flying. I try to duck behind the island, but Tina hits me squarely across the chest. I haven't been in a food fight since middle school, but I grab a tub of pink and fling a small handful at her—just paying her back for the sweater—and then I'm out.

"Ooh-hah!" They are laughing hysterically. The boys roll on the floor, mushing frosting in each other's hair. Tina grabs some silver balls and sprinkles them over the boys like snow.

"What's going on down there?" Lizzie's stern English voice calls from upstairs.

"Ooh, we're in trouble," she says. "Carter, I think we're in trouble." They all crack up again. Lizzie comes into the kitchen in her terry bathrobe and slippers.

"Oh, my God." She looks around. There is frosting everywhere, dripping off the French tiles and the topiaries lining the window.

"Oh, Lizzie, we were just having fun. Loosen up! Don't be so British."

"Tina!" Lizzie uses my Wicked Witch voice. "Go get in the tub!" Tina looks crestfallen and starts to cry, sinking in her robe and revealing a bit too much of her impressive superstructure.

"But I . . . We were . . . We were just having fun. Please don't tell John. You had fun, didn't you, boys?"

"I had fun. Don't be sad." Grayer gently touches her head, patting bits of pink frosting into her blonde hair.

Tina looks at Lizzie and wipes her nose on her sleeve. "Okay, okay." She hunkers in front of the boys. "Mommy's gonna go take a bath, okay?" She pats each one on the head and then walks over to the banister. "You come back real soon, Grayer, you hear?" she murmurs to herself as she disappears down the stairs.

"Good-bye, Tina!" Grayer shouts. And with a little backward wave she's gone. I wait for Carter to protest, but he's quiet. We strip the boys and Lizzie gives me a pair of Carter's pajamas and a plastic bag for Grayer's clothes. We put on *The Jungle Book* and try to clean up the kitchen.

"Dammit," Lizzie says, scrubbing on her hands and knees. "Mr. Milton might come home tonight and if he sees this he'll send her back to Hazelden and it's terrible for Carter, her disappearing for weeks at a time when his father travels so much. It absolutely devastates him." Lizzie wrings out the sponge. "He asked me to go with her—to Hazelden. So I could, you know, figure out when she would use again and intervene."

"What's she on?" I ask, though I already have a pretty good idea.

"Coke. Alcohol. Prescription stuff when she can't sleep."

"How long has this been going on for?"

"Oh, years," she says, squeezing out her sponge into the bucket. "I think since she came to New York. She fell in with some really posh junkies, celebrities and the like. He leaves her alone here all the time, so it's hard for her. But there's no prenup, so I guess he's just waiting for her to OD." Well, this certainly puts panties in perspective. "I know I should quit, but my visa extension is attached to this job. If I leave Carter it means going home and I really want to stay in America." I just wring out my sponge, not knowing what to say. "Here, why don't you guys push off? I'll finish this."

"You sure?"

"Oh, yeah. Tomorrow it'll be something else."

Grayer and Carter are loath to be parted, but we manage to get all the way downstairs and out the door.

"Good-bye, Carter!" he shouts as I hail a cab. "Good-bye, Tina!" Since we're only going four blocks it seems ridiculous, but in addition to everything I was carrying before, I'm now sporting a plastic bag of Grayer's clothes and my raincoat in a shopping bag so my sweater doesn't shed sprinkles on it.

"What happened to you all?" James asks as he helps us out of the taxi.

"We got in a food fight with Tina," Grayer explains as he pads ahead of me in Carter's Tigger pajamas.

Upstairs I turn on the bathwater and put some tofu dogs on the stove while Grover plays in his room. "Hello?" a strange voice calls from the maid's room.

"Hello?"

A woman I've never seen before emerges from the darkness, wearing Connie's uniform.

"Hello, I'm Maria," she says in a South American accent. "I was waiting for Mrs. X and must have fallen asleep. I didn't want to just leave on my first day without saying good-bye."

"Oh . . . hi. Hi, I'm Nanny. I take care of Grayer." I introduce myself for the third time today. "Actually, Mrs. X is out to dinner and probably won't be back till late. You go on home and I'll tell her you waited when she gets back."

"Oh, great. Thanks."

"Who are you?" Grover stands blocking the doorway in his briefs.

"Grayer, this is Maria." Grayer sticks his tongue out, turns and runs back to his room. "*Grayer.*" I turn back to her to apologize. "I'm sorry. Please don't take it personally. He's had a really long day." I gesture to my buttercream sodden self with a half-smile. "Actually I was just gonna go give him his bath. Really, it's okay to leave. Not to worry."

"Thanks," she says, folding her coat over her arm.

"No problem. See you tomorrow." I smile at her. I walk through the apartment, turning on lamps Connie cleaned only two days ago.

I go into Grayer's room, where he's still dancing in his underwear in front of his closet mirror. "Come on, Baryshnikov." I plunk him in the bath.

"That was so fun, Nanny. Remember when she threw the frosting and it hit my butt?" He convulses in giggles again. I sit down on the toilet while he soaps up the wall, plays with his frogmen, and hums a little Donna.

"G, you almost done?" I ask when I'm tired of using his baby comb to scrape the frosting from my sweater.

"Beep-beep. Toot-toot. Beep-beep. Toot-toot." He shakes his soapy tush in the water.

"Come on, it's late." I hold up the towel.

"What did the girls do?"

"Who?"

"The bad girls. You know, Nanny, the bad, bad girls." He shakes his hips. "Why are they bad?"

"They didn't listen to their nannies."

✧

Mrs. X didn't seem to notice as she breezed past me to her bedroom that, in a torrential April downpour, I left wearing only a T-shirt, carrying my sweater and coat in a shopping bag. I wait for the elevator, gingerly putting my sweater back on so I don't freeze. I got as much frosting out of my hair as I could in the laundry room, but I'm still crumbling out a few hardened bits when the elevator door opens.

"Oh, shit." He looks flustered. "Hi!"

"Hi!" I can't believe it! "What are you doing here?"

"Oh, man," he says, crestfallen, "I was going to surprise you. I had this whole plan, with flowers and everything—"

"Well, mission accomplished! What happened to Cancún?" I step into the elevator, shaking at the unexpected sight of my H. H. in muddy jeans and my NYU sweatshirt.

"That was just to throw you off the scent—I was going to be waiting in the lobby tomorrow night—in a suit. We were going to go dancing." I beam at him and he gives me a once-over. "Looks like you and Grayer have been doing performance art again."

"Well, I've just returned from the Play Date in Hell with a crackhead mom. And I'm not being metaphorical, I mean an *actual* crackhead. She was coked up out of her mind, determined to be Betty fucking Crocker and we got dragged right into it—"

"God, I missed you," he interrupts, grinning from ear to ear as the door opens to the lobby. He leans over to wipe traces of frosting gently off my eyebrow and, without a second thought, I reach my arm under his to press the button for the eleventh floor. The door politely slides closed.

It is a carnal frosting frenzy.

◇

Wrapped in his navy flannel sheet, I perch on the edge of H. H.'s kitchen table as he throws a dryer sheet in with my clothes. He closes the metal door. "Hungry?" He turns, illuminated by the light from the neighbors' kitchen.

"What do you have?" I ask as he opens the fridge.

"My mom usually leaves a pretty stocked kitchen when she knows I'm going to be here by myself. Tortellini?" He brandishes a package.

"Ugh, if I never see another tortellini—" I shuffle over to peer into the refrigerator alongside him.

"Lasagna?" he asks.

"Ooooh, yes, please."

"How about some wine?"

I nod, grabbing a bottle of red and pushing the door closed with my hip. I lean against the fridge and watch him pull out plates and set us up at the table in his polka-dot boxers. Go me.

"Should I heat this up?" he asks, kissing my bare shoulder as he passes.

"Probably. Want some help?"

"No, you sit down." He hands me a wine glass. "You've had a hard day, frosting girl." He pulls silverware out of a drawer and carefully lays it out on the table.

"So, where are your parents?"

"They took my brother to Turkey for his break."

"Why aren't you in Turkey?" I sip my wine.

"Because I'm here." He smiles.

"Here is good." I pour a second glass and hand it to him.

He looks over at me, illuminated by the light from the microwave. "You look beautiful."

"Oh, this old thing? It's a toga from the L. L. Bean collection." He laughs. "You know, I'm doing Latin with Grayer now. How old were you when you started Latin?"

"Umm . . . fourteen?" He pulls the lasagna out of the microwave and comes over with two forks.

"Well, you must have been a late bloomer, because he's four. He's wearing a tie now, have I mentioned that? Not a child's tie, the full-grown, hangs-to-the-floor-on-him kind."

"What does his mom say?"

"She doesn't even notice. She's been pretty off the deep end— she fired Connie for, like, no apparent reason and Connie's been there since before Grayer was even born."

"Yeah, that man drives his wives to the brink."

"Wait—what?"

"Yeah, when Mr. X was cheating on his first wife, she completely laid into James in the lobby right in front of some board members."

I start choking on lasagna. "His first who?!"

"His first wife, um, Charlotte, I think, maybe." He looks incredulously at me. "You didn't know?"

"No, I did *not* know. He was married before?" I have to stand up, hoisting my sheet with me.

"Yeah, but it was, like, a long time ago. I just assumed you knew."

"Why would I know?! Nobody tells me anything. Oh, my God. Does he have any other kids?" I start pacing around the table.

"I don't know—I don't think so."

"What was she like? What did she look like? Did she look like Mrs. X?"

"I don't know. She was pretty. She was blond—"

"Was she young?"

"I was a kid. I dunno—she just seemed like a grown-up to me."

"Not helping. Think. How long were they together?"

"Jeez, maybe seven, eight years—"

"But no kids, huh?"

"Unless they kept them in their storage bin." I pause by the sink to entertain the idea for a brief moment.

"So, why'd they split?"

"Mrs. X," he says, taking a big forkful of lasagna.

"What do you mean, 'Mrs. X'?"

"Can we talk about you in the sheet some more?" He reaches out for me as I pass.

"No. What do you mean, 'Mrs. X'?"

"He was having an affair with Mrs. X."

"WHAT??!!" I nearly drop the sheet.

"Will you please sit down and have some lasagna?" He points his fork at the chair opposite him.

I sit down and take a gulp of my wine. "Okay, but you have to begin at the beginning and leave nothing out."

"Okay, according to my mom, Charlotte X was a big art collector. She bought everything at Gagosian, where your Mrs. X worked. Apparently, Charlotte sent Mr. X over to approve one of her larger purchases and . . . they hit it," he says, grinning.

"Mrs. X??!!" I cannot imagine Mrs. X hitting it. Period.

"Yeah, and sometimes he would bring her here when his wife was away and the doormen started talking. So pretty soon everyone in the building knew." He stares into his wine glass before sipping.

"I just cannot. Cannot, cannot, cannot believe it."

"Well . . . it's true. I saw it with my own twelve-year-old eyes. She was hot."

"Shut up," I splutter.

"No, she was red lipstick, tight dress, heels, the whole thing. She . . . was . . . hhhooot."

"Just finish the story."

"Well, Seven Twenty-one Legend goes Charlotte found stockings that didn't belong to her and went racing down to the lobby, clutching them in her hand, and completely lost it at James, wanting to know who had been up in the apartment. She moved out a few weeks later and your Mrs. X moved in."

I put the wine glass down. "I cannot believe you didn't tell me about this," I say, suddenly a little cold in my sheet as the high tenor of emotion from the ninth floor catches up with me.

"Well, you've been so stressed out—" He puts down his fork.

I push sharply back from the table and step over to the dryer. "So, if I don't know about it, then it doesn't affect me." I pull out my damp clothes. "Such fucking Boy Logic. I'm sorry—have I been bringing you down with this little job of mine?"

"Look, Nan, I said I was sorry." He stands.

"No you didn't. You did not say you were sorry." Warm tears fill my eyes as I try awkwardly to pull on my damp sweater without revealing myself beneath the sheet.

He comes around the table and gently takes the sweater. "Nan, I'm sorry. Lesson learned: tell Nan everything." He reaches his hand around my bare waist.

"It's just that you're the only person in my corner and to find out you're holding out on me—"

"Hey, now," he murmurs, pulling me against him. "I am the *mayor* of your corner."

I mush my face into his collarbone. "I'm sorry, I'm just so burned out. I know I'm way too consumed by this job. I really don't want to care if he had a first wife. I really don't want to spend tonight talking about them."

He kisses the top of my head. "Well, then, how about some music?" I nod up at him and he goes to the stereo on the counter. "So I guess Donna Summer is out?"

I laugh, willing myself to return to the eleventh floor. I shuffle up behind him and wrap us both in the sheet.

✧ ✧ ✧

I take another sip of my third cup of coffee and try to stay awake as I wait for Grayer's dinner to finish steaming through. Despite my afterglow it's still been a very long day on only two hours' sleep. I push up the sleeves on the faded heather crewneck H. H. gave me this morning so that I wouldn't be coming to work in the same clothes I wore yesterday. Not that these people would notice if I came to work wearing a clown nose and pasties.

As I slide the steamed kale onto his plate, Grayer slides down, stomach first, off his booster seat.

"Where you going, little man?" I ask, popping a steamed carrot in my mouth.

He pads over to the refrigerator and turns to admonish me. "I said not to call me that! No more 'little man'! I want some juice. Open the refrigerator," he says with his hands on his hips and his tie dangling over his pajamas.

"Please," I say over his head.

"Please! Open it! I want juice." His exhaustion from this afternoon's round of tutorials is starting to show.

I pull the fridge open and reach for the milk. "You know there's no juice with dinner. Soy milk or water, take your pick."

"Soy milk," he decides, reaching up with both arms.

"I'll get it for you, Grove. Why don't you get back up in your seat?" I walk back to the table with the Edensoy.

"NO! I want to. I want to, Nanny. Don't walk with it. Let me—" He's so cranky when it gets near my time to leave, making the last part of my shift the most trying.

"Hey, take it easy. Come on over and let's do it together," I suggest cheerfully. He pads back and stands at the table, his head level with the cup. She hates it when I let him pour. Not that I'm a huge fan of the task myself, as it can take forever and frequently concludes with me down on my hands and knees with a sponge. However, given his bad mood, I'd rather just do it with him than send him into a tantrum fifteen minutes before I have to leave for my eight o'clock class. He reaches his hands up to place them below mine on the box and we pour the soy milk together, spilling only marginally.

"Great job! There you go, little ma—Grover. Climb back up and let's knock dinner off." He climbs onto his booster seat, stabbing halfheartedly at the limp vegetables, completely forgetting the glass of milk. I look at my watch and decide rinsing off the dishes will be the most productive way to pass my last few minutes here, as he seems in no mood to chat.

I place the last pot in the dryer rack and turn to check on Grayer just in time to see him lift up the cup and very deliberately pour it on the floor.

"*Grayer!*" I run over with the sponge. "Grayer! Why did you do that?" I look up from the floor. He is sheepish, biting down on his bottom lip, clearly a little shocked at himself. He shifts away from me in his booster. I crouch next to him. "Grayer, I asked you a question. Why did you just pour your milk on the floor?"

"I didn't want it. Stupidhead Maria will clean it up." He drops his head back and looks up at the ceiling. "Stop talking to me." Soy milk seeps up my wrists where the sweater has come unrolled. A wave of exhaustion breaks over me.

"Grayer, that is not okay. It's a waste of food. I want you to climb down here and help me clean this up." I push back his chair and he kicks out at me, narrowly missing my face. I swerve back, stand up, and turn away from him to count to ten. I look at my watch to make a plan before I turn around and do anything I'll regret. Jesus, she's fifteen minutes late. My class starts in forty-five minutes.

I turn back to him and respond steadily. "Fine. Stay there, then. I'm going to clean this up and then it's time for bed. You are breaking rules and that tells me that you are very tired. Too tired for stories."

"I'M NOT HUNGRY!" He bursts into tears, slumping down in the booster. I wipe up the milk, trying to keep H. H.'s sweater away from the wet floor, and squeeze the sponge out into his plate.

By the time I've gotten everything into the dishwasher Grayer has tuckered himself out and is ready to forget about the whole incident. I place his tie over his shoulder and carry him back to his room, noting that I now have a leisurely twenty minutes to make it to Washington Square for Clarkson's lecture and have not received so much as a phone call from this child's mother. I keep hearing the whir of the elevator and perking up, ready for her to walk in the door and take over so I can cab it to class.

I peel Grayer down to his birthday suit. "Okay, go in the bathroom and pee, please, so we can put on your nighttime pull-ups." He runs into the bathroom and I pace; I only ask to leave before eight on Thursday nights, for God's sake. You'd think she could manage just one night out of five.

The bathroom door swings open and Grover stands in the door frame in a naked ta-da, arms over his head, tie hanging over his privates. He runs past me to the bed and grabs his pajama top.

"If I put 'em on can we read a book? One book?" He struggles to pull the striped shirt over his head and my heart goes out to him.

I sit down on the comforter to help, turning him to face me between my knees. "Grayer, why did you pour the milk on the floor?" I ask softly.

"I felt like it," he says, resting his hands on my knees.

"Grove, it hurt my feelings because I had to clean it up. It's not okay to be mean to people and it is not okay to be mean to Maria. It makes me very sad when you call her 'stupidhead' because she's my friend and she's going to do nice things for you every day." I lean forward and circle him in my arms as he puts his fingers up in my hair.

"Nanny, sleep over on the floor, okay? Just sleep over and then we can play trains in the morning."

"I can't, G. I have to go home and feed George. You wouldn't want George not to have any dinner. Now go pick out one book and we'll read it. One." He heads over to the bookcase. The front door mercifully clicks open and Grover runs out into the hall. Five minutes! I have five minutes to get to class! I follow right behind him and we both catch up to Mrs. X, clad in a Burberry trench, about a foot from her office. It is clear from her hunched shoulders and quick step that she had no intention of coming into Grayer's room.

"Mommy!" Grayer wraps around her from behind.

"I have class," I say, "I have to go. Um, it's at eight on Thursdays—"

She turns to me as she attempts to spatula Grayer from her leg. "I'm sure you can still make it if you take a cab," she says distractedly.

"Right. Well, it's eight now, so . . . I'll just get my shoes, then. Good night, Grayer." I scurry into the hall to pull my stuff on, hoping the elevator hasn't gone down yet.

I hear her sigh. "Mommy's exhausted, Grayer. Go get into bed and I'll read you one verse from your Shakespeare reader and then it's lights out."

Down on the street I run past the doorman to the corner and flail madly for a cab, hoping, at least, to make it downtown for the closing summary. I unroll the window completely, promising myself that I'll clarify my hours before next week's class and knowing that I probably won't.

✧ ✧ ✧

A few days later I pull out from my mailbox, in addition to the usual barrage of J. Crew and Victoria's Secret catalogs, two envelopes which give me pause. The first is on Mrs. X's cream business stationery, usually reserved for her committee work.

April 30

Dear Nanny,

I would like to share with you a matter of concern to Grayer's father and myself. It has come to our attention that after you left in such a hurry last night there was a puddle of urine found beneath the small garbage can in Grayer's bathroom.

I understand that you have your academic obligations, but I am, frankly, alarmed by your lack of awareness of such a situation. As per our agreement, in the hours during which you work here we are to receive your utmost and constant attention. Such a glaring oversight gives me pause as to the consistency of your performance.

Please review the following rules:

1. Grayer is to wear pull-ups when he gets into bed.
2. Grayer is not to drink juice after five P.M.
3. You are to be supervising him at all times.
4. You are to be familiar with the cleaning supplies and use them accordingly.

I trust you will review the consistency of your care and note that if an incident of this nature repeats itself I shall not have to pay you for that hour. I do not expect that we will have to discuss this again.

Hope you both have fun on your play date with Alex! Please be sure to pick up my coat at the tailors', it should be ready after two.

Sincerely,

Mrs. X

Right.

The second envelope is lined in Crane's tomato red. I pull out a wad of hundred-dollar-bills held together by a sterling money clip engraved with an X.

Dear Nanny,
I will be returning from Chicago the third week of June. I'd appreciate it if you could see that the apartment is

stocked with the following:
Lillet—6 bottles
foie gras—6
Teuscher champagne truffles—1 box
steaks—2
Godiva chocolate ice cream—2 pints
oysters—4 dozen
lobsters—2
lavender linen water

Keep the change.
Thanks, Ms. C

What is up with these women and lavender water?

The quadroon nurse was looked upon as a huge encumbrance,
only good to button up waists and panties and to brush and part
hair; since it seemed to be a law of society that hair must be
parted and brushed.

—THE AWAKENING

CHAPTER NINE

Oh . . . my . . . God

Sarah cracks her front door open to the extent the chain will allow, revealing flannel cloud pajamas and a pencil holding her blond bun in place. "Okay, half an hour—that's it. I mean it, thirty minutes. I'm home to cram for my orgo final, not sort through the Xes' dirty laundry."

"Why did you schlep yourself all the way back into the city to study?" Josh asks as Sarah unlocks the chain and lets us into the Englund family's front hall.

"Have you ever met, Jill, my roommate?"

"I don't think so," Josh says, taking off his jacket.

"Don't worry—you're not missing much—she's a theater major and her 'final' is performing five minutes of her life for the heads of the department—throw your stuff on the bench—so she's constantly standing up in our room, saying 'Dammit!', and sitting back down. I mean, how hard is it to sit and read a magazine for five minutes?" She rolls her eyes. "Do you guys want something to drink?" We follow her into the kitchen, which still has the same yellow daisy wallpaper that it did when we were in kindergarten.

"Sing Slings." I request Sarah's speciality.

"Coming right up," she says, stretching to pull a cocktail shaker and sour mix out of a high cabinet. "Have a seat." She gestures to the long green table by the window.

"It would be much cooler if this were a round table, like we could be the Knights of the Panty Roundtable," Josh says.

"Josh," I say, "the panties aren't the focus right now—the letter is—"

"We have a round coffee table in the living room," Sarah offers.

"We are totally doing this at a round table," Josh decides.

"Nan, you know the way," Sarah says, handing me a bag of Pirate's Booty. I lead Josh into the living room and plop down on the Persian carpet around the coffee table. Sarah follows with a tray of Singapore Slings. "Okay," she says, carefully sliding the tray onto the coffee table. "The clock is ticking—spill it."

"Let's just see the goods," Josh says, taking a sip.

I reach into my backpack and pull out the Ziploc baggie, along with Ms. Chicago's letter, and lay them ceremoniously in the middle of the table. We sit in silence for a moment, staring at the evidence as if they were eggs about to hatch.

"Man, it really is a fucking panty roundtable," Josh murmurs, reaching out toward the bag.

"No!" I say, slapping his hand. "The panties stay in the bag— that is the one condition of the Round Table. Got it?"

He folds his hands primly in his lap, sighing. "Fine. So, for the edification of the court, would you care to review the facts of the case?"

"I found Ms. Chicago practically hanging out in Mrs. X's bed four months ago, and then, all of a sudden, I received a letter *at my home*—"

"Exhibit A," Sarah says, waving the letter.

"Which means she knows where I live! She's hunted me down! Is there nowhere for me to hide?"

"It's so over the line," Sarah confirms.

"Oh, does Nan have a line?" Josh asks.

"Yes! I have a line. It's drawn right across Eighty-sixth Street. They cannot come to my home!" I feel myself starting to get hysterical. "I have a thesis paper to write! Exams to take! A job to find! What I do not have—is time. I cannot be running around NYU with Mr. X's mistress's underwear in my bag. I *cannot* be juggling their secrets on a full course load!"

"Nan, look," Sarah says gently, reaching around the table to put her hand on my back. "You still have power here. Disengage. Just give it all back and call it a day."

"Give it all back to who?" I ask.

"To the skank," Josh says. "Mail that shit back to her and let her know you don't want to play."

"But what about Mrs. X? If this all comes out and she finds out I had the panties and didn't tell her—"

"What's she gonna do? Kill you?" Sarah asks. "Put you in jail for the rest of your life?" She holds up her glass. "Send 'em back and quit."

"I can't quit. I don't have time to look for another job and my Real Job—at whatever school I can convince to hire me—won't start till September. Besides"—I open the bag of cheese poofs, finished with my bout of self-pity—"I just can't leave Grayer."

"You're gonna be leaving him at some point," Josh reminds me.

"Yeah, but if I want to stay in his life I can't end on bad terms with her," I say. "But you're right. I'll send this stuff back."

"And look, that only took us twenty minutes," Sarah says. "Which still leaves ten minutes for you to run my orgo flashcards with me."

"The fun never stops," I say.

Josh leans over to give me a hug. "Don't sweat it, Nan, you'll be fine. Hey—let's not overlook the fact that you guessed Ms. Chicago's panties would be black lace thongs, like, months before we found 'em. That's gotta be a marketable skill."

I empty my glass. "Well, if you know a game show on which I can turn that into ready cash, lemme know."

✧ ✧ ✧

I survey the disheveled piles of books, highlighted photocopies, and empty pizza boxes strewn all over my room that I've accumulated since I got home from work Friday. It's four A.M. and I've been writing for forty-eight straight hours, which is significantly less time for my thesis than I allotted myself. But, short of leaving Grayer to care for himself in the apartment, I didn't really have a choice.

I glance over at the brown manila envelope that's been resting against my printer since The Panty Roundtable a week ago. Taped and stamped, it only remains to be ceremoniously deposited in a mailbox after I deliver my thesis in four hours. Then Ms. Chicago and NYU will be well on their way to becoming a distant memory.

I grab another handful of M&M's out of the quarter-pound bag. I probably have all of five pages to go, but can barely keep my eyes open. A loud snore erupts from behind the screen. Fucking hairy pilot idiot.

I stretch my arms out to yawn, just as another guttural snore punctuates the silence, sending George darting with intense purpose across the room and diving into a neglected heap of dirty clothes.

I'm so tired I feel like my eyes are filled with playground sand. Desperate to regain some semblance of lucidity, I step carefully around the debris to locate my headphones and plug them into the stereo. I pull them onto my head and crouch down to spin the tuner until I find thumping dance music. I rock my head to the rhythm, turning the volume up until I feel the beat make its way down to my lucky turtle socks. I stand up to dance around in the small radius allowed me by the headphone cord. Bongo drums fill my ears and I shimmy wildly amid the books, eyes closed, willing my adrenaline to perk me up.

"NAN!" I open my eyes and slightly recoil at the sight of Mr. Hairy in a T-shirt and boxers, one hand carelessly scratching in his shorts. "WHAT THE HELL? IT'S ALMOST FOUR IN THE MORNING!" he bellows.

"Sorry?" I slide the headphones off my ears, noticing that this action does not decrease the volume. He points exasperatedly at the stereo where my floor show has unplugged the headphones.

I lunge for the off button. "God, sorry. My thesis is due tomorrow and I'm so tired. I was just trying to wake up."

He stomps off to the other end of the studio. "Whatever," he grumbles into the darkness.

"As long as you're comfortable!" I mouth silently in his direction. "As long as you're happy, sleeping here even when Charlene is flying all-nighters from Yemen! As long as my rent-paying-utilities-paying-can-only-get-to-the-bathroom-during-daylight-hours self is not disturbing you." I roll my eyes and head back to the computer. Four hours, five pages. I grab another handful of M&M's; let's go, Nan.

❖

The alarm wakes me at six-thirty, but it requires quite a few bleeps and one very disgruntled "WHAT THE HELL?" to raise my weary head off the pillow. I look at the clock; sixty minutes of sleep in forty-eight hours ought to do me just fine. I uncurl from the tight fetal position in which I passed out mere seconds ago and reach down to pull on a pair of jeans.

Pink light spills in through the open window, illuminating the disarray, which looks as if librarians came over and partied very hard. The computer hums loudly, mixing with the chirps of birds outside. I lean over the chair and wiggle the mouse to get past the screen saver and click Print. I click again on OK, appreciating that my computer feels compelled to check in with me at least twice regarding all major decisions. I hear the Style Writer run its warm-up swipe and shuffle groggily off to the bathroom to brush my teeth.

By the time I return not a stitch of progress has been made. "Jesus," I mutter, checking the Print Monitor to see what's In the Queue. A message pops up on the screen to notify me that Error Seventeen has occurred and that I should either reboot or call the service center. Fine.

I press save and shut down the machine, careful to pull out the disk on which I saved the five-thirty A.M. version. I restart as instructed, while pulling on boots, tying a sweater around my waist, and waiting for the screen to light up again. I check my watch: six-fifty. One hour and ten minutes to shove this behemoth under Clarkson's door. I press a myriad of buttons, but the screen remains dark. My heart pounds. Nothing I press can cajole my computer back to life. I grab the disk, my wallet, keys, the Ms. Chicago package, and run out of the apartment.

I jog up to Second Avenue, both arms waving over my head to hail a cab. I leap into the first one that languorously pulls over, trying to remember where, in the maze that is NYU's campus, the computer center is located. For some reason I have been unable to commit most campus locations to memory and suspect some Freudian connection between logistics and my fear of bureaucracy is responsible.

"Uh, it's off West Fourth, um, and Bleecker, I think. Just head in that direction and I'll tell you when we get close!" The driver takes off, braking sharply before each light. The streets are pretty empty, save the street cleaners whirring past and the men in suits and overcoats disappearing, briefcase first, down subway steps. Why this paper has to be in at eight A.M. is utterly beyond me. Some people get to mail in their final papers. Oh, who am I kidding? If that were the case, I'd just be in a frantic cab ride to the post office.

I hop out of the taxi on Waverly Place, taking the disk, my wallet, and keys just as a girl in a shiny outfit and smeared makeup shoves me aside to get in the cab. I catch the unmistakable whiff of a long night out—beer, stale cigarettes, and Drakkar Noir. I am comforted by the reminder that my life at this moment could be worse— I could be a sophomore doing the Walk/Cab Ride of Shame.

It's a little past seven-fifteen by the time I find my way, almost by smell, to the main computer center on the fifth floor of the education building.

"Need to see your ID," a girl with green hair and white lips mumbles from behind a large Dunkin' Donuts cup clutched at chin height. I riffle through my wallet a moment before remembering that the card she's referring to currently sits at the bottom of my backpack, upon which George is probably peacefully asleep.

"I don't have it. But I just need to print something out; it'll only take five minutes, I swear." I grip the counter and peer intently at her. She rolls her heavily kohled eyes.

"Can't," she says, pointing halfheartedly at the list of rules printed out in black-and-white on the wall behind her.

"Okay! Okay, here, let's see, I have my sophomore ID and . . ." I tug cards madly out of their leather slots. "Um, and a library card to Loeb. See, it says 'senior' on it!"

"No picture, though." She flips through her X-Man comic book.

"*PLEASE*, I am begging you. *Beg-ging*. I have, like, twenty-eight minutes to get this printed and handed in. It's my thesis; my entire college career hangs in the balance here. You can even watch me while I print!" I am starting to hyperventilate.

"Can't leave the desk." She pushes her stool back a few inches, but doesn't look up.

"Hey! Hey, you, in the ski hat!" A stick-thin boy with a name tag dangling from the chain around his neck glances over from where he lounges near the Xerox. "Do you work here?"

He saunters over in blue patent leather pants. "Wants to print, but doesn't have ID," the help desk girl informs him.

I reach out and touch his arm, stretching to read his name. "Dylan! Dylan, I need your help. I need you to escort me to a printer so that I can print out my thesis, which is due, four blocks from here, in, like, twenty-five minutes." I try to breathe steadily in and out while the two confer.

He eyes me skeptically. "The thing is . . . we've had some people coming in to use the center for their own purposes. Not students, I mean, so . . ." He drifts off.

"At seven-thirty in the morning, Dylan? Really?" I try to get a handle on myself. "Look, I can even pay you for the paper. I'll make a deal with you. You watch me print and if *TOGETHER*, you *and* me, *we* generate anything other than a thesis paper you can throw me out!"

"Well . . ." He slouches against the counter. "You could be from Columbia or something."

"With a sophomore ID from NYU?" I wave the plastic card in front of his face. "Think, Dylan! Use your head, man! Why wouldn't I just print up there? Why would I come all the way down here to sneak past you and your partner if I could just waltz into the computer lab three feet from my dorm room, *all the way uptown*? Oh, God, I do not have another minute to argue with you two. What's it going to be? Am I going to fail out of college and have a cardiac arrest *right here* on the linoleum or are you two going to give me FIVE FUCK-ING MINUTES AT ONE OF YOUR GAZZILLION FREE COM-PUTERS?" I pound my keys on the countertop for emphasis. They stare at me blankly while Patent Leather Pants weighs the evidence.

"Yeah . . . Okay. But if it's not your thesis then . . . I'm going to have to rip it up." I am already way past him, disk jammed into ter-minal number six, clicking Print like a madwoman.

◇

I slowly emerge from the deepest of sleeps, pulling my sweater off my face to check the time. I've been out cold for almost two hours. Too tired even to make it to Josh's, somehow, in a total fog, I found this stanky couch in the far corner of the Business School lounge where I could finally give way to my exhaustion.

I sit up and wipe the drool off the side of my mouth, getting a lusty gaze from a man highlighting his *Wall Street Journal* in a chair nearby. I ignore him and pull my wallet and keys from where I had stored them for safekeeping, under my butt in between the orange cushions, and decide to treat myself to the fancy coffee from the gourmet espresso shop.

As I walk down LaGuardia Place spring is in full bloom. The

May sky is warm and bright and the trees in front of Citibank are thick with buds. I smile up into the cloudless sky. I am a woman who has taken this place by the horns and made it! I am a woman who will, against all bureaucratic odds, probably graduate from NYU!

I take my five-dollar cup of coffee to a bench in Washington Square Park, so I can bask in the sun, resting against the shiny black luster of the wrought-iron bench. There are few people in the park at this hour, mostly children and drug dealers, neither of whom can disturb my reverie.

A woman strolls over to the bench across the way pushing a toddler in a plaid stroller and clutching a McDonald's bag under her arm. She sits, rolling the child to face her as she unwraps two Egg McMuffins and passes one to the stroller. The pigeons cluster around my feet, pecking at the brick. I have an hour before I have to pick up Grayer; maybe I should window-shop for a cute little sundress, something to wear in the warm summer nights to come as I sip martinis with H. H. on the Hudson.

I watch the woman pull another container out of the bag and mull over how lovely hash browns would taste right now, gazing absentmindedly at the little backpack hanging loosely on one of the stroller handles. Yes, hash browns and a milk shake, maybe chocolate. My eyes trace the pink border of the cartoon on the front of the backpack. Little pear-shaped figures. All in different colors with shapes on their heads. They are all . . . I squint to make out their names . . . They are all Teletubbies. I spit coffee in a good three-foot projectile in front of me.

Oh, my God. OH, MY GOD. I struggle to breathe as the pigeons jitter away. Flashes of Halloween, the dark limo ride home, the mink held close around Mrs. X's face, Grayer racked out beside me. I remember Mr. X snoring and Mrs. X talking and talking. Chattering on and on about the beach. I am in a clammy sweat. I put my hands over my forehead, trying to piece together the memory.

"Oh, my God," I say out loud, causing the woman to grab her

food and stroll quickly to a bench closer to the street. Somehow I have managed to suppress for the last seven months that I sat in the back of a limo and agreed to go to Nantucket with the Xes, that too many vodka tonics actually made me request that she "bring it on."

"Oh. My. God." I pound the bench with my fists. Shit. I mean, I do not, *do not* want to *live* with them. It's bad enough here in the city where I can go home at the end of the day. Am I going to see Mr. X in his pajamas? His underwear? Are we even going to see him at all?

What would she possibly be hoping for? A little family vacation? Are they going to thrash it out over the hooked rug? Beat each other senseless with canoe paddles? Put Ms. Chicago up in the guest house? Ms. Chicago—

"FUCK!" I leap up, patting myself down. "Fuck. Fuck. Fuck." I have keys, I have coffee, I have a wallet. "I have no fucking enve-lope." I jerk in about five different directions as I run through the last two hours and the multitude of places I could've left it. I sprint back to the coffee place, the orange couch, Dr. Clarkson's mailbox.

I stand, wheezing and sweaty, in front of the computer center help desk.

"Look, man, you've gotta clear out or for real we're gonna have to call security." Dylan tries to sound authoritative.

I can't speak. I'm *sick*. I was *trying* to have integrity. Instead, I'm the girl who stole eight hundred dollars and a pair of dirty under-wear. I'm a felon *and* a freak.

"Dude, I mean it, you better get out of here. Bob's on the noon shift and he's not nearly as cool as me." Noon. Right. Gotta go grab Grayer and drag him to Darwin's birthday party.

◇

"STOP IT! I DON'T LIKE THAT!" Grayer screams, his face flat-tened into the metal rails that line the upper deck of the boat.

I crouch down to whisper in his assailant's ear. "Darwin, if you do not step away from Grayer in the next two seconds I'm going to throw you overboard." Darwin turns in shock to my smiling face. Good Witch/Bad Witch on three hours of sleep and out eight hundred dollars; kid, you don't want to mess with me today.

He falters a few feet back and Grayer, a red imprint running across his right cheek where it was pressed against the pipe, wraps himself around my leg. Grayer has only been the focus of Darwin's torture for the past few minutes, joining the ranks of fifty other terrorized birthday-party guests, held prisoner for the last two hours on the Circle Line Jazzfest Cruise.

"Darwin! Honey, it's almost time for your cake. Go on over to the table so Sima can help you with the candles." Mrs. Zuckerman glides over to us in her Gucci ballet flats and matching pedal pushers. She is a vision in pink and gold and, coupled with her multitude of diamonds, practically blinding in the afternoon sun.

"Well, Grayer, what's the matter? Don't you want cake?" She tosses her three-hundred-dollar highlights in Grayer's direction and leans against the rail beside me. I'm far too tired for small talk, but am able to put on what I hope is a charming smile.

"Great party," I finally muster, hauling G up onto my hip and out of harm's way, so he can look over my shoulder into the white-crested wake behind us.

"Sima and I have been planning it for months. We really had to put our heads together to top last year's overnight at Gracie Mansion, but I just said 'Now, Sima! Creativity is part of the special something you bring to our family, so go to it!' And I tell you, she has really done it." Screams emerge from the stern of the boat and Sima races past us, panic-stricken. Darwin follows closely behind, lunging out after her with a flaming Tiffany's lighter.

"Darwin," Mrs. Zuckerman admonishes him lightly, "I said to help Sima, not set her on fire." She laughs gaily, taking the lighter from him and clicking the top down. She hands it sternly to a red-faced Sima. "See that he doesn't run around with this next time. I shouldn't have to remind you that it was a gift from his grandfather."

Sima accepts the sterling silver box, without lifting her eyes. She takes Darwin's hand and pulls him delicately back to his cake.

Mrs. Zuckerman leans in to me, the gold Cs on her glasses gleaming. "I'm so lucky, really. We're like sisters." I smile and nod. She nods back at me. "Please give my regards to Grayer's mom and please be sure to tell her that I have the name of a great d-i-v-o-r-c-e lawyer for her. He got my friend Alice ten percent above her prenup."

I instinctively put my hand on Grayer's head.

"Well, you two have fun!" She tosses her hair to the other shoulder and walks back to the cake melee. I guess Mr. X's residence at the Yale Club has become common knowledge.

"So, Grove, ready for some cake?" I shift him to my other hip, straighten his tie and touch his cheek where the pipe imprint had been. His eyes are glassy and he's clearly as exhausted as I am.

"My tummy hurts. I don't feel good," he mumbles. I try to remember where I saw a bathroom sign.

"What kind of hurt?" I ask, attempting to define the nuances of motion sickness versus heartburn to a four-year-old.

"Nanny, I—" He moans into my shoulder before pitching forward to throw up. I manage to aim him over the edge so that the Hudson can receive the thrust of his vomit, leaving my sweater dripping with only about a third.

I rub his back. "Grover, it's been a very long day." I wipe his mouth with my hand and he nods his head into my shoulder in agreement.

✦

Two hours later Grayer is holding the front of his pants and bouncing on his Nikes in the Xes' vestibule.

"Grove, please just hold it one more second." I give the front door a last shove and it finally gives way. "There. Go!" He runs past me.

"Oof!" I hear a thud. I push the door farther open and see Grayer sprawled on a pile of beach towels, felled by a Tracy Tooker box.

"G, you okay?"

"That was so cool, Nanny. Man, you should have seen it. Stand there, I'm gonna do it again."

"Yeah, no." I squat down to take off his sneakers and pull off his pukey windbreaker. "Next time you might not be so lucky. Go pee." He runs off. I gingerly tiptoe over the hatbox, the pile of towels, two Lilly Pulitzer shopping bags, three L. L. Bean boxes, and a bag of charcoal briquettes. Well, we're either going to Nantucket, or moving to the burbs.

"Nanny? Is that you?" I look over and see that the dining room table is completely covered in Mr. X's summer clothes, the only things of his that Connie and I hadn't packed up.

"Yes. We just got home," I call, moving two Barneys bags out of the way.

"Oh." Mrs. X comes out, holding an armful of pastel cashmere sweaters. "You're covered in vomit." She recoils slightly.

"Grayer had a bit of an accident—"

"I really wish you'd keep better track of what he eats at those parties. How is Mrs. Zuckerman?"

"She sends you her regards—"

"She's so creative. She always throws the best birthdays." She stares at me expectantly, eagerly waiting for me to reenact the afternoon, complete with sock puppets and commedia dell arte. I am just too tired.

"She, um, wanted to pass on a referral."

"Yes?"

I take a deep breath, bracing myself. "She said that she, uh, knows a really good lawyer." I look down at Mr. X's clothes.

"Nanny," she says icily, "these are my husband's clothes *for the trip*." She turns away from me and her voice becomes resiliently perky. "I haven't started packing myself, yet. No one can tell me what the weather will be like. Some of our friends broiled, some nearly froze." She drops the sweaters onto the table, sending several balled-up tennis socks rolling onto the floor. "Maria!"

"Yes, ma'am." Maria pushes open the swinging door to the kitchen.

"Can you fold these?"

"Yes, ma'am. Right away." She ducks back in the kitchen.

"I don't want to overpack, but I also don't want to have to do laundry while I'm there and I have no idea if they even have a decent dry cleaner on the island. Also, that reminds me, we'll be leaving on the fifteenth, promptly at eight A.M.—"

"Is that Friday?" I ask. She looks up at me. "I'm sorry, I didn't mean to interrupt you, it's just that the fifteenth is the day of my graduation."

"So?"

"So, I won't be able to leave at eight—"

"Well, I don't think we can delay our departure on your account," she says, walking to the bags in the front hall.

"No, the thing is, my grandmother is throwing a party for me that evening, so I really can't leave until Saturday." I follow her.

"Well, the rental starts on Friday, so we can't leave on Saturday," she says, as if explaining to Grayer.

"No, I understand that. I'm sure I could take a bus up on Saturday. I'd probably be there by five or so."

I follow her back to the dining room table where she adds her shopping bags to the stockpile. "So what you're basically telling me is that, of the fourteen days we need you, you will not be available for two of them. I don't know, Nanny. I just don't know. We're invited to the Blewers' for dinner on Friday and the Pierson barbecue on Saturday. I just don't know—" She sighs. "I'll have to think about this."

"I'm really sorry. If it were anything else. But I really can't miss my graduation." I bend down to pick up the errant socks.

"I suppose not. Well, let me discuss it with Mr. X and I'll let you know." If I can miss my graduation?

"Okay, also, I wanted to ask you about getting paid, because my rent is due this week—" And you haven't paid me in three weeks. And I now owe your husband's girlfriend *eight hundred dollars.*

"I've been so busy. I'll try to get to the bank this week. That is, as soon as you write up your hours for me, so I can go over them—"

She is interrupted by naked Grayer peeking around the doorway.

"GRAYER!" she shouts. We both freeze. "What is the house rule?"

He looks up at her. "No penises in the house?"

"That's right. No penises in the house. Where do penises stay?"

"Penises stay in the bedroom."

"Yes, in the bedroom. Nanny, would you see that he gets his clothes on?" Grayer walks solemnly ahead of me, his bare feet making sliding noises on the marble.

I see the balled-up clothes on the floor of the bathroom.

"I had an accident." He pushes at one of his wood cars with his toes.

"That's okay." I pick up the clothes and turn on the bathwater. "Let's get you cleaned up, okay, bud?"

"Okay." He puts his arms out for me to pick him up. I pull off my dirty sweatshirt and lift him up. As we wait for the tub to fill I bounce him a little and walk back and forth. He gives the weight of his head to my shoulder and I wonder if he might be falling asleep. I walk him over to the mirror, wrapping him in a towel to keep him warm, and discover in the reflection that he's sucking his thumb.

✧ ✧ ✧

Nanny,

I don't know if you were factoring the ferry into your calculations, but I have to point out that it can add another full hour to the journey. I was wondering if you could either (a) catch the eleven o'clock bus Friday night, which would get you to Nantucket at 6 A.M. or (b) take the 6 A.M. bus

Saturday morning, which would get you there by one, in time for the barbecue if we go late.
Let me know.

Dear Mrs. X,
I really appreciate your looking into alternate transportation for me. While I in no way want to inconvenience you, I feel it would be impractical to commit to an earlier start time as I have to attend a number of graduation events on Friday evening. I will be in Nantucket by 7 P.M. and, of course, anticipate you will adjust my pay accordingly.
Speaking of which, I was wondering if you've had the chance to get to the bank as my rent is due. Please find attached a list of my hours as you requested. Again, I really appreciate the options. Thanks!
Nanny

Nanny,
I am a little puzzled by your recalcitrance regarding our departure. However, I still hope that we can reach a compromise. Perhaps you could arrive by three and take a taxi to the Piersons'?

Dear Mrs. X,
As I, of course, do not wish to be anything other than accommodating I might be able to make it there by six.
Nanny

Nanny,

Never mind. The woman the housecleaning agency furnished us with will look after Grayer until you get there.
P.S. I would like to have a conversation regarding the hours you listed for Wednesday the third. I believe I took him shopping that day.

Dear Mrs. X,
I defer to your records regarding the 3rd.
Also, as I mentioned, I'll need to leave by two on
Thursday because I have my thesis defense.
Thanks, Nanny

Dear Mrs. X,
Just a quick reminder that my thesis defense is
tomorrow, so I'll need to leave at 2 o'clock sharp.
Also, if you could pay me, that would be great.

Dear Mrs. X,
I'll see you at two!

"Where is she!" I look at the oven clock for the millionth time in
five minutes. 2:28. I am supposed to be defending my thesis in
exactly forty-seven minutes. My entire academic career is about to
culminate without me as a panel of professors interrogates an empty
chair about child development!

"Don't shout." Grayer looks up, his eyebrows scrunched.

"I'm sorry, Grove. Will you excuse me for a second?"

"Are you gonna pee?"

"Yes. Don't forget your milk." I leave him finishing his melon
and walk into the maid's bathroom, turn on the faucet, shut the

door, flush the toilet, and scream into a hand towel. "FUCK!" My voice is absorbed by the terry cloth. "Where the fuck is she? Fucking fuck." I sit down on the bathroom floor, tears starting to well at the corners of my eyes.

"Fuck."

I should have written "two o'clock" with lipstick on every mirror in the apartment! I should have pinned a huge number two on the end of her pashmina when she wandered out this morning! I debate grabbing Grayer and running down Madison screaming her name like Marlon Brando. My frustration becomes a hysterical silent giggle, tears still running down my face.

I take a deep breath, slap my cheeks a little, dry my eyes, and try to compose myself for Grover. But I'm still giggling a bit when I walk back into the kitchen to find Mrs. X standing over him.

"Nanny, I'd appreciate it if you didn't leave Grayer unattended with silverware."

I look down at the spoon on his Linnaeus place mat. "I'm sorry—"

"My, you're dressed up." She picks a piece of melon off Grayer's plate.

"Thanks, actually it's for my thesis defense which starts in thirty-five minutes." I head for the door.

"Oh, right. I thought there was something." She saunters over to put her alligator Kelly bag on the counter. "I made it to the bank this morning. Let's sit down in my office and go over the list you gave me—" She pulls an envelope out.

"Great, thanks, but I really better run," I say over my shoulder.

She stands with one hand on her hip. "I thought this had to be done today."

"Well, if I don't go I'll be late," I call back from the front hall where I left my notes.

She sighs loudly, bringing me back into the kitchen.

"Be smart, Nanny!" Grayer cranes his head from his booster seat. "You'll be smart!"

"Thanks, Grove."

"I'm extremely busy and right now is the only convenient time for me to do this. I don't know when I'll be able to sit down with you again, Nanny. I went all the way to the bank—"

"Great. No, let's do it. Thank you." I pull out of my stack of papers a typed, revised list of all the hours I worked in the last five weeks. "So, as you can see, it averages between four and five hundred a week."

She looks down at the paper for a few moments while I shift my weight from foot to foot. "This is a little higher than we originally discussed."

"Well, the original list I gave you was two weeks ago and I've accrued over sixty hours since then."

She sighs and starts counting out twenties and fifties, slowly sliding them back and forth between her fingers to ensure that none of the bills are stuck together. She hands them over, her Hermès limoge bangles clanking together. "It sure is a lot of money."

I smile back at her. "Well, it adds up over five weeks." I turn on my heels, brushing Grayer's head as I pass him. "Have a great afternoon, guys!"

◇

I slather conditioner into my hair and massage the idea of quitting into my head. I imagine myself, under the awning in front of 721 Park, giving Mr. and Mrs. X a good, swift cartoon kick that lands them in the meridian shrubbery. Lovely. However, the image becomes much less clear with the addition of Grayer. Grover, in his big tie, looks up at me expectantly while his parents flail around in the manicured shrubs. I sigh, pushing my face under the hot water. And then there's the money. I'm nauseated at the thought of having to mail Ms. Chicago nearly half of what Mrs. X finally paid me today.

A little meow breaks my thoughts and I pull the curtain aside to see George, silhouetted in the candlelight, sitting primly beside the tub, waiting for me to splash him. I drop a little water on his head and he darts behind the toilet into shadow.

At least I have a quiet night to myself to celebrate a successfully defended thesis. And an eleven P.M. phone date with H. H. to look forward to. I wrap the towel around my torso, scoop up my clothes, and blow out the candle. Opening the bathroom door, I freeze at the sound of voices coming from the far end of the apartment. My end, to be precise.

"Hello?" I call out into the bright light. I can always tell when Charlene is home because she turns on every single light.

"I'm home," Charlene calls back flatly. My heart sinks. I pull the towel tight and walk past her screen to my side of the room. My desk lamp shines down on the candle I'd lit before getting in the shower. She stands with Hairy Pilot measuring my bed.

"It's kind of a mess in here, Nanny," she says, rolling up the tape measure. "Go over there and let's do that side of the room," she instructs Hairy, who pushes past me, nearly stepping on George to stand near my stereo.

"I had my thesis defense today, so I've been at the library every night." I step out of the way, tucking my underwear into a less visible spot in the ball under my arm as she walks with purpose to join her mate. "I'm sorry, can I help you two with something?"

She hands him one end of the tape measure and walks it back to the other wall. "I wanted to see if his couch would fit here." My stomach tightens. This is the antithesis of the relaxing evening I had in mind. She stands straightening her navy skirt. "Nanny, I wanted to talk to you this week, but you never answered the phone—"

"My lease is up. I'm moving in at the end of the month," Hairy volunteers. Fabulous.

"So that gives you, like, two weeks to find something else. That should be plenty of time," she says, grabbing a pen off my dresser to write the measurements on a Post-it. "Julie and her fiancé are coming over to play cards in an hour. Are you cool with that?" She steps past me. "God, it's so steamy back here. Are you taking showers in the dark again? That's so weird." She shakes her head.

I regain my composure as Hairy follows her, barely evading George's stealth attack. "I'm just on my way downtown, actually," I say to the floor. George stands under my chin to receive a drip. I reach for the phone, hoping Josh'll be pleased to hear from me.

✧ ✧ ✧

The next morning I dig through every pocket until I find the napkin on which Josh wrote the real estate people's name. I do a quick prayer for the apartment-deprived and dial the office number.

"Hehlow!" A horrendous New York accent answers on the seventh ring.

"Hello, I'm looking for Pat."

"She doesn't work here anymore."

"Oh. Well, perhaps you can help me? I'm looking to rent a studio for July first."

"Can't help you."

"What?"

"Can't help you. It's only the beginning of the month. You want a place for July you show up at the end of the month with a fistful of cash, say at least twelve thousand to start, and we'll tawk."

"Cash?"

"Cash."

"I'm sorry, twelve thousand in cash?"

"Cash. For the landlord. You've gotta come with the first year's rent in cash."

"The entire first year?"

"And you have to bring documentation *proving* that you net, *net*, mind you, forty-four times the month's rent, and your guarantors—"

"My what?"

"Guarantors—the people who are going to guarantee that the rent gets paid even if you die, typically, your parents. But they must live in the tristate area so their assets can be seized and they have to net *at least* one hundred times the rent."

"That seems a little extreme. I just want a small studio, nothing fancy—"

"Oh, my Gawd. This is June! June! Every American under the age of thirty is graduating from *something* and moving here."

"But all that in cash?"

"Honey, the Wall Street kids all get relo money from their companies. You want to beat them out you gotta pay up front."

"Oh, my God."

She takes a deep breath. "What were you looking to spend?"

"I don't know . . . six, seven hundred."

"A month?" She holds the phone away from her mouth while she cackles. "Honey, do us all a favor and look in the *Voice* for a share."

"But I don't want to share."

"Then I would get myself an apartment in Queens and a can of pepper spray."

"Well, do you have any listings in Brooklyn?"

"We don't do the boroughs." She hangs up.

The hairs on the back of my neck stand up as I hear the distinct tear of a condom wrapper from the other side of Charlene's screen. Ugh! I throw myself down on the bed, pulling the pillows over my ears. Forget quitting, by graduation I'll be begging Mrs. X to let me move in.

✧ ✧ ✧

H. H. gives Grandma another twirl around the dance floor to the strains of the salsa band she has hired for the evening from her favorite Mexican restaurant. Her apartment is aglow in colorful paper lanterns.

"*And* he can dance!" she calls out to where my parents and I are sitting on her terrace, her flamenco skirt swinging as he turns her.

Mom leans in toward me. "He's adorable."

"I know," I say with pride.

"Hey, watch it. Father's present," Dad says jokingly from where he sits in the chaise beside us. The evening is warm and Grandma set the food up out here where my friends mingle with my parents' friends around the candlelit tables.

"That guy over there wants to *pay* me to sculpt my *elbows*," Sarah says, coming over with two plates of cake and handing one to my mother.

"Yeah, sure—it starts with the elbows . . ." Dad warns her.

The song finishes and H. H. and Grandma applaud the band.

"Darling!" Grandma comes out on his arm. "Did you get some cake?"

"Yes, Gran," I say.

"You." My grandmother snaps her fingers at my reclining dad. "Get out there and give your wife a twirl." Mom stands, extending her hand in Dad's direction. They shuffle off in step to the music. "How are my darlings?" Grandma asks as she and H. H. sit down on the chaise. "Has everyone had enough to eat and drink?"

"The party is divine, Frances," Sarah thanks her. "Now, if you'll excuse me, I'm going to make sure our friend Joshua isn't off losing his paella." She disappears onto the dance floor.

I lean back to look up at the stars. "It's strange to actually be finished with school—"

"Life is school, darling," Grandma corrects me, taking a forkful of Dad's unfinished cake.

"Then I'm in Real Estate 101," I say, picking up my fork to join her. "I only have the weekend after I get back from Nantucket to find an apartment and get all my stuff out of Chez Charlene."

"That's Mrs. Hairy to you," H. H. interjects.

Grandma reaches out her bangled arm to squeeze my hand. "I'm so sorry you can't stay with me, but I've already rearranged the guest room for Orve's potting wheel." This will be Orve's second summer-in-residence with Grandma. She has a long-held summer tradition of hosting fledgling artists from all parts of the globe—they teach her technique in exchange for sumptuous room and board. "You'll find something—I have faith."

"So do I, darling," H. H. says, mimicking my grandmother's ebullient tone.

She winks at him as she stands and I notice a glint of blue at her throat.

"New necklace, Grandma? It's charming."

"Isn't it? I was in Bendel's last week and there were these little blue lacquer letters." She fingers the tiny ℱ and ℚ hanging on the gold chain around her neck. "They were all by themselves in the display case, the rest of the alphabet must have sold. I just had such a good laugh, get it? FQ, say it real fast." She laughs deeply as she merengues her way back inside and, for the first time since this afternoon's ceremony, I am alone with H. H.

"Come on," he says softly, taking my hand and leading me over to the stone balustrade overlooking the park. "I think your family rocks."

"Believe it or not, I can't complain," I say, placing my arms around him as we look out across the city.

"I'm going to miss you so much," he says, giving me a squeeze.

"Sure you are. While you're off in Amsterdam with all the porn stars, smoking the pot—"

"It's *The Hague*. A full twenty minutes from all that. No porn stars. No pot. Just me, missing you, and a whole lot of political prisoners with grievances."

I turn my head and reach up on my tiptoes to kiss him. "Those political prisoners, whine, whine, whine," I murmur.

He kisses the top of my nose and then my forehead. "And what about you? Stuck at the beach with all those lifeguards, pool boys, cabana boys—"

"Oh, my god. I'm not going to the Riviera—I'm going to stinky little Nantucket." I smack my hand on top of the railing. "Shit. I forgot to check my messages!"

He rolls his eyes. "Nan—"

"Wait, wait, wait—it'll only take me two minutes. I just have to call my machine and find out what time they're picking me up from the ferry tomorrow. Don't move, I'll be right back!"

I go into Grandma's bedroom to use the salmon-pink Princess phone on the night table, moving aside a few of her needlepoint pillows to sit on the sateen bedspread. As I punch the answering-machine code into the keypad the soft light of the room reminds me of sleep-overs from my childhood when she would leave the lamps on until I fell asleep.

Mrs. X's voice comes through like ice cubes dropped down the back of my dress. "Oh, Nanny, good news—our friends the Horners are flying up tomorrow at nine and have graciously offered to let you come along. So you'll be in Nantucket by nine-thirty in the morning. Now, Nanny, these are *very* dear friends of ours so I'm *counting* on you to be timely about this. Plan to meet them at the Westchester County Airport in the private-plane departure area. You'll need to take the seven-fifty Metro-North train to Rye and a taxi or something to get out to the airport. They have three girls, so they should be easy to spot. Now, they're doing this as a favor, so you really can't be late. Actually, you might want to plan to be at Grand Central Station by six-fifty just to give yourself time—"

Beep.

"Your machine cut me off. I'll need you to stop by while you're out and about and pick up an article I've left with James for you on Lyme disease. Horrible. Also, I'll need you to find deer-tick repellent suitable for a four-year-old and make sure it's hypoallergenic, so it won't irritate his skin. And I would appreciate it if you could go to

Polo and pick up six pairs of knee-high cotton socks, white. Take one of Grayer's shoes with you so you get the right size. I've left a pair with James so you can get them when you pick up the article and then just stick it all in your carry-on. Perfect. See you tomorrow!"

Beep.

"Nanny." I have trouble placing the voice at first. "As per my letter of instructions, I'll be arriving at the apartment tomorrow. I trust you had no trouble finding the foie gras. Have a good time in Nantucket and please say hello to Grayer for me."

*All right. I grew up and then became a governess. [Pause] I'd
really like to start a conversation, but there's no one to start a
conversation with . . . I don't have anybody at all.*
                    —THE ANDRYEEVICH FAMILY GOVERNESS,
                                    THE CHERRY ORCHARD.

CHAPTER TEN

And We Gave Her an All⸱
expenses⸱paid Vacation

"Good-bye!" the Horners shout from their car as it pulls out of the
Nantucket Airport parking lot, leaving me alone by the side of the
tarmac.

I sit down on my duffel bag and fight the urge not to throw up as
only someone can who's just flown twenty-five minutes on a six-
seater plane through torrential downpours, unrelenting fog, and
massive turbulence with four adults, three children, a goldfish, a
guinea pig, and a golden retriever. Only my consideration for the
Horner girls prevented me from screaming at every drop.

I pull my sweatshirt closer around me against the salty wind
and wait.

And wait.

And wait.

Oh, no, that's okay, that's fiiine. No, I wasn't out late at my *graduation party.* No, you take your time—I'll just sit here in the cold
drizzle. No, I think what's important is that I'm here, in Nantucket,
and that you and your family can rest easy just knowing I am somewhere within a ten-mile vicinity of you. I think what's important,

you know, paramount really, is that I'm not off living *my* life, attending to whatever I need to be doing, but am permanently on pause for you and your fucking family—

The Rover pulls in and barely slows to a roll as they motion for me to jump in.

"Nanny!" Grayer screams. "I got a Kokichu!" He holds up a yellow Japanese toy as I open the door. There is a very large canoe precariously angled in the trunk so that it sticks out over half the back passenger seat.

"Nanny, be careful of the boat. It's an antique," Mrs. X says proudly.

I maneuver myself under the canoe, pull my bag between my feet, crouch low, and reach around to pat Grayer's leg in greeting. "Hey, Grove, I missed ya."

"The antiquing here is wonderful. I'm hoping to find a new couch table for the second guest bedroom."

"Dream big, honey," Mr. X grumbles under his breath.

Ignoring him, she looks up at me in her visor mirror. "So, what was the plane like inside?"

"Um, it had brown leather seats—" I say, my head wedged into my chest.

"Did they serve you anything?"

"They asked if I wanted peanuts."

"You're so lucky. Jack Horner designs fabulous shoes. I absolutely adore Caroline. I worked on a benefit last year for her brother's campaign. It's such a shame they live in Westchester or we'd just be the best of friends." She checks her teeth in the mirror. "Now, I want to go over the plan for the afternoon. It turns out the Pierson barbecue is formal, so I thought it'd be nice for you guys to just enjoy some downtime at the house. Relax and enjoy the place."

"Great. That sounds like fun." I attempt to look over at Grover in his car seat with visions of us passed out in matching chaises on the lawn.

"Now, Caroline was supposed to call about dinner, so just give her my cell number when she rings. I've tacked it up next to the phone in the kitchen." Thanks, because it usually takes me about nine and a half months to memorize a ten-digit number.

We pull off the main road onto a densely wooded drive and I'm surprised to see that quite a few of the trees are still bare.

"They've had a cold spring." Mrs. X reads my thoughts. The drive opens into a loop in front of what can only be described as a sprawling, ramshackle 1950s bungalow. The white paint is peeling, the screen door has a hole in it, and a piece of roofing dangles at a precarious angle from the gutter.

"Well, we're here. Casa Crap," Mr. X says, stepping down from the car.

"Darling, I thought we agreed—" She gets out and chases after him, leaving me to unbuckle Grayer and get my bag out of the back. I hold what's left of the screen door open for Grayer, although he probably could just crawl through.

"Honey, it's not my fault the realtor's photographs were outdated."

"I'm just saying that for five thousand dollars a week, maybe you could have done a bit more research."

Mrs. X turns to us, beaming. "Grayer, why don't you show Nanny her room?"

"Come on, Nanny, it's reallyreally cool!" I follow him up the stairs to a little room at the end of the hallway. There are two twin beds close together under the sharply slanted low ceiling and Grayer's stuff is on one of them. "Isn't this cool, Nanny? We get to have a sleep-over every night!" He sits, bouncing on his bed. I stoop, careful not to bump my head, to fish a warm sweater and jeans out of my bag, as it was actually summer back in New York and I optimistically wore shorts.

"Okay, G. I'm just going to change."

"Am I going to see you naked?"

"No, I'll go in the bathroom. Wait here. Where's the bathroom?"

"There!" He points to the door across the hall.

I push it open. "AAAAaaaaaaaaaaaaaaaaaaahhhh!" And am confronted by a red-haired little girl, shrieking on the toilet. "This is my privacy!"

"Sorry!" I slam the door closed.

"Grayer, who's that?" I ask.

"That's Carson Spender. She's staying the weekend."

"O-kay." Just then I hear a car pull up the gravel drive. I go over to the window and watch Mr. X direct a Range Rover around to the side of the house. I walk down the hall to the dingy clerestory window facing the ocean and see the car pull in next to four others parked by the overgrown hedge. There are at least ten children on the back lawn.

"Grover?" I call, and he comes thumping down the hall. I heave him up so he can see out the window. "Who are those kids?"

"I dunno. They're just kids." I kiss him on the top of his head and put him down as the bathroom door opens. Carson shoots me a dirty look before marching downstairs.

"G, why don't you head down and I'll change quickly?"

"I want to stay with you," he says, following me back into our room.

"Okay, you can stand outside the door." I try to close it.

"Nanny, you know I don't like that." I pull it back, so it's barely cracked, and pull off my shorts. "Nanny? Can you hear me?"

"Yes, Grove." He sticks his little fingers under the door.

"Nanny, try to catch my fingers! Come on, catch 'em!" I look down for a moment, then kneel and gently tickle the tips of his fingers with my own. He giggles at my touch.

"You know, Grove," I say, recalling that first week when he locked me out. "I got mye thung thitikin outta, too, and you can't see it."

"No you don't, silly."

"How do you know I don't?"

"You'd never, Nanny. Hurry up, I'll show you the pool. It's really really freezing!"

Out back are men in summer suits, and women shivering in lawn dresses, all standing like traffic cones as children whiz chaotically around them.

"Mommy! She took my privacy!" I can hear Carson pointing me out to her mather.

"Oh, Nanny, there you are," Mrs. X says. "We should all be beack around six. There's plenty of stuff in the fridge for lunch. Have fun!"

A chorus of "Have a great time, guys!" erupts around us as the adults head over to their cars, which take off, car seats empty.

I look down at twelve expectant faces, as visions of an afternoon on the chaises quickly disappears. "Okay, guys, I'm Nanny. I have a few ground rules. NOBODY goes near the pool. Is that clear? I don't want to see anybody going past that tree over there or you will sit in the broom closet for the rest of the afternoon. Got it?" Twelve heads nod solemnly.

"But what if there was a war and the only place to go for safety was by the pool and—"

"What's your name?" I ask the freckled brunet with glasses.

"Ronald."

"Ronald, no more silly questions. If there's a war we go to the shed. Okay, everyone, go play!" I run inside, looking out every window I pass to make sure no one is even creeping toward the pool, to find Grayer's art kit.

I set up crayons, construction paper, and scotch tape on the patio table. "Okay, listen up! I want you all to come over here, one at a time, and tell me your name."

"Arden," a small girl in OshKosh B'Gosh tells me.

I write "ARDEN" and a big "1" on her impromptu name tag and then tape it to her shirt. "Okay, Arden, you're one. Every time I call out 'Head count!' you shout 'One!' Got that? All you have to remember is 'one.' " She climbs up into my lap and becomes my assistant, passing me the tape and pens, alternately.

For an hour everyone runs around on the grass, some play with Grayer's toys, others just chase each other, while I look out at the fog-covered ocean. Every fifteen minutes I call out "HEAD COUNT!" and they sound off.

"One!"

"Two!"

"Three!"

Silence. I tense to run down to the pool.

"Jessy, you're four, dummy."

"Four!" a small voice squeaks.

"Five!"

"Six!"

"Seven!"

"Grayer!"

"Nine!"

"Ten!"

"Eleven!"

"Twelve!"

"Okay, time for lunch!" I survey the troops. I am wary about leaving them outside while I inspect the supplies. "Everyone inside!"

"Awww!"

"Come on, we can play outside after lunch." I slide the wobbling glass door closed after number 12.

"Nanny, what's for lunch? I'm reallyreally hungry," Grayer asks.

"I dunno. Let's go take a look." Grayer follows me into the kitchen, leaving 7, 9, and 3, who are turning the living room couch into a fort.

I pull open the fridge. "Okay, let's see what we've got!" Umm, three fat-free yogurts, a box of SnackWell's, a loaf of fat-free sourdough, mustard, brie, local jam, and a zucchini.

"Okay, troops! Listen up!" Eleven hungry faces look up at me from their various tasks in the group mission to destroy the living room. "Here are the choices: we have jam sandwiches, but you may not like the bread. Or we have brie sandwiches, but you may not like the cheese. Or we have Cheerios, but no sugar to sprinkle on top. So, I would like you to come in the kitchen *one* at a time to taste the bread and the cheese and see which one you want."

"I want peanut butter and jelly!" Ronald shouts.

I turn around and shoot him a quick Look of Death. "This is war, Ronald. And in war you get the supplies your commanding offi-cer sends you." I salute him. "So let's all be good soldiers and eat the cheese."

I'm making the last sandwich when the first raindrops fall, blan-keting the sliding doors with a thick sheet of water.

◇ ◇ ◇

"Bye, Carson!" Grayer and I call out as the Spenders begin to pull out of the driveway Sunday night.

"Bye, Grayer!" she calls back from her car seat and then puts her right thumb up to her nose and waves her fingers at me. Despite my best efforts all weekend I was evidently never able to work my way back into her good graces after "taking" her privacy.

"Grayer, are you ready?" Mrs. X comes outside in a green and cream silk coat, Prada's signature look this spring, putting in her right pearl earring.

"Mommy, can I bring my Kokichu?" he asks.

We've been invited over for a "casual Sunday supper" at the Horners' and Grayer feels he needs to come equipped with some-thing to share, since Ellie, their four-year-old, has a guinea pig.

"I suppose that'll be okay. Why don't we leave it in the car when we get there and then I'll let you know if it's okay to bring it out? Nanny, why don't you run upstairs and change?"

"I am changed," I say, glancing down to confirm that I am still wearing clean chinos and a white turtleneck sweater.

"Oh. Well, I suppose it's okay. You'll probably be outside with the children most of the time, anyway."

"Okay, everybody in the car!" Mr. X comes by, swooping Grayer up, and carries him, sack-of-potatoes-style, outside.

As soon as we get in the car Mr. X plugs his cell phone into the dashboard and starts dictating instructions to Justine's voice mail. The rest of us sit quietly, Grayer clutching his Kokichu, me balled up under the canoe staring at my belly button.

As Mr. X unplugs his cell phone he sighs. "This is a really bad week for me to be away from the office. It's terrible timing."

"But you said the beginning of June was going to be quiet—" she says.

"Well, I'm just warning you I'll probably have to go back on Thursday for a meeting."

She swallows. "Well, when will you be back?"

"I'm not sure. It looks like I'll probably have to stay over the weekend to entertain the execs from Chicago."

"I thought your work with the Chicago office was done," she says tightly.

"It's not that simple. Now there's the issue of layoffs, merging divisions—reorging and making this thing run."

She doesn't reply.

"Besides, I *will* have been here a whole week," he says, making a left turn.

"Why are you turning away from the water?" she asks edgily.

We have trouble finding the house because, according to the instructions, it's on the inland side of the main road.

"I just can't believe they wouldn't have an ocean view," Mrs. X says, as she forces us to round the same traffic circle for the third time. "Give me back the instructions."

He balls up the piece of paper and throws it at her without taking his eyes off the road. She smooths it out methodically on her knee. "You must have copied them down backward."

"Let's be crazy and just follow the fucking directions and see where we end up," he hisses.

"I'm starving. I'm gonna die if I don't eat," Grayer moans.

Dusk is falling when we finally pull into the Horners' shingled, three-story house. Ferdie, their golden retriever, is sleeping peacefully on the wraparound porch under the hammock and the crickets chirp loudly in greeting. Jack Horner pushes the screen door open, wearing faded jeans and Birkenstocks.

"Take off your tie! Quick!" Mrs. X whispers.

"Park anywhere!" he shouts with a broad smile from the porch.

Mr. X is divested of his blazer, tie, and cuff links before we can get out of the car.

I stretch out my cramped back as I walk around to the trunk. I fish the rhubarb pie Mrs. X bought at the supermarket this morning out of the cooler. "Here, I'll take that," she says, walking off after Mr. X, who's holding a bottle of wine, and followed by Grayer, holding his Kokichu in front of him, like the three wise men.

"Jack!" The men shake hands and clap each other on the back.

Ellie peeks around the door. "Mom! They're here!"

Jack ushers us into the cozy living room, where one wall is completely covered in the children's art and a macaroni sculpture sits on the coffee table.

Caroline comes out of the kitchen wearing jeans and a white blouse, wiping her hands on her apron. "Hi! I'm sorry, don't shake my hands—I was just marinating the steaks." Ellie attaches herself to Caroline's leg. "Did you guys have any trouble finding the place?"

"Not at all, your directions were perfect," Mrs. X quickly responds. "Here." She hands off the pie box.

"Oh, thank you. Hey, Elle, why don't you show Grayer your room?" She bumps the girl gently with her hip.

"Wanna see my Kokichu?" He takes a step forward, proffering the fluffy ball. She looks down at the yellow fur and runs off, Grayer's cue to follow, and they scamper upstairs.

"Nanny, why don't you go watch the kids?" Mrs. X says to me.

"Oh, they're fine. I took away Ellie's Ginsu knives, so Grayer should be safe," Caroline says, laughing. "Nanny, would you like some wine?"

"Yes, drinks. What's your pleasure?" Jack asks.

"Do you have any Scotch?" Mr. X asks.

"Wine would be great," Mrs. X says, smiling.

"Red? White?"

"Whatever you're having," Mrs. X says. "Where are the other girls?"

"Setting the table. Would you excuse me? I'm just going to finish getting dinner together," Caroline says.

"Would you like any help?" I ask.

"Actually, that'd be great, if you don't mind."

Jack and Mr. X go outside to do manly things with the barbecue, while we follow Caroline into the kitchen, where Lulu and Katie, ages eight and six, are sitting at the table, rolling up napkins and putting them in rings.

"Nanny!" They leap up as soon as I come in, throwing their arms around me, much to Mrs. X's chagrin. I pick up Katie and quickly dip her backward, holding on to her legs, then give Lulu her turn.

"Would you mind tossing the salad?" Caroline hands off the bowl and a Mason jar full of dressing.

"Not at all." As I start flipping the lettuce I notice the sweet aroma of a pie baking.

"What can I do?" Mrs. X asks.

"Oh, nothing. I wouldn't want you to ruin your beautiful coat."

"Honey?" We hear Jack calling from the backyard.

"Lu, would you run outside and see what Dad wants?" The little girl comes running back a second later.

"He says the grill's ready."

"Okay, will you carry the steaks out to him, but be careful or we're all having grilled cheese for dinner."

Lulu picks up the metal tray and walks slowly to the door, staring intently at the pile of meat.

"Where are the kids eating?" Mrs. X asks casually.

"With us."

"Oh, of course," she says, covering.

"I wanted to ask you a favor," Caroline says, circling the island to put her hand on Mrs. X's arm.

"Of course, anything."

"I have a friend from college coming out next week. She's getting divorced and moving back to New York from L.A. and I wonder if you wouldn't mind taking her under your wing a bit."

"Not at all—"

"It's just that being up in Westchester I can't do as much to introduce her around as I'd like. Also, if you know a good real estate agent, she's looking for a place."

"Well, there's a three-bedroom in our building that's on the market."

"Thanks, but she's looking for a studio. It's a horrible situation—even though her ex-husband was the one c-h-e-a-t-i-n-g, none of the assets were in his name. He's incorporated or some crap, and she's gotten nothing."

Mrs. X's eyes widen. "That's terrible."

"So anything you can do to help, I'd really appreciate. I'll call you when she gets here."

When we all get to the table, I'm charmed to see that the girls have made place cards by taking leaves and writing our names on them in silver pen in three markedly different handwritings. Katie and Lulu have asked to have me seated between them, while Mrs. X is placed between Grayer and Ellie and spends much of the meal cutting meat and answering Ellie's questions about her coat.

Ferdie comes over and starts whimpering for scraps at Jack's feet. "We had a retriever when I was a boy," Mr. X says, spooning mustard onto his second steak.

"Ferdie's a local, actually," Caroline says. "One of the top breeders lives just down the road, if you're thinking of getting a puppy—"

"This is such a fabulous house," Mrs. X says, changing the subject as she plays with her salad.

"It was built by Caroline's grandfather," Jack says.

"With his own two hands, no nails, in the driving rain, if you believe him," she laughs.

"You should see the overpriced beach shack my wife picked out. We'll be lucky if the roof doesn't blow off," Mr. X laughs, corn in his teeth.

"So, Nanny, where are you in school?" Jack turns to me.

"NYU—I just graduated on Friday, actually."

"Congratulations!" He smiles at me, while buttering another ear of corn for Lulu. "So, have you figured out your plans for next year?"

"You're such a dad." Caroline laughs at him across the table. "You don't have to answer that, Nanny." She stands up. "Who wants pie?"

"ME! ME!" the little Horners and Grayer all shout.

As soon as the door swings behind her I stand to clear, but Jack stops me. "Come on," he mock-whispers. "She's gone. What are your plans?"

"I'm going to be the program associate of a children's organization in Brooklyn," I tell him in a stage whisper.

"Honey!" he shouts. "It's okay! She has a plan!"

Caroline comes back in, smiling, with a carton of ice cream and nine bowls.

"Jack, you're hopeless." She puts down the carton and the bowls. "Lulu, will you take coffee orders?"

A gracious hostess, Caroline serves both pies, but there's little demand for the cold one in the aluminum dish.

✧

"Mommy, I want a guinea pig," Grayer says sleepily from his car seat. He's out almost immediately and the Xes begin rehashing the evening, as I try to find a comfortable way to slump beneath the canoe.

"He was telling me by the barbecue that he's managed to expand into twelve new markets this year—" Mr. X is impressed with Jack's business acumen.

"You know"—she turns slightly toward him, putting her hand on his arm—"I was thinking I could go back with you on Thursday—we could have a romantic weekend in the city."

He pulls his arm away as he makes a left turn. "I told you, it'll just be a lot of client entertaining. You'd be bored out of your mind." He plugs in his cell phone and dials with his free hand.

She pulls her Filofax out and flips through the empty pages. "Nanny, one thing I would like to mention—" she calls back reprovingly.

"Yes," I say, starting to nod off.

"I'm not sure if it's appropriate for you to monopolize the dinner conversation. Just something I'd like you to be a little more aware of from now on."

✧ ✧ ✧

Darling, I've gone over to the Sterns' for tea. I'll be back by five. Just a thought—if you have to go, why not see if you can come back to the island early Sunday morning, because the Horners have invited us over for brunch. Have a great match! Love you.

✧

I hope your golf game went well. In case you're worried if I'll be lonely Caroline has offered to keep me company while you're gone, so don't worry about me. Although they're quiet busy, but I'm sure other people will think of me. See you at the club at six. Love you.

❖

Darling, I didn't want to wake you from your nap——I'm going into town.

I called the rental agent and she said that it's really pretty safe out here. She said she'd be surprised if anything happened to Grayer or me while we're here all by ourselves, so please don't spend your time in the city worrying about us all the way up here.

❖ ❖ ❖

Wednesday night, on the eve of Mr. X's departure, the three of us sit waiting in the Rover for Mrs. X. The original plan was to leave Grayer and myself home for the evening "to relax," while they had dinner at Il Cognilio with the Longacres. But when they came home to change, Grayer screamed hysterically until Mr. X insisted that they bring him along, so he would, quote, "shut up."

After five straight days of running a virtual day-care center for all of the Xes' friends on at most five hours of sleep a night, I start to nod off as soon as I slump down under the canoe.

Mr. X jerks the cell phone away from his head. "We're going to lose the reservation—go see what's taking her so long." I open the car door just as Mrs. X teeters out onto the gravel on uncharacteristically high heels, clad in a strapless black dress with a red cashmere wrap around her shivering shoulders. Mr. X barely glances at her before starting the car.

"Honey, what time do you want me to drive you to the airport tomorrow?" she asks, pulling on her seat belt.

"Don't bother—I'm taking the six A.M. flight. I'll just call a cab."

"I want to fly with Daddy." Grayer, hungry and, of course, napless, begins to squirm in his car seat.

"Mrs. X? Um, you didn't get a chance to see if you brought any mosquito bite stuff, did you?" my voice echoes from beneath the canoe.

"No, are you still being bitten? I just don't understand it. None of us has any bites."

"Do you think it might be possible for me to run into a drugstore and grab some After Bite?"

"I really don't think we have time." She retouches her lipstick in the yellow light of the visor mirror.

I give my leg a good going-over through my pants. I am on fire. The itch is so bad it's keeping me awake on the alternate hours Grayer or Mr. X isn't snoring. I just. Want to go. To a drugstore.

After a tense twenty-minute drive we pull into the parking lot/ gift shop of the famous restaurant whose annual signature T-shirt, featuring a rabbit in silhouette, is a bizarre, nationwide status symbol. Of course I want one.

Mrs. X ushers us into the restaurant, a glorified bait-and-tackle shop that serves up twenty-five-dollar bowls of pasta on splintered tables.

"Darling, how are you?" Mrs. X is accosted by a woman with large, blond hair that looks as if it could stand up to the fiercest Nantucket wind. "You're so dressy, my God, I feel like a bumpkin." She pulls her Aqua Scutum barn jacket closer around her.

The men shake hands and Mrs. X introduces Grayer. "Grayer, you remember Mrs. Longacre?"

Mrs. Longacre absentmindedly pats his head. "He's getting so big. Honey, let's get our table." We are shown to a drafty corner table and handed a green booster seat, which Grayer tries to squeeze himself into.

"Mrs. X, I think it's too small."

"Nonsense." She looks over at him sitting sideways, straining to fit his whole tushy in the seat. "Go see if they have a phone book."

I finally unearth three filthy Nantucket directories and slip them under his derriere, while the adults order cocktails. I pull crayons out of my bag and start telling Grayer a story, illustrating on the paper tablecloth as I go.

"Well, of course, I love it up here, but I don't know how I'd do it without my fax," Mrs. Longacre says. "I don't know how people went anywhere before the fax and the cell phone, I really don't. I'm putting together a small dinner for a hundred people for the week we get back. You know, I planned Shelly's entire wedding from here last summer."

"I know, I wish I'd thought of bringing ours from home," Mrs. X says, adjusting the wrap around her naked shoulders. "I'm waiting to hear from the board if they're letting me buy one of the studios on the second floor."

"Your building has studios?"

"Well, they were all maids' quarters originally and most are owned by people who have larger apartments in the building. I'd love to have someplace for a little private time, you know? I'm just so torn when Grayer's home. I want to be with him, but sometimes I need to get things done for my committee work."

"Oh, honey, cheers to that! Our eldest daughter just did the same thing—she has two kids and needed someplace where she could do her own thing, but still be close enough to be involved. I think it's a great idea."

The waitress comes over with the six drinks on a tray just as a small child goes whizzing by her at knee height, nearly knocking three highballs onto Mrs. X's head.

"Aaaan-drew . . . Come to Mommmyyy." We hear a plaintive

voice whine as the human tumbleweed flies under tables and between diners.

The maître d' looks pleadingly at the oblivious parents, willing them to discipline their child.

"Oh, honey, isn't that the Cliftons?" Mrs. X excuses herself to go over and kiss cheeks.

"Nanny, draw me a chicken," Grayer asks, while the men compare this week's golf scores.

"Isn't that great?" she says, sitting back down. "They're here with their son, so I told Anne that Nanny would take everyone out to the parking lot until the food comes." Everyone? Am I to lead Mrs. Clifton in a rousing rendition of "Michael, Row Your Boat Ashore" by the Dumpster?

I pull myself out of my seat and take Grayer and the whirling dervish out into the cold, dark, sandy parking lot to play. They climb up and down a piece of oiled driftwood a few times and then Andrew suggests making dirt angels.

"Yeah, no. How about we wash hands before the food comes?" I try to steer them back inside toward the ladies' room.

"No!" Andrew shouts. "I'm a boy. I'm not using some girl's toilet. No way."

Mr. Clifton rounds the corner to the bathrooms. "I'll take them," he says to me, leading the boys into the bathroom and leaving me to enjoy a whole two minutes in the ladies' room by myself.

I've just latched the door on the stall when I hear Mrs. X and Mrs. Longacre come in. Mrs. Longacre is agreeing about something. "Absolutely! You can never be too cautious these days. Do you know Gina Zuckerman? She has a boy about Grayer's age—Darwin, I think. Apparently the woman they had watching him, some South American, grabbed him by the arm. Gina caught it all on the Nannycam. Sent that woman right back to whatever third world village she crawled out of."

I try not to breathe as Mrs. Longacre pees beside me.

"We just set up our Nannycam a few weeks ago," Mrs. X says. "I haven't had time to review the tapes, but it gives me peace of mind knowing I'm able to be virtually right there with my son."

Shut up. Shut up!

"Don't you have to go?" Mrs. Longacre asks, coming out of the stall.

"No, I'm just washing my hands," Mrs. X says from the sink.

Grayer pounds on the bathroom door. "Nanny!"

Mrs. X opens the door. "Wha—Grayer? What are you doing here?" I hear her leave and wait for Mrs. Longacre to finish washing her hands before I unlatch the stall.

NANNYCAM?! NANNYCAM???!!! What's next? Periodic drug tests? Strip searches? A metal detector in their front hall? *Who are these people?*

I splash my face with cold water and try, for the umpteenth time in nine months, to put my six-foot employers out of my mind so I can focus on the needs of the three-foot one.

I walk back to the table. Mrs. X is struggling to balance Grayer on the phone books. She looks up, openly glaring at me. "Nanny, where have you been? I found Grayer unattended and I think it's unacceptable—"

An unprecedented level of rage shows on my face, momentarily silencing her. I readjust Grayer on his phone books, cut up his chicken for him, and take a forkful of mashed potatoes.

"Well, then, Nanny, why don't you take the kids outside till we're done?" she asks sweetly.

And I spend the rest of the meal in the damp wind, feeding Grayer sandy chicken out of a Styrofoam container. Pretty soon Andrew joins us, then three more. I play Head, Shoulders, Knees, and Toes. I play Mother May I. I play Red Light, Green Light.

But there is only so much you can do with five children in a dark parking lot before you want to sell them.

✧

After putting Grayer to bed I ransack the kitchen for ammonia. While searching under the sink, I hear the tap of Mrs. X's Manolos on the linoleum as she opens the cabinets above. She maneuvers awkwardly around me in silence.

"What are you doing under there?" Mr. X comes in, holding the paper.

"I'm looking for ammonia to take the sting out of my mosquito bites," I say, my head tucked between the pipes and a bottle of bleach as I hunt for this emergency Girl Scout solution.

"And I'm looking for the Scotch, so I can fix you a nightcap." Her feet swivel so she can face him and her wrap slides slowly to the floor, landing in a scarlet-red heap beside her goose-pimpled ankles.

"Ammonia?" he asks. "Huh."

His heavy footsteps move from the linoleum of the kitchen to the wood of the hallway.

"Honey?" she says in a slightly husky tone as she follows him to the door frame. "Why don't we read in bed?"

I hear the rustle of him handing the paper over to her. "I've got to confirm my flight out tomorrow. I'll be in when I'm done. Don't wait up. Good-bye, Nanny." I see Mrs. X's calf muscles clench.

"Bye, have a good flight," I say. Give Ms. C my regards.

I hear her follow him down the hall, leaving me alone to rummage under every sink in the house, but all I find is a lot of Mr. Clean and some Pine-Sol.

An hour later, when I turn out the bathroom light, I see Mr. X slowly pushing their bedroom door open, a shaft of light illuminating the hallway.

"Darling," I hear her say quietly. The door slides closed.

✧ ✧ ✧

"Daddy, you're here!" Grayer jumps up in front of *Sesame Street* when Mr. X enters the living room late the next morning.

"Hi," I say, startled. "I thought you were—"

"Hey, sport." He comes over to sit on the couch.

"Where's Mommy?" Grayer asks.

"Mommy's in the shower." His father grins. "Have you had breakfast?"

"I want cereal," he says, skipping in circles around the couch.

"Well, let's rustle you up some food. I could go for eggs and sausage." It *is* Thursday, right? It's not still Wednesday? Because I already scratched Wednesday off on the little calendar I've carved into the wall by my bed.

Mrs. X saunters in wearing a bikini top, sarong, and miles of exposed gooseflesh. She's flushed and has the aura of victory about her.

"Morning, Grayer. Morning, you." She languorously comes up behind Mr. X, putting her hands on his shoulders and giving him a little massage. "Darling, would you mind going to pick up the paper?" He rolls his head back to look up at her and she grins, leaning down to give him a kiss.

"Sure." He comes around the couch, brushing his lips over her shoulder as he passes. Well, I've officially found the only scenario more uncomfortable than being around when they fight.

"Would you mind if I went with Mr. X to the store to get some After Bite?" I ask, trying to capitalize on her postcoital glow.

"No. I'd rather you stayed here to watch Grayer while I get ready." Mr. X grabs the keys from the table by the door and heads out. As we hear the car start she asks, "Grayer, how'd you like a baby brother or sister?"

"I want a baby brother! I want a baby brother!" He runs over to her, but she spatulas him and rebounds him back to me, like a field hockey ball.

The phone begins to ring as Mr. X pulls out of the driveway. Mrs. X takes his sweatshirt from the back of the couch and pulls it on over her head before picking up the heavy olive-green receiver. "Hello?" she stands, listening expectantly. "Hello?" She adjusts her sarong. "Hello?" She hangs up.

She eyes me across the room. "I hope you haven't been giving this phone number out."

"No, only to my parents in case of an emergency," I say.

She's halfway up the stairs when the phone rings again, bringing her back down into the living room.

"Hello?" she asks a fourth time, sounding annoyed. "Oh, hi . . ." Her voice is strained. "No, he's not in . . . No, he decided not to leave today, but I'll have him call you when he gets back . . . Chenowith, right? I've got it. Are you in Chicago or New York? . . . Okay, bye."

No Teuscher truffles for you, Ms. Chicago.

When Mr. X gets back I go into the kitchen to help him unload and pull out the usual assortment of carcinogenic sugar-free yogurts, tofu dogs, and SnackWell's.

"Did anyone call?" he asks, pulling a single cheese pastry out of a small wax-paper bag for himself as Mrs. X comes into the kitchen.

"Nope," she says. "Why, were you expecting someone?"

"Nope."

Well, then, that's settled.

◇ ◇ ◇

Ring. Ring. Ring.

The next afternoon as a plane flies low over the backyard, I wake to the shrill sound of the phone from inside the house. Again. Slapping at the mosquitoes feasting on my bare legs, I unpeel my flesh from the rubber slats of the dilapidated lawn chair and stand up to answer the ringing. But it abruptly stops. Again.

Earlier this morning I stood warily staring at a truck in our driveway as an old man unloaded three large rental bikes, wondering with a heavy heart if this implied that I was to ride with Grayer up on my shoulders. At this point, I doubt I'd so much as bat an eyelash if they suggested that I load him into my womb to make more room in the Land Rover.

Grayer had to explain to his father that he could only ride the red ten-speed propped up in the driveway if it had training wheels. I still can't tell if the man is totally clueless or just insanely optimistic about Grayer's capabilities. At any rate, one adult bike was exchanged for a smaller one and, to my surprise, I was permitted to bow out of their excursion. They rode off toward town, leaving me with grand plans for a long jog, a leisurely bath, and a nap, but I seem only to have made it as far as sitting down on this deck chair in my running shorts and sports bra to put on my sneakers. Well, one out of three ain't so bad.

I grope under the chair for my watch, grimacing as a sliver of wood slides under my fingernail. I pull the watch out and suck gently on the afflicted finger. They've been gone for over an hour.

I head back inside, turn on the hot water in the kitchen sink and thrust my hand under it. I finally get a free moment to myself for the first time in a week and I have to spend it coaxing this damn house out of my very skin!

Ring. Ring. Ring.

I don't even bother to move from where I'm leaning against the counter. She gives up after the fifth ring. She seems to be losing her subtle edge.

The hot water proves to be unsuccessful, forcing me to gather a makeshift emergency kit, consisting of a corn holder, matches, and a neglected bottle of Ketel One from the freezer. As I set up shop at the kitchen table I stare down at the cracked green linoleum. I wish I could call up and order a fill-in friend, like a guy orders a stripper. Some fabulous young woman would show up with Cool Ranch Doritos, margaritas, and a copy of *Heathers*. Or at least some old *Jane* magazines. If I have to flip through *Good Housekeeping* from July of '88 one more time I'm going to bake myself into an apple pie.

I reach for the vodka, freezing when I think I hear the crunch of gravel in the driveway signaling their return. I untwist the top, pour a shot into a juice glass, and feel it roll onto my tongue. I pound the glass back on the table, turning it over like a cowboy.

I look over at the old, decrepit AM radio on the sideboard, and turn on the power.

Ring. Ring. Ring.

"He's not here!" I shout over my shoulder.

I start rolling the knob, dropping my head on my arm as I spin past dribbles of news and oldie stations blurring through the ancient speakers in tiny bursts of static. I move the knob slowly, an astronaut listening for signs of life, trying to make out a Billy Joel song amid the fuzz. My head lifts. It's not Billy . . . it's Madonna!

I roll the knob a millimeter, standing with excitement at the familiar sound of "Holiday." I grab the corn holder and shove it in by the knob to hold it in place, crank the volume up as high as it will go, and sing along with the next best thing to a fill-in friend. There is life beyond this place, my glitter-eyed, badass, blond friend reminds me, life without *them*!

" 'If we took a holiday, oohya—' " I shimmy my Lycra-clad self around the kitchen, tossing the vodka back in the freezer to chill, forgetting completely about my finger, mosquito bites, and severe sleep deprivation. Within moments I am right there with her as she insists that I take some time to celebrate, (oohya), and kick, eighties style, into the living room, grabbing Grayer's monster truck for a microphone and belting it out for all I'm worth.

I am just sliding off the back of the couch, when Mr. X throws open the screen door in his Donna Karan running pants. I freeze in a squat, truck in hand, but he barely notices me as he hurls his cell phone onto the rickety wing chair and strides to the stairs. I jolt up to look out the front door, where the silhouette of Mrs. X moves closer from a heap of Grayer in the middle of the driveway. I leap over Grayer's toys, run into the kitchen, dislodge the corn holder, kill the power, and run back into the living room just as the front door swings closed.

She eyes my midriff. "Get him ready for his play date, Nanny. He claims he scraped his knee, but I can't see anything. Just quiet him down—my husband has a headache." She breezes past me to the stairs, rubbing her own temples. "Oh and something's wrong with his cell. Check it, will you?"

Mr. X screams from upstairs, "Where's my suitcase? What have you done with my suitcase!"

Strains of a sobbing Grayer ripple through the house as I reach for my sweatpants, finger throbbing back to life. I pick up Mr. X's cell phone. The caller ID shows that all the calls are coming from the Xes' apartment.

✧

Ring. Ring. Ring.

I struggle to open my heavy eyelids in the darkness.

Ring. Ring.

I don't know why he doesn't just call her and tell her he's not coming back!

"Nanny!" Grayer cries out as the phone wakes him for the third time tonight. At this point I'm about one ring from calling her and telling her where she can stick her phone *and* her foie gras.

Reaching across the two-foot divide between our beds, I squeeze Grayer's sweaty hand. "The monster," he says, "is really scary. It's going to eat you up, Nanny." The whites of Grayer's eyes shine in the dark room.

I roll over onto my side to face him, while not letting go of his hand. "Think real hard, what color was the monster? I want to know, 'cause I'm friends with a few."

He's quiet for a moment. "Blue."

"Oh, yeah? Sounds like Cookie Monster from *Sesame Street*. Was he trying to eat me?" I ask sleepily.

"You think it's Cookie Monster?" he asks, his death grip lightening as he relaxes.

"Yup. I think Cookie wanted to play with us, but he scared you by accident and was trying to tell me he was sorry. Want to count sheep?" Or rings?

"No. Sing the song, Nanny."

I yawn. " 'Ninety-nine bottles of beer on the wall, ninety-nine bottles of beer,' " I croon softly, feeling his warm breath on my wrist. " 'Take one down, pass it around, ninety-eight bottles of beer on the wall.' " His hand grows heavy and by ninety beers he's back to sleep for at least a few more hours.

I turn over on my right side and watch him, his chest gently rising and falling, his hand curled under his chin, his face for the moment relaxed and peaceful. "Oh, Grove," I say quietly.

✧ ✧ ✧

The next morning, after indulging in three cups of unflavored coffee, and buying a case of After Bite. I stand against the only pay phone in town, frantically dialing the numbers on the plastic phone card.

"Hello?" H. H. answers.

"Oh, thank God. I thought I wasn't going to catch you before you left." I slump against the pay phone.

"Hey! No, I was just packing—my flight's not till eight. Where are you?"

"At a pay phone. They left me in town while they went to a dog breeder." I fish the box of cigarettes I bought along with the phone card out of the plastic bag and rip off the cellophane wrapper.

"A dog breeder?"

"Mr. X is hoping to buy a small furry replacement for himself. He's leaving this afternoon. I guess one week of family vacation was about all he could take." I stick a cigarette in my mouth and light it, inhaling and exhaling quickly. "This town must have some rule against businesses selling anything but scented candles, boats in a bottle, or flavored fudge. Hell is a yacht-shaped candle—"

"N, just come home." A family walks by, each member in various stages of finishing ice-cream cones. I turn my body into the booth, guiltily hiding the cigarette.

"But I've got to get moving money together. Ugh! When I think of all those times after work that I marched straight to Barneys and blew half my paycheck just to cheer myself up, I could shoot myself!" I take one last inhale and stub the cigarette out on the top of a nearby fence. "I'm so unhappy," I say quietly.

"I know, I can hear that," he says.

"Everyone here looks *through* me," I say, feeling my eyes welling up with tears. "You don't understand. I'm not supposed to talk to anybody and everyone acts as if I should be *grateful* just to be in Nantucket, as if this were the Fresh Air Fund or something. I'm so lonely." I'm really crying now.

"I respect you so much. You've made it through seven whole days! Hang in there for the Grayermeister. So, what are you wearing?" I smile at the familiar question, blowing my nose onto the brown paper bag.

"A G-string bikini and a cowboy hat, what else. You?" I button the top button of my cardigan and pull up the wool turtleneck close around my chin as a biting wind blows off the Atlantic.

"Sweatpants." God, I miss him.

"Listen, fly safe and remember, no pot smoking with the porn stars. Repeat: tulip barges and Anne Frank museum—okay. Porn stars—not okay."

"Got it, partner, keep your hat on and shoot straight from—" The phone abruptly clicks and a dial tone blares into my ear, signaling the death of my phone card. I bang the receiver into the Plexiglas. Damn, damn, damn.

I turn away from the phone booth, prepared to go buy a lot of fudge, when the old cell phone explodes in shrill beeping, causing me to trip into the hedge and bang my elbow on the wooden fence lining the pathway.

Tears spring to my eyes again as I march solemnly to Annie's Candle Shack, their appointed meeting place. I shove the cigarette pack deep into the pocket of my jeans just as the Land Rover pulls into the parking lot. I can hear barking coming from the trunk of the car, but Grayer looks joylessly out through the window.

"Let's get going. I want to make the noon flight," Mr. X says as I strap myself in beneath the canoe and heavy raindrops splatter the windshield.

Sharp barking ricochets through the car.

"Make it stop, Nanny!" Grayer says grumpily. "I don't like that."

Mr. X turns off the car and the Xes jog into the house, evading the last of the drizzle, while I struggle to unbuckle Grayer and carry the whimpering crate in after them. I set the wooden box down on the shag rug, lifting the retriever puppy out, just as an elderly woman with shoulder-length gray hair emerges from the kitchen.

"Grandma!" Grayer cries out.

"Ah, there you are. I thought I must have the wrong house," she says, untying her scarf and maneuvering carefully so as not to touch the mildewed walls.

"Mother." Mr. X looks as if he's just been zapped with a stun gun, but then recovers, moving forward automatically to kiss her on the cheek. "What are you doing here?"

"Well, that's a fine way to greet your mother. Your charming wife called me yesterday and invited me to enjoy this refugee camp you probably paid a bundle for," she says, looking up at the peeling paint. "Although, honestly, I don't know why I couldn't have come tomorrow," she says to Mrs. X. "I caught the nine thirty. I tried calling from the ferry, but the line was busy, and as much fun as it would have been to wait in the rain and eat one of the fried bread products available for purchase at your charming station I decided to hail a cab." I stand just outside of their triangle, taking in the grande dame who has spawned this family. I've only met women like Elizabeth X when my grandmother has dragged me to Vassar reunions for the class of 1862. She's real Boston Brahmin, part Katharine Hepburn, part Oscar the Grouch.

"Elizabeth, welcome." Mrs. X glides forward to give her mother-in-law a guarded kiss. "Can I take your coat?" Call the union—Mrs. X is taking a coat!

Elizabeth slips out of her beige Burberry trench, revealing a blue and white polka-dot pleated dress. "Darling?" Mrs. X says to Mr. X, who still looks stunned. "You're always saying how you two don't get to spend enough time together, so I thought I'd give you a little surprise."

"I said hi, Grandma," Grayer says impatiently.

She bends her knees slightly with her hands on her thighs. "You look just like your father. Now, run along." She straightens up. "Who's this? And what's that?"

"Elizabeth, this is Nanny. She looks after Grayer." I shift the puppy to my left arm and reach out to shake her hand.

"Lovely." She ignores the gesture and reaches into her purse to pull out a pack of Benson and Hedges.

"That's Grayer's new dog," Mr. X says jovially.

"I hate it," Grayer says from the couch.

"Would you like a cocktail, Mother?"

"Scotch and soda, dear, thank you."

"Oh, I think we only have vodka, Elizabeth," Mrs. X says.

"Send—I'm sorry, what was your name?" Elizabeth asks me.

"Nan," I say.

"I can go, Mother."

"I just traveled three hours through torrential rain to spend time with my son. My son who, from the look of it, might have a heart attack any day." She pats his protruding stomach. "Send Nan."

"Well, Mother, the insurance doesn't cover—"

She turns to me. "Nan, can you drive?"

"Yes."

"Do you have, on your person, a valid driver's license?"

"Yes."

"Son, give her the keys. Do we need anything else?" she asks Mrs. X.

"No, I think we have everything, Elizabeth."

"The Clarks and the Havemeyers are coming by tomorrow, and knowing you, dear, there's only rabbit food. Nan, come with me to the kitchen. I'll make a list."

I dutifully follow her into the avocado-green kitchen, dragging the dog crate behind me as I go. I park the box near the table and place the puppy gently back on her towel. As soon as I latch the cage door she resumes her yapping.

Elizabeth throws open a few cupboards, while I take a piece of paper from the pad by the phone. "This place is quite a shithole," she mutters to herself. "Okay." She starts dictating. "Scotch, gin, tonic, Clamato, tomato juice, Tabasco, Worcestershire, lemons, limes." She opens the fridge and tuts with disgust. "What the hell is soy milk? Does a soybean have udders? Have I missed something? Carr's water crackers and more brie. Can you think of anything else?"

"Um, macadamia nuts, pretzels, and potato chips?"

"Perfect." My grandmother taught me that when entertaining WASPs, the key is to put out only a tiny silver bowl of each item and suddenly even Pringles have class. "Son! Can you please put that goddamn dog in the garage! The yelping is giving me a migraine!" she shouts.

"Coming, Mother." Mr. and Mrs. X enter the kitchen.

"I couldn't agree more, Elizabeth. Nanny, help Mr. X carry the crate into the garage," Mrs. X instructs me.

I take the front end of the crate and try to make reassuring noises to the puppy as we carry her out to the cold garage. Her brown eyes stare up at me as she tries to steady herself. "There, there, good girl," I murmur.

Mr. X looks at me as if he can't quite figure out who I'm talking to.

Mrs. X follows us down the rickety wooden steps as we lower the crate onto the damp cement floor. "Nanny, here are the keys." She holds them up as she comes over. "Oh, good." She looks down with disdain. "I think it'll be much happier out—"

Mr. X grabs her by the elbow and steers her into the corner by the boiler. "How dare you invite her without consulting me," he growls through clenched teeth. Still waiting for the keys, I crouch down to adjust the puppy's towel, trying to make myself as unobtrusive as possible.

"But honey, it was a surprise. I was just trying to—"

"I know exactly what you were trying to do. Well, I hope you're happy. I really hope you are." He pivots in his loafers and storms back into the kitchen.

She stands with her back to me in the corner, facing the rusting trash cans. "Oh, I am." She reaches up and smooths her fingertips across her forehead. "I'm so happy. Really fucking happy," she says quietly into the darkness.

She walks shakily past me, back up the steps to the kitchen, the car keys still clenched in her fist.

"Um, Mrs. X?" I say, standing as she reaches the splintering door. She turns, her mouth pursed. "What?"

"Um, the keys?" I ask.

"Right." She hurls them at me and steps through the kitchen door to rejoin her family.

He was determined to show who was master in that house, and when commands would not draw Nana from the kennel, he lured her out of it with honeyed words, and seized her roughly, dragged her from the nursery. He was ashamed of himself, and yet he did it.

—PETER PAN

CHAPTER ELEVEN

A Bang and a Whimper

Moments after finally surrendering to unconsciousness I wake to sobbing. I pull myself out of bed and lie down beside Grayer as he thrashes around, battling the monsters who have chased us out of our rest.

"Shhh. Shhh." I try to take him in my arms, but not before one of his flailing limbs manages to whack me in the eye. "Ow, shit." I sit up.

"I would appreciate it if you didn't use that kind of language in front of Grayer." I look over to see Mrs. X silhouetted in her mutton-sleeved nightgown by the doorway. "Well?" she asks, making no attempt to come closer.

"I think he had a nightmare."

"Okay, then. Just try to keep him quiet. Mr. X has his tennis tournament today." She disappears back down the hall, leaving us alone.

"Shhh, I'm right here, Grove," I whisper as I stroke his back.

He shakes, turning his head into my neck. "No you're not. You're gonna go away." He begins to sob against my shoulder.

"Grove, I'm here. I'm right here."

He pulls back slightly and raises himself onto his elbow, puts his small fingers on my cheek and turns my face to his. In the dim glow of the Grover night-light he looks intently into my eyes. I hold his gaze, taken aback by the intensity of his expression, as if he were trying to memorize me. When he's finished he lies back down, his body slowly relaxing as I curl around him, whispering our monsters away.

✧

Unable to get back to sleep, I exhale the last of my cigarette into the shed, stubbing the smoke out into the wet grass, and look back at the house framed by the moonlight.

"Woof!" The still unnamed X pet nestles against my ankles.

"Shhh, you," I say, reaching down to scoop her up like a baby, her slick paws brushing my chin. I carefully make my way through the wet grass up to the back door, pulling it open slowly and cringing at the unavoidable creak. I step out of my damp tennis shoes into the kitchen.

She wriggles to get free as I nestle her into the crate. Shaking with agitated exhaustion, I stare at the refrigerator. I tiptoe over and open the freezer door to pull out the vodka, desperate to be knocked out. But the icebox light reveals that my little survival swigs have made a noticeable dent in the reserves. I hold the bottle under the tap before returning it to its spot under the frozen veggie burgers. I hate what this trip has reduced me to. I swear, another week and I'd be mixing crack in the bathroom.

On my way upstairs I see that someone has finally taken the receiver off the hook in the living room. It's about time. I crawl under the scratchy wool blanket to await sleep, half-dreaming of Ms. Chicago parachuting onto the front lawn at breakfast.

I'm awakened two hours later by Grayer trying to scramble over me to get to the bathroom.

"Nanny, it's time for breakfast."

"In where? France?" I'm so exhausted I can barely see. I hold on to the wall as I follow him to the bathroom and help him pull down his pajama bottoms. While he's relieving himself I pull open the shade, squinting as the bathroom is bathed in orange light.

I pull a sweatshirt on over my pajamas and we shuffle downstairs. "What do you want for breakfast?" I ask, bending over to pick up the puppy.

"No, Nanny, leave it," he whines, turning his back on the cage. "Leave it in the box."

"Grayer, what do you want for breakfast?"

"I don't know. Froot Loops?" he mumbles as I heave her up onto my shoulder. She barks and licks my face.

"Sorry, bud, you know we only have Soy Flakes."

"I hate Soy Flakes. I said I want the other kind!"

"I want a personal life, Grove. We can't always have what we want." He nods. I give him Soy Flakes, which he pokes at while I take the puppy outside to relieve herself.

At eight o'clock I wake at the sound of footsteps on the stairs. Mrs. X descends in yet another Nantucket outfit she bought at Searle and casually places the phone receiver back on its cradle. "Grayer, let's turn off the TV. What do you want for breakfast?"

"He al—" I start to say.

"I want Froot Loops! I wanted it, but Nanny wouldn't give it to me."

"Nanny, why didn't you feed Grayer?" she asks, turning off the television.

"I WANT IT! I NEED IT!" he screams like a baby into the dark screen, rousing the dog into a yelping frenzy.

"Cut it out," I say quietly, and it silences him for a second until he remembers this isn't my show. Full-on screaming ensues and doesn't stop until he's eating his second chocolate doughnut and the

TV is back on. I yawn, wondering if they'd get him a hooker if he cried hard enough.

"I believe I've made it clear, Nanny," she says, looking down at the retriever as if she were vermin. "That I don't like the dog in the living room. Please put it back in the garage." I pick up the puppy. "Have you packed Grayer's activity bag for the club?"

"No, I've been keeping him company."

"Well, he seems occupied for the moment," she says.

I nod, picking up the bag with my free hand.

"Also, did you get more wipes?" What, with the private chauffeur you got me? I can't even get myself to a drugstore, you fucking freak.

"Um, did Mr. X pick them up when he was at the store?" I ask just as the phone rings.

Mrs. X picks up the receiver. "Hello?" She stares at me while gripping the receiver. "Hello!" She slams the phone down, shaking the bamboo table. "I don't know if he did. Did you put it on the shopping list?" She rests her hand on her hip.

"I never saw yesterday's shopping list."

She sighs. "Honey?" she calls upstairs. "Did you get more wipes?"

Silence. We all stare expectantly at the ceiling. Finally we hear the sound of slow footsteps on the stairs. He descends wearing his tennis whites and makes a direct beeline for the kitchen.

"Did you get wipes?" she asks his back. "Honey? You know— those little cloths I use to clean Grayer?"

He keeps walking, then stops at the door, turns to *me* and says, "Tell my wife I got what was on the list," and disappears into the kitchen. I can hear Mrs. X exhale slowly behind me. Won-der-ful. Ladies and gentlemen, for the remainder of the show the role of Fucked will be played by Nanny.

"*What*, in the name of Christ, is all this racket?" The senior Mrs. X stands in a Pucci zip-front robe in the doorway, flinging a bejeweled hand toward the television. "Can we please turn off that god-awful purple dinosaur?"

"No!" Grayer spews chocolate crumbs on the couch.

"I'm sorry, Elizabeth," Mrs. X says, rubbing her temples. "Would you like some coffee?"

"Black, like ink." Neither woman moves, indicating that the onus is on me to produce this inky coffee.

"Elizabeth, why don't you go sit on the porch and Nanny'll bring your coffee out there?"

"Do you want me to catch pneumonia?"

"How about the kitchen, then?" Mrs. X asks, buttoning her cardigan.

"I don't suppose my lazy son has gone to get the paper yet?"

"No, but yesterday's is still on the table."

"Well, now that would have been useful yesterday. Honestly, I don't know why you insist on spending your vacation here in this . . . *hut* when you could have come and stayed with me on the Cape and Sylvia would be serving us all eggs right now."

"Next year, Elizabeth, I promise."

After returning the dog to her crate on the kitchen floor, I'm scooping grounds into the filter when Mrs. X comes in. Mr. X abruptly stands up from where he's been studying *The Economist* at the kitchen table and goes out the back door.

She takes another long exhale, biting the side of her mouth. She opens the fridge, grabs a yogurt, holds it for a second and puts it back. She brings out a loaf of bread, flips it around to look at the nutrition information and returns it to the shelf. She closes the door and pulls down the box of Soy Flakes from on top of the fridge, giving it a once-over.

"Do we have any grapefruit?" she asks.

"I don't think Mr. X got any."

"Never mind, I'll eat at the club," she says, putting back the box.

She walks slowly over to me, tracing her fingers along the counter. "Oh, a boy called here for you a few days ago. It was a terrible connection, though . . ."

"Really? I'm sorry—"

"He's not the kid who lives on eleven, is he?" she asks.

"Actually, um, yeah." I get a coffee cup out of the cupboard, silently willing her to drop the conversation.

"I recognized the name, but it took me a few hours to realize from where. I was wondering how you knew him. Did you meet in the building? Was Grayer with you?" The lurid image hangs between us of me not only having sex on her bed, but enabling said sex by letting Grayer take a nap. Hard to say which she'd find more alarming.

"Yeah . . . It's funny . . ."

"Well, he must be quite a catch for you." She walks toward the windows and looks out at Mr. X standing in the yard with his back to the house as the fog lifts. "His mother was telling me that his last girlfriend—she was so beautiful. Every time I saw her in the elevator I'd tell her she should go in for modeling. And always so pulled together." She turns to eye my pajamas. "Anyway, she just went to Europe on a Fulbright. I don't suppose you'd ever consider applying for a program like that? Though I doubt NYU students are eligible for awards of that caliber."

"Well . . . I wanted to work after graduation . . . that is, I'm not really interested in international fieldwork so—" But she's already walked out. I lean against the avocado-green linoleum counter, my jaw gaping. The coffee machine clicks off.

"Dear Mrs. X, you suck," I mutter as I pour.

"Pardon?" I whip around. Mr. X stands behind me, stuffing a doughnut in his mouth.

"Nothing. Um, can I help you?"

"My mother said you were making coffee."

I pull down another chipped cup, still having a minor Fulbright attack. "Does your mother take milk and sugar?"

"Nope, black, black, black."

"Should I not have used a filter?" He laughs and for a second he looks just like Grayer.

"Nanny! Where's that coffee?" I hustle back to the living room, trying not to spill.

"So I said to him, if he thinks he's going to screw me he's got another think coming!" Mrs. X has a pained expression as Elizabeth regales her with the trials of getting her pool properly serviced.

"Nanny, why don't you get him dressed? We're going over to the club. Honey, you and Mommy are going to spend the whole day together watching Daddy play tennis." Grayer barely looks over from the TV.

I kneel to dress him in front of *Sesame Street*.

"No, Nanny. I want to wear the Pooh shirt, I hate that one," he says when I hold up the Power Ranger shirt.

"Poo shirt! That's disgusting!" Elizabeth X cries as she stands to go upstairs.

"It's Winnie-the-Pooh, actually," I clarify as she passes.

I'm tucking the offending shirt into his shorts when Mrs. X comes in from the kitchen.

Ring.

She pauses briefly to raise the receiver a few inches and then slams it back down again. "No, that won't do." She waves down at me. "We're going to the club. Get one of those Lacoste shirts I bought him."

"No! I want to wear this one!" He prepares for another gale.

"Grayer, that shirt isn't appropriate," she says definitively. She picks up her handbag to wait for us while I wrestle him into the new shirt and rebrush his hair.

"Nanny, his shorts are wrinkled. Oh, well, I suppose they'd just get wrinkled on the ride over anyway." I wonder if she's considering making him stand in the car, hugging the front seat all the way to the Nantucket Yacht Club.

⟡

"Grayer, stay by the car while Mommy and Nanny get our beach things," Mrs. X calls after him as he runs up onto the golf course abutting the club's parking lot. She sighs, opening the trunk, and begins to load me up. Mr. X and Elizabeth have already trotted off to the courts for his first game.

"There you go." I have a straw bag containing everyone's clothing changes swinging off my right elbow, a duffel bag full of lotions, sand toys, and sporting goods hanging from the other elbow, and an enormous pile of beach blankets and beach towels in my arms, to which she adds two fully inflated floaties. I lift my chin obediently so that she can tuck the orange plastic securely beneath it.

"Grayer Addison X, I SAID WAIT!" she screams into my face and over my shoulder, sliding her little yellow Kate Spade tote up to her elbow and sauntering forward, hand in hand with Grayer, yellow silk sarong billowing in the cool breeze. I tighten my arms around the pile, trying not to trip as I precariously navigate behind her. She greets the entire club as she passes, remembering each mother and child by name. I follow her, thankful that the floaties have positioned my head at such an angle that no one can tell if I'm rolling my eyes. Which I am. A lot. We kick off our sandals and walk down the wooden planks to the sand.

She weaves in and out of umbrellas, before pointing her head at a plot of empty beach to indicate where I'm to set up camp. Grayer skips in circles around the blanket as I lay it out.

"Come on! Let's go swimming! Right now. Right now." I look over at Mrs. X, as I anchor the blanket with a bag, but she's already immersed in conversation.

"Let's get your suit on, Grover." I take his hand to walk up to the cabana that someone named Ben's brother has lent us for the week while he's in Paris. I close the wooden door, leaving us in damp semi-darkness, with only slivers of sunlight peering in through the slats and onto the white boards. He pulls open the door the moment his other foot is through the top of the shorts.

"Wait, G! Got to lather up." I hold up the Chanel Bébé SPF 62, which I am constantly forced to slather on him.

"I hate that stuff!" He tries to make a run for it, but I grab his arm.

"How about you put it on my face and I'll put it on yours," I offer.

"Me first." He gives in. I squirt the white cream on his fingers and he smears it over my nose. I gently cover his, trying to get his cheeks at the same time so we can get out of the cabana before sunset.

"Nanny, we are taking turns! Don't cheat," he admonishes, generously slathering my ears.

"Sorry, Grove. I just want to hurry up and get this stuff on you so we can get out there and go swimming." I cover his ears and chest.

"I'll do it myself, then." He smears his hands on his arms and legs, covering about a fifth of his exposed skin. I bend down in the doorway, attempting to even it out, but he runs away from me back down to the sand. Ten pedicured toes stop in front of me.

"Nanny, don't forget to put sunscreen on him. Oh, and there's a jellyfish warning today so you better bring everything up to the pool. See you later."

I schlep our stuff back up to the pool, only to discover that the water is slowly being drained out after a small child had an "accident." We head over to the Little Schooners Playground, a bit of an overstatement for a rusted swing set in a shadeless, fenced patch of sand. The sun beats down mercilessly as Grayer attempts to play with the seven other children, none of whom is close to him in age. We all pool beach supplies, taking turns coloring, throwing a ball, and picking our noses.

After he threatens to hurl a two-year-old off the swing set for her juice box, I leave our stuff and lead Grayer over to the clay courts to get drink money from Mr. X. For a good twenty minutes, we stumble along the bleachers in the heat searching for his match, but find it difficult to pick him out of the crowd of middle-aged men wearing visors.

"That's him! That's my dad!" Grayer keeps shouting hopefully, pointing at various men in tennis whites, only to have them turn around with disconcertingly unfamiliar faces.

When we finally spot him on the last court Grayer throws himself against the fence, gripping the wire with his fingers and screaming, like Dustin Hoffman in *The Graduate*.

"*DaaAAAAaadddDDdyyyyYYYYyyyyyy!!!!*"

Elizabeth hisses at us disapprovingly as Mr. X marches over with a murderous look in his eye. I guess Grayer "the political prisoner" doesn't fit in with the image he's been cultivating all morning.

"Come on now, sport, don't cry," he booms for the whole court to hear. I put my hands gently on Grayer's shoulders to pull him back. "Get him out of here!" he whispers fiercely as soon as he's close enough that he won't be overheard. "And here." He pulls his cell phone from his belt and thrusts it through the fence at me. "Take this goddamn thing with you."

He stalks back to his game before I can ask him for the money. I look up to Elizabeth, but she glares straight in front of her, blowing smoke coolly to the side. I shove the phone deep into my pocket, and pick up Grayer, who's screaming, and lug him, still screaming, to the parking lot, because I have no idea where else to go.

When I am about two minutes from teaching Grove how to drink from the sprinklers we finally track down Mrs. X at the golf course.

"There you are!" she exclaims, as if she's been looking for us for hours. "Grayer, are you hungry?" He droops to the grass, still holding my hand.

"I think he's thirsty, actually—"

"Well, the Benningtons have invited a few families to their

house for a barbecue. Won't that be fun?" He plops down on the lawn, red faced and sweating, forcing me to pick him up and follow her as she strolls back to the car, sipping from her Perrier.

✧

When we pull into the Benningtons' drive the first thing I notice is the Filipino man in a white jacket walking a poodle around the fountain. The second is that there are at least fifteen cars parked on the gravel. How do you throw together an impromptu barbecue for fifteen families when the Benningtons left the club only minutes before us? As we walk through the white gate at the side of the house to the pool area the answer becomes apparent. You call the house on your cell phone and mobilize your staff.

I stand there, absorbing the realization that there is no way my wedding is going to be as nice as this informal little barbecue. It's not just that the impeccably manicured lawn goes right down to the water, or that everything is in full bloom, or that another man in a white jacket is tending bar, serving ice cubes that all have grapes frozen in them, while a third flips filet-mignon burgers; it's not even that tables with starched floral tablecloths have been set up all over the lawn; what finally gets me are the watermelons sculpted into the busts of former presidents.

I am startled by Grayer, fully revived from the contraband can of Coke his dad absentmindedly handed him, dumping a hot dog on my foot. He has ketchup all over himself, including his Lacoste shirt. I couldn't be more pleased.

"Come on, Grover, let's get you another dog." He and I eat our lunch, and then I sit nursing a vodka-tonic while he runs around the lawn with the other kids. By now I know better than to talk to any of the guests.

I see the Horners arrive with an attractive tan woman in tow. Caroline brings her over to meet Mrs. X while Jack takes the girls to the grill. I watch with curiosity as Mrs. X switches herself on, her hands going to her pearls, her face a mask of compassion. This must be Caroline's divorcée from California. After a few minutes Mrs. X loses steam, holds up her empty glass to signal her need for a refill, and departs.

Jack joins the two women, bringing with him a hot dog and Mr. X. The foursome engage in animated conversation for some time until Lulu skips over and pulls her parents away. Mr. X and the tan woman start to walk over to where I'm sitting. I quickly slump down in the chair and close my eyes. Not that Mr. X could pick me out of a lineup.

"Well," I hear him say as they pass by, "I have season tickets, so if you'd like to go . . ."

"Doesn't your wife go with you?" she asks.

"She used to, but she's so wrapped up with our son lately . . ." Your who?

I sit back up to check if Mrs. X has noticed her husband's stroll down to the water, but she's embroiled with Mrs. Longacre. My pocket starts to vibrate.

"What the . . . ?" I pull Mr. X's pulsing phone out and try to switch it off without spilling my drink, hitting buttons at random.

"Hello?" I hear a voice call out from my palm.

"Hello?" I instinctively raise the phone to my ear.

"Who is this?" a woman's voice demands.

"Nanny," I say. There's no need to ask who she is.

"Nanny?" She sounds like she's crying. "Is he there?"

"No," I say, craning my neck to see down to the water, but Mr. X and his new friend have disappeared. "I'm sorry, look, I've gotta go—"

"No. Don't hang up. Please. Please just tell me where he is," she begs tearfully.

I crane my head around. "Wait a sec." I hold the phone down low at my hip and walk swiftly up to the house and into the first French door off the porch. I close it shut behind me, keeping Grayer steadily in my gaze. I take a deep breath before lifting the phone back up to my ear. "Look, I'm not really sure what to tell you. Not to be trite, but I really just work here."

"What is he still doing up there? He won't answer his phone, he—"

"He's, he's . . ." I don't know what to say. "Playing tennis . . . and eating doughnuts, I guess?"

"But he hates her, he hates going away with her. He can't be having fun—"

"Well, yeah, no, he doesn't really seem to be having fun."

"Really?" she asks. I look out the window at the party, such as it is: balding paunchy men and their second or third wives, who're just biding time till their next peel or tuck, all oblivious to their children running back and forth on the lawn, savoring a few moments away from their monsters. And the nannies, all sitting quietly on the damp grass, awaiting their next order.

"No," I say, "nobody is having any fun."

"What? What did you say?"

"Look, I just have to ask, because you seem so intent on being here. What is it here that you want? What about any of this is appealing to you?" I gesture out at the window.

"You don't know what you're talking about. What are you? Eighteen?" Her tone changes as she sobers up from her crying jag. "I don't see how this is any of your business."

"Oh, oh, you know what? I don't think this is any of my business, either!" I want to hurl the phone straight through the window and have it land right in Mrs. X's Perrier. "*You* came to *my* house. How much more of my problem could you have made this? Having a covert affair, okay, means *nobody* knows about it. You do not get to have a crew of little helpers." I stare at the phone. "Are you still there?"

"Yes."

"Well, for whatever it's worth, I've been all up and in here for nine months, as in as a girl could get, and I can tell you: there is nothing good here—"

"But I—"

"And don't think it's all her, either, because it's not. She was *you* once, you know. So you can play all the Cole Porter you want, turn the heat up as high as it will go, but in the end you'll spend your life chasing him down, just like everybody else in that apartment." I look back out the window at the children playing tag on the lawn.

"My," she says, "that's quite an impressive moral analysis from the girl who stole eight hundred dollars from me—"

Suddenly Grayer trips and goes flying through the air. My breath catches and it seems to take hours for him to land.

"Are you listening?" she asks. "Hello? Nanny? I said I fully expect—"

"What, do I have to say it in Spanish? Get out of this relationship while you still have a pulse! And this advice is worth way more than eight hundred dollars, so you just consider us even." I click the phone shut. There is an interminable pause and then a bloodcurdling wail. The entire party is struck silent, no one moves.

I run out to the porch and down onto the lawn. I weave through the immobile linen shifts and khaki pants, immediately locating Mrs. X in the parting crowd.

"Nannnyyy!" he cries. Mrs. X gets there first. "Nannnyyy!" She tries to bend down to him, but he hits out at her and flings his bleeding arm around my legs. "No! I want Nanny." I sit down on the grass and pull him onto my lap. Mrs. Bennington comes over with the first-aid kit, while the other adults look on.

"Here, why don't you let Mommy take a look at it," I say. He holds out his arm, allowing her to bandage it, but curls his face away from her into my shoulder.

"Sing the bottle song," he asks tearfully as Mrs. X awkwardly applies iodine.

" 'Ninety-nine bottles of beer on the wall,' " I sing quietly, while rubbing his back. " 'Ninety-nine bottles of beer . . . ' "

" 'Take one down and pass it around,' " he mumbles into my shoulder.

"Where's my husband?" she suddenly asks, scanning the crowd just as Mr. X rounds the hedgerow with his arm around Caroline's friend. They're both a little flushed and clearly hadn't been anticipating that all eyes would be on them when they returned.

✧

I hold G's bandaged arm as he swishes in his bath, a reminder not to get the Batman Band-Aid wet. He leans his head against my hand. "I'm going to get a boat when I get big. It's going to be blue and have a pool on it."

"I hope it'll be warmer than the one at the club." I wash his back with the washcloth in my free hand.

"Oh, man. It will be so hot! Like this bath! And you can come and swim with me."

"Thanks for the invitation, Grove. You know, when you're all grown-up you'll have lots of friends and I'll be real old—"

"Too old to swim? No way, Nanny. You liar."

"You're right, G, I'm lying, count me in for the cruise." I drop my chin to the cool porcelain beside his head.

"You could bring Sophie, too! She could have her own pool. A pool for all the animals. And Katie could bring her guinea pig. Okay, Nanny?"

"What about your puppy, Grove? Have you thought of a name for her yet?" I ask, hoping if we name her she might not get left in the yard all day again.

"I want a guinea pig, Nanny. Ellie can have the puppy."

"They already have a dog, Grove."

"Fine, no dogs on the boat. Only guinea pigs. And we'll all

swim forever and ever and ever." He tugs his plastic aircraft carrier in circles.

I nuzzle my nose in his hair and rest my eyes while he finishes parking his boats. "It's a date."

I wait until Grayer is completely asleep and Elizabeth has turned in before going down to the living room. Mr. and Mrs. X are reading the paper, sitting silently across from each other in the worn arm-chairs on either side of the couch. Both of them tilt their sections toward the flickering side lamps in the darkened room. I take a seat in the middle of the empty couch, but neither X bothers to look up.

Taking a deep breath, and in the most supplicating voice I can muster, I say, "Um, I was just wondering if it would be possible if, instead of driving back on Saturday—"

Mrs. X lowers her paper. "I'm pregnant," she says steadily.

His paper doesn't move. "What did you say?" he asks.

"I'm pregnant," she says in a steely, even tone.

His paper drops. "What?"

"Pregnant."

"Are you sure?" He looks at her, his eyes wide, his voice shaking.

"Once you've been pregnant you know how to recognize the signs." She smiles slowly at him, laying down her Full House.

"My God," he says, a trickle of sweat forming on his brow.

"And tomorrow at breakfast we'll tell your mother."

They stare at each other, tacitly acknowledging the arrangement she has made on their behalf. I pray to fall between the couch cushions.

"Now, Nanny." She turns her cold smile to me. "What is it I can do for you?"

I stand. "You know what? It's totally not a big deal. We can talk about this later. And congratulations," I offer as an afterthought.

"No, this is a perfect time, isn't it, honey?" She smiles at him.

He just stares back at her.

"Sit down, Nanny," she says.

I swallow. "Well, it's just that I have to find a new apartment this weekend, so if there's any way that you could drop me off at the ferry Friday night on the way to your party . . . It's just that there'll be so much traffic on Saturday and I haven't even started packing and I need to have everything boxed by Monday and I was just thinking, you know, if it's not any trouble . . . Of course, if you need me I'm happy to stay—I just thought . . ."

Mrs. X fixes me with a steely gaze. "Well, I have a better idea, Nanny, why don't you just leave tonight? Mr. X can drive you to the ferry. Elizabeth's here—we're really covered."

"Oh, no, really, I don't need to leave tonight. I just thought, you know, there might be so much traffic on Saturday. I'm happy to stay, I want to stay—" My heart pounds as I become fully cognizant of what is at stake. I am staggered by the vision of Grover, waking in a few hours, terrified and alone.

Mrs. X cuts me off. "Don't be silly. Honey, when's the next ferry?"

He clears his throat. "I'm not sure."

"Well, you can just drive Nanny over to the dock—they go pretty regularly."

He stands. "I'll get my jacket." And exits.

She turns back to me. "Now, why don't you go up and pack?"

"Really, Mrs. X, I don't need to leave tonight. I just wanted to have my apartment sorted before Monday."

She smiles. "Frankly, Nanny, I just don't feel that your heart's in it anymore and I think Grayer can sense that, too. We need someone who can give Grayer their full commitment, don't you agree? I mean, for the money we're paying you, with the new baby coming, we should really have someone more professional." She stands. "I'll give you a hand, so you don't wake Grayer."

She follows me toward the stairs. I walk up ahead of her, frantically running through scenarios that might give me a chance to say good-bye to him. She comes behind me into the small room and stands between our beds with crossed arms, watching me carefully as I hastily stuff my things into my bag, awkwardly moving around her in the cramped space.

Grayer moans in his sleep and rolls over. I ache to wake him.

I finish collecting my things in her shadow and sling my bag up over my shoulder, mesmerized by the sight of Grover's hand in a tight fist flopped over the side of the bed, the Batman Band-Aid sticking out beneath his pushed-up pajama sleeve.

She gestures for me to walk past her to the door. Before I can help it, I reach out to smooth the damp hair off his forehead. She grabs my hand an inch from his face and whispers through clenched teeth, "Better not to wake him." She maneuvers me to the stairs.

As I start down ahead of her my eyes fill with tears, causing the stairs to pitch beneath me and I have to grip the banister to steady myself. She bumps against the back of my bag.

"I . . . I . . . I just wanted—" My voice is coming out in little gulps. I turn up to face her.

"What?" she hisses, leaning menacingly forward. I pull back, the weight of my bag drawing me off balance as I start to fall. She instinctively reaches out and grabs my arm, swinging me against the banister as I right myself. We face each other, eye to eye on the same step. "What?" she challenges me.

"She was in the apartment," I say. "I just thought you should know, I mean, I—"

"You fucking child." She comes back at me in this two-and-a-half-foot space with all the force of years of suppressed rage and humiliation. "*You. Have no idea. What you're talking about.* Is that clear?" Each word feels like a punch. "And I'd be very careful. If I were you. How you regard our family—"

Mr. X honks the car from the driveway, startling the puppy, who begins a round of sharp barking from the kitchen. As we reach the bottom of the stairs the noise wakes Grayer. "Nanny!" he cries out. "NAAANNYYY!!"

Mrs. X pushes past me. "Ugh, that dog," she mutters, marching to the kitchen. She shoves the swinging door open and the dog bounds out, yapping fiercely at her.

"Just take it," she says, roughly lifting the puppy up by her rib cage.

"I couldn't—"

"NANNY, COME HERE. I NEED THE LIGHT ON. NANNY, WHERE ARE YOU?"

"I said, take it." Mrs. X. thrusts her out at me. Her paws flail for solid ground, forcing me to instinctively receive her before she's dropped. Mrs. X jerks the front door open, grabbing her purse off the side table. She pulls her checkbook out and scribbles furiously while I look over toward the stairs. "Here." She hands me the check.

I turn and walk past her onto the gravel driveway, as Grayer's increasingly hysterical cries echo out into the darkness.

"NAAAANNNNYYYY! I NEEEEEED YOOOOUUUUU!"

"Have a good trip!" she calls out from the doorway as I make my way shakily down the path lit by the Rover's headlights, willing my knees not to give out.

I get in the front seat and try to steady my hands as I pull the seat belt across the puppy and myself.

"Oh," Mr. X says, looking at her. "Yeah, I guess Grayer's a little young. Maybe in a few years." He starts the car and peels out of the driveway, and before I can look back to fix the house in my mind, it is eclipsed by the woods as he races the car across the empty country roads.

He pulls into the deserted ferry dock and I open the door to get out. "Well," he says as if it's just occurred to him. "Good luck with the MCATs—they're a killer!"

As soon as the door slams, he peels out of the parking lot and drives away. I walk slowly into the nearly empty ferry terminal and look around for the schedule. The next ferry isn't for an hour.

The puppy wriggles under my arm and I scan the waiting room for anything that could serve as a carrier. I go over to the guy who's closing up the Dunkin' Donuts counter and ask him for a bunch of plastic bags and some string to fasten a makeshift leash. I pull all my clothes out of my tote, shove them in the plastic bags, line the tote with the remaining ones and place the dog in on top.

"There you go," I say. She looks up at me and barks before hunkering down to chew on the plastic. I slouch back against the peeling orange seat and look up into the fluorescent light.

I can still hear him screaming for me.

But nobody ever knew what Mary Poppins felt about it, for Mary
Poppins never told anybody anything.

—MARY POPPINS

CHAPTER TWELVE

It's Been a Pleasure

"Yo, lady!" I jolt awake. "Last stop—Port Authority!" the driver
shouts from the front of the bus. I hastily gather my things together.
"I wouldn't be trying to sneak on any animals again, girlie. Or next
time you'll find yourself walking back to Nantucket," he says, leering
at me over the steering wheel.

The puppy lets out a low growl of indignation and I stick my
hand in the tote to quiet her.

"Thanks," I mutter. Fat gut.

Stepping down into the stench of the terminal, I squint in the
brightness of the orange-tiled hallway. The Greyhound clock reads
4:33 as I stand for a minute to get my bearings. My adrenaline completely spent, I lower the tote to the ground between my feet and
peel off my sweatshirt. The humid summer heat is already trapped in
the tunnel, along with the stench of commuter sweat.

I walk hurriedly up to the street level to find a cab, past closed
bakeries and newsstands. Outside the Eighth Avenue exit hookers
and cab drivers await their next jobs while I let the puppy out on her
string leash to pee by a sweating garbage can.

"Where to?" the cabbie asks as I slide in behind my bags.

"Second and Ninety-third," I say, rolling down the window. I
root around in the plastic bags for my wallet and her brown furry

head pushes its way out of the tote, panting. "Nearly there, little one. We'll be there soon."

"Bethune?" he asks. "I thought you said Upper East."

"Yeah, I'm sorry. Ninety-third," I clarify. As I open my wallet Mrs. X's check flutters to the floor of the cab. "Damn." I bend over to retrieve it in the darkness.

"Pay to the order of: Nanny. Five hundred dollars."

Five hundred dollars. *Five* hundred dollars?

Ten days. Sixteen hours a day. Twelve dollars an hour. So, that's like sixteen hundred dollars—no, eighteen hundred—no, nineteen hundred!

FIVE HUNDRED DOLLARS!

"Wait, make that seven twenty-one Park."

"Okay, lady." He makes a sharp U-turn. "You're paying."

You have no idea.

I unlock the Xes' front door and carefully push it open. The apartment is dark and silent. I put the tote down and the puppy wriggles out of it as I drop the rest of my bags on the marble floor. "Pee anywhere."

I reach for the dimmer on the hall switch, bathing the center table in a taut circle of light. The spot lamp pours beautiful cold ripples through the cut-crystal bowl.

I lean forward and rest my hands on the glass top that protects the brown velvet swags. Even now, even as it's gotten this out of hand, I'm distracted from my thoughts of the Xes by the trappings of the Xes. And really, it strikes me, isn't that the point?

I pull back to see the two perfect palm prints I've left on the glass.

Walking determinedly from room to room, I switch on the brass lamps, as if illuminating their home will shed some light on how I could have worked so hard and been hated so much.

I open the door to the office.

Maria has stacked Mrs. X's mail carefully on her desk just the

way she likes it—envelopes, catalogs, and magazines each in separate
piles. I riffle through them and then flip the pages of her calender.

"*Manicure. Pedicure. Shiatsu. Decorator. Lunch.*"

"Vice president in charge of bullshit," I mutter.

"*Monday 10 A.M. Interview: Nannies Are Us.*"

Interview? I flip quickly back through the last weeks.

"*May 28: Interview Rosario. June 2: Interview Inge.
June 8: Interview Malong.*"

They start the day after I said I couldn't make the drive to Nantucket because of my graduation. My mouth goes dry as I read the
notes scrawled in the margin of that afternoon.

"*Reminder: call problem consultant tomorrow. N's behavior is unacceptable. Completely self-centered. Providing
poor care. Has no respect for professional boundaries. Is
taking complete advantage.*"

I close the book, feeling as if I've been punched in the solar
plexus. An image flashes into my mind of Mrs. Longacre's crocodile
handbag resting by her feet under the stall partition in the bathroom
of Il Cognilio and something snaps.

I head to Grayer's room, throw the door open, and see it immediately—the stuffed bear that arrived on Grayer's shelf after Valentine's Day without explanation.

I pull it down, flip it around, and pull the back panel off to
reveal a small videotape and control buttons. I rewind the tape while
the puppy races across the room and into Grayer's closet.

I press record and place the bear on top of Grayer's dresser, shifting it around until I think I've set up the shot.

"*I'm* completely self-centered? My behavior is unacceptable?" I
shout at the bear.

I take a deep breath, trying to channel my rage and begin again.
"Five hundred dollars. What is that to you, a pair of shoes? A half day
at Bliss? A flower arrangement? No way, lady. Now I know you were an
art major, so this might be a little complicated for you, but for ten

straight days of unmitigated, torturous hell, you paid me three dollars an hour! So, before you wrap up a year of *my* life to be trotted out as an anecdote at the next museum benefit, keep in mind that I am your own personal sweatshop! You've got a handbag, a mink, *and a sweatshop!*

"And I'm the one taking advantage of you?"

"You have. No idea. What I do. For you." I pace back and forth in front of the bear, trying to formulate nine months of swallowed retorts into some sort of coherent message.

"Okay listen up. If I say 'Two days a week,' your response should be 'Okay, two days a week.' If I say, 'I have to leave by three for class.' This means, wherever you are—all those important manicures, those crucial lattes—you drop and come *runing*, so that I can leave—not after dinner, not *the next day*, but at three o'clock, pronto. I say 'Sure, I can fix him a snack.' This means *five minutes* in your goddamn kitchen. This means microwave. This does not involve steaming, dicing, sautéing, or anything at all to do with a soufflé. You said 'We'll pay you on Fridays.' Now listen, genius, this means every one—last time I checked you were not Caesar, um, it's not up to you to rewrite the calendar. Every. Single. Week."

Now I am really rolling. "All right—slamming the door in your child's face: not okay. Locking the door to keep your son out when we're all home: also not okay. Buying a studio in the building for 'private time' *definitely* not okay. Oh, oh, and here's one: umm, going to a spa when your son has an ear infection and fever of one hundred and four? News flash; this officially makes you, not just a bad person, but like, officially, a *terrible* mother. I don't know, I haven't birthed anyone, so I may not be an expert here, but if my kid was peeing all over the furniture like a senile fucking dog—umm, I'd be just a tad bit concerned. I might, oh, you know, just on a whim, eat dinner with him at least one night a week. And, just a heads-up here, people hate you. The housekeeper *hates* you—the might-kill-you-in-your-sleep kind of hates you."

I slow down to be sure she gets every word. "Now let's review:

there I was—innocently strolling through the park. I don't *know* you. Five minutes later, you've got me cleaning your underwear and going to 'Family Day' with your son. I mean, how do you get there, lady? I really want to know—just where do you get the balls to ask a perfect stranger to be a surrogate mother to your kid?

"And you don't have a job! What *do* you do all day? Are you building a spaceship over there at the Parents League? Helping the mayor map out a new public transportation plan from a secret room at Bendel's? I know! Thinking up a solution to the conflict in the Middle East from behind the locked door of your bedroom! Well, you keep right on plugging away there, lady—the world can hardly wait to hear how your innovations are going to launch us right into the twenty-first century with a discovery so fantastic that you can't spare a moment to give your son a hug."

I lean down and stare deeply into the bear's eyes. "There's been a lot of 'confusion,' so let me make this perfectly clear for you: this job—that's right, j-o-b, job—that I've been doing is hard work. Raising your child is hard work! Which you would know if you ever did it for more than five minutes at a time!"

I stand back and crack my knuckles, ready to take this all the way to the top. "And, Mr. X, who *are* you?" I pause to let that sink in. "And, while we're making introductions, you're probably wondering who I am. Here's a hint: I did not (*a*) come with the rental or (*b*) show up out of the goodness of my heart, asking your wife if she had any chores I could do around the house. What do ya think, X— wanna take a guess?"

I look at my nails, pausing dramatically for effect.

"I'VE BEEN RAISING YOUR SON! I've been teaching him how to talk. How to throw a ball. How to flush your Italian toilet. I am not a med student, a business student, an actress, or a model and I am in no shape or form a 'friend' to that crackpot you married. Or purchased or whatever." I shudder in disgust.

"Here's the update, big guy. This is not the Byzantine empire—

you do not get a camel and a harem with each plot of land. Where's the war you fought? Where's the despot you've overthrown? Making seven figures a year, with your fat ass in a chair, is not heroic and, while it may win you a trophy wife or two, or five, it most definitely does not qualify you for the door prize of fatherhood! I'll try to put this into terms you can understand: your son is not an accessory. Your wife did not order him from a catalog. You cannot trot him out when it suits you and then store him in the basement with your cigars."

I pause to catch my breath, looking around at all the toys he's paid for and never once enjoyed with his son. "There are people—in your home—*human beings*—drowning in their desire for you to look them in the eye. You made this family. And all you have to do is show up and like them. It's called 're-la-ting.' So get over whatever totally-absent-buying-your-affection parenting that you received and *get here*, man—because this is your *LIFE* and you're just pissing it away!"

"Woof!"

The puppy pushes the closet door open, gripping the bus-pass holder in her mouth. "Hey, give me that," I say gently, kneeling down to take it from her. She drops it, rolling onto her back to play. I stare at the dirty shreds of paper inside the plastic, all that remains of Grove's business card.

I blink, looking around Grayer's room, so familiar to me that it feels like my own. I see him sashaying down the imaginary runway of our Christmas fashion show, wassailing his heart out in the bathroom, falling asleep against me as I finish *Goodnight Moon*.

"Oh, Grover." And then I am crying, curled tight in a ball by the foot of his bed. Waves of sobs rack through me at the fresh realization that I will never see him again. That this is it for us, Grayer and me.

When I'm finally able to catch my breath, I crawl over to the dresser and press stop. I set the bear on the floor, leaning against Grayer's bed as I gently rub the puppy's soft belly. She stretches out, resting her paw on my arm, her warm eyes so appreciative of the attention.

And then I know.

Nothing I've said so far will make them love him the way he needs to be loved.

Or allow me to leave with any grace.

I hear Grayer: "Be smart, Nanny. You'll be smart."

I rewind the tape back to the beginning. I press record and return the bear to the carpet in front of me.

"Hi. It's Nanny. I'm here in your apartment and it's . . ." I glance down at my watch. "Five in the morning. I entered with the key you gave me. And I have all those possessions you value so highly within arm's reach. But here's the thing. I just don't wish you harm. If for no other reason than you have the profound privilege of being Grayer's parents." I nod, knowing it to be true. "So I was just going to leave. But I can't. I really can't. Grayer loves you. I have borne witness to his love for you. And he doesn't care what you're wearing or what you've bought him. He just wants you there. Wanting him. And time is running out. He won't love you unconditionally that much longer. And soon he won't love you at all. So if there's one thing I could do for you tonight, it would be to give you the desire to know him. He's such an amazing little person—he's funny and smart—a joy to be with. I really cherished him. And I want that for you. For both of you, because it's just, well, priceless."

I reach out for the bear and press stop. I hold it in my hands for a moment. Looking over at the bottom shelf of the bookcase, I see a small framed picture of Caitlin tucked behind the Playskool garage.

Right.

I hit record and plop the bear back down.

"And if not, then at the very least you owe me, and whoever else you bamboozle into doing it, some fucking respect!"

I pick up the bear and eject the tape.

✧

Wending my way back to the front hall, I turn off all the lights as I go. The puppy comes scampering into the foyer as I stand over the glass table once again. I set the tape down in between my palm prints and rest their house keys on top of its white label.

I pick up my bags and pull open the Xes' front door for the last time.

"Grover," I say quietly, willing with all my heart, as if I were standing over my birthday cake, making the most important wish of my life. "Just know that you are wonderful—fabulously wonderful. And I hope somehow you'll know that I'll always be out here rooting for you, okay?" I flick the last light off and scoop up the puppy. "Good-bye, Grayer."

The sun is just coming up as I lead her into the park. She pulls her string leash taut as we walk up the bridle path to the reservoir. The first joggers are already making their steady orbit around the water as the sky brightens and the last star disappears. Over the treetops the buildings framing the western skyline are bathed in the pink dawn.

The water laps against the stones as I stand against the wire fence, taking in the beauty of this open vista in the center of the city.

I reach into one of the bags and pull out the Xes' cell phone. I take a moment to feel its weight in my hand before lobbing it over the fence. She jumps up to press her front paws against the wire, barking as it makes a satisfying splash.

I look down at her. "How do you like that for leaving with grace?" She barks in agreement, tilting her head up at me, her brown eyes looking affectionately into mine.

"Grace."

She barks.

"Grace," I say again.

She barks again.

"I see. Well, then, Grace, let's go home."

ACKNOWLEDGMENTS

We wish to thank: Molly Friedrich and Lucy Childs of the Aaron Priest Literary Agency for their unflagging support—should Nanny ever have to go head-to-head with Mrs. X, these are the women we'd want behind her! Christy Fletcher for seeing the potential. Jennifer Weis for letting us know when there was no there there. Katie Brandi for reading this book almost as many times as we have. Joel for taking Nanny on the honeymoon. George for keeping us going on the tough days, and Le Pain Quotidien for the supplies.